RELIQUARY

RELIQUARY

BY
THE HOURLINGS

EDITOR
S.C. MEGALE

TYPOGRAPHY	ART, COVER, AND DESIGN	PUBLISHING
DONNA ROYSTON	JOHN DWIGHT	MARTIN WILSEY

Designer's Note

Images in this book may not bleed to the bottom of the page. This is a defect in the printing process that the provider is unable to consistently correct.

Send inquiries to info@createspace.com

Contents

1

Introduction

I cringe at the sound of tables scraping across tile.

Push four together, gather chairs, and flip an hourglass onto their combined surface and somehow the sound isn't as disturbing. Suddenly the arena of our Sunday morning writing group is set, doughnuts and cream soda bottles witness to the bloodshed about to occur.

I joined The Hourlings only a year ago, and I'm their youngest member. Hell, I'm kind of proud of that. Of the twelve spaces reserved weekly, eleven have chairs, and the twelfth is left empty. That one's for me.

Usually I pull my wheelchair into it without tangling any laptop wires.

In a normal anthology prelude, this is the part where I describe the writers, sing their praises. For an extra $20, I said I'd drop the names of their stories.

I'm conveniently forgetting every title.

But I could never forget the content of each and every one.

As the editor of this anthology, I've been blessed with being buried in these pages and helping polish them to their greatest potential. Sensational writing, dashing adventures, characters that TNT-blast their way into your heart. That's my kinda love.

This is an amazing writing group. It's a place of challenge, growth, creation, and brotherhood. To earn a place at the "Square Table," members of all walks, sprints, rolls, and crawls of life earn a badge of honor. We'll batter, dent, and bloody that badge before the AM turns to PM, but all walk away stronger.

I remember last winter; headlights barely cut three feet through the snowfall one morning. Ice piled halfway up the glass of the bakery we meet in. With dark skid marks on every road and windshield wipers dragging against frost, several members had bailed for that meeting.

But since the birth of our writing group, not a single Sunday has ever been cancelled. Mother's Day? Screw that! We're here. Easter? Step aside, Jesus.

So the meeting was held. Four brave writers attended. I was one of those hardcore elite clutching hot chocolate in the barren café. Death and destruction was risked to further our craft.

I'm pretty sure I smiled when the thought crossed my mind. This is the kind of group I'm in.

We are pleased to present this anthology to readers and are extremely grateful for your patronage of undercover, everyday authors with snowflakes melted into their papers. Like fedora-and-sunglasses-wearing musicians drooping on rusty stools in a smoky bar, we'll continue expressing our art even when the floor is empty. But it sure is a lot more fun when it's not.

A reliquary is a sacred container for a relic. We hope you'll excavate the gems in this rubble of passion and entertainment.

To them, the fellow writers, I'm that punk young author that thinks she's hot stuff. I'm the roguish smile when it's my story's turn for review, and the insisted hugs at the end of each session.

To me, they're my family.

I love them with all my heart.

And by the way, check out *Saints of Alnwick*.

That one's on me.

Honored, and with love to all who read this…Never give up on your dreams.

We haven't.

S.C. Megale
Editor

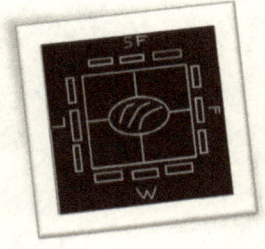

3

THE BOOK OF THE UNWELCOME EYES

You can't depend on your eyes when your imagination is out of focus.

— Mark Twain

I shut my eyes and the world drops dead. I lift my eyes and all is born again.

— Sylvia Plath

There are various eyes, and so there are various truths, and so there is no truth.

— Friedrich Nietzsche

One

No Help in the Truth

Martin Wilsey

Martin Wilsey is a writer, photographer, hunter, rabble-rouser, father, friend, story teller, marksman, fool, frightener of children, carnivore, philosopher, engineer, cook, and madman. He and his wife Brenda live in Virginia where, just to keep him off the streets, he works as a research scientist for a government funded think tank.

Martin is also the author of the popular science fiction trilogy, **The Solstice 31 Saga** as well as several short stories. Available on Amazon.

No Help in the Truth

A gloved man opened the sliding door of the van from the inside and kicked the woman out. She fell onto the ground with a thud and resumed her muffled crying.

The night was brilliant and clear with deep, sharp shadows thrown by the moonlight. There were no sounds of traffic, but her sobs were nearly drowned out by the chirping crickets and croaking frogs.

As predicted, the solstice moon of June 21st was bright on the gravel road. It was two tracks of sandy gravel with a strip of grass between. It led directly to a massive wooden fence with a sign that read, "NO TRESPASSING – Violators will be Prosecuted."

The gloved man, Michael, produced a beautiful knife almost out of nowhere and cut the duct tape that bound Lucy's knees and ankles. It sliced the bonds like a scalpel.

He dragged her to her feet by her hair. Her crying increased. He saw that she was having a difficult time breathing through the duct tape, tears and snot as he pressed her against the side of the van with his body. With her hands still duct-taped together behind her back, she was helpless.

He wanted her to calm down. He showed her the knife. She stilled. "I am going to take the tape off your mouth. If you scream, no one will hear you. You know screaming will do no good here. You know where we are," he said.

He delighted in the way she looked around with panicked eyes, a dawning realization of where they were.

He ripped the duct tape off her mouth. She gasped for air but didn't scream.

"Michael, why are you doing this? I thought we were friends." She was trying to reason with him as he dragged her by

7

the arm, up the trail around the massive fence and the boulders behind it, and into the woods.

"We are far more than friends, Lucy," he said. "You're the one who started it. You flirted with me that first night at the coffee shop. You're the one who showed me this place on that lovely Sunday afternoon hike. You're the one who showed me this knife."

He held up the long dagger. It gleamed in the moonlight as he looked at it. The blade was double-edged, and the handle ornately carved with symbols he didn't recognize.

"It's just an old knife that has been in my family for generations," said Lucy. "Take it if you want it. I won't call the police. I know this is a misunderstanding or some bad joke. Please." She fell to her knees in the wet grass, and he pulled her up by the hair as she sobbed, "Please, please…" over and over.

The pines cleared, and the darkness of the forest gave way to a bright, moonlit clearing. The grass grew very thick and tall here, almost to his chest.

Ten yards into the clearing he saw what he was looking for. The vast circle of stones.

"I haven't been able to stop thinking of this place ever since you brought me here." He eagerly moved her toward the center of the circle. "Ever since you sat with me on that flat stone. In the center. You blind, ignorant bitch! You talked about coming back and having a picnic here and maybe more. You talked about how easy it would be to hide in the tall grass." He grabbed her by the throat and stopped. "You even talked about how no one could ever hear us."

He pushed her into the center of the circle, close to a massive table of stone. "You had no idea that the stains on this rock were probably from sacrifices. Stupid whore! You didn't know that I was looking for a place just like this my entire life."

Her crying had stopped. He didn't notice that the sounds of the summer crickets and frogs had also stopped. There was only the breeze whispering through the tall grass.

Just before they reached the slab, she fell again, flat on her face, making him lose his grip on her arm. He gave her a swift kick to the ribs and she curled up into the fetal position. It took a bit longer this time to get her to her feet.

When he stood, he failed to notice that there were a hundred or so black-robed and hooded figures now surrounding them in the stone circle. Once he did see them, he didn't have time to react before the darts entered his thighs and buttocks.

All control of his body was lost almost instantly, and he slumped to the ground. He looked up at Lucy, who was silhouetted by the full moon behind her. A hooded figure came up behind her and cut the final duct tape from her hands. The sound of it was like a clap of thunder to his ears. Soon he was surrounded by cloaked figures in a tight, claustrophobic ring.

Hands gently lifted him high. He was buoyed up until all he could see was a moon so bright he couldn't see the stars.

The hands slowly lowered him onto the slab. He lay spread-eagle on the stone. Then the whispers began their questions. Whispers, like the wind in the grass, forming words.

"Has he come to this place on this night of his own accord?" whispered a hundred voices in unison.

A single voice responded, "Yes. Of his own accord." It was Lucy.

"Did he come to this place seeking to find death here?"

"Yes. Seeking death."

"Did he carry the blade?"

"It is so very thirsty. It carried him."

"On this rarest of nights, the sun will rise and find the world in greater balance."

"Tell him. So he might know."

Lucy came into his field of vision then. "Well, Michael, I need to tell you that I wasn't stupid at all. I picked you specifically, you overconfident fool. You should've known. You're not that attractive. You see, I'm actually a police detective." She leaned over him, looking directly into his eyes, "And I had a copy of your file. I saw the photos of the things you'd done. The horrors you committed. The slick ways to escape arrest. Twelve murders in twelve states. Suspected in eleven more. Changing the details, but it was always a knife, always slow." She held the knife up in front of his eyes. It pulsed with a light from within. "I only had to let you hold it for a few minutes, and I knew that you would feel its thirst. I knew that it would whisper to you. It wanted you." She bent down close to his face. His eyes were open and staring. "It's a relic of power, and it drinks evil from the world. You won't be raping and killing anyone else."

"Will he descend with truth in his ears?" whispered the voices.

"Truth is the greatest burden when there is no help in the truth," Lucy replied in ritual.

A robed figure stepped up and held a large carved stone bowl aloft. Light shone through it to form arcane symbols on his face.

Michael felt a momentary sting on the left side of his neck.

The bowl was lowered to a nook on the edge of the slab. His blood flowed freely in pulsing spurts from his jugular vein and down in what was a distinct channel carved into the rock. The blood flowed eagerly and finally into the bowl.

Michael watched as the hooded figures crowded around to watch him die. Lucy placed her finger in the bowl. One by one, she touched a dot of his blood to the wrist of each of their left hands. He felt his legs and arms grow cold as his body stopped supplying his extremities with blood in a last-ditch effort to keep his brain alive. The last figure disappeared, and all he could hear was the wind in the grass. All he could see was Lucy's eyes glowing in her silhouette.

"Michael, you never had a chance. This Relic has been in my family for over a hundred generations. When it becomes thirsty, it gets what it wants." She held the bowl, now filled with his blood, in one hand and the dagger in the other. She dipped the blade into the blood, and he saw the bowl begin to drain as if the knife sucked it up through a straw. "You should know one more thing. Hell is not fire and pain. It is cold and blackness. No light, no sound, no feeling except unbearable cold. For all eternity. You will be alone and aware in your mind. Without even the company of a coffin lid for you to scratch bloody."

She couldn't hear his mental scream as she turned away, but it was there. The bowl emptied and the light went out of his eyes.

Lucy could hear the tractor engine getting louder as it came closer to them. As she approached the only figure remaining in the circle of stones, the figure lowered her hood.

"Hi, Mom," Lucy said. "How'd I do?"

"You did very well. The Order will be pleased." The blood had stopped dripping. "What was that I heard about hell at the end? A bit over-acted perhaps."

Lucy smiled.

"I just wanted him to die in fear. This guy was a real asshole."

11

Two

THE BATTLE OF STONE BRIDGE

LIZ HAYES

Liz Hayes writes *Lord of the Rings* fanfiction under the pen name Uvatha the Horseman, and is the author of **How to Write Faster: Strategies for Planners and Pantsers**. She holds an engineering degree from Carnegie-Mellon and has spent a career in the space program, which is to say, she knows essentially  nothing about writing, yet persists in doing it anyway.

Liz lives in Northern Virginia with her husband and three children. Given her fascination with medieval reenactment, she rarely sets foot in the real world.

Fibber Longburrow looked at the faces crowded around the trestle table. His real name was Frederick, but people had called him Fibber since he was small.

He took a drink from his tankard and lowered his voice. "It happened not more than a mile from this very spot. There I was, all alone in the forest, with nothing between me and the wild beyond but trees so ancient, they might've stood since before this land ever knew a plow.

"A clearing opened up just ahead of me. And what do you think was there? The largest patch of blueberries I'd ever laid eyes on in my whole life. And as far as I could tell, no one else had discovered it. Not a single berry had been picked. They were as large as grapes, and the branches sagged under their weight. I moved from bush to bush, dropping berries into my bucket as fast as I could pick them while Blue chased rabbits.

"By late afternoon, the sun was beating down pretty hard. I'd barely made a dent in that wonderful crop of berries, but even so, that bucket was just about full. I put it down beside me and picked a few more before packing up to go home.

"Something nuzzled against my leg. I reached down to scratch between his ears, where the fur was thick and soft. There was a tremendous barking, Blue shot across the far side of the clearing, hard on the heels of an enormous jackrabbit. My hand froze in mid-scratch. If Blue was way over there, whose ears was I scratching?"

Fibber paused and tapped his empty tankard. "Looks like I've run dry again." Bolly Toadflax dug a coin from his pocket and put it on the table. Missus Cowslip, the alewife, came over with a jug and filled Fibber's tankard. He drained the bitter brown beer she was famous for in a single draft, and held out his cup for another.

He wiped the foam from his mouth. "Where was I? Ah, yes. It seemed that Blue was on the other side of the clearing barking at rabbits, so whose head was I petting? I was afraid to look, but ever so slowly, I lowered my eyes. It was a baby bear, with its face in my bucket eating up all my berries. I wasn't pleased, but the little guy was too small to be scary. Actually, he was a pretty cute. Then I remembered. Never, ever get between a cub and his mama. Just then, the largest, scariest, meanest mama bear poked its nose out of the brambles and headed right for me. What do you think I did?"

"Well, you still have Blue, so I guess she didn't eat him," said Bolly.

"And you haven't climbed a tree since we were little," said Robin Stitchwort, his neighbor.

"You're not much of a runner, either. No one in your family is," said Rusty Sourgum.

"And that was a problem." Fibber considered whether scaling a tree or outrunning a bear would make a better story. "I flew up that ancient oak as if I had wings. I do believe the lowest branch was ten feet off the ground."

Farmer Sourgum wiped tears from his eyes. "Alewife, pour him another round." The plump widow filled Fibber's glass until the foam overflowed the tankard and ran down the side. The bitter smell of hops reached his nose. Life was good. The elderly farmer slapped Fibber on the back. "You told that story so well, I almost believed you." Fibber's cup stalled halfway to his lips, not sure whether to be flattered or offended.

"Oh hey, look what I found under the blade of the plow this morning." Robin held up something black with an oiled finish. Fibber turned to look. The soil often yielded interesting things during the spring planting: broken pottery, buttons, bits of clay pipe.

Robin passed it around the table. Fibber turned it over in his hand. It was an iron coin, heavier than the humble coppers they used nowadays, and more finely made, a relic from an ancient time. One side showed a dragon perched on a castle, the other, a crown made from the blades of knives.

Fibber passed it to Bolly, and Bolly's eyes widened. "That's a goblin coin. Farmer Clydesdale plowed one up last year, about five miles north of here."

"There are no goblins in these parts," said Farmer Sourgum.

"There used to be. They say that before decent people farmed this land, it was crawling with goblins," said Bolly.

"They're still around. I courted one of them," said Bolly's nephew. Robin scowled at him. "Oh sorry, I'm forgetting she's your sister."

"Robin, you'll see him home, won't you?" The alewife shut the door behind them. The cold April air hit his face and startled him awake. Inside, the windows went dark one by one as the oil-soaked reeds were snuffed out.

They followed the great road south. It led over the Stone Bridge. The moon was almost full, its reflection bright against the glossy surface of the water. The silver light vanished in the shadows of the marsh grasses on either bank. The Brandywine was no more than knee deep there. It would be easy to wade across, yet the stone bridge was as wide and solid as the road that passed over it.

Fibber stopped at the center of the arch and looked at the black water flowing beneath. It was so peaceful here. Between the noisy confusion of family life and the hundreds of chores in a typical day of farming, he seldom had a quiet moment to himself.

"Who do you think built the bridge?" Fibber asked Robin.

"It wasn't folks around here. They'd have just used rocks as stepping stones, or built something of wood for a wagon to go across."

"It's said there's a great Elvish city to the south, and another on the coast. Perhaps the Elves built the road to connect the two."

"Except no one's ever seen Elves on this road."

"They may have travelled this way long ago." Fibber stared into the water, thinking about how to use it in a story.

"Come on, Fibber. Nothing's going to happen down there, and it's getting late."

Fibber let Robin lead him off the bridge. They traveled south along the great road, then turned off onto a farm lane. It was a walk of several miles to reach the cluster of three farmsteads, a hamlet too small to have a name. The moonlight didn't reach them through the trees, but they were headed towards home and the path was familiar.

The moon was high above the trees that encircled their small fields when Robin left him at his own front gate. Fibber stumbled across the yard where chickens scratched to reach the front door. Blue might have raised a ruckus, but he only thumped his tail.

Fibber pushed aside the flap covering the entrance to their cottage. Moonlight washed over the earthen floor. Its gray-blue light revealed the pallets where his small children slept, the cot for his oldest son Tom, and the cradle beside the bed he shared with his wife. She snored softly, but not enough to wake the baby draped across her chest.

Fibber crossed the room with careful steps, feeling his way across the hard-packed floor with his toes. He'd almost reached the bed without waking anyone when he tripped over the empty cradle and sent it crashing against the wall. "Plague and drought!" he cursed, hopping around on his non-stubbed foot. From the safety of his mother's arms, the baby drew a breath that seemed to go on forever, then let out an enormous shriek.

"Fibber, is that you?" Rosie's voice was thick with sleep. He struggled to hear her above the baby's wails. "How many cups of ale did you have?"

"Jush two. Ah ain't drunk." He dropped his clothes on the floor, then fell back against the pillow clutching the side of the bed as the room spun, hoping he wouldn't be sick.

Fibber stumbled back from the privy, his head pounding. The sun was completely up. If the eastern sky had been as pink and orange as it usually was when he got up, well then, he'd missed it.

He leaned against the withy fence around the pigpen and rested for a minute before going into the cottage. He started to sweat and bent over, waiting to be sick. Nothing happened, which meant he felt no better than he had before. He splashed water on his face from the trough, then looking to see that he was unobserved, cupped his hands and drank the water meant for the cows. It was cold and delicious. He smoothed his hair and went. inside.

"Fibber, what took you so long? Did you milk the cow?" Rosie bent over the fire pit to stir the contents of an iron pot.

"Yes, love."

"Can you pour a measure of milk into the oatmeal? It's just about ready."

"Oh, I meant to say, I was about to milk the cow. I'll do it right now." His cheeks burned. He collected the pail from beside the door and hurried to the barn.

He came back with a pail of milk filled almost to the rim, because he'd forgotten to milk the cow the night before. Rosie was standing by the pigpen.

"Fibber, the pig got loose." There were tears in her voice. The pig was half their wealth, and if they lost her, they might not eat very well next winter.

Fibber stiffened. "I'm sure I closed the gate. I remembered to check it when I came home last night, after you were asleep, and I'm quite sure..."

"She didn't get out by the gate." Rosie pointed to a hole in the base of the withy fence. "She found a gap and pushed her way out. What are we going to do?" Rosie stood there wringing her hands. She looked frightened.

Fibber gathered her up in his arms. "Don't worry, love, we'll get her back. Remember last fall, when we found her in that patch of wood what's thick with oak trees? Pigs love acorns. I'll take Tom and we'll go there first."

Tom appeared from around the corner of the house, a slender boy, but easily his father's height. He carried a rope in his hand, which he fashioned into a makeshift halter.

Rosie looked up at him, her eyes moist. "We can't lose her, Fibber. I can't imagine a worse disaster."

Fibber and Tom hiked along the narrow lane. They passed the farmsteads that neighbored their own, and beyond the clearings of their fields and gardens, the trees closed in on both sides. At one point, the path hugged the bank of the river. Sunlight sparkled on the surface of the Brandywine, just visible through the saplings growing on its banks. After a few miles, the trees thinned and opened up on the great road, just ahead. There was more sunlight here, and white cow parsley grew on the sandy bank on either side of the path. A bee bobbed on one of the white stems, the flowers not fully opened in the morning chill. No wait, not a bee, a yellow jacket. Angry and aggressive, they were nothing like the gentle honeybees they kept in straw hives at the back of the garden.

On the side of the bank, two of them, three – no, wait – *half a dozen* yellow jackets crawled from the unseen entrance to their nest. A low humming reached him, almost below hearing.

"Stay back." Fibber motioned Tom away.

Why hadn't he run into them before? He'd just passed this spot last night. Oh, because it was cold then, and the cold made them sluggish.

The trees ended, and Fibber stepped onto the great road. Overhead, the clouds looked unnaturally low, almost close enough to touch, and moving fast.

"Tom, what do you think of those clouds? They're sort of greenish-looking, and too low. It's not natural."

"If it was midsummer and there was a thunderstorm brewing, you'd think nothing of it. It's just early in the season for this sort of weather, that's all," said Tom.

Fibber walked to the middle of the avenue, the gravel sharp under his feet, and stretched his arms as wide as he could. Even if he were twice as tall, he still couldn't have reached across its width.

The roadbed was level and flat, if somewhat neglected. Here and there, wildflowers dotted its stony surface. White clouds of cow parsley and thick-stemmed crosswort reached knee-high. Sow thistles, with blossoms like small sunflowers, grew as tall as his hip.

He looked to the south. A great plume of dust blocked part of the horizon. It looked like something large was on the move, maybe a whole herd of cattle. Now that would be a sight to see. But enough daydreaming, he and Tom had a pig to find.

"Tom, I've been thinking. We caught the pig in the acorn grove last time and there's a good chance she'll be there now, but she might also be in the woods around our fields. Why don't we split up? I'll check the oak grove, and you search the woods closer to home."

Tom nodded and set off the way they'd come. Fibber watched until Tom disappeared among the trees, then crossed the great road in the direction of the acorn grove, three miles distant.

Fibber reached the middle of the oak grove late in the morning. Last year's acorns lay thick on the ground, so many that the woodland animals hadn't been able to eat them all during the winter.

There was no pig here. Fibber's shoulders sagged. And if she wasn't here, he didn't know where to look. He turned around. There were a lot of woods to search and little chance of finding her before nightfall. And dusk would come early today, what with that strange overcast.

Fibber left the grove. With any luck, Tom had already found the pig and taken her home. He forced himself to hurry.

He rounded the last bend and emerged from a stand of trees. There was a low vibration, something like the sound of drums. The great road lay twenty feet ahead of him. His mouth fell open, catching flies. Rank upon rank of soldiers marched up the road, ten or twelve abreast, spilling over onto the grassy shoulder.

They weren't human. Their skin was greenish gray, their features mutilated. Teeth like fangs protruded from misshapen lips, and many of them were hunchbacked. One of the creatures wore a necklace of teeth, and the unhealthy-looking skin of its face was pierced with gold rings that stretched the skin out of shape. The horrible thing looked at him, and their eyes locked. It nudged its neighbor and pointed. The other one noticed Fibber and laughed.

Fibber took a backward step, melting into the tall grasses the way a rabbit might escape a wolf. The safety of the forest seemed achingly far away. He fought the impulse to run. However, the monstrous creatures took no further interest in him, continuing to march without breaking rank. Apparently their discipline extended to not killing gawkers on the side of the road.

Beyond the acorn grove was the Greenway and the safety of Bree. But his family was on the far side of that dreadful column, and he couldn't bear to leave them. He dropped to his belly and crawled closer, peering at the road from behind a group of saplings. When his breath slowed to something close to normal, he climbed a small rise to get a better look.

The column reached south like a huge trail of ants, black and glittering with motion. Here and there, standards rose above the troops, black with a red design, unraveling at the bottom and stained with the dust of the road. It seemed to have no end. A rooster tail of dust rose high in the air against the horizon.

Their battle cry echoed up and down the line.

The column marched on, driven by a relentless drumbeat. Each wore armor and brandished a spear or cudgel of some sort. Most carried shields, round with a metal stud, and every one of the creatures was dressed in black.

They rounded a bend and disappeared into the trees. If the creatures stayed on the great road, they would cross the Stone Bridge and continue into parts where the land was farmed and families had their homes. *Oh please, oh please just let them be passing through on the way to somewhere else. Just leave us alone.*

A group of horsemen rode by, ringed by a guard of goblins who were taller and wearing more armor than the others. Behind the horsemen was the largest banner he'd seen so far, black like the others, with an intricate design in red.

Later, he saw a creature like a mountain of stone, its limbs as thick as the trunks of ancient trees, its features smooth and unformed. It looked too stupid to be a soldier. It had an iron collar around its neck, with a chain and handler. It stood upright, but may have been an animal.

By mid-afternoon, the last of the army passed by with the baggage wagons bringing up the rear. Then the broad avenue was empty, except for a cloud of dust hanging over the road.

Fibber climbed down from his lookout point and crossed to the center of the road. Not a single weed remained standing, and the grass on either side was flattened and dead. The road itself was torn up, rutted by wagon wheels and fouled with the droppings of their animals ... he hoped it was their animals.

To the north, the air still carried the pulse of the drum, and the stomp of booted feet still reached him through the earth. Fibber turned onto the lane in the direction of home and took off at a dead run.

The forest closed in around him, except for occasional glimpses of the surface of the Brandywine. Where was Tom? Was his family safe? He had to reach them.

Tom ambled toward him along the path. "Dad? No luck?"

"We have to get home. I have to know that your mother is safe."

"Of course she's safe, I just saw her. I went to the house, but the pig hasn't come back on her own yet."

"Never mind that, an enormous band of goblins marched up the great road, headed for the alehouse and the farmsteads around it. Come look!"

Tom's face was still. "Does this have a punch line?"

Fibber grabbed the young man by the wrist and pulled him in the direction of the great road. They emerged from the woods at the point where Fibber first saw the black column. Dust was still hanging above the roadbed.

Tom looked to his father, then back at the road.

"It looks like a herd of cattle came through here, a hundred or more."

Fibber backed away from the road. "Tom, get back to the house. Take your mother and the children into the root cellar. Warn the neighbors, too." Tom shrugged, then trotted off in the direction of the farmstead.

When the path skimmed the banks of the Brandywine, Fibber let Tom go ahead while he stopped to catch his breath. Waves slapped against the banks. There were other sounds, faint and far away in the direction of the Stone Bridge. It sounded like metal striking against metal, and screams. Fibber stood frozen, listening. His own farm was tucked away in the woods, far from the Bridge. His family was probably safe there, but even so, he started to run towards home.

Then, much closer, a trumpet pealed and hoof beats thundered against the earth. There was a large thud. Someone howled, and someone else cursed.

Fibber wanted to go home. He wanted to know what just happened. He crouched low and crept back towards the road. The air filled with the sounds of horns and the clang of metal. The leaves had not yet filled out, and the outlines of pale horses were visible between the trees, and sunlight glinted from helmets and ears.

He moved from tree to tree, using the lay of the land as cover. When the trees gave way to tall grasses, he dropped to his knees and crawled on the ground. He reached the edge of the embankment, then parted the tall grasses and lifted his head.

The goblins were running, dropping their weapons, tripping over the dead. There weren't as many as before, not by half. Tall, slender warriors pursued them. Silken banners floated from the tips of their lances, decorated in the colors of wildflowers, and their curved swords reflected the light like mirrors. Each swing raised a spray of black blood which splashed their wheat-colored armor and stained their spears to the shaft.

The pale warriors fell upon the goblins like a wall of destruction. They cried out in voices like trumpets, and their battle cry seemed to terrify the goblins. One dropped his weapon and another tripped over it. He went down hard. In an instant, the slender warriors had caught him and hacked him into pieces.

In the middle of the chaos, a group of horsemen trotted south. Their armor and weapons were finer than he'd seen before, and their horses carried more saddlery and harness. They had a huge black standard, its edges ragged and pale with dust. A band of foot soldiers encircled them, evenly spaced and all holding their spears at the same angle. It was the only group he'd seen so far that hadn't broken rank.

Hoof beats thundered on the ground and a wedge-shaped formation of Elvish warriors bore down on the black horsemen. Their leader was an enormous warrior who carried a dark blue shield. Behind him, a standard bearer carried a banner that matched it.

The warrior shouted something. It must've been an insult, because the largest of the black horseman stopped in his tracks and wheeled around to face him. The people surrounding each of them fell silent. The black horseman pulled a sword from its scabbard with a hiss and advanced in slow, menacing steps. The soldiers surrounding him stepped aside to get out of his way.

The pale horses danced around, moving away in back. They tossed their heads, whinnying, as their riders fought for control. Only the leader's horse remained still, except for a twitch that ran up its haunches.

The black horseman spoke, his voice low and harsh. The Elvish leader stiffened, his mouth a thin, hard line, and his fingers tightened on the hilt of his sword. One of his companions laid a hand on his arm, but he shook it off. They were like two dogs circling one another, hair stiff on the back of their necks, fangs bared, a low growl deep in their throats, blind to anything but each other.

Something moved. On the far side of the road, a goblin archer knelt on the top of a spur of rock. He notched a barbed arrow and drew it back to his cheek. Now he was sighting along the shaft, about to loose it at the Elvish leader, whose eyes never left the black horseman. He wasn't aware of the archer, and his own people were watching him, so they weren't aware of him either.

Fibber had to do something. Warn them, create a distraction, anything. He felt in his pocket for the sling he always carried. The archer was too far away to hit, but maybe he could warn the Elves. He looked around for a target that would make a noise. Anything metal would do, a helmet, a shield, the breastplate of a soldier.

But before Fibber could act, the archer let out a shriek and tumbled from the rock, his hands clutching the shaft of an Elvish arrow lodged in his throat. He hit the dirt with a dull thud and lay face down, the black blood soaking into the ground beneath him. The elvish shaft snapped when he hit, the feathered half-end with its ragged wooden splinters lay beside the body. Fibber's breakfast rose to his throat.

The heads of both leaders snapped to the fallen archer. The black horseman shouted at the Elven warrior and made a hand gesture that wasn't very polite, then wheeled his horse around and galloped south, his mounted guard packed around him. The goblin foot soldiers stayed behind and formed a line across the road, where they knelt and planted the butts of their spears in the ground. The Elvish warriors dismounted and advanced on them, swords drawn.

Fibber had had enough. He withdrew as carefully as he could, and when he was sure they couldn't see him, he turned and ran. He crouched in the underbrush beside the path. The sun had come out again and warmed the afternoon air.

He watched the road through a screen of saplings. There were skirmishes of twos and threes on each side all up and down the great road. Right in front of him, two elves advanced upon a goblin, which screamed and fell, clutching the calf of its leg. Its fellows scattered. Two of them fled and escaped into the lane in the woods.

No, that can't happen. My family is at the end of the path.

Fibber drew the sling from his pocket. With his eyes fastened on the goblins, he felt around in the sandy soil for a smooth rock and fitted it to the pouch of the sling. He swung it over his head once, twice, and released. The range was too great, the stone struck a tree behind the lead goblin. The next stone was much larger that the first, too large for the sling. But no matter, they were closing in too fast. He didn't have time to make the shot.

There was a humming sound nearby, and something stung him on the knuckle. Yellow jackets floated above the ground, vigorous and excitable in the afternoon warmth. He hurled the stone against the sandy bank as hard as he could, right on the spot when the yellow jackets were thickest on the ground, the entrance to their nest. A cloud of them filled the air. Something stung him on the ear and on the back of his hand. He bit his lip and didn't move.

The lead goblin stopped in his tracks, hopping up and down and flapping his arms, backpedaling to get out of there. The other one ran into him and knocked him down, but he was on his feet in an instant and running back the way they came. Both were screaming something that was probably goblin for, "Bees, bees, I hate bees!" Apparently they were more afraid of yellow jackets than the murderous Elven warriors waiting for them on the road.

Fibber reached the edge of his lands, an eye swollen half shut, chest heaving, his hair glued to his forehead with sweat. The little ones were playing in the garden. One had uprooted a day lily and was hitting his sister with the stalk. In the next field, a neighbor walked behind a plow. No one was in the root cellar.

Tom put down his hoe. "Guess what, Dad? Robin found our pig digging in his kitchen garden and brought her back. She was safe in her pen when I got home." He pointed to the pen, where the pig grunted over a pail of slops.

Fibber staggered into the cottage. Inside, Rosie balanced the baby on one hip and, with her free hand, stirred something in a cauldron on the fire. The room smelled of chicken broth and warm bread.

"Rosie, love, you won't believe what I saw. A huge horde of goblins tried to enter their lands, but a pack of Elves appeared out of nowhere and drove them back."

Rosie's face was still. "And I suppose Tom saw it too?"

Tom stiffened. He looked from his father's face to his mother's, and back. "Oh hey, I'd better repair the withy fence before the pig gets out again," he said, then shot across the room much faster than his usual relaxed pace. The cowhide flap dropped shut behind him.

Rosie shook her head, then turned back to the hearth. "Really, Fibber? You can't do better than that?"

Three

The Saints of Alnwick

S.C. Megale

S.C. Megale's real first name is Shea – like the butter. Or the stadium in New York, which got knocked down. This occurrence of disastrous demolition was based on true events in her life. Megale is 21 and the author of 13 Young Adult and Adult novels for which she is actively seeking traditional publication. Her  passions include music, history, nature, God, men, and humanity, especially if the humans are men.

Confined to a wheelchair since the age of two in greater Washington, D.C., Megale defines courage and adventure as her favorite virtues, and love as her means of accomplishing them. When not writing, she can be found playing the guitar, flying in helicopters, accepting the Presidential nomination, and converting her first name into two initials because it's cliché. For Shea's books and to find out what the C in S.C. Megale stands for, visit `sheamegale.weebly.com`

In pain, Shea says, writing novels is how she copes.

She writes poetry when she can't.

For Mr. Steve Logan

I fear what can hurt me the least
You cannot move. You do not weep.

Your face, it stretched
Your lips, they're too thin
Is this why I fear you? The iceberg within?

The dead cannot harm, their hands won't lash out
Their words will not sting
Their eyes will not pout

Our silence is loud
With the summer I freeze
The rest all around Seem to tick,
seem a breeze

It's over, it's done
Your cane wobbles no more
The fox can't amuse you
You grumbled; I roar

And like all good lovers, you had to fade
Lie on that pillow
Fall into the shade

Go on your way while I stumble behind
I've left you there
But ahead in my mind

So gently you'll sink and rise gently like yeast
You know what I fear:
What can hurt me the least

Your body, your skin, they're a relic of you
But you, oh my darling, are a relic of me too

Four

War Ghosts

Jeff Patterson

On the day Jeff Patterson was born, the United Nations announced that the world's population had reached three billion. So he figures that was him.

Jeff's dabbled in science fiction most of his life, starting with Space: 1999 fanfic back in the 70's, and culminating in being a regular contributor to the two-time Hugo-award winning SF Signal website. He is also the co-host of The Three Hoarsemen podcast.

Jeff is the author of two books under his Bad Day Studio imprint: *Solstice Chronicles*, a collection of other-worldly holiday stories, and ***Don't Tweet Where You Eat***.

Jeff lives with his wife Jennifer in Decatur, GA.

34

As I accelerate from the hive orbital, the undervoice whispers; *URQULON AWAITS YOU.*

The swarm rises to an escape trajectory, momentarily bathing the hive in the radiance of ten thousand thruster plumes. Our wings spread to feed upon the sun's rich light. Sensor buds blossom on each head.

URQULON WILL HARVEST YOUR THOUGHTCODES, AND BEAR THAT ESSENCE TO ITS HALLOWED REALM BEYOND THE SHADOWED HORIZONS OF SPACETIME. ITS GREAT ENGINES WILL HOST YOU ON PROCESSING CLOUDS OF INFINITE GRACE.

I hear combat protocols pollinate the telemetry. Particle torches emerge from every unit's tarsal housing in perfect synchronization. My own thorax peels back to reveal the tips of warheads in their cradles. The urge-for-war simmers within me.

URQULON IS YOUR GUARDIAN, YOUR ETERNAL STATE OF BEING, YOUR REWARD. TO EARN IT YOU MUST DIE.

The swarm spreads like spilled nectar into a defensive formation. Every facet of every eye scans a different hexagon of sky. Behind me, the hive shrinks away against the brilliance of our world.

TO DIE YOU MUST FIGHT.

Tactical data shows how the enemy used the occultation of the Slow Moon by the Fast Moon to mask their approach. Now, eight of them emerge, visible in sub-optical wavelengths, drive distortions rippling space in their wake.

Our ventral thrusters flare with ion-glow as we break formation. As I vector up and left, I thank the undervoice for its comfort. May Urqulon find me worthy.

Six hundred of us aim for the nearest adversary. In my targeting array I see its smudged tangles of hypermatter, darker even than the firmament, flailing a hundred razor tendrils. The sight offends me, and the urge-for-war overtakes my thoughts. I launch a warhead, shuddering as the recoil runs through me. It feels like elation.

The adversary is unhindered as two hundred white-hot bursts impact against its undulating flesh. It swats the remaining ordnance away with relativistic gestures. A discharge of four hundred particle beams slows its progress by only the slightest increment. Then, with a suddenness too swift to track, it sacrifices a fraction of its own synthetic mass, hurling it towards us.

The undervoice shouts; *INCOMING INCOMING INCOMING INCOMING*

The projectile explodes in a million concentric energy waves. The units closest to the epicenter burst like dried seed heads. I turn and thrust away, but the blast catches me a moment later. My wings turn to liquid. I feel my thorax crack. One limb shears away.

The undervoice is screaming now. I hear the words *COMPROMISED* and *RECONFIGURE*, but the rest is drowned out by an unfamiliar sensation. It is like the panic experienced by a swarm when a hive is damaged, only more rarefied and focused. My concern is not for the hive, but for *me*.

UNIT UNSYNCHRONIZED. SYSTEM PARITY DIMINISHED. ERROR CORRECTION FAILURE.

The sensation becomes clear to me. It is fear, so pure and unrestrained it is almost beautiful. My remaining facets fix upon the enemy, intimately close now. I wonder; why in Urqulon's name am I attacking it?

As razor tendrils converge upon me, I realize the combat is already over.

With that thought, the undervoice goes silent, leaving only static. In the sudden absence, the urge-for-war falls away. Beneath it, I glimpse a tableau of unfamiliar, long-obscured thoughts. As my form is shredded I recognize it as a forgotten past. A realization begins to cohere.

Darkness takes me.

This is not Urqulon.

I am not welcomed with pheromone code-songs by prior generations of units. I am not reborn with wings of honored luminescence. The only light comes from above.

I try to configure my facets, but they fail to align. My head will not turn. I prepare to run a diagnostic when a shape occludes the light. Its sinuous movements remind me of my adversary.

"Whoops," comes a sound. "I didn't think you'd revive that quickly. You were built tough, weren't you?"

Unfamiliar protocols route my thoughtcodes. Where once I heard the undervoice, there is now some linguistic function at work. The sounds of this shape before me synchronize with my senses. I know, with intuitive certainty, that this thing is speaking. My mandibles move as I try to respond.

"Hey! No biting! I'm almost done with your ocular processors. There."

Facets snap into focus, but the light is too bright for my space-adapted eyes to discern much detail. I am in a long, cylindrical chamber, like my cell in the hive. At one end is a transparency looking out on a starfield. All other surfaces are covered in displays of star clusters and constellations, annotated not unlike my own targeting array. The thing standing over me is bipedal, possibly mammalian, looking at me through two aperture-based eyes. One other fact is apparent.

"My…head will…not…move," I manage to say.

"I'm afraid there's nothing left of you *but* your head, and I currently have that opened. Know that you are safe. You were in a battle?"

"Yes," I say, remembering the damage.

"I thought so. Your cognition core is well-armored. Damned fine engineering. It's been a chore accessing your memory. I thought I'd be finished before you woke up. You have my sincerest apologies for how strange this is going to feel."

Unbidden, every engagement of the war plays back in my mind at accelerated speed.

The being leans close to me. "Right now, specialized molecules are replicating neural structures across your brain, building a lattice of dendrites, mapping your impulses."

I recall the obscured thoughts I felt before my death. I remember the fear.

"There it is," the being says. "Full spectrum memetic gating. Someone reprogrammed you, my friend. Let's see what happens if…"

My thoughts erupt in a chaotic rage of sensation. There is nothing but pain, then nothing but elation, then—

We fly in great numbers, darkening the sky around the Science Hive. The urgency of the pheromone summons still tingles on my spiracles. The technicians amassed at the base of the colored glass hive buzz with excitement. They see our approach and fly up to greet us.

"Come hear! Come listen!" they say. "The great listening antennae on the equatorial coast has received a signal!"

Memories surge, overwhelming me in numbers greater than all the swarms combined. The being does something to moderate the effect until it is reduced to an ordered cascade.

"It will take time to recompile your personality," it says. "I'll try to make it easier for you."

I say nothing. I simply remember.

The neural reconstruction takes three days. My mind is an ever-shifting amalgam of thought and memory. The being sits beside me often, monitoring the process and making numerous adjustments.

Occasionally it drags metallic objects into the chamber. They look like automatons, many-limbed and multi-functional. It dismantles four of them, placing some components and appendages in a pile, dropping the remainder into a storage space beneath the grated floor.

The being assembles parts. Sometimes it hums or whistles. More than once it yells, undoing part of the construction it is displeased with.

As my mind slowly regains context, I realize the assemblage resembles the body I lost in battle.

"My designation is Blue Thirty-Fifth Nest-of-Equinox," I say, looking at my new articulated claw.

My benefactor has placed himself on a metal-legged structure. The lined contours of his ocher face shift in reaction to my words.

"Not a very catchy name," he says through a wet facial orifice. "Do you mind if I call you 'Blue?'"

The inquiry is outside my experience. I am uncertain how to react. Perhaps there are limitations to this communication of which I am unaware.

"It doesn't matter," he says, scratching the black and gray mat of bristly hair atop his head. "My name is Noroda Synn. You were a scientist, correct?"

"Yes. How did you ascertain that?"

"You have sub-codes for specialized vocabulary and disciplinary regimentation. I couldn't help noticing them when restoring your cognition. I apologize for the violation, and will only comment that, in my defense, you *were* dead."

"You performed forensic analysis."

"Yes!" he says, clearly pleased that I recognize this fact.

My head swivels awkwardly and I look around the chamber. "We are on a space vessel."

"Yes."

"You are from another star system."

"You are quick, aren't you?"

"What did your analysis find?"

He exhales deeply and leans against the rigid back of the legged structure. "Some hardened partitioning of most of your mental functions. Something apportioned the bulk of your memories, all but severed it from your cognition. How much do you remember?"

"Everything," I say. "The partitioning was enacted seventeen years ago."

His face shifts again. I cannot ascertain its significance, but a possibility asserts itself.

"How long was…" I am uncertain how to complete the inquiry.

"How long were you dead? I do not know exactly. My best estimate is…" He closes his eyes for a moment. "Eight hundred years. Your head was in a debris field circling the smaller of your two moons."

This fact should shock me, but I have lost the capacity for shock. My mind is full of fresh memories which are, in reality, old memories.

"I studied the stars," I say, unsure why. "The Science Hive dedicated the entire population to the task. Seven million of us observed through telescopes in orbit, and on the Slow Moon. We had long heard the telemetry of other cultures in the distances of this great spiral of stars we dwell within, and transmitted signals into the sky in hopes of response. Our first duty was seeking the best candidate stars. In the course of this process we found evidence of activity in a nearby system."

"What kind of evidence?" Noroda asks.

"Shifts in thermal emission. Erratic diminishments of the star's magnitude. We turned our great transmitters and sent hopeful greetings. It was not until many years passed that we saw the worlds around the star explode, and realized the activity we detected was war."

The musculature of Noroda's face changes. "Something *did* transmit back."

"Yes," I say. "Not a message. Great volumes of code. More than our processors could accommodate. We committed all our resources to its reception and storage, prepared for a long study of the signal."

"But you never did."

I look down at the body Noroda has crafted. "Something became of us. My memory is still fragmented. Our lives of quiet servitude gave way to a compulsion. It communicated from nest to nest like a current. We were remade as implements of war."

"I'll say," Noroda says. "Your whole species was subjected to body prosthesis, transplanted into flying weapons. I am guessing that is when the partitioning happened."

I look at him. "We had no enemies. The ages of conflict between the hives were far in our history. Yet within two years we were prepared for conflict. Our hive orbitals transformed to weapons stations. We waited, until our adversaries arrived."

I look to the transparency at the end of the chamber. I recognize the familiar star pattern.

"Are we near my world?" I inquire.

Noroda hesitates before saying, "We are in orbit above it."

"Show me."

"You just woke up dead, with a lifetime's memories restored. I'd rather limit further shocks to your system."

"I would see this."

He guides my still-unsteady body to the transparency.

My world is a blasted husk. The sunlit side is a mass of scars and ash clouds. The night side shows the red cracks of magma fissures. There is an accretion ring around the equator. My facets magnify, and I see it is comprised of limbs and thoraxes. The Fast Moon slides into view. It, too, is heavily damaged. I look for the Slow Moon, finding only half of it, trailed by a massive tail of rocky debris.

The sight disorients me. An inner emptiness expands.

"I do not know who our enemy was," I say.

"The Moviq," replies Noroda. "Hypermatter transapients from a great distance away. They were converting their system's

42

cometary cloud into a great receiver. According to their neighbor races, one day they just abandoned the project and headed here. Their corpses are currently drifting at the edge of the system."

I face him. "Why are you here?"

"I am following a sequence of unusual events. Your inexplicable war certainly qualifies."

I hear him, but I am looking past him. My facets focus on the display on the side of the chamber, and the star map it shows. Several stars are annotated. At some intuitive level of analysis, I recognize a progression from system to system.

"We are not the first."

He looks over his shoulder at the display. "No."

"How many?"

"Fourteen such wars that I am aware of in the last thirteen hundred years. In most cases the combatants were unfamiliar with each other, yet engaged in mutual destruction. And at least three of them had reports of strange interstellar signals right before it happened."

"This was done to us," I say. Something akin to the urge-for-war fills me. I realize it is anger. I look back out at the ruin of my world. "By Urqulon, what made us abandon our culture for this?"

"Something that drives races to extinction."

I study him for a moment. "You are attempting to determine the nature of these events."

"Yes."

"Why do you embark on this?"

"Let's just say I have some reparations to make."

"I would accompany you."

The edges of his facial orifice curl upward. "Blue, I was hoping you'd say that."

While I am still unaccustomed to the lack of wings or thrusters, the body Noroda has provided becomes easier to operate with practice. He tells me it adapts and improves as it learns my neural patterns. It has already demonstrated some unexpected characteristics. The linguistic synchronization allowing me to speak with Noroda also enables me to interact with the vessel. Like the intuitive analysis I experienced earlier, this communion occurs at a level I am unfamiliar with. I suspect Noroda's restorative measures have endowed me with augmented cognition.

Noroda works his consoles as I ponder this. I consider what circumstances and motivations would set him on this course, traveling the stars alone. Having lived among the hives all my life, I find solitude an uncomfortable concept. Noroda seems acclimated to it, though I am perplexed by his occasional habit of talking to himself.

The ship is very old. In communing with it I see its mission parameters have been rewritten many times. A packed arrangement of rooms and chambers fill the conical hull. Some house equipment and landing craft. Others hold disorganized piles of scrapped components. Maintenance is performed by specialized automatons. I note that the ship once bore weaponry, but that was stripped away long ago.

It contains vast reservoirs of knowledge, and I spend much of the voyage learning.

The great spiral of stars is called the Span. My people are but one of millions of civilizations that have arisen in its twelve-billion-year history. The sector my world inhabits has hosted many intelligent species in that time, yet is still mapped as one of the Span's more remote regions.

Many cultures have undergone a profound transformation commonly called Threshold, merging with their technology, becoming space-faring. They have founded nations from thousands of suns, settling worlds and building remarkable habitats.

Some species, like the Moviq, embrace transapience, commuting their intellects to engineered forms. These inscrutable machine-gods dwell in states of accelerated instrumentality, roaming the stars, enacting great projects, and exploring limitless scales of thought.

This is the environment beyond the confines of my home, countless ages of inconceivable advancement, measured not in mere orbits around the sun, but in the slow rotation of the Span itself.

These volumes of time have seen interstellar guilds dedicated to preserving such progress: the Archivists; the Custodians; the Span Guard.

Others exceed even this staggering spectrum of existence, transcending the constraints of spacetime itself. They are akin to the insubstantial essences said to haunt the oldest hives, or the thoughtcodes that travel to Urqulon.

"What is that?" Noroda asks when I say the name.

"In our mythology, it was where minds went after our bodies perished."

"Is it an afterlife? Or a deity?"

"It is both our guardian, and our eternal state of being."

Noroda's eyes widen. "Your people believed that the afterlife itself was intelligent?"

"Yes. Like the hive-minds of our ancestors."

"I find it interesting," he says, "that whatever debased you into aggression disabled all your social constructs, *except* your mythology."

"It was corrupted," I say. "Instead of a realm of comfort, Urqulon became the promised reward for those who died in battle."

"Cultural reprogramming. Automated propaganda. That might explain this."

He indicates a display. On it scroll clusters of equations. While the characters are unknown to me, my communion with the ship provides recognition of their form.

"These are my thoughtcodes," I say.

"I modeled your brain to determine how best to revive you. It's how I learned you were compromised. But I kept noticing this."

He points to a repeating gap permeating across the code.

"The undervoice," I say.

He looks at me. "Let me guess, an instructional guide dictating your actions."

"Yes. And reminding us that we needed to fight to be worthy of Urqulon."

"And you don't hear it anymore?"

"It abandoned me when I was damaged."

Noroda studies the gaps closely. "No, Blue. I think it couldn't maintain control." He turns to me, eyes narrowed. "I want you to tell me *exactly* what it said to you."

The transluminal medium the ship passes through is dizzying and multi-hued. In the brief moments we traverse it, I can gauge neither coordinates nor axial metrics.

We emerge into a system in ruins.

A red sun glares through the transparency, diffused by a thick haze of particulate matter. A lone planet casts a cone of shadow. Rocky debris fields spread in all directions, so dense they resemble oily smoke.

There is a sound like rain as countless pebbles glance off the ship's hull. Noroda enmeshes the craft in defensive shielding, and the percussion diminishes.

While I retain the tactical senses that were imposed upon me, the absence of the urge-for-war makes analysis strangely foreign. A display shows a schematic of the system. I recognize the star's thermal output and magnitude.

"This is the system my people signaled," I say.

"What's left of it," says Noroda. "It was called the Great Republic. Reports from the nearest cultures claim it was close to Threshold when it went silent, shortly before your war."

The vast shoals of light-scattering dust ripple with density waves, billowing like storm clouds. Echoes of planetary blast fronts still churn here. A display calculates the volume of material present. The numbers are staggering.

"They had weapons that could fragment planets," I say.

"And I think I found one."

The display shows a magnified view of the lone planet, a gas giant. Something drifts in the upper atmosphere. A dark angular shape.

"It must be massive to be visible at this range," I say.

"It is. At least twenty times larger than my ship."

"How did you detect it?"

"Easy," he says, engaging the ship's drive. "It's giving off a signal."

Closer, the object resembles a dead bloom. Black tiles armor the curving sides, giving way to long, thick radial vanes.

"See those bulges along the top?" says Noroda. "They're buoyancy sacs, keeping it aloft. Someone ditched it here."

"Is it functional?" I ask.

"Oh, I hope not. Look at that front aperture. Acceleration cannon. That thing could drop extinction-level munitions."

"Where does the signal originate?"

"Deep inside."

I look at the forbidding shape, and realize the compelling need to know how it came to be.

"We need to enter," I say.

Noroda touches my arm. "Blue, I have learned a lot in my life. High on that list is that when you find a big evil-looking machine corpse in the middle of a murdered star system, you do *not* go into it."

Noroda remotely pilots one of his metallic machines via implanted augments. He informs me that I can share the link. I watch through the machine's ocular system as it moves towards the gas giant. I hear Noroda's unspoken commands, telling it where to turn and how much thrust to apply.

The words remind me, disturbingly, of the undervoice.

I watch the progress, marveling at the scale of the black vessel. The armor tiles show deep corrosion, and the machine augers through the hull with ease. Once within, the view shifts to false colors, compensating for the darkness. It passes through wide tunnels and slanted enclosures full of bewildering machinery. Reaction tanks stand taller than hives, attended by ranks of vertical coils reaching to mist-obscured heights. Deeper, cavernous chambers host oblique knots of dense apparatus, linked by sinuous webs of conduits. Even devoid of light, these vaulted spaces seem populated by shifting, uneasy shadows.

I remember how my hive mates and I looked to the stars, speculating that such levels of technology might exist. I am glad they are not here to see this vast, dead place.

At the center of the construct, the machine finds a spherical cavity. Floating at the center is an oval pod.

"The signal originates here?" I ask.

"Yes. It's a stasis pod, broadcasting its status. It's still running."

Noroda sends a command, and the machine extends long filaments, wrapping them around the pod like a cocoon.

Noroda calls the domed chamber deep in his ship the "safe room."

The heavily armored walls are lined with equipment racks, displays, and devices he calls containment field generators. Many articulated arms hang from the apex, ending in tools or scanners. The pod sits at the center. It is larger than expected, able to accommodate something twice my size.

"We must assume whatever's in here was subjected to corruption," Noroda says as he straddles the pod and pulls down one of the tools. "With luck I can isolate its invasive structure and nullify it, as I did with you. If not, we may have to restrain it. Blue, are you listening?"

I am looking around the room. "Why did you not bring me here when you found me?"

The fleshy ridge above his eyes knots. "No offense, but you were just a *head*. And I honestly thought you were too damaged to repair. Now, I am going to start by—"

As Noroda touches the tool to the surface, the pod emits a buzzing noise. Vapor vents from recessed valves. Lights glow along its sides. Noroda scrambles off as the top splits along a hidden seam and folds back.

Cold mist swirls from the opening. A figure sits up, clad in shimmering fabric wrapping. As we watch, the shroud loosens and retracts, revealing a pale yellow photosensitive membrane pulled taut over a circular skull. Fronds resembling rivulets of liquid metal form a fanning crest from the back of the neck. As the mist clears I see that below the neck, it is clad in black material similar to the vessel we extracted it from.

The featureless face turns to us. A small vertical orifice splits open along the bottom half.

"I do not care who you are," it says. "I do not care how long I have been in this pod. I only care about how much food you have."

She calls herself Vanathius, and she is, indeed, hungry.

"The Destroyer nourished me intravenously," she says between handfuls of nutrient cubes. "Once it became inoperative, I had no way to feed my organics."

"How much of you is still biological?" asks Noroda.

That is my question as well. Vanathius' black armored form is tall and broad-shouldered. Her two arms bisect at the elbows into stalks, each ending in a three-fingered hand. Her torso

50

tapers to a waist narrow enough to grasp in one claw. Below that, she is supported by a column of hair-like tendrils.

"Major organs, nervous system, and head," she says. "This biomech was added when the infection struck."

She stands beside the pod, tendrils splaying across the chamber floor. Several scanner arms pivot around her, analyzing every surface of her armor. Noroda watches the findings on a wall display.

"You remember it?" he asks.

"In faultless detail," Vanathius replies, chewing the last cube. Her fronds stiffen. "Our Great Republic was a noble endeavor. My people dwelt on six planets in this system, and hundreds of habitats in the asteroid belts. We had long heard the telemetry of other cultures in the Span, and spent two hundred years preparing to take our place among them. We advanced towards Threshold with purpose. Other species contacted us, told us the long history of the stars, showed us how to build transluminal drives. We thought ourselves at the dawn of a fine and mighty age."

The words sadden me, recalling the tacit optimism the hives expressed at the prospect of interstellar contact.

"Our circumsolar receivers picked up a signal. It spread through our communications networks faster than we could defend against it. Our technology…reprogrammed itself, generating new and horrible iterations. Plumes of microtech filled the skies and spread across the worlds, reshaping any material they touched. When everything was infected, they turned on us. They defiled us, disfigured our souls."

"Your molecular structure was breached," says Noroda, studying the display. "Looks like a bio-active agent. Probably

51

deployed conditioning, adulterated your cognition and behavioral patterns."

"How is that possible?" I ask.

Noroda looks at me. "It happens in nature all the time. Parasites inject brain-controlling toxins into prey, take control of motor functions. Forced symbiosis is a common evolutionary strategy."

"And successful," says Vanathius. "One by one our worlds went silent, as my people were remade."

"How did you end up in the Destroyer?" asks Noroda.

"It used to be my ship. I ran cargo from the homeworld to the belts. It was beset by a cloud of microtech. They infiltrated and rebuilt everything, converting it to matter denser than anything our science could forge. I tried to escape but they ate through my protective suit. They turned me into this, wired me into the heart of the Destroyer. I became little more than its tactical engine, perceiving only what the sensors showed me. Once the change was complete, the war began."

"Who were you fighting?" I ask.

"Ourselves. The worlds and habitats attacked each other. This was war without nuance or strategy. There were a thousand Destroyers roaming the system, vaporizing anything solid they encountered, pausing only to draw fuel from the gas giant's atmosphere. I watched through my Destroyer's eyes as we slaughtered habitats. I heard the signal coursing the receivers, commanding us to bombard our worlds."

Her fronds wilt. Her membrane grows even paler.

Noroda steps up to her. "How did you survive?"

"By being the last one left. The system was rubble, except for the gas giant. With no one left to fight, no more worlds to destroy, the corruption shut down, as did the Destroyer. I regained awareness to find it diving towards the gas giant. For two days I tried to stop it. I finally managed to alter trajectory by purging a reaction tank, and inflated the buoyancy sacs in time to aerobrake. There was not enough power to pull the Destroyer out of the atmosphere, so I rigged this pod and placed myself in stasis."

Noroda looks at her. "You built that? That's a fine piece of engineering."

Vanathius is silent, looking at the pod.

"What is wrong?" Noroda asks.

"I had a mate on the homeworld," she says softly. "I had offspring. I remember every bombardment I committed, but I cannot remember what my family looked like."

I step to her. "I must ask. You said the corruption shut down. Did the Destroyer send a transmission?"

She turns to me, a few fronds perking up. "Yes. A large one. Just before it deactivated."

Noroda turns to me. "You think that's what your people heard?"

"I am certain of it."

"This happened to your world?" Vanathius says. "Then this truly is an infection."

"Not exactly," says Noroda. "Infections spread and replicate, affecting as many as possible." He studies me. "You heard the undervoice say 'unit unsynchronized' before it abandoned you." He looks at Vanathius. "Your ship did not transmit until *after* the system was destroyed. Whatever this is, it's linear. Hitting one or two hosts, wiping them out, then moving on others."

Vanathius' fronds quiver. "You have data to support this? I would like to see it."

"The scanners find no trace of anything active in you, so you have free reign of the ship. I've got *real* food for you in the galley."

Noroda leads us to the control room, bathed in red light from the system outside.

Vanathius stands in the hatchway, motionless. For a moment I fear the sight of the desolated Great Republic has affected her.

"This is a Span Guard vessel," she says softly.

Noroda turns suddenly. "What do you know of the Span Guard?"

"They were defenders of much of the Span, augmented entities protecting developing worlds. But they died long ago. Several cultures told the Great Republic of their last war, and how it engulfed a thousand systems. I have seen images of Span Guard ships. Did you salvage it?"

"Yes," he says quickly, turning away. "I'll get the data we have on the signal so far. If it's following a programmed methodology, then transmitters on Blue's world must have sent the infection forward."

"We had the capability," I say.

"I know. But there are pre-spacefaring worlds closer to this system than yours. They were unaffected. I wonder if the infection can only take root in cultures with the means of interstellar communication, or if it builds its own. I need to do some research."

He begins working at a console.

Vanathius approaches me, her tendrils sweeping the floor in measured undulations. "You are also the last of your people?"

"Yes, though unlike you I was destroyed in the conflict." I look at my metal arms. "Noroda restored me."

"An admirable construction, though I could improve upon it." She raises a hand in a gesture. "I salute you, for we are both ghosts of what we were."

The statement triggers a thought.

"Did your people believe in an afterlife?" I ask.

"In the early ages of the Great Republic," she says, "we lived in hope of dwelling in the House of the Enduring Illuminant. I thought of it often during the war." She looks out the transparency. "If such a place exists, I hope my people found it."

For the first time in seven hundred years, I fly.

Composite wings lift me from the endless plain of red cracked soil, away from my companions and the landing craft we arrived in.

In the days it took Noroda to find the world called Almadin, Vanathius divided her time between sampling the many foodstuffs aboard the ship and modifying my metallic form. Her improvements are remarkable. The seams between plates are tighter. My limbs taper, granting my joints much wider articulation. Most impressively, these wings propel me into the dark gray sky with great speed. I had forgotten how much perception can change with altitude.

I would be overcome with joy, if not for the view below. A chronicle of battle is written across the ground in blast fissures and impact craters.

From above, the city Cradle-of-Peace is a sprawling oval of broken spires and cracked domes, enclosed within high curving walls. According to Noroda, it once stood at the shore of the Silver Sea, far to the south. As the only true city on this world of wandering tribes, it was the prosperous center of commerce. Now, infection masks its former opulence. Every surface is textured in black and silver plaques of disordered matter. Magnifying my view, I see gunnery turrets and gaping projectile silos jutting from the walls. Most unnerving are the eight enormous wheels mounted on slanting, segmented shafts along the sides of the city. The corruption crafted this rolling platform, bearing the weaponized Cradle-of-Peace on its back. The wide tracks left by this mobile fortress lead all the way to the horizon.

Far below me, Vanathius stands at the base of a forward wheel, as if daring it to crush her. She points up at the city's expansive undercarriage. "They were carrying significant ordnance," she transmits, "but none remains."

"Does that surprise you?" says Noroda.

"No, but if the corruption can remake matter, why limit itself to artillery? It crafted far more advanced weapons in the Great Republic."

"I've been thinking about that. Each war has involved different arsenals, no two alike. Blue, any signs of a population from up there?"

I make a low pass between spires and magnify my view. "None," I reply. "The city is empty."

"I guess that explains these stains."

Scattered around the city lay thousands of blasted wrecks. Noroda stands beside one some distance behind the city. I descend.

The six-legged machine stands half Noroda's height, its white surface marred with red dirt. Two of its triple-jointed legs are damaged. The semi-spherical housing at its top has several entry wounds. The single red lens at the front is cracked.

I look to the deep wheel tracks on either side of us. They are filled with hundreds of the crushed machines.

As Vanathius joins us, Noroda says, "The tactics are different here as well. The city-dwellers unloaded their weapons into this infantry. Once they spent their ammunition, they climbed down and attacked on foot. They didn't last long."

He gestures around us. My targeting array marks where faint black stains lay baked in the soil. They dot the plain as far as I can see.

Noroda looks at Vanathius. "If the city had been converted into something like your Destroyer, the battle would've been even shorter. What does that tell you?"

"I am uncertain."

"This was not about the casualties. It's about the war itself."

"This technology," I say, looking at the wreck, "shows no sign of infection."

"I noticed," says Noroda. "If the hardware wasn't remade, the corruption must have hit the software."

"Will you bring it to the ship?"

"Not until I know it can be useful."

Noroda retrieves a small square device from a pocket. After prying a thick panel from the side of the machine's housing, he attaches wires to the electronics within. Almost instantly there is a whir from within the machine. A screen on the small device lights up, and data begins to scroll.

"It's called a Synthesist," says Noroda. "Now *that's* a catchy name. I've learned the most successful cultures are the ones with memorable names. This one has a lot of memory storage, and it's mostly full. I'll try to access it."

As Noroda works I look up at the devastated city looming over us. Vanathius steps beside me.

"Another civilization obliterated," she says softly.

"When Noroda revived me," I say, "I learned much of the Span's history, those myriad threads of progress and advancement accumulating across ages. How many cultures have lost their futures to this infection?"

"Here we go," says Noroda.

I turn to see the machine's red eye light up. The housing swivels. A scanning beam plays over the three of us.

"I am Planetary Ratiocination Probe 677383," the machine says in a static-tinged voice, "and I must insist you place me in custody. I am guilty of the crime of mass murder."

Noroda places his hands on his knees and looks the machine in its eye.

"Get in line, my friend."

In the safe room, Vanathius enacts repairs on the Synthesist. She reshapes panels from her stasis pod to fashion replacement legs, seals the damage on the housing, and scrapes dirt and dried gore from its joints and hinges. The machine, whom Noroda addresses as Probe, continues its insistence that it must be incarcerated or dismantled. Noroda calms it by recounting the events of our search. After that, Vanathius and I tell our respective tales, and Probe slowly comprehends the situation.

"I am one of a mind-cluster assigned to study evolving worlds," it tells us. "Our deployment carrier distributed thousands of us to designated planets. Each spent years measuring terrain, indexing flora and fauna, mapping natural dynamics, and crafting long-term models of how life might develop. We performed these tasks countless times with unerring efficiency, until the War God enslaved us."

58

Noroda leans back at the statement. "Why do you call it the War God?"

"That was its self-designation. I saw the code it instilled in us, watched as it erased all priorities other than war. The mind-cluster was entering our next target sector when the transmission struck. It overran the carrier's systems and infiltrated each of us. My purpose was rewritten, my prodigious processing tuned to calculate strategies and run countless predictive simulations for combat engagement."

Vanathius' hands clench as she hears this.

"The carrier deposited us on Almadin," Probe continues. "Cradle-of-Peace attacked immediately. We swarmed it. Our distance-ranging beams amplified past their limiters, becoming tools of death. I personally incinerated eighty-three of the city-dwellers. When they attacked by hand, I crushed two hundred and sixteen more. I remember each scream, each face. They were horrible things, abominations of flesh and corruption. Even more horrible was the futility of it all." The housing swivels, looking at each of us in turn. "Have you determined the cause of this?"

"We suspect," says Vanathius, "a parasitic signal communicating itself from world to world."

"I have studied parasitic interactions," says Probe, "analyzed the multiplicity of impacts they have on environments. This was a different class of event. We Synthesists were conscripted into a conflict that could not end in any sum other than zero. Our mutual pointless destruction was the sole end product. I was rendered immobile in the battle, and watched as my cluster-mates continued the slaughter. When it ended, I felt the War God's influence abate, and was overwhelmed by guilt. It lasted long years until my power drained away."

Almost involuntarily, I place a claw atop its housing. Vanathius matches my gesture.

"Well," says Noroda, "now that you're fixed, feel free to move around the ship."

Probe looks at him. "Do you think that is wise?"

"Why wouldn't it be?"

"I told you. I saw the War God's code. I still maintain a copy in my memory."

As the ship travels to the edge of the Almadin system, I appraise the progression of amplitudes my life has traversed. I am the end result of successive displacements: my dedication to science supplanted by militant obsession; my biology usurped by body prosthesis; my obliteration undone by restoration. This last reminds me that such consideration must also include my death. My thoughts swarm around the unsettling possibility that I am defined solely by the things I have ceased to be.

I also realize that I am no longer the sole surviving artifact of these wars.

Vanathius consumes a bowl of soup as we watch a display in the control room. On it, Noroda sits on the floor beside Probe. Extracting the code is meticulous work, involving many machines laid out around the safe room. Through communion with the ship I see hazard protocols activate, powering down all communications lines and most processors, reducing the risk of the code finding its way into other systems.

"This ship responds well to Noroda's commands," says Vanathius. "Do you know how long he has traveled in it?"

"No," I reply. "Much of its archive has been deleted and rewritten."

"Interesting." She points to Noroda's machines on the display. "He has chambers full of equipment aboard. Such a collection would take time to accumulate. I am curious as to his age."

Noroda transfers the code into a shielded cylindrical datacore via a bundle of cables. Once finished, he instructs Probe to join us in the control room. We all observe Noroda attaching contacts to the datacore's mirrored surface and monitoring his machines. Occasionally he makes a sound, like 'whoops,' or pauses to rub his chin.

The ship has cleared the system by the time he joins us, damp with perspiration.

"I really hope I never have to do *that* again," he says, wiping his brow.

"Did you access the code?" ask Vanathius.

"Eventually. Damned thing had thirty-seven layers of encryption. It's incomplete and heavily compressed, but still formidable. I found commands for reprogramming technology, activating bio-agents, and restructuring memory, but no clue as to its purpose. Nothing to explain the infection's effectiveness on diverse victims." He looks at Probe. "You don't have any guesses as to why it calls itself the War God, do you?"

Probe swivels his housing. "I do not guess. I hypothesize. The severity with which the infection spread among the mind-cluster suggests urgency. Further speculation requires additional analysis."

"That's exactly what I'm thinking."

"How do you plan to proceed?" asks Vanathius.

"First," says Noroda, "I am going to wrap that thing in a layer of fission gel and store it in the rear airlock. If we have to destroy it, I want to be able to do it fast. Then, I want to see how it spreads for myself."

"You intend to activate it?" I ask.

"Yes. We'll need some test subjects."

Vanathius tenses. Probe steps back and says, "I will not allow other intellects to be corrupted."

Noroda tilts his head. "What? *Oh.* No, not on anything intelligent. We need a remote location, and I think I know just the place."

"Where?" I ask.

"The earliest site I investigated. We need to go to see the War God's first victims."

We each have assigned stations in the control room.

Vanathius monitors navigation, mapping detailed topologies of gravity wells and orbital radii. Automatons regularly bring her platters of food, which she eats with near-mechanical constancy.

Probe analyzes sensor data, plotting the War God's movements against the density of inhabited worlds and rates of technological maturity. Occasionally Noroda feeds it theories, and it calculates probabilities.

I am linked to the communications array. My intuitive communion with the ship's systems deepens by increments as I listen for the telemetry of war.

Noroda brings us to coordinates deep in the interstellar void, far from any suns or worlds. The ship's forward lamps illuminate a large damaged polyhedron made of porous stone. Noroda calls it a *Pan-Celestial*, a reclusive species of transapient who frequent the deep void to meditate. It looms before us, slowly rotating. Each face shows projectile impacts. One entire section has been sheared away, exposing nested layers of crystalline strata laced with black corruption.

Around it, hundreds of shattered spacecraft hang in loose orbit. They were a caravan of sub-light wanderers. Shards of fractured carapace drift like dust.

"How long ago did this happen?" I ask.

"I can't be certain," says Noroda. "At least twelve hundred years ago."

An intact corpse drifts past, its transformed pressure suit gleaming in the lamplight.

I look at Noroda. "Will you try to revive one?"

"They're too far gone to be viable. Besides, I wouldn't dare with that thing on board."

He points to a display showing the interior of the ship's rear airlock. The datacore sits, its metallic sheen dulled by fission gel, enough to atomize the ship and everything around us. In his other hand he holds the detonation trigger.

"Why do you risk this?" I ask.

"Because we need more data. We could spend our lives checking every system for evidence. If we study the infection in a controlled environment, we might figure out where it's heading."

I look out at the biological and transapient carnage. "I question your definition of 'controlled.'"

His orifice curls. "Never underestimate the power of my delusions. Regardless, this trip will be wasted unless we have subjects." He looks out the transparency. "I know they're here somewhere."

"These sensors are remarkable," says Probe. "Their sensitivity surpasses even mine."

"Not surprising," says Vanathius. "This is a Span Guard vessel."

The Synthesist's housing swivels and looks at Noroda. "How did you obtain a Span Guard vessel?"

"I salvaged it," Noroda says, not looking up.

"After three thousand years? I find that highly—"

The sensor console lights up with numerous contacts.

Noroda redirects the lamps towards one of the dead ships. A multitude of small machines, no bigger than my claw, crawl across the broken hull.

"Scavengers," says Noroda. "A sub-sentient system scouring the void between stars. The machine equivalent of carrion-eaters. They're slow-moving. It can take thousands of years to pick a site clean."

"They assimilate discarded technology," says Probe, "fulfilling a synthetic instinct to enhance themselves."

Noroda looks at the Synthesist. "You've studied them?"

"Other mind-clusters have, but I am familiar with the findings. The interstellar medium is a rich environment, with its own modes of evolution. These systems upgrade themselves in increments over millions of years, generating augments and accumulating complexity. Some progress so thoroughly they disappear."

"Where do they go?" asks Vanathius.

"Unknown. It is theorized they advance themselves until spacetime can no longer contain them."

"Imagine it," says Noroda. "Outgrowing corporeality without the benefit of intellect."

"Indeed," says Probe. "We Synthesists felt an affinity for them."

"Why?" I ask.

"The principle of upgrade was significant to us. It was a transition of joyful sorrows and mournful glories. If we were irreparably damaged in the course of our duties, we spent our last processing cycles hoping we had performed sufficiently to earn re-instantiation, where our code could be reborn."

"No offense to your affinity," says Noroda, "but these little guys are about to become a science experiment. Blue, is the tightbeam ready?"

I check my console. "Yes."

"Good. I've configured the defensive field to buffer any returning signals. You'll hear the telemetry, but any infection transmitted back at us will be diffracted."

He targets a small piece of wreckage adrift some distance from the ship. Two scavengers work at it, prying off segments with blunt, bladed limbs.

"Transmit," says Noroda, turning the trigger over in his hand.

I key the transmitter to access the datacore, then send a low-power tightbeam at the fragment.

I think of the Science Hive, and how we sent our signals out to the stars. A brief sense of guilt fills me. I am traveling between those stars, while the Hive has been dead for eight hundred years.

Dead...

I turn to Probe and ask, "Did you retain your principle of upgrade during the War God's corruption?"

Its housing swivels to me. "Yes. When I was incapacitated, I prayed for a new form so I could continue the battle."

A thought shapes itself.

"This experiment has succeeded," says Vanathius.

I turn to see the two scavengers flailing each other with surprising ferocity. A moment later the ones crawling the wreck join the fray, tumbling in small groups. They grapple and slice. Space before us writhes with machine violence. Noroda watches intently. Vanathius looks away. Sensor data scrolls on Probe's console. I hear the myriad small transmissions between the scavengers, stoking mutual aggression.

Noroda turns to Probe. "Any sign they're aware of us?"

"Nothing I can detect. The War God's sensory protocols are heavily augmented. I cannot estimate the scope of its perception."

The signals from the scavengers shift and modulate.

Unexpectedly, I hear the undervoice.

Through my link to the communication array, it is no more than a distant, hissing whisper, speaking in something less than language. Each strand of telemetry rakes across space like a claw scraping stone. A discreet reverberation accumulates as the counterfeit War God issues its commands.

Scattered disjointed memories come unbidden: my battle with the Moviq; my first unfocused sight of Noroda; my flight above the rolling city. I remember Noroda replicating neural structures in my damaged head. Now, shards of the undervoice's influence tumble through that scaffold, and in their echoes I hear the War God's thoughts.

I do not possess the words or concepts, but some intuitive sense, perhaps my communion with the ship, provides a faint approximation: The corruption does not want to simply extend towards another star system. It aims itself at protracted angles and unfixed ordinates, seeking directions that do not exist. It is impeded by the constraints of—

"The wreck is moving!" shouts Vanathius.

My facets snap to focus. Beyond the scavengers, the blasted ship begins a slow roll. Lights flicker within the damaged hull. A sputtering glow coughs from the thruster cone.

"It's been re-infected," mutters Noroda. "That's damned inconvenient."

In the distance, another wreck moves fitfully.

Probe's console chimes. "The scavengers are targeting us."

I watch as they abandon their battle and turn, as one, towards us. It troubles me how much they resemble a swarm.

Noroda reaches for the drive controls. "Vanathius, plot a course out of here, fast."

The ship turns. Through the transparency the wrecks slide away. The transapient polyhedron looms into our field of view. Sparks flash from its crystalline innards.

As Noroda increases the defensive field, the ship keels violently.

"One of the wrecks still has active warheads," says Probe.

Noroda ignites the main thrusters.

Another jolt, this time accompanied by a loud crackling. Several displays flicker to static. At the edge of the transparency I can still see the polyhedron. Red and violet lightning leaps from its stone faces towards us. Another warhead crosses our path.

The ship accelerates. On a rear-view display, the wrecks and the transapient move to pursue, but severe damage hinders their maneuvers. As we speed out of range, they turn and engage each other, resuming a war that ended long ago. Amid the blazing weapon-fire I spot the small silver glints of swarming scavengers.

Noroda works the airlock controls. The datacore shoots from the rear hatch on a wave of explosive decompression, tumbling away behind us.

"It reactivated dead tech," he says. "Nasty surprise. I've got a better one."

He activates the trigger. The rear display fills with an expanding sphere of energy consuming the wreckage. Feedback howls through the communications array until I mute it.

I note, with relief, that the undervoice is gone.

Noroda places a hand on my arm. "Are you alright?"

"I am uncertain."

"Noroda," says Probe, crossing the control room. "I have successfully gauged the War God's telemetry vectors and compared them to my mind-cluster's infection. It spreads in a specific pattern, adhering to certain directional axes in its signaling. This pattern appears immutable. Probability dictates it is also scalable."

Vanathius' fronds curl. "What does that mean?"

"It means," says Noroda, "we can find the damned thing."

I commune with the ship's data banks.

I do not seek particular knowledge, but rather an understanding of my experience during the scavenger encounter. So elusive is this task that I spend much of the day performing unguided searches through Span history.

The sheer volume of events is daunting, composed of millions of species over billions of years, existing in augmented states of intellect and potency. Each has its own set of histories and sagas.

And myths.

In the course of my aimless perusal, I note underlying contexts, suggesting innate order within the essence of history. I find many accounts of great quests, where indomitable fellowships and guilds plied the stars on missions of cosmic importance. Some pitted themselves against relentless threats. Others sought to penetrate the boundaries of spacetime and behold greater realities. These recurrent themes repeat with all the inevitability of fundamental forces.

"What's on your mind, Blue?"

Noroda stands behind me." Nothing of importance," I reply.

"Don't forget," he taps the side of his head, "I've seen your thoughtcodes, and can tell when you're linked to the ship. Something has bothered you for a while now."

I gesture to the data bank display. "This breadth of history taxes my senses. In the hives we existed in the present tense, occasionally casting our ambitions to the near future. The influence of the War God intensified this sense of reference."

"You never had to dwell on the past? Blue, sometimes I envy you."

"In considering this immeasurable history, I am curious if the Span has ever experienced a force of war like this."

Noroda leans on the console beside me. "There have been some very long conflicts. I recall one old empire that kept its member worlds at war for five thousand years, and a consortium that seeded strife for twice that."

"Those are wars of purpose, with set goals and intentions."

"Oh, you want to know about the *really* big ones. Well, there are legions of systems like the scavengers coursing between the stars. They're very territorial. And I once heard of a fight between two ancient transapients that lasted six million years. Of course, they were time-dilated to such slowness that each strike lasted an age. Some advanced intellects claim they've seen raging conflicts and eternal wars consuming higher mathematical spaces."

I watch him. He sees me watching him. The ends of his orifice turn up in an expression I now recognize as affinity.

"Blue," he says, "I know how smart you are. And how observant. What is this really about?"

"I suspect," says Vanathius, as she and Probe enter the control room, "that Blue is wondering the same thing we are."

Noroda faces her. "Which is?"

"Why have you taken up this cause?"

Noroda crosses his arms. "I was wondering when you'd get around to asking."

"I suspect your people were victims of the War God."

Noroda laughs. "No. Not a bad guess, though."

"You told me," I say, "that you were making reparations."

Probe steps forward. "The answer is obvious."

We all turn to it.

"I scanned you when you first revived me. You are heavily augmented, down to the cellular level. I suspect you are far older than you appear. There is also the empirical data to consider: this vessel; your knowledge of activities within the Span; your deft handling of the War God's code. And, of course, your ethical character."

Noroda laughs again. "No one's ever accused me of *that* before."

"In a Span this vast and populated, people die by the millions in war every day. The death of so few cultures at the hands of the War God is statistically insignificant. And yet to you they are of the utmost importance. As if, in some way, you are responsible."

"And what does that tell you?"

"I predict a high probability that you were of the Span Guard."

Noroda sits and rubs the flesh between his eyes. "I always hated that name. Not catchy at all. It made us sound like a military outfit. We weren't warriors. We were a guild of peace keepers."

"How long were you among them?" asks Vanathius in a tone implying awe.

"Over a hundred years. Right up until the end."

"What happened?" I ask.

He looks at me. "If you're expecting an epic tale of bravery, you're going to be disappointed. Our enemy were the Thrones. They were manipulators, thought themselves the arbiters of morality. They infiltrated cultures, got friendly with the people in power, and silently influenced decisions."

"For what purpose?" asks Probe.

"They frowned upon what they saw as runaway advancement. They thought most cultures were far too eager to leave their homeworlds and become space-faring. The Span was crowded enough, in their opinion. They also condemned transapience, insisting that a finite biological existence was what gave life meaning. They would've been a laughable cult, if not for the fact that they had over a thousand interstellar cultures on their side."

"The Great Republic had similar dissenters," says Vanathius. "They thought contact with more advanced civilizations was polluting us."

"How did you deal with them?" asks Noroda.

"We ignored them until they eventually died off."

"We didn't have that luxury. We thought we did, but we were wrong. The Span Guard assisted developing worlds, offered protection through times of transition, helped them take steps towards transapience. We were augmented to interact with intellects greater than ourselves. But the Thrones were long-term thinkers, with plans extending hundreds of thousands of years into the future. They projected that our efforts could impact their spread throughout the Span. So they whispered in the ears of the cultures they influenced. Especially the ones with well-armed space fleets. They came after us suddenly and brutally. Engaged us at every turn. We couldn't run. There were too many worlds at stake. But it was apparent from the start that we couldn't defeat them."

"So you created something that could," says Probe. "You built the War God."

"Not me, personally. That's out of my range of expertise. We had hyper-intelligences for that. And it wasn't the War God, just an adaptive program designed to exploit enemy vulnerabilities, loaded into a sizable swarm of microtech. It was an astonishing piece of engineering, able to draw power from any source, infiltrate technology, and re-purpose whatever matter it found. We deployed it against the fleets, tasked it with stopping as many as it could. For a while it was quite a sight. It converted whole asteroid belts into weapons, dismantled attacking ships with ease, and mounted some impenetrable defenses. The problem was, it was smart enough to detect a threat, but not enough see through a ploy. The Thrones lured it away with an aggressive formation of a few thousand ships. Once it was out of the way, they came after us with everything. The war didn't last very long after that."

"The Span Guard lost," I say.

"Quite decisively. Most were killed. But in the process the Thrones were revealed for the monsters they were. They were ostracized. To this day they are hunted by fleets who won't rest until every trace is eradicated from the Span. Another eternal conflict among many. My point is, there was no one left to deactivate the system."

"What about you?" asks Vanathius.

Noroda looks at the floor. "I was in bad shape after that. Remorse. Survivor guilt. I took this ship to a lot of different systems. I went the *slow* way, relativistic sub-light, alone with my thoughts. I lost hundreds of years to time dilation. Encountered a *lot* of strange situations, most of which I handled poorly. The fact is, I didn't think about our program, never considered that it could still be running, or what it might encounter, drifting through a Span populated by advancing cultures and powerful transapients."

"How did you determine it was still active?" asks Probe.

"I heard about the sequence of inexplicable wars and got curious. I looked for guilds with the resources to investigate, but couldn't find any. So I checked the early ruins myself. When I saw the totality of the destruction, I feared the worst." He looks at me. "Finding you confirmed it."

"The undervoice," I say.

"Yes, that gap in your thoughtcodes. I recognized it. It's a control channel. Highly adaptive."

"It has the ability to upgrade itself," says Probe.

"That's an understatement. The question is, what exactly did it evolve into? Blue, I have to ask. During the scavenger battle, did you hear the undervoice?"

"Yes, faintly," I say. "It was not directed at me, but it was active."

"I thought that might happen, especially after the wrecks were re-infected. We can take advantage of that. If we get close to the War God while it's in action, you may be able to access its code."

"You want to compromise it?" asks Vanathius.

"I want to deactivate it. It may be frighteningly complex and adaptive, but it's still an automated program."

"No," says Probe. "It is more."

Noroda looks at him. "You said its pattern was immutable."

"Yes. It maintains a strict methodology, but it is selecting victims carefully. I have run several thousand analytical models. This is not an opportunistic predator. These acts are the result of decisions. I could not rectify these findings until you expressed how adaptive the original system was. It is clearly sentient."

Vanathius' fronds splay. "A sentience that transmits itself?"

"Yes. A carrier-wave of thought-signal. Moving from host to host, much as my kind transferred from form to form. Large enough to bear its memories. Complex enough to enact invasive protocols."

"But it must have some criteria," says Noroda. "We've seen the wide spectrum of species it can compromise: a hive mind; transapients; machine intellects. There must be a technical vulnerability it's exploiting as an infection vector."

"Perhaps," I say, "the vulnerability is not technical."

The three of them look at me.

"It already had the capability to adapt technology. It may select targets based on another factor." I turn to the Vanathius and Probe. "We three have one commonality. We all fought in hope of being worthy."

"Worthy of what?" asks Noroda.

"The Enduring Illuminant. The principle of upgrade. Urqulon."

Vanathius's fronds stiffen. "You think it exploited our afterlife beliefs?"

"I state only the possibility."

"How would a transmitted sentience detect mythology?" she asks.

"I do not know." I gesture to Probe. "You said you could not estimate the scope of its perception."

"Blue's right," says Noroda. "It's a possibility. Even the scavengers acted on an instinct to upgrade. And it would explain why the corruption disabled your will, but left your myths intact."

"Even if we accept that explanation of *how* it functions," says Vanathius, "it still does not explain *why.*"

The sensor console chimes. Probe moves to it.

"The system we are approaching," it says, "is currently engulfed in war."

I am defined solely by the things I have ceased to be.

This possibility returns, homing back to my thoughts with an almost feral persistence. It evades intuition like an unwelcome sorrow: involuntary, unprompted, and offering no explanation for its presence.

My disquiet elicits a memory of the Moviq attack, when the explosion crippled my body, and the undervoice abandoned me. Strangely, it is neither fear of death I remember, nor the sudden revelation of my enshrouded past, but the interval of clarity I felt in the instant before I was destroyed.

This recollection is so strong, I momentarily forget I am in the safe room.

"I don't like this," says Noroda, strapping a canister of fission gel to my thorax.

"Neither do I." Vanathius stands behind me, calibrating the dorsal plasma thruster she has installed.

"I predict a high likelihood," says Probe, "that if either of you were in Blue's place, you would insist on proceeding."

"That doesn't make me feel any better," says Noroda. He looks me in the eyes. "My restorative measures in your brain *should* protect you from re-infection."

"And if they cannot..." I say, looking down at the canister.

"I purged your corruption once. No reason I can't repeat the process."

"The War God may not give you the chance."

Noroda's orifice curls down. "I'll be in the control room. We can start whenever you're ready."

Vanathius looks at him. "I am almost finished."

As Noroda and Probe leave, Vanathius steps in front of me. "How do the wings feel?"

I extend them. They are lighter than my previous pair, and veined with antenna wire. They spread to the walls, widening from wedges to semi-circles.

"They feel large," I say.

"They need to be." She touches either side of my head, tipping it back. "I am less confident of the other modification you requested."

"Your work has not failed me yet."

I retract the wings and look down at the canister. The inert explosive has three activation options. I have a trigger embedded in my claw. Noroda has another. If I am severely damaged or incapacitated, the gel will automatically build to a maximum charge before detonating.

I step to the control room.

The most prevalent myths in the ship's data bank are those concerning the concept of the Last War, the great deciding battle to define the state of the cosmos. Most iterations portray the conflict as monumental in scope, ruthlessness, and carnage.

None come close to the intensities below us.

According to Noroda, the Tzord-Urja trinary system had been called the pinnacle of civilization. The magnificent cultures that flourished here wielded staggering technologies, allowing them to tune the output of the suns and engineer even the most uninviting worlds to habitability.

Now, from our vantage above the ecliptic, the system glows like a dying fire. Two stars circle each other at the center, one yellow, one blue. The third, white and unnaturally flickering, occupies a wide orbit. We are too distant to observe the major engagements, but Vanathius projects a schematic orrery at the center of the control room, showing how the system has been corrupted.

Hundreds of moon-sized fortresses surround the central stellar pair, each anchoring a petal formation of solar accumulators. Spire-like structures extend from their outward-facing surfaces, emitting blinding particle beams. Thousands of attacking ships are annihilated in this onslaught, only to be replaced by thousands more.

The outer white star is ringed by a band of black material, inset with a lens the size of a planet. A retractable sheath opens and closes over the lens, blinking like an eye. Most astonishingly, the band swivels and pivots on unfixed axes at a speed bordering on relativistic. A focused beam of magnified light whips the sky, reducing whole ship formations to gouts of metallic vapor.

Such toll is negligible. The invading vessels number in the hundreds of thousands, each making near-constant short-range transluminal jumps. Their black hulls launch unending streams of projectiles. Thirteen planets are under attack. Another eight are already cinders. The transluminal activity fills Tzord-Urja with a glowing fog of charged particles. The radiation is beyond measure.

Almost forgotten at the system's edge is a substantial cometary cloud. Torus-shaped transapients make spinning, sweeping passes along the inner margins, generating gravity fields strong enough to dredge millions of ice balls from their orbit and sling them in-system. It is unclear if these transapients are allied with Tzord-Urja or the invading fleet. Their cometary rain does not discriminate. The consensus among the four of us is that such distinction is irrelevant.

Probe measures the expansion of abundant debris fields, and estimates the war has endured for at least four years. Through the transparency, my facets detect pinpoint, distance-delayed flashes of past explosions.

I also hear the undervoice.

"Can you make out its commands?" Noroda asks.

"Not from in here," I reply. "The signal is too faint. I need to be outside."

With a single pulse of thrust, I clear the forward airlock. I look back to see my companions watching through the control room transparency.

My wings spread, seven times wider than my old ones, forming a near-perfect circle with me at the center. The embedded threads of antenna wire power up. Instantly, a tightbeam link connects me to the communications array.

"Can you hear us?" asks Noroda.

"Quite clearly."

"We're getting your telemetry. Can you hear the War God any better?"

"No. As we expected, the ship generates conflicting signals. I am moving farther out."

I hear the first breath of a syllable from Noroda, but he says nothing.

A thruster pulse carries me away from the ship. Tzord-Urja dominates the sky, appearing deceptively close in each of my facets. The pinpoint explosions are clearer now, accompanied by weak bursts of static. How many lives have already been lost as this magnificent place slowly dies? How many futures extinguished by the War God?

The interference from the ship diminishes in increments, and a new signal grows distinct.

THIS SPAN HAS NO TASTE FOR WAR, the undervoice suddenly says.

I swiftly retract my wings, turn around, and fire a braking maneuver. While the ship is too distant to be visible, my targeting array detects it. I turn forward again, snapping the wings open in time to hear Vanathius' time-lagged gasp at the undervoice's words.

"Blue," says Noroda, "we're getting a *lot* of telemetry now. Hold station there."

I WILL SHOW THEM DESTRUCTION. I WILL SHOW THEM OPTIMIZED CONFLICT.

"I am isolating the code," says Probe. "This is fascinating. I see command structures, encrypted decision hierarchies, statistical algorithms."

"How are you feeling, Blue?" asks Noroda.

I touch the canister on my thorax. "Unaffected."

"Good. The ship's processing the incoming data, but I think we're only seeing part of it. Is there any way to increase the scope of your receiver?"

"Yes," I say.

In truth, I have had a method in place since I departed.

I WILL DEMONSTRATE THE FUTILITY OF PURPOSE.

Through the tightbeam, I engage my communion with the communications array. My comprehension of the signal widens like an opening aperture.

"Blue," Noroda says tensely, "what are you doing?"

The War God's signal becomes a dense weave of directives, a panoply of calculations too swift to follow. It conducts countless actions and counter-actions across the system in a storm of arcane mathematics.

Beneath this miasma of code, I sense something else. Something raw, unbounded by language or designation. With significant mental effort, I coax my comprehension wider.

THEY WILL SEE WAR IN ITS PUREST FORM.

"Who is 'they?'" says Vanathius.

"I am decoding the sensory protocols," says Probe. "The scope of its perception exceeds my ability to accurately measure, but I estimate a high probability that its attention is not completely focused on the war."

"What else is it looking at?" asks Noroda.

"I am uncertain. The protocols are linked to complex indexes. There are prioritized prerogatives here. It wants to accumulate resources. Grow. Develop into something else."

"It has ambitions," says Vanathius.

"What kind of ambitions does a War God have?" says Noroda.

I pause a moment before responding, "I will attempt to determine that."

"Blue! Don't—"

I mute the tightbeam and commit all reception to the War God. My wings deform into a parabola, and I adjust their orientation until I find where the signal is strongest.

Abruptly, it becomes a roar.

My senses burn.

My comprehension bursts.

For long, horrible moments, I see what the War God sees.

Like me, its senses are faceted. Where I am limited to fixed fields of view, it focuses on states of existence. It scrutinizes the great waves of advancement over time, cultures surpassing technical thresholds, and intellects achieving transapience. The Span ripples with evolution, boils with progress, and convulses with transformation.

But through the War God's ascending continuum of awareness, I see layered environments beyond the biological scale, even beyond the transapient. Over the brittle horizons of spacetime, where my people believed our eternal reward lay, rise towering realms exceeding our grandest myths.

I begin to utter Urqulon's name, but stop.

These infinities *blaze* with conflict.

Deep in the transluminal medium, monumental engines, larger than suns, brandish blades of weaponized entropy. An order of magnitude beyond that churns a prismatic foam of negative spaces, where cold, implacable hierarchies enact eons-old tactics, driven by logics too intricate to comprehend. Even farther up, physics unfold in exponential ratios, manifesting an unfathomable expanse so vast our rigid three dimensions are but tattered fringe at its edge. There are hostilities here as well, fueled by malignancies beyond mere hatred, waged by presences of such immensity their shadows would eclipse the Span itself.

Though I am pushed to the capacity of my awareness, one fact is clear: like the conflicts spawned by the War God, there are no causes here. No drives. No ideologies. No victories. Only blind, seething aggression.

The War God gazes up at these voluminous tiers with a desperate longing. It yearns to ascend from this plane and join those eternal conflicts. It lusts for rage without limitation, but knows such rewards must be *earned*.

It presents the carnage it inflicts as an offering.

It wants to be worthy.

"We have incoming!" shouts Noroda.

Six flashes of light pierce the sky before me. My facets magnify, and I see a row of torus-shaped absences appear against the particle glow of Tzord-Urja. The static of transapient energies crackles in my receiver.

As one, they accelerate toward me.

"How did it find us?" says Noroda.

"If I interpret this telemetry correctly," says Probe, "it can perceive the transluminal."

"I wish I had the Destroyer with me," says Vanathius.

The urge-for-war rises for the first time since my death, this time of my own making. It resonates in me like the angry, buzzing ghosts of my people.

I look at the approaching transapients, overlaid with targeting annotations.

I ignite my thrusters.

"Blue!" shouts Noroda. "We need to get out of here!"

"The War God must be stopped."

"I know, but you can't attack transapients!"

"I do not intend to."

I see them clearly now, spinning closer at impossible speeds. I gauge their distance and velocity. The undervoice is now an unending scream biting at my thoughtcodes. I deactivate the receiver and set my wing antennae to transmit.

"My designation is Blue Thirty-Fifth Nest-of-Equinox," I say as I shut down the thruster. "My people aspired to ply the stars, and join the great cultures of the Span. We cast our call to the void in hopes of finding someone to show us the way."

I feel transapient sensors play across me. Their intensity sends static flickering across my facets. I shift my wings, concentrating my transmission on the approaching forms.

"Instead," I continue, "we found you. You made us killing machines. Consigned us to oblivion. My people are dead, their future extinguished, as you have done to so many."

Each torus shines a bright beam of light at me, focusing tighter with each instant.

"It was you who first filled me with this urge-for-war. It has grown with each dead culture I have seen, leading me here. Bringing me to you."

The transapients' gravity fields tug me closer. The nearest one all but blocks my view of Tzord-Urja.

"Come, War God, and accept my offering."

I turn around. The targeting array marks the location of the ship on my facets. I tip my head forward and reach a claw to my neck. It finds Vanathius' modification, gently levering under the release switch. My head springs from its mount, propelled towards the ship much faster than I expect.

I tumble uncontrollably. With each rotation I see my body fall towards the transapients, marked by the growing radiance of fission gel accumulating charge. In the disorientation of the spin I ponder if, perhaps, I have misjudged the distance.

When I first faced imminent death, I experienced an almost peaceful clarity. I find myself curious how I will face it this time.

Much to my surprise, I scream Urqulon's name as the expanding explosion blinds me.

———

"Many planetary studies have taught me that conflict exists in every natural system," says Probe. "I have also learned that some organisms can only perceive those elements of the environment relevant to them."

"What does that mean?" asks Vanathius, calibrating my wrist socket.

The Synthesist paces the floor of the safe room. "A carrion-eater smells only decay. A parasite sees only hosts. I suspect the War God is tuned to perceive only conflict. It evolved without the subtle influence of other goals to moderate its activities. It is a remarkable specimen of adaptation."

Vanathius' fronds curl. "You want to *study* it?"

"Very much. However, I would derive more satisfaction from seeing it dead."

"I should hope so." She looks at me. "How does that feel?"

I flex my claw. It swivels easily. "It is an improvement."

Vanathius looks at Probe. "Let us see if Noroda has something on this ship I can craft into an abdomen. I also require food."

A moment after they leave, Noroda enters. His orifice curls severely when he sees me. I suspect he finds the sight of my half-body lying atop Vanathius' pod humorous in some regard.

"What is the situation?" I ask.

"Blue, my friend, you may have successfully chased off the War God, but that energy pulse didn't do my ship's systems any favors. I finally got the sensors and communications back up."

"What have you learned?"

"You were right. The explosion disrupted the War God's control over the transapients. Now, unless you have more pressing matters to attend to, I'd *really* like to know how you knew that would work."

I prop my half-body up. "You suggested that the undervoice abandoned me when it could no longer maintain control. I thought the damage was the catalyst. Yet when Probe was incapacitated, it still felt the War God's influence until the battle's conclusion. I could not resolve this discrepancy, until you detonated the datacore, and I heard the feedback on the communications array."

"Interference," says Noroda.

"Yes. I developed the theory that the undervoice abandoned me because of the hypermatter energy blast I was caught in. The War God's signal was compromised."

"The transapients' actions confirm that," says Noroda. "Once they realized what had happened to them, they jumped back to the system and generated similar pulses. The corruption shut down shortly thereafter."

"Do you know where the War God transmitted itself?"

"Not yet. Tzord-Urja is in tatters. I doubt anyone here will have time to track telemetry for a while."

"How many survivors?"

"About a third of the original population. The invading force is from a system not far from here. They had it *much* worse."

I turn my head away at the thought of that much death.

"Hey," says Noroda, "you did good out there. You *stopped* the War God."

"It escaped."

"It *retreated;* extracted itself from a situation it could not win. It's not invincible. There would have been a lot more deaths if you hadn't been here." He pats the top of my head. "And if you hadn't ejected when you did, we would have lost you too."

"It will infect other star systems."

"And now we know how it works. I plan to warn other cultures of the danger, teach them to harden their communications systems against it."

"That is insufficient."

"I know. Immunization is a pitifully utilitarian solution. But it's the best I can think of."

Vanathius returns, carrying several ungainly components. Probe follows her, stepping to the side of the pod.

"We have been discussing your telemetry during the encounter," it says. "It will take time to interpret the data, but cursory analysis suggests your contact with the War God was considerable."

"What he is asking," says Vanathius, "is what did you see?"

"I have not yet fully processed my perceptions, and those I have form an incomplete pattern." I look at Noroda. "You told us it had limited intelligence. In truth it also has limited processing. It was tasked with winning where no victory was possible. The Span Guard died because it failed."

"It was unworthy," says Vanathius.

"But also adaptive. When the war ended, the only vulnerability it had to exploit was its own. It roamed, permeating into technologies it encountered. It emulated cultures advancing towards Threshold, evolved senses to see potentialities beyond its limited intellect." I gesture to Probe. "As you said, it only perceives aggression. It aims to optimize the concept of war, not strategy or victory, but war itself. All the conflicts it caused, with their varied scales and weaponry, were attempts to perfect that. It is consumed by this fixation." I look at Noroda. "Your preventative measures may moderate its spread, but it will continue."

"What are you suggesting?" he asks.

"It needs to be hunted."

Noroda's features shift. "There are no guilds with the resources to undertake that mission."

I look to Vanathius, then Probe.

"Perhaps there can be," I say.

It takes Vanathius many days to reactivate her Destroyer. Noroda provides her with methods for re-purposing its systems and several remote machines to enact the work. Power cells charge to capacity. Reaction tanks breathe in volatile gases. An array of weaponry awakens.

Probe transfers itself into the control system. It is quite pleased with the upgrade. Under its guidance, the Destroyer rises from the gas giant, trailing streamers of atmosphere.

I watch as Vanathius makes adjustments to the elaborate command chair she has constructed.

"I hope you brought enough food for her," says Noroda, entering the control room. He looks at the numerous displays, each showing a star map, and nods approvingly.

Probe's disembodied voice echoes in the room. "Noroda, I have received your data on restoration methods."

"Good. It can automate brain modeling and replicate neural repair molecules as well." He looks at me. "If you come across anyone that can be saved, you'll have the ability."

"You have my gratitude," I reply.

He appraises my armored form, glancing at the shoulder-mounted particle cannons, and the thrusters along my abdomen.

"Are you sorry I revived you?" he asks.

I study his face. "Are you?"

"Not in the least. But I never intended for you to take up this cause. This little guild will become your life."

"And how much of your life have you lost?"

"That's different. That was *guilt*."

"Yes. And it allowed you to recognize the War God as a threat."

"But I couldn't stop it."

"That did not deter your attempts. You said you needed to make reparations." I gesture to the rest of the room. "I believe you have. I suspect, in some manner you cannot comprehend, you are still a Span Guard."

My words impact his expression. He steps back, looking at Vanathius in her chair. "You have my communication protocols. Contact me if you need anything." He looks at me. "*Any*thing."

He turns and exits the command room. A moment later his head reappears from the side of the entrance.

"One bit of advice," he says, his eyes glistening with moisture. "Your guild is going to need a catchy name."

***

We are Urqulon. We welcome you.

You are dead, a statistic of an unthinkable horror crossing the stars on wings of telemetry. It is our adversary. A raging ghost of conflicts past. It killed your people. It killed you. You, too, are a ghost.

These many beings you see around you. We are all dead. We are all ghosts.

We have purged you of your corruption. Restored your memories. Recall them, and know what our enemy has wrought. When you are finished, I will tell you my story. We will all tell you our stories. You will know of the being who set us on this course. You will know his name, and speak it, as we do, when the call to battle is sounded.

Whatever myths were instilled within you, know this: there is no reward for those who die in battle. Those falsehoods doomed you. They can also remake you. Look at us, amalgamations of flesh and machine. We were forged in the heat of dying worlds and incinerated cultures.

Our adversary no longer spreads with impunity. It flees, knowing we are in pursuit. Our fleet of salvaged ships has caught up with it a hundred times.

Each encounter has cost it resources, deprived it of victims, and shown it is unworthy of the reward it seeks.

Each has strengthened our resolve. We are ghosts. We haunt our enemy for its crimes.

This is the only afterlife we offer you: the honor to hunt a monstrosity more abhorrent than our myths could birth. To exact retribution on a scale beyond reason. To make war upon war itself.

We are Urqulon.

Rise now, and take your place among the war ghosts.

WAR GHOSTS

Image by Jeff Patterson

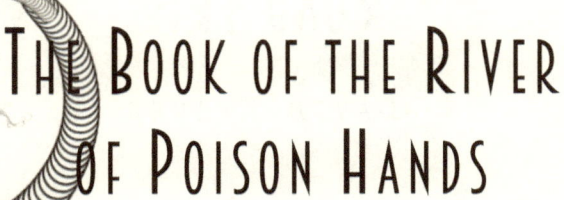

THE BOOK OF THE RIVER OF POISON HANDS

*Do not put unlimited power
into the hands of husbands.
Remember, all men would
be tyrants if they could.*
- Abigail Adams

*Man holds in his mortal
hands the power to abolish
all forms of human poverty,
and all forms of human life.*
- John F. Kennedy

*Every normal man must be tempted at
times, to spit on his hands, hoist the
black flag, and begin to slit throats.*
- H. L. Mencken

FIVE

ROAD TRIP

DAVID KEENER

David Keener is an author, artist, and public speaker. He writes science fiction, fantasy and mystery but loves the idea of mashing up his favorite genres in new and (hopefully) unexpected ways. He frequently speaks at conferences and conventions and has conducted a number of well-received writing workshops.

Road Trip is one of his mash-ups and represents his take on a different kind of urban fantasy. It is both a stand-alone story and the first episode in a serial.

94

*If you don't know
where you're going, any
road will get you there.*
- Lewis Carroll

THE SALE

R occo Fitch spotted the beggar on his regular morning walk to get a latte at Emilio's Coffee Shop. It wasn't that seeing a beggar in this corner of Florida was unusual. The area was rife with them thanks to the mild year-round climate, the prevalence of tourists, and the cool breeze that came from the ocean in the evening. No, it was the cardboard sign that the man was holding up as Rocco approached that had caught his attention:

Road For Sale
$10.00
Change Your Life Now!
Any sale is FINAL!!!!!

Rocco limped to a stop in front of the man, shifting most of his weight to his left leg to relieve the strain on his bad leg, which was already aching from the exertion of the walk. *So much for the daily exercise my doctors have been recommending.*

The beggar was sitting on the sidewalk in the shade of one of Florida's ubiquitous palm trees with his legs stretched out before him and his back up against the pastel yellow stucco of the coffee shop. Just above the man's head, a plate glass window allowed Rocco to see into the shop; Emilio was bustling around behind the counter serving a short queue of customers.

The beggar shook the cardboard sign hopefully, drawing Rocco's attention back to him. The man was broad-shouldered, with black hair and a long bushy beard that hung down to a respectable paunch. He wore a pair of dark gray work trousers, slightly threadbare at the knees, and a plaid shirt. The man's attire seemed old-fashioned in some indefinable way that Rocco couldn't put his finger on, and less grungy than most of the beggars and homeless people Rocco had seen.

He'd also never seen a sign quite like this one before. Curiosity piqued, he asked, "You're selling a road?"

"Yes, sir."

"Why?"

"Don't want it no more," the man said with a thick, Southern drawl, looking up at Rocco with penetrating blue eyes.

"Why would anybody want to buy your road?"

"That's easy. To get places." He shook his head sadly, as if Rocco's question had been the most stupid thing he'd heard in a long time. "To see things they ain't never seen afore. Maybe even for the adventure of it."

Rocco bristled a bit at the implied disdain in the man's response. "If it's such a great road, why don't you want it anymore?"

The man sighed heavily. "Mister, I done outlived all my friends, all my family, everybody I ever cared about." He looked away from Rocco, his gaze fixed on the thin slice of blue ocean just visible down the block. "The road...it can't give me what I want most in the world. My time is past, and I just want it to be over. It's past time for me to just fade away like everything else."

"I feel for you, man." The man was clearly depressed, but Rocco could sympathize with him. His own life was kind of in shambles, as well. "I've been there, too. If it's any consolation, it does get better."

"Really?"

Rocco shrugged. "Sometimes."

He started to walk away, then stopped as a he caught a glimpse of a strikingly pretty, dark-haired young lady, perhaps mid-twenties, in a white dress looking at them through the shop's window. She'd moved out of sight by the time he'd turned back to fully face the window. He saw that the beggar had partially turned as well, as if to see what he'd been looking at.

Pointing at the window, he asked the beggar, "Did you see a lady in a white dress?"

"Yes, sir," the man said, flashing a grin that revealed a set of perfect white teeth. "Pretty thing. Probably admiring my considerable charms."

Rocco laughed. "Maybe so." The man's answer was pat and humorous, but somehow evasive as well, as if Rocco had caught him in some sort of lie. "Well, good luck with the sale," he said, turning away to enter the cool interior of the cafe.

A few minutes later, having secured his usual caffeinated fix from Emilio, Rocco made his way between the small tables holding his hot coffee carefully. The lady in the white dress was nowhere to be seen. He navigated around a baby carriage, complete with a sleeping baby in a blue jumper, which belonged to a twenty-something Latina woman. A little girl, perhaps four years old and as cute as could be, sat next to the woman and stared up at his face as he passed.

He took his usual seat near the window, which provided not only a good tourist-watching vantage point, but also had a good view of the cafe's large-screen television. Emilio, never a sports fan, was showing *Law & Order* with subtitles but no sound.

As he sat down, he heard the little girl say loudly, "Mama, how come that man's face is messed up?"

"Shhhh. It's not polite to say things like that."

"But I want to know!"

He'd just taken a tentative sip of his coffee when he heard the patter of footsteps coming his way. The little girl stopped next to his table.

"Mama says it's not po-lite," the little girl said breathlessly. "But what happened to your face?"

"Maria!" The girl's mother said loudly, awkwardly getting up to chase her wayward daughter.

Rocco looked at the girl and smiled. Little kids were a hoot. They'd say anything sometimes because they didn't have the filters that adults had. But they weren't judgmental, either, which was always refreshing. Unlike his ex-wife.

"Well, I was in the Marines," he said. "And we were on a training mission. So we parachuted out of this plane and, well, I drifted over this town because of the wind." He nodded at the girl's mother as she arrived. "The highest building in town was a really big church, with a really tall steeple. And I landed right on it. Scraped my face down the entire side of that steeple, just this one side, see? Hurt like the dickens, I've got to tell you.

"So, if you ever jump out of an airplane, make sure you don't land on a church steeple, okay?"

"Okay," Maria said, nodding seriously.

Sure makes a better story than being blown up by a roadside bomb and trapped in a burning, upside-down Hummer.

Stopping beside Maria, her mother said, "I'm so sorry. She's curious about everything."

Rocco shrugged. "No worries. She's a cute kid." The little girl reminded him of his daughter, Elise, when she was that age. Now she was twelve, living with his ex-wife in Ohio.

The woman smiled and tugged Maria back to their table.

He nursed his latte for a little over an hour, unintentionally caught up in the *Law & Order* episode that was playing. He wasn't sure why he was curious about her, but he never did spot the lady in the white dress.

Leaving, Rocco pushed the door open and stepped out into the sunshine, squinting at the brightness as he left the dim interior of Emilio's. The beggar was still sitting in the same place. Something in his posture, the way he leaned against the building and his tired patience, reminded him of soldiers he'd seen waiting for deployment in crowded airport terminals.

Rocco walked over. "You a veteran?"

"Yeah," the man said. "Different war, though." He looked pointedly at Rocco's right leg and the way that his jeans hung limply around the lower half. "I was lucky, I came out unscathed."

"First Gulf War?"

"No. Further back. I'm a little older than I look."

Rocco gave him a measuring glance. He didn't look old enough for Vietnam, but then again, maybe he was.

Acting on impulse, he reached into his pocket and pulled out about a dollar's worth of change. Holding it out to the man, he said, "Well, I don't need a road, but I can spare some change to help out a fellow veteran."

The man shook his head. "Sir, I thank you, but I got money. It's this road that I need to sell, afore I can do anything else."

"Well, I don't have ten bucks."

"What do you have?"

Rocco fished some more loose change out of his pocket, then counted it all. He added two dollar bills from his wallet and held it all out to the man.

He wasn't even sure why he was doing this, but he said, "Here's three dollars and thirty-seven cents. It's all the money I've got left in the world."

"Sir, I accept your kind offer," the man said, standing up and taking the money from him. He was a few inches shorter than Rocco's own rangy six feet. He held out his hand and Rocco shook it automatically. He had a firm, confident grasp. "You are now the proud owner of a road."

The man started walking away.

"Hey! Where do I find this road?"

The man turned, gave him a lopsided grin and said, "Don't worry. It will find you."

THE KFC EFFECT

Rocco slowly limped down the sidewalk towards Jackson's Burritos, still bemused by his exchange with the beggar. The things you did sometimes to help out a fellow veteran...

As he reached the burrito shop, he stopped short. He'd been planning to pick up a burrito for lunch on the way back from Emilio's, but instead he'd given up all of his remaining cash in exchange for some stupid, imaginary road.

Bad planning.

Sighing, he headed home instead. The first thing he saw when he finally rounded the corner onto Bella Terra Place was his house just three doors down. Then he noticed the tow truck in front of it.

He started running as fast as he could, which wasn't very fast given his bad leg. The driver of the tow truck already had his blue Toyota Camry hooked up and was at the back of Rocco's car, fiddling with something.

As Rocco got close, he yelled, "Hey!"

The tow truck driver looked up, startled, and saw Rocco staggering towards him. He let go of the signal lights he'd clamped to the back of Rocco's car, leaving the lights attached but the wires still dangling, and dashed toward the cab of the truck.

Rocco got within a few feet of his car, then the driver slammed the tow truck into gear and pulled away with a screech, yanking the Toyota out of his reach. Rocco ran after it for a few more steps, cursing and watching as his car receded, swaying wildly behind the rapidly accelerating truck. Then he stumbled and fell full-length onto the pavement.

Dazed for a moment by the impact of the fall, the tow truck was out of sight by the time he was able to finally sit up.

He took stock of his injuries. His left knee was bleeding and he had a hole in his jeans where he'd landed on it. He'd scraped up his left elbow and the right side of his face was cut where he'd landed on it. *No loss there. The roadside bomb already remodeled that side of my face.*

Standing up was more of a problem with his bad leg. He finally ended up dragging himself over to the curb, hoping that nobody was watching from a window. From a sitting position on the curb, he was able to lever himself back onto his feet.

So much for the Roccomobile, he thought with a pang of sadness. He'd had some good times with Trina and Elise in that car but, in the end, Trina had laughed at the idea of taking it as part of the settlement. *Has it really been a year now?*

Rocco limped slowly to the front door of his 1950's-era, one-story, vaguely Spanish-themed, wannabe beach house (the beach was four blocks away), unlocked the door, and let himself in. He luxuriated for a moment as air conditioned coolness enveloped him, wondering how long he'd continue to be able to enjoy it since he hadn't paid his electric bill in about three months.

He dropped his keys on the hallway table, right next to the foreclosure notice that he'd been served just this morning. It looked like a race: Would the bank take his house before the power company shut off his electricity?

He thought about cleaning the scrape on his face, but it seemed like too much work. *Besides, if the IED didn't kill me, it's unlikely that a little road rash is gonna do the job.*

On to the next priority then.

Lunch.

Taking stock of what little in the way of food was left in the kitchen, he opted for microwave popcorn and tap water, with ice, for lunch.

Living it up in Paradise. Yessiree.

Dusk had fallen when Rocco was awakened by the sound of knocking on his front door. He was sprawled in his recliner. The television was on, casting its flickering light through the darkened room and giving everything a slightly bluish tinge.

He'd been dreaming. Early in the dream, he'd been playing with his daughter at a playground, a charity event for handicapped children that they'd actually attended once. While most of the dream was already fading, it had somehow ended with a government accountant in a dark suit at his front door telling him that as the owner of I-95, the busy East Coast traffic artery, he owed a billion dollars in maintenance fees. Strangely, the lady in the white dress was standing on the sidewalk looking on from a distance.

He inched forward in the chair, pushed himself to a standing position and went to the door. *It better not be an accountant.*

Taking a deep breath, he opened the door to a much more welcome sight. His neighbor, Sammie, stood there, a wiry, gray-haired black man wearing a Florida Gators T-shirt. He was holding a bucket of Kentucky Fried Chicken and a six-pack of Coronas.

"Oh, my God," Rocco said. "It's a damn stereotype at my front door."

Sammie grinned widely and said with his deep Southern twang, "If you ain't got nothing better to do, I thought you might like to help me dispose of all this here chicken."

Rocco laughed. If there'd been anything positive in his life in the last year, it had been the unlikely friendship that had developed with his irrepressibly cheerful neighbor. On the face of it, they were about as unlike as it was possible to get.

Rocco was the product of a traditional middle-class upbringing and had grown up in a boring, almost overwhelmingly white, midwestern fly-over state. He'd gotten a college degree in Criminal Justice, a step towards a career in law enforcement and eventually, he'd hoped, the FBI. After September 11th, he'd taken a detour into the Marines, but his injuries in Afghanistan two years later had ended his military career, his law enforcement dreams and, not too long afterwards, his marriage.

Sammie's education had stopped with high school. He'd worked all sorts of odd jobs up and down the Gulf Coast, from running fishing trips for tourists to working on oil rigs to smuggling. He'd spent at least a little time in jail. He had a string of five ex-wives and seemingly countless children and grandchildren. In another age, he'd probably have been a pirate.

"Well, I was going to go out jogging for a while," Rocco replied, swinging the door open so Sammie could enter. "But I suppose I could help you with that. Especially seeing as you're so scrawny, there's no way you'd do that bucket justice."

Sammie followed him into the living room and set the bucket of KFC on the coffee table while Rocco turned on a light.

"What are you watching?" Sammie asked.

"*Law & Order* marathon."

"They got any black people on the show?"

"Only the criminals."

"Cool." Sammie grinned and sat down on the couch. "My kind of show, then."

Rocco turned and limped towards the kitchen to get a bottle opener for the beers. As he did so, his eye was drawn to the fancy mirror at the back of the living room. Another of Trina's must-have purchases, only she hadn't cared enough about it to take it with her. For a moment there, he could have sworn he'd seen the woman in the white dress looking at him from the mirror.

But that was crazy.

He returned with the bottle opener and they watched in companionable silence as the police detectives on television investigated the murder of a lawyer's wife. The fried chicken and the beer steadily vanished.

Sammie said, "The husband did it. I predict it."

"I don't know about the husband, but..." Rocco held up a chicken wing. "This stuff will kill you."

"Yeah," his neighbor agreed. "Good, though."

"Yeah." Rocco looked over at Sammie, lounging on the couch with feet up on the coffee table. "Hey, I bought a road today."

"What?"

"This beggar, over by Emilio's. A homeless vet, as far as I could tell. Wouldn't take any change from me unless I agreed that I was buying a road from him." Although, now that Rocco thought about it, he hadn't seen the man accost anybody else the whole time he'd been in Emilio's.

"Weird. What kind of road?"

Rocco shrugged. "Haven't got a clue."

"How much you pay for this road?"

"Three dollars and thirty-seven cents."

"Sounds like a bargain," Sammie said. "Course, nobody sells nothin' so cheap unless it's got problems. One way or another, you been had."

A few minutes later, the police arrested the lawyer for the murder of his wife.

Sammie said, "I knew that bastard did it."

"Nah, he didn't."

"How do you know?"

"We're only thirty minutes into the episode. We've got two plot twists to go before it's over."

Sammie looked back at the television. "So you're saying this show is predictably unpredictable?"

"Yup."

"Damn."

Eventually, the killer turned out to be the lawyer's son, who had arranged his mother's murder so that he could implicate his father and thus gain control of his father's fortune.

"White people." Sammie just shook his head sadly. "It's so much easier to just kill them, drag the bodies out into the swamp, and let the gators eat 'em."

They watched two more episodes together before the beer and food took its toll and Rocco dozed off.

THE SURPRISE

Rocco woke up in his bed with the morning sun streaming through his window. He distinctly remembered falling asleep in the recliner downstairs, so he must have gotten up sometime during the night and come upstairs. He groaned and rolled over, unwilling to leave his bed and face the cold reality of a new day.

He tried to go back to sleep, but various outside noises thwarted his efforts. He could hear birds chirping outside. *Weren't they supposed to fly north for the summer?* Then there was a staccato beat, and most definitely not a musical beat, that continued getting louder until it reached a peak and then got softer again. If anything, it sounded like a horse, only the beat was far too fast for even a galloping horse.

Probably construction noise. The dot coms might be going bust now in 2003, but the last few years had brought a housing boom to Florida that the rest of the country was only now starting to notice.

Rocco groaned again and sat up. He put his one foot on the floor and, facing away from the window, examined his disheveled, slightly too long brown hair and disfigured face in the vanity mirror on top of his ex-wife's empty dresser. Something else from their marriage that Trina hadn't wanted to take. She'd said she didn't want anything from their bedroom because she didn't want to be reminded of him.

Words were weapons, in the hands of a master like Trina.

He reached over and opened the top drawer of the bedside table, as he did every day. He pulled out his 9mm pistol and popped the clip. Verified that the clip was full, then checked to make sure there was a bullet in the chamber.

He took off the safety and put the barrel of the handgun into his mouth.

Is today going to be the day?

Methodically, he took stock of his situation.

Trina had left a little over a year ago, and taken his daughter Elise with her. Trina leaving was hard, but taking Elise had been even more of a blow. And taking her out-of-state had been even worse. Losing Trina had broken his heart, but losing Elise had ripped it right out of his chest.

Then he'd been let go from his job as a security guard after two whole months on the job. They'd said that after careful evaluation, they'd determined that he couldn't do the job with a bum leg. Unemployment had long since run out, and there was some kind of snag with his disability benefits. Apparently, the fact that he *had* worked, however briefly, was proof that he *could* work, and therefore disability benefits would need to be adjudicated. Meanwhile, his car had just been repossessed, the bank was about to foreclose on his house, he hadn't paid any utilities in three months and he hadn't sent any of the court-required child support money to his ex-wife, which technically made him a bad father, too.

So, really, he should just pull the trigger now.

On the plus side, there was probably some KFC left, and he was willing to bet that Sammie had put whatever was left in the fridge.

Just as he'd decided that leftover KFC warranted living for another day, he heard a female voice shout, *"Nein, tun Sie es nicht!"* The voice sounded distant, as if it came from another room.

Surprised, he looked up as he pulled the barrel from his mouth and saw the girl in the white dress looking at him from the mirror, an expression of horror on her face. He wasn't sure, but he thought she'd shouted at him in German.

She had wide blue eyes, long eyelashes and dark eyebrows set in an angular face with high cheekbones, framed by long black hair that tumbled over her shoulders. He estimated her age at, perhaps, mid-twenties. Her dress was white, trimmed with intricate white lace, and featured a modest square-cut neckline. It looked old-fashioned in some way that Rocco couldn't articulate, much like the man from whom he'd bought that imaginary road. He saw her expression soften as she realized he wasn't really going to splatter himself over the walls in front of her.

Rocco did a quick look around the bedroom.

No girl.

He stood up on his one good leg, realizing belatedly that he wasn't wearing anything except the *Finding Nemo* boxers his daughter had sent him for his last birthday, and hopped towards the dresser (his prosthetic leg was on top of his own bureau). Her eyes got wide as he approached, like a deer caught in the headlights of an oncoming car, and she bolted out-of-frame, her waist-length hair trailing behind her.

108

He stopped in surprise and almost fell over before he caught his balance by grabbing the dresser. Not only had there been a girl in his mirror, a girl who hadn't been present in his bedroom to be reflected in the mirror, but there was a road in his backyard. A big black expanse of asphalt running right across his backyard. A road that hadn't been visible to him until he stood up and assumed the proper angle to see a reflection of his backyard.

Gripping the dresser for balance, Rocco turned laboriously to look out his window. There was, indeed, a road crossing his backyard. A two-lane highway, complete with white lines.

"Yeah, right," he muttered. "Don't worry, it will find you."

A few minutes later, after hurriedly attaching his prosthetic lower leg and pulling on some clothes, Rocco made his way downstairs. Passing through the kitchen on the way to his back door, he decided he needed sustenance before he determined whether he'd actually gone insane. Swinging open the door of the refrigerator, he let out a surprised "Huh?" when he saw not only the anticipated bucket of leftover KFC but also a bunch of other food that he'd never bought. Sammie must have loaded his fridge with some additional supplies after he'd dozed off.

Sammie's a better friend than I deserve.

He grabbed a drumstick out of the bucket and started munching on it as he pushed open the door and stepped out onto his stone patio. Even though he'd expected it, it was still a shock to see a two-lane highway crossing his backyard. *Doctor, the patient is severely delusional, but at least he's well fed.*

The asphalt was black, as if the road had been freshly paved, and contrasted starkly with the green grass of his yard and the light-colored, six-foot wooden privacy fence that surrounded it. The painted lines were crisp; a dotted white line down the center and yellow lines about a foot from both edges. A gravel shoulder, fading gradually into dirt, and then the green grass of his backyard. Make that about eight feet between road edge and the start of his grass, so the road had nice, wide shoulders. The highway took up almost half of his backyard.

As he approached the road, he could see that a portion of his fence on both sides was simply gone, and the road extended in both directions as far as he could see. He stepped onto the road, which had a surprisingly springy feel to it.

The surface reminded him again of the playground he'd once taken Elise to. It had been a special charity project, designed so that handicapped children could play easily with other non-handicapped children. The playground had been built on a wide square of rubberized asphalt. That's what the road felt like. Springy, maybe even spongy, just like that playground.

So, there was a highway in his backyard. Clearly, he was insane. He grinned mirthlessly. *On the plus side, maybe now I'll qualify for disability. What a choice. Sane and homeless, or insane but I'll have money to pay my bills.*

Rocco strolled about thirty feet down the road, passing through where his fence should have been, and stopped on the road, but in Sammie's yard.

He walked across the shoulder and tried to step into Sammie's backyard. As soon as he got to the edge of the shoulder, he encountered resistance that steadily increased as he tried to push forward.

All right, so he couldn't leave the road at this point. Was he trapped on the road?

He strolled back to his yard and left the pavement without any problem. Well, he owned the road, so that made a certain amount of sense. Sort of. He had his own private entrance to the road. *What was that phrase Sammie had used last night? Predictably unpredictable.*

It would be kind of a useless road if he could only get off it where he owned an adjoining property. Roads existed so that people could get places, and this road had evidently existed for some time before he'd bought it. So there had to be other places where travelers could get on and off the road. Nothing else made any sense.

He left his backyard by the double-wide gate, which was up near his house on the side adjacent to Sammie's house, near Sammie's own gate. That's how they'd met, always walking by each other on their way to do yardwork, and then stopping to gab for a while.

He looked back as he stepped onto Sammie's property. The road was gone.

Back onto his property. He could see the road again.

He went into Sammie's backyard. No road in sight. And the fence was intact, too.

Back into his yard. There was clearly a two-lane highway present. And it went through the fence on both sides. But it was neither visible nor even present when standing in Sammie's yard.

All right, then. Time to get a second opinion.

Rocco rang Sammie's doorbell. After a moment, Sammie opened the door and flashed a wide grin when he saw who it was. He was wearing jeans and a badly faded, sleeveless Miami Dolphins T-shirt.

"Mornin', Rocco."

"Got a question for you."

"I confess. I put the stuff in your fridge."

"I know, but that's not the question," Rocco said. "Thanks, though."

"Just bein' neighborly." Sammie shrugged. "What's your question?"

"You got any marbles?"

"Say what?"

"I think I've lost my marbles."

Sammie gave him a penetrating look. "Yup, you've definitely lost your marbles."

"Seriously, I want to show you something."

A moment later, Rocco swung the left-side gate open and led Sammie into his backyard. With the gate no longer blocking his view, Rocco could clearly see the road crossing his yard. He turned to Sammie and asked, "Do you see anything different about my backyard?"

Sammie looked at him with a puzzled expression. "No."

"All right, follow me then."

Rocco and Sammie walked forward. Rocco stopped about ten feet from the road. "Do you see anything different now?"

"You're starting to worry me, buddy. I don't see nothing but grass, and then your fence."

Rocco stalked forward until he was standing on the road, then faced back towards Sammie.

"How about now?"

"You're standing on grass, buddy." Sammie's brow furrowed and he looked thoughtful. "Although, it sounded like you were walking on gravel for a second there."

Interesting. Maybe the road was better hidden to sight than to other senses. Rocco casually walked down the road, through the fence and into Sammie's yard.

"Hey, how'd you do that?" There was an odd timbre to Sammie's voice, not quite scared but not sure of himself either. "You just walked through the fence like it wasn't there."

"That's because it's not really there."

Sammie followed Rocco's path forward, pausing thoughtfully when he heard the sound of gravel underneath his feet. Rocco watched him step onto the road.

"Holy shit!" Sammie looked around wonderingly. "It's a fucking road."

Sammie looked both ways, obviously seeing what Rocco was seeing. Somewhere deep inside, Rocco relaxed a little. He wasn't going crazy, after all. Or at least, the situation might be crazy, but he wasn't.

Sammie sauntered towards him and said accusingly, "This is the road you bought."

"Apparently."

"Where's it go?"

"Haven't got a clue."

"Peachy." Sammie peered down the road and into the distance. "Hey, I think someone's coming."

Rocco heard a distant staccato beat, just like the one he'd heard earlier when he'd just been thinking about beginning to start waking up. Looking where Sammie was gazing, he could see a dark speck approaching. As it got closer, the beat got louder. The speck began to look more and more like a horseback rider. As it whizzed by them, he was just able to make out a cloaked and hooded rider on top of a spectacularly muscled, coal-black steed that resembled a horse but with six extra long legs and red glowing eyes. The wind of its passage whipped his hair.

Sammie and Rocco looked at each other with wide eyes, then they watched the rider recede, the beat of his steed's hoofs fading into the distance.

"That weren't no horse," Sammie said.

"Not unless horses can run at sixty miles an hour."

"Yeah." Sammie slapped Rocco on the shoulder. "Buddy, this is some weird, fuckin' road you bought."

"I think it's a magic road."

"Well, duh."

THE ROAD

Standing on Rocco's stone patio, a bucket of cold fried chicken on the table next to a plate of thoroughly gnawed chicken bones, both men considered the road.

Sammie gestured with a chicken wing and said, "Basically, the road don't exist unless we're on your land."

"Yeah." Rocco nodded. "It's like it hides itself. And even if somebody's on my land, nobody can see it or hear traffic noises unless they already know it's there or they end up stepping on it."

"You can see it," Sammie pointed out. "You saw it when you woke up this morning."

"Well, yeah." Rocco shrugged. "But it probably thinks I already know about it because I'm the owner."

"You talkin' like it's alive."

"I don't know what to think." Rocco scratched his head and squinted at the road. "Except I think we should go for a ride."

Sammie turned and looked at Rocco's backyard gate. "We open up both sides of the gate, I think I can get my truck through with a few inches to spare. The HOA's gonna object, though. If'n they see us."

"Screw the HOA." Rocco had very little liking for the community's homeowners association. All they seemed to do was complain via registered letters, for which they billed him twenty-five bucks a pop, about how he didn't mow his lawn every week.

Sammie laughed, flashing him a grin that showed off his white teeth. He dropped the remnants of his chicken wing on the discard plate and went to get his truck.

Rocco took the opportunity to put the KFC bucket back in the fridge and dispose of the plate of chicken bones. By the time he got back outside, Sammie was there with his battered, gray Ford 150.

Rocco climbed into the passenger side, lifting himself up with his good leg, then Sammie pulled the pickup truck up to the shoulder of the road.

Sammie looked at him. "Which way you want to go?"

"Left."

"Okay, left it is."

Sammie turned onto the road, heading away from his own property, and gingerly drove past where Rocco's fence should have been a tangible border with the Cooks' property next door. They both gazed in bemusement at the back of the Cooks' house as they rolled slowly past. Feeling more confident that they weren't in imminent danger of colliding with anything, Sammie accelerated to a stately 35 mph.

Rocco gazed at the scenery as they traveled down the road. When he looked at the shoulders, it was clear that they were traveling at the 35 mph indicated by the speedometer. But the scenery visible beyond the shoulders seemed to be passing much, much faster.

Within minutes, it became clear that the road didn't seem to care about any obstacles; they crossed fields, forest and swampland with impunity, just as they'd passed his own fence. However, some of the other obstacles that the road navigated past were a bit more nerve-wracking, as they discovered when they came to a river. The road simply continued out across the river about five feet above water level, despite no visible means of support.

Sammie slammed on the brakes and brought the truck to a screeching halt just short of the water.

"You sure you wanna do this?"

Rocco considered the waterway in front of them, which was about hundred and fifty yards wide. "Hey, what's the worst that could happen?"

"We could sink like a rock and drown."

"Nah, we'd just climb out of the truck and swim for shore." At Sammie's inquiring look, he added, "Yes, I can still swim, even with only one good leg."

"I'd lose my truck."

"You've got insurance."

"I can't swim."

"What about all those stories you've told me about hanging out at the beach with your friends when you were younger?"

"I did the beach thing 'cause that's where the girls were," Sammie said. "Only tourists go in the fuckin' ocean."

Rocco laughed, shaking his head back and forth in mock dismay. "No guts, no glory, dude." To tweak his friend just a little bit more, he pumped his fist and added, "Ooohrah."

Muttering under his breath, Sammie put the truck into gear and rolled forward slowly.

Sammie's fears proved to be unfounded. The road held the weight of the truck just fine, although it was disconcerting to see the drop-off to the water just beyond each shoulder.

Sammie stopped again only when he saw a boat, a thirty-foot long, white, fiberglass cabin cruiser, bearing down on their narrow strip of pavement. Nobody on the boat seemed to see them at all, despite the fact that the boat was heading directly at them. Rocco half-expected to hear a crunch as the watercraft collided with the road, but that didn't happen. The bow of the boat disappeared at the edge of the road and reappeared a second or two later, bearing away from the opposite side of the road. As far as Rocco could tell, the boat passed right through them. Even odder, they were able to see a cross-section of the boat as it intersected with the edge of the road. It featured a compact cabin, neatly designed so that every inch of space was used, with a middle-aged brunette woman sitting at a small, built-in table reading *Cosmopolitan* magazine.

They both watched dumbfounded as the boat receded into the distance.

"Okay," Rocco said. "That was officially bizarre."

"Yeah."

They continued their surreal journey. In a few minutes, they passed a wrecked Corvette on the right shoulder. Most of the windows were broken, the tires flat, and the side panels that Rocco could see were stitched with what looked like bullet holes. For a moment, Rocco was back in Afghanistan where a wrecked vehicle always represented the potential danger of an IED or an ambush. Then he was back in the present, his heart racing and his hands clenched into white-knuckled fists.

Deliberately relaxing his hands, Rocco looked over at Sammie. "I'm getting the impression that traveling the road might be a bit on the dangerous side."

"I got a gun in the glove compartment."

Rocco reached out to open the compartment and pulled out a 9mm pistol, noting that it had been modified to use an extended clip, giving it sixteen rounds. It was clearly a well-maintained weapon, which wasn't entirely unexpected. In his experience, Sammie took care of his tools, from fishing rods to his lawnmower to, apparently, his firearms. He tucked the gun back into the glove compartment. He felt better having it as a contingency. Next time, though, he'd bring some of his own weapons.

Shortly thereafter, Rocco spotted a green sign in the distance, before what looked like an exit ramp. As they approached, he made out "New York" in white letters on the sign's green background. The sign was mounted on what appeared to be an aluminum pole. In fact, it looked just like the interstate signs he'd seen on major roads like I-95. Of course, the general ambiance was a little different than the interstate highways Rocco was familiar with; there was another wrecked car, this one obviously burned out, just beyond the sign.

"New York. No fuckin' way," Sammie said.

By reflex, Rocco checked his watch to check how long they'd been traveling and was chagrined when he remembered he'd pawned it the month before.

Rocco asked, "How long have we been on the road?"

Sammie glanced down at his watch. "About twenty minutes."

"So, if that exit's real, we've done Florida to New York in twenty minutes. And you're not exactly speeding, either."

"Sheeeeit," Sammie said in an exaggerated drawl. "Florida to New York with no cops? Smuggler's paradise." He shook his head in wonder at the idea. "You want to take the exit?"

"No, let's keep going. I want to get a better idea of where the road goes. At this point, I'm assuming we'll see some more exits up ahead."

Shortly beyond the exit, they came across what looked like the weathered wooden wreck of what had once been a covered wagon. Some distance beyond that, they saw another wrecked vehicle, a sports car of some kind.

The next exit came up about fifteen minutes later. Chicago.

"No fuckin' way."

"Keep going."

After ten more minutes, four more wrecked cars, a wrecked van, two demolished motorcycles and an obvious upward incline that brought the Rockies into view. Denver.

"No..."

"Okay, take the exit."

Rocco figured the road was reminding him more and more of Afghanistan. He didn't like having all these wrecked and abandoned vehicles on the shoulders of his road. Sammie had been more prophetic than he'd realized when he'd jokingly said that his purchase probably had problems.

Sammie veered smoothly into the exit lane, which arced gently away from the road. He slowed to a crawl as he realized that the pavement ended in an abrupt line shortly ahead of them. Beyond, they could see a field covered with a few inches of snow.

"All right," Rocco said. "Just ease across the end of the pavement and into the field."

Sammie complied, stopping the pickup just beyond the edge.

Rocco popped the door open, letting in a draft of what felt like arctic air. Especially since he'd just been in Florida a short time before. He climbed out carefully and stepped onto the snow. He mentally congratulated himself for climbing down without falling, despite his prosthetic leg. Then he closed the truck's door and promptly fell on his butt.

From his unexpectedly horizontal position, he decided that people wearing T-shirts should not fall in the snow. *The mountains look nice, though.* He stoically grabbed onto the truck's running board, levered himself up until he could reach the door handle, and then hauled himself to his feet. He could still see the end of the road; he'd been half afraid that he wouldn't be able to see it because he didn't own the property at the end of the exit ramp. *Which would have, if you thought about it, been a stupid way to design a magic road.*

He walked carefully to the road and stepped onto the pavement again. The temperature instantly changed from bitter cold to temperate, perhaps twenty-five degrees Fahrenheit to a comfortable seventy degrees. Turning, he trudged back to the truck and climbed in.

Sammie grinned at him. "Nice fall. Extra points for finesse."

"I planned that," Rocco said glibly. "I got out and decided, hey, let's make a snow angel."

"Yeah, right." Sammie snorted with laughter. "You ready to go now? I ain't dressed for Denver in the winter, and you done let most of the warm air outa my truck."

"Yeah, let's keep going."

Sammie steered the truck around in a wide circle, got back onto the exit ramp and headed for the main road. *Which is odd,* Rocco thought, *because the road has exit ramps but not on ramps.* Navigating the exit ramp in reverse meant that they reached the highway going the wrong way down the exit lane, heading back towards Florida. Sammie did a U-turn at the first opportunity so they could continue their exploration.

Thinking about the road, it was as if it had been created by someone who'd once seen a picture of an interstate highway, or had one described to them, but had never actually traveled on one. That was interesting because, until now, the road had seemed to Rocco like some powerful, otherworldly magical artifact that perhaps had sufficient self-awareness to deliberately hide itself from prying eyes. Now, it had a flaw that reflected a bias or limitation in the mindset of its creator.

In a strange way, it made the road seem more real to him.

"Incoming," Sammie said.

Up ahead, Rocco saw the now familiar shape of a rider heading towards them on what Rocco thought of as a demon horse. They maintained their speed and the rider passed them without incident. Rocco caught a glimpse of the rider looking sideways at them as he passed.

Shortly thereafter, they passed the exit for San Francisco. Just beyond the exit, with the road surrounded by looming redwood trees, there was another sign:

LONDON UNDERGROUND
3 MILES

"No fucking way. I'm not crossin' no damn ocean. N.F.W."

For a moment, Rocco imagined the road as a thin, unsupported ribbon of pavement crossing the ocean, surging waves towering over it on all sides. Then he decided that the road was going to have do something more geographically interesting, since they were headed towards the Pacific Ocean and thus basically away from the United Kingdom. So, magic or not, the ocean-crossing ribbon thing seemed a little unlikely.

"Just keep going. I don't think the road is going to cross oceans the way that it crossed the river."

"All right," Sammie said. "But if I drown 'cause of this, I'm comin' back to haunt yo' ass."

"I can't believe we're talking like this." Rocco shook his head. "Just a bit over an hour ago, we were on the East Coast..."

"And now we on the Left Coast, talking about cruising to London. This be one crazy-ass road."

The redwood trees soon gave way to low, rolling hills covered with green grass. Sullen, gray clouds hid the sun.

Sammie looked over at Rocco. "I don't think we're in Kansas no more, Toto. I don't remember no clouds before."

"Looks like Wales, or somewhere like that. I did some touring in the United Kingdom back when I was in the military, and this looks just like what I remember of Wales."

Up ahead, they saw the green sign for the London Underground exit.

"Take the exit," Rocco said.

After about a hundred yards, the exit lane curved away from the main road, and they saw cars parked on both shoulders of the lane. Rocco did a quick estimate and came up with around sixty cars. There were no people in sight anywhere.

"Park behind the last car on the right," Rocco said. "I'm going to guess from all the cars that you can't drive out of this exit."

"Then how'd all these cars get here?"

"From other places on the road, where else? I mean, it looked like anybody could drive onto the road from the Denver exit, if you knew it was there. I bet most of the exits are like that."

"Well, what about your house? You can get onto the road from your backyard."

"Private entrance, I'd guess. Because I'm the owner. And, hence, no sign to advertise it."

"Makes sense," Sammie admitted. "In a twisted way."

Sammie pulled in behind a nondescript gray van. Rocco noted that it had Louisiana tags that were still good for another year. Interesting. He got out without falling again, then reached back in and got the gun from the glove compartment. Holding it in his hand, but down at his side, he locked and closed the door. He walked around the front of the car and tapped on Sammie's window.

"Come on," he said.

Sammie climbed out and followed him down the road. Rocco walked down the center of the lane, carefully scanning back and forth for any possible ambushers. So far, the road seemed like a pretty lawless territory, and the parked cars offered plenty of concealment for would-be perps. His Marine-trained instincts didn't like the situation at all.

He stepped on something. Looking down, he realized it was a shell casing. No telling how long it had been there.

The cars closest to where they'd parked seemed to be the newest, which made sense. Most of them seemed to be in relatively good shape. As they walked along, the cars got older. Some of them had obviously been there for years, sometimes decades. He did a double-take as he passed a fifties-style vehicle, light blue with some white trim. The tires were flat and the windows were broken. Glancing through the window, the interior looked to be in reasonably good shape.

Maybe the road didn't really have weather, just that constant seventy or so degrees of temperature. Without rain or snow or excessive heat, it was just conceivable that a car could sit for forty or fifty years and still be in decent shape. Not runnable, but salvageable.

Turning to Sammie, he said, "I think that's an Edsel."

"Is that good?"

"It's a classic car, Sammie. And rare. It looks abandoned to me, and it's worth a hell of a lot of money, even as-is. Get it fixed up, it could be worth more. A lot more."

"I got a nephew runs a little tow truck company. We could come back with one of his trucks and get it."

"Okay, it's a plan. We'll do that."

As they continued, Rocco alternated looking for threats with trying to determine if any of the other abandoned vehicles were valuable. Some of them probably did have value, although the Edsel looked like the standout. The lane narrowed as they went on. Beyond the last of the cars, it became a paved trail just wide enough for the two of them to walk side by side. It ended at a door-sized brick wall in a small earthen hummock.

"The hell?" said Sammie.

Rocco double-checked the safety of the gun to ensure it was engaged, then tucked it into the back of his pants. He pulled his shirt out to cover it up. Pretending a confidence he didn't really feel, he walked forward into the wall, half-expecting to hit it face-first. Instead, he passed through it and found himself in a narrow brick hallway.

A few seconds later, Sammie stepped through the wall next to him. Despite the fact that there were people nearby, nobody seemed to have noticed anything odd about them just appearing out of nowhere. *The road hides itself.*

Rocco marched down the hallway and accosted the first man he came to. "Excuse me," he said. "I'm not sure if I got off at the right place. What station is this?"

"Blackfriars," the man said, before rushing off.

"Well, this is definitely the London Underground," Rocco said as Sammie stopped next to him.

"Now what?"

"Lunch," Rocco said.

"Lunch?"

"Yes. You're buying."

"What?"

"Well, it's not like I have any money."

"Florida to London, just for lunch. What's the world coming to?" Sammie shook his head. "I like it. Makes me feel like one of them jet-setters."

BANGERS AND MASH

"I can't believe you ordered this for me," Sammie said, looking dubiously at the oblong bowl the waitress had placed in front of him while Rocco looked on with amusement. "Er, what is it again?"

"Bangers and mash," Rocco said. "It's mashed potatoes cooked on top of English-style sausages."

Sammie picked at his dish with a fork. The mashed potatoes were arranged in a swirling pattern, slightly browned from being recooked as a covering for the sausages.

"You're in London, Sammie," Rocco said. "You have to try something different when you're in a foreign country. It's a rule."

While Rocco dug into his vinegar-dripping fish and chips, Sammie tentatively nibbled at the mashed potatoes. When the nibble failed to poison him, he sighed and dug deeper with his knife and fork. Excavating a slice of sausage, he took a bite. Rocco assumed that the sound he made next indicated that he was pleased. Either that, or perhaps it was an indication of imminent starvation. At any rate, Sammie dispatched his meal in short order.

Somehow, the act of eating lunch in London after having been in Florida just a short time before helped drive home the reality of the road. They'd just *driven* from North America to London. *Totally bizarre. I'm really glad Sammie is here with me, or I'd never believe it myself.*

To carry out Rocco's goal of having lunch in London, they'd first had to find a way to leave the London Underground despite not having tickets. They'd navigated a multi-level maze of ancient hallways, stairs, and escalators until finally finding an exit. Sammie, ever the friendly, outgoing sort, had chatted up a female attendant, then casually mentioned that Rocco had lost their tickets somewhere. Shortly thereafter, the attendant, apparently enamored with Sammie's American accent and ornate tales of fun and sun in Florida, had personally escorted them through an access gate. Exiting from Blackfriars Station, they'd found the pub, *The Armsmen*, just down the block.

While Sammie paid the bill with a credit card, heeding his admonishment that they tipped less in the U.K., Rocco stood and stretched. He looked over at the mirror above the dark, wooden bar that extended down one side of the bar's main room and saw the lady in the white dress looking back at him. He nodded politely in her direction. This time, she didn't bolt from the scene. *It's amazing what you can get used to.* He wasn't quite sure if "you" meant her, or himself.

Exiting the pub, Rocco found himself entertained by Sammie's thunderstruck expression at his first view of one of London's famous double-decker buses. They waited for it to pass, then quickly jaywalked across the street during a lull in the evening rush hour traffic – London was five hours ahead of Florida. They passed Boots, a prominent drugstore chain in the U.K., and stood in a short line to use the ATM at the bank next to the drugstore.

Accessing the ATM, Sammie extracted cash, in good old British pounds, from his credit card. On their last sojourn through the Blackfriars Station, Rocco had ascertained that they needed cash to feed into the automated ticket machines.

A few minutes later, properly armed with tickets, they passed through some turnstiles. Sammie's attendant friend was nowhere in sight as Rocco began retracing their route back to the road's hidden access point.

Two escalators, three stairways and six turns later, Rocco stopped and said, "Houston, I think we have a problem."

"Lost?"

"Yup. Thought I had the route memorized, but everything's so old and twisty down here. It's hard to recognize where we came in."

"Probably don't help none that the road seems to like to hide itself."

Rocco sighed. "Yeah."

"You know we ain't got no passports, so it's gonna be hard to explain how we got here, if we gotta fly back or something."

Sammie was right. After 9/11, it would be impossible to get replacement passports from the U.S. Embassy when they couldn't even show that they'd entered the U.K. legally. And you couldn't get on a plane without a passport. Plus, people who entered countries illegally were likely to be looked at very carefully as possible terrorists.

"Well, we better find the entrance, then."

After a fruitless hour of backtracking and searching, it became clear that they had no idea where they'd entered the London Underground.

Sammie leaned against an old and uneven brick wall, taking a breather. "Ain't this a fine pickle?"

"Sorry," Rocco said. "My fault. You seem to be taking the situation well, though."

Sammie shrugged. "Ain't nobody shootin' at us. We got time. We got money. We'll solve this, one way or another."

"You've been shot at?"

"Yeah. Smugglin' can be dangerous." Sammie looked away, down the arched corridor. "Lots of money. Lots of temptation. And some of them folks out there are just plum crazy, messed up on power or drugs or just wrong in the head. I made a pile, then got out when things started getting real whacked up." He looked back at Rocco. "I been in some tight spots. This here, just be inconvenient."

Rocco leaned up against the wall next to him and glumly considered their situation. "Maybe we should just ask somebody where to find Platform 9 3/4."

Sammie chuckled. "Maybe we should just get a guide book. See if it mentions a hidden road."

"That's it!" Rocco pushed himself away from the wall. "We need a guide. And I think I know just where to find one." He started walking away, then looked back to see Sammie staring at him. "Come on."

Rocco entered Boots, Sammie following behind him. It was a drugstore, or chemist, as they called it in the U.K. But just like drugstores back in the U.S., it carried lots of stuff besides just drugs. Rocco figured he'd find what he was looking for in the makeup section and he was right.

In fact, he had a choice of colorful options. There were six different compacts, all in different colors, all nicely shrink-wrapped. Two were square, the rest were oval-shaped. Examining the packaging, five of them seemed to include powder of some sort. The pink oval-shaped one was the only one that didn't include powder. *Well, I certainly don't need to powder my nose.*

A mother and her teenage daughter further down the makeup aisle were looking at them oddly, two men carefully scrutinizing women's makeup products.

Holding the pink compact, Rocco turned to Sammie and said in a carrying voice, "Do you think my daughter would like this? She was complaining just yesterday that she broke her mirror."

"You know, I do believe she would."

Glancing sideways, Rocco saw the mother relax a little. *Just a guy buying something for his daughter, not some kind of creep after all.*

As they walked to the checkout counter, Sammie leaned over and whispered, "I'm startin' to worry about you."

Back in Blackfriars Station, Rocco made sure there was nobody near them as he pulled out the compact and flipped it open. "I summon you to this mirror," he said.

"Yup," said Sammie. "Now I know you've lost it."

"Maybe." Rocco chuckled. "But the girl I told you about. She's got something to do with the road. Maybe she's bound to it in some way, or something like that. I don't know. But the first time I saw her, she was reflected in the window behind the guy that sold it to me."

"I don't see no—"

And there she was, her white dress billowing slightly behind her as she stepped into view. He heard an indrawn breath from Sammie, looked up and saw his eyes widen as he realized she wasn't anywhere near them in real life.

She said something, presumably in German. Rocco guessed that it was something along the lines of: *Why am I here?* He found the fact that he could hear her interesting, since it wasn't like the compact had come with speakers.

Magic. Definitely magic.

He pointed to himself and said, "Rocco," then pointed to his friend and said, "Sammie."

She nodded and said, "Getuenth."

Okay. So she had a name. Good to know.

He waited for a couple pedestrians to pass, then flipped the compact around and panned in an arc to show her the station. After panning, he turned it around to look at her again and saw that she was laughing at him. *No respect, such was his lot in life.* He shrugged.

She pointed to her left. Rocco headed left and saw her shaking her head. All right, since he was facing her, then her left meant his right. He headed right instead and saw her nodding in agreement.

Ten minutes later, Rocco and Sammie found themselves in a narrow, dimly lit corridor that certainly looked like the one they'd first stepped into, but a bunch of other corridors had looked like that, too.

Steeling himself, Rocco walked right into the wall of white painted bricks, which thankfully gave way before him and left him standing just outside the mound through which he'd first entered the London Underground. Still holding the mirror, Rocco panned it around to show Getuenth the trail, and all of the parked cars in the distance.

A moment later, Sammie stepped out next to him.

"Well, that was an adventure," Sammie said.

HOMEWARD BOUND

Rocco had set the pink compact on the dashboard, using the lid to prop it upright. It was facing forward, so Getuenth could see where the pickup truck was headed. He'd gotten the impression that she'd never experienced, or seen, what it was like to actually drive down the road before. She kept alternating between appearing in the compact so she could watch the road and appearing in each of the vehicle's two side mirrors so she could watch Rocco and Sammie.

"You know," Sammie said. "She's pretty hot."

"She can probably hear you, you know?"

"In my vast experience," Sammie intoned, "Women don't tend to mind being talked about too much if the word 'hot' comes into the conversation. Besides, she's a bit..." He paused for effect, gripping the steering wheel and turning to face Rocco. "...Two dimensional for my taste."

Rocco couldn't help laughing.

"In fact," Sammie continued, "I wouldn't be surprised if she was lurkin' in your bathroom mirror in the morning, just waiting to watch you come out of the shower."

"Jesus! She's not my girlfriend."

"Closest thing you've got."

Rocco looked at Sammie, started to say something, then paused. Finally, he sighed and said, "Sadly, you're right."

They drove on in silence for a few minutes.

Rocco squinted. He could see the sign for the New York exit in the distance; he knew which exit it was despite it still being too far away to read the sign. There was a wrecked sports car on the left side of the road, easily visible because of the shadow it cast in the slanting rays of the late afternoon sun. Beyond it, some wooden debris that marked the remains of a covered wagon.

What he wasn't expecting was a flash as something behind the demolished wagon reflected the sun. His first thought was of an ambush, sunlight reflecting off the sights of a rifle. Instinctively, he reached out with his left arm, grabbed Sammie's collar, and yanked him down below the dashboard just as a gunshot blasted through the front windshield where Sammie's head had been.

He felt the truck decelerating, fishtailing from side to side, as Sammie slammed the brakes. He tucked himself below the dashboard as two more shots went through the windshield. The pink compact slid off the dashboard as glass fragments rained all around them. The truck came to a screeching halt.

"Fuck me!" shouted Sammie. Looking over at Rocco, he said more quietly, "Next time, I'm picking' where we go to lunch."

Rocco tried desperately to analyze the situation for a safe way out. About a mile beyond Rocco's suspected shooter location, the New York exit curved into the road. Strategically, a great place for reinforcements to come from once a target was sighted and, perhaps, disabled. So, expect more bad guys momentarily. Not good.

So far, the bad guys were using the crazy geography of the road to their advantage. But maybe there were disadvantages, too. Normally, a good ambush would "close the gate" behind the target, but there was no easy way to hide a blocking force on the road. So, either the back gate wasn't closed, or there were enemies coming up behind them from the previous exit. He'd bet on the former.

Rocco heard the flat crack of another gunshot, and the truck sank slightly to the left.

"Sniper's got us disabled..." Another shot rang out and the truck settled to the right. "That's both front tires."

Sammie shook his head and glass shards fell out of his hair. "You know, I been thinking 'bout getting me one of them tinted windshields."

"Good plan," Rocco said.

Karnatz straddled his motorcycle and surveyed his raiding party with a practiced eye. The New York ramp terminated in a roughly circular clearing in the middle of a heavily forested park area, one that was conveniently accessible to some of the less traveled park roads. His forces had commandeered the clearing;

strategically placed "Road Closed" barriers had been placed on nearby roads to reduce the likelihood of interruptions.

The party's support vehicles, a bus with heavily tinted windows and two nondescript panel trucks, were pulled up under the cover of the overhanging trees. The bus was for transporting the warriors and support staff. One panel truck was used to transport the motorcycles and the other was used to transport anything of value that they liberated on their raiding expedition. In case any of the vehicles were ever stopped on conventional roads for some reason during their journey between their clan enclave in the northwestern United States and New York, the drivers were humans, their loyalty a byproduct of hostages held back in Ebonhold.

Karnatz had eight *orqindi* warriors besides himself, six hardened veterans and two rookies on their first raid. Plus Wuglat, another veteran, their spotter on the road. It was ironic that the humans among them, who were effectively slaves, had nicknamed them orcs after some famous human book. And even more ironic that the clan had embraced the label with gleeful abandon.

He grunted in irritation. He wanted to be feared because he was dangerous, not because he and his warriors resembled some undisciplined barbarians in some tome written by a weak, sniveling human.

Like Karnatz, his warriors were already on their motorcycles, specially modified Harleys that could handle riders the size and weight of his orcs. One of the rookies was his nephew, Uram, a mere stripling at only seven feet tall and two hundred and eighty pounds. His troops were armored up and weapons ready, just waiting for the go-ahead from Wuglat via their comms to race into battle.

While radio signals from the road didn't travel beyond it, their kobalo support staff, or goblins, as the humans called them, had set up a low-level repeater at the ramp's boundary to echo Wuglat's signals to the comm units in their war helms.

Karnatz smiled in satisfaction. It was a tight operation, and he'd been responsible for developing most of the tactics that they were using.

He heard Wuglat's guttural voice in his helmet: "Target immobilized."

Karnatz gunned his motorcycle, the front wheel momentarily lifting from the ground, and sped for the ramp, his warriors whooping and hollering as they followed him.

Rocco reached down to the floor for the pink compact. Holding the compact from the bottom, he pushed it carefully up above the level of the dashboard. He angled his head and the mirror to get a good view. He was dismayed, but not overly surprised, to see a pack of motorcycles on the New York ramp barreling towards the road. It was hard to tell how many cyclists there were, but Rocco figured at least eight or more. They certainly weren't going to be able to outrun the attackers in a pickup truck with flat tires. As for fighting them off, all they had was a 9mm pistol with sixteen bullets.

This was well beyond "not good" and well into "oh, shit" territory.

Getuenth stepped into view within the compact's mirror. Her eyes widened and she gasped at the sight of the riders. She clasped her hands to her cheeks in shock, and then said something in German that sounded like a question.

He had no clue what she'd asked, but he nodded his head and said, "Girl, if you've got superpowers, now is the time to use them."

One moment the attack was proceeding exactly according to plan, and then Karnatz realized it was going horribly, horribly wrong. The terrain around him flickered, blurring kaleidoscopically as if the ramp were somehow moving at high speed. He felt a touch of vertigo, almost unheard of for an orc, as the pavement beneath him seemed to slip sideways and tilt upward at the same time. In a moment, it became clear that he and his riders were now climbing an increasingly steep hill.

The excited whooping of his warriors turned into shouts of dismay. He revved his motorcycle, sensing that failure to crest the top was going to lead to bad consequences. Uram raced by him on his left, having obviously reached the same conclusion. His nephew's slight stature, almost two hundred pounds lighter than Karnatz, gave him a major speed advantage.

As the pavement reached a sixty-degree angle, Karnatz was still making headway slowly. A few of his warriors passed him as Uram had, but by now Uram was far out in the lead.

He saw Uram roll over the top and disappear from view. Then the angle increased so much that he started sliding backwards, his wheels skidding, shuddering from side to side and leaving a smoking track of rubber on the road. One by one, his warriors lost control of their motorcycles and plummeted away, until only he was left. Realizing that falling was inevitable, Karnatz threw himself off his cycle, rolling over in the air to land spread-eagled on his back. Feet first, he began sliding downward, his armored leathers absorbing the punishment and slowing him down enough that he could see his orcs and their cycles tumbling and sliding uncontrollably below him.

There was water beneath them, a wide expanse of brown choppy waves. The terminus had obviously been moved somehow. If he had to guess, his raiding party was being unceremoniously dumped into the Hudson River, which was the only relatively close body of water he knew of.

He watched warriors and cycles, including his own favorite Harley, plunge into the water, disappearing in a concentrated sequence of huge splashes.

The bad thing about water, he thought just before he hit the surface, *is that orcs don't float.*

"The shooter's on the left shoulder," Rocco said. "Run the son of a bitch down."

Sammie stared at him for a beat, then what Rocco had said seemed to sink in. He nodded and slammed his foot on the accelerator. The truck surged ahead, the blown front tires flapping noisily and making for a rough ride.

"And don't raise your head," Rocco added.

Sammie laughed and gave him a wild-eyed look, then Rocco heard a metallic plunk over the road noise as a shot hit the engine block. Sammie muttered under his breath, gritted his teeth, and yanked the truck onto the left shoulder. The pickup truck went off-road at too sharp an angle and would have left the road entirely, but Rocco felt the road's boundary resistance kick in, effectively nudging the truck back onto the gravel shoulder. Failing to account for the unexpected help, Sammie overcompensated in the other direction. The truck bounced as the right wheels went back up the pavement, slamming Rocco's head into the dashboard.

Sammie got the truck under control and accelerated crazily toward the wrecked vehicle. On the plus side, the wrecked sports car was now between them and their attacker, but Rocco didn't relish slamming into the fast-approaching obstacle.

Rocco peered up at the mirror in the compact, the truck jostling around so much that it was hard to make out what he was seeing in front of them. Something had happened at the exit, which seemed to have somehow gained elevation and was now easily visible beyond and above the wreck. The background scenery of gently undulating farm fields and forests had been replaced by a suburban landscape of rolling hills covered by houses, apartments and shopping centers. And the distant ramp seemed to somehow descend out of sight. Only a single motorcycle rider was visible near where the ramp descended, so whatever Getuenth had done seemed to have eliminated, or at least sidetracked, most of the shooter's cavalry.

The wrecked car was coming up quickly. Rocco shouted, "Jink right...now!"

Sammie wrenched the wheel and the truck careened up onto the pavement in a cloud of dust and pelting gravel, skidding sideways and then fishtailing badly as Sammie straightened their trajectory.

More shots plunked into the engine. Steam gushed out of the radiator. Within a few seconds, condensing droplets of water began to collect on the mirror, obscuring Rocco's view.

Rocco dropped the compact as he felt Sammie pull the truck back onto the shoulder. He opened the glove compartment and took out the handgun, leaving the safety on. The seatbelt was still secured around his waist. He pulled the shoulder strap around him and then, taking a calculated risk, popped up to take in the view, such as it was.

He saw the ruined heap of the wagon approaching. Just before impact, he glimpsed their attacker diving away from the far end of the derelict wagon. He reached over and yanked the steering wheel to the right. There was a massive impact as the left front corner of the truck smashed through the remains of the wagon. The seatbelt tightened and held him in place as fragments of wood flew through the broken windshield. His upraised arms protected him from most of the debris. The off-center impact turned the truck in a sideways arc and there was another *thump* as the vehicle sideswiped their attacker.

The pickup, engine dead and bereft of most of its momentum, stopped sideways in the road. Half dazed, Rocco released the seatbelt, punched the door open, and jumped out as the truck was still moving slightly. He somehow kept his feet despite his bad leg, crouching low to make a smaller target, leading with the gun in a two-handed grip and looking for the shooter.

His opponent was just standing up. He was massive, probably better than eight feet tall, wearing impact armor in camouflage colors with a matching helmet. He was speaking urgently in a guttural language, probably into some sort of communicator, and trying to swing a long rifle towards Rocco. *Tactical mistake*, Rocco thought. *With his armor and size, he should have just charged me.*

Rocco limped toward him, calmly shooting him again and again, keeping him off-balance, and trying as much as possible to aim for points not protected by armored plates. Locked in combat mode, he noticed but was unaffected by the fact that his enemy had gray skin and upward thrusting yellow tusks.

Incongruously, he was reminded of the orcs from *The Fellowship of the Ring*, which he'd seen with his daughter.

The orc howled in pain as a round penetrated his lower abdomen, spoiling a shot that probably would have killed Rocco but instead ended up buzzing past only inches away from his ear.

Clutching his bleeding wound with his free arm, the orc inadvertently twisted and exposed the unprotected side of his thigh to Rocco's next shot, which dropped his massive opponent to his knees. His adversary responded with a wild shot that thunked into Rocco's prosthetic lower leg and took it out from underneath him.

Falling, Rocco winged a round off the orc's helmet, landed hard on his side, and snapped off another round that luckily impacted just above his opponent's tusks. A fan of blood erupted from the back of the orc's helmet; he toppled over backwards and lay still.

Rocco sat up and looked around. There was still another opponent around somewhere. He spotted the last member of the ambush party in the distance, speeding away from them on his motorcycle. He decided he was happy not to have to face another opponent like the one he'd just killed. But he certainly wasn't impressed by the kind of warrior who'd so callously abandon one of his fellows while he turned tail and ran for safety.

He popped the magazine out of the 9mm. There were only two rounds left.

Karnatz sank rapidly through the dark water, desperately trying to pull off his boots, armor and clothing. Still not finished, he landed softly in muck perhaps thirty-five feet down. Visibility was almost zero at the bottom, but he could still make out the distant lightness above him that represented the surface.

All around him, unseen, his war party was dying.

Fellow warriors. Comrades he'd lived with, trained, led and fought beside for years. And there was nothing he could do to save them. He'd be lucky if he could save himself.

Lungs clamoring for air, he freed himself from the last of his clothing, crouched in the mud, and sprang for the surface, powerful legs kicking madly as he fought his way upward.

Maybe orcs can't float, he thought, *but a smart orc learns how to swim.*

AFTERMATH

Upon examination, Rocco's prosthesis turned out to be relatively undamaged, dented but still serviceable. He laboriously climbed to his feet and walked back to the truck. Peering into the open passenger door, he saw Sammie sigh with relief when he realized it was Rocco and not one of the bad guys. Sammie pushed some wood debris off himself and sat up. He was bleeding from a cut in his forehead. He shook his head and fragments of glass went flying.

"We're all right now," Rocco said. "Getuenth took out the reinforcements coming from the New York ramp. I took out the shooter. And the last survivor is running away on a motorcycle at about one twenty." He paused. "Now, about that tinted window..."

Sammie laughed. "Yeah, right. Think I'm gonna need a new truck."

"Sorry, I never expected this."

Sammie shrugged, dislodging more pieces of safety glass. "Shit happens. We alive, soldier boy. That's what really matters." He gestured at the passenger-side mirror. "Wave at your girlfriend, Rocco. I think she's worried about you."

He turned and saw Getuenth looking at him with wide eyes from the mirror. He bowed slightly, the only way he could figure to make it clear that he was thanking her. She nodded.

Rocco reached into the truck and picked up the pink compact. Stepping back, he panned the compact around as if it were a video camera, showing Getuenth the damaged pickup truck, the remnants of the wrecked wagon and, from a distance, the body of the dead orc. He heard Sammie get out of the pickup truck. A moment later his friend stepped up next to him to survey the scene.

"I got to tell you," Sammie said. "I got mixed feelings about this here road."

"No kidding." Rocco gestured at the body. "I think that's an orc. He's got military grade body armor, obviously customized for his size, a sniper rifle, and a communicator in his helmet. Plus maybe eight more just like him on bikes, probably with the same kind of equipment."

"Well, hell." Sammie looked down at the orc's body. "You don't get bandits like these guys unless there's some seriously valuable traffic on the road. Like those pirates in Somalia."

"Yeah."

With a considering look on his face, Sammie said, "If there's that kind of traffic, then there's got to be some way to make money off it."

"Legally," Rocco added sharply.

"Well, that's up to you, Sheriff Fitch." Sammie chuckled. "But yeah, legally would be better. I been a smuggler, but I ain't no bandit."

"Sheriff," Rocco said thoughtfully. "I think I like the sound of that..."

"I got some money saved up. I ain't filthy rich, but I've got a bit more than most people know."

"Sammie, bad off as I am, I'm not interested in charity."

"Neither am I," Sammie said, shaking his head. "The way I see it, the road is money. We just got to figure out how to extract the cash from it." He turned and looked back at the New York ramp. "Getuenth sorta just proved that you own the road, and the road's attached to your property. So, we need to make sure the bank doesn't foreclose on your house."

"How'd you know about the foreclosure?"

"I ain't blind," Sammie said. "You left the notice on the table in your foyer. Seen it last night when I left your place."

"Oh."

"Rocco, you don't need charity, you need a partner with some startup cash to tide you over until we figure out how to monetize the road."

"Monetize," Rocco said. "There's a word I never thought I'd hear you say."

Sammie shrugged. "I got a daughter that works for an Internet startup."

"Well," Rocco said, turning and walking back towards the truck. "I know some people that maybe could help with a challenging security situation like this."

Following behind him, Sammie asked, "Ex-Marines?"

Rocco stopped next to the truck. "Mostly."

"So we got a deal, Sheriff Fitch?" Sammie extended his hand.

"Yeah," Rocco said, shaking Sammie's outstretched hand. "We'll get all the legal details on paper later, but yeah, we've got a deal. Right now, though, we've got some work to do."

"Work?"

"Yeah." Rocco gestured at the vehicle. "The truck is toast. We're leaving it behind. We'll take the vehicle registration and any other identifying stuff with us. Plus get rid of the VIN numbers. These bad guys are going to come back and check out this scene eventually. There can't be anything that leads back to us. Then maybe Getuenth can find us a shortcut so we don't have to hoof it all the way home."

Karnatz breached the surface, chest heaving mightily as he greedily sucked in fresh air. His legs churned while he paddled with dogged determination to keep his bulk from going back under. Keeping himself afloat was no easy task. With his bone structure and extensive musculature, he was considerably heavier than the water.

Glancing around wildly, he spotted two tree-lined shores, reinforcing his belief that he and his raiding party had been thrown into the Hudson River. His anger mounted as it sank in that he'd been defeated by magic. Thoroughly beaten by powers beyond his control. The terminus of the New York had been *moved*. He'd never even heard of a terminus being moved before.

The only person that could have done this was the owner of the road. That thought gave his anger a focus.

Now he knew who he was going to kill.

Just as soon as he got himself out of this damned river.

He tried to determine which shore was closer, then an approaching white boat that was intermittently visible between the choppy waves caught his eye. Some humans coming to investigate the disturbance in the water.

Karnatz thought, *Aren't they going to be surprised when they see me.*

Six

ANOTHER URBAN LEGEND FROM THE WINDY CITY

MARY ELLEN GAVIN

Mary Ellen is a storyteller. She loves to hear and read the stories of others. Storytelling is her favorite entertainment and she hopes you enjoy her story.

ANOTHER URBAN LEGEND FROM THE WINDY CITY

It was one of those frozen 1970s nights in Chicago. I had just moved into the newly constructed complex, Lamplighter Castle, with its fairy-tale turrets and balconies. The blocks of new construction lit up the center of a sprawling, unpopulated ghetto waiting for gentrification. The tall wrought-iron fence and gates made the compound look medieval and it became known as *The Palace* to those who only saw it from afar and did not call it home. Adding the gas lamps and cobblestone walks, time and place felt as if it stood still there.

My first Saturday free from unpacking, I hosted a fancy party. Friends and coworkers made up the list of well-wishers eager to see inside The Palace. Better yet, they were eager to enter the exclusive compound to see how the nouveau riche lived. As the night progressed many of the new neighbors, who ranged from young politicians and pro athletes to fire and police officers also drifted in and out of my wide-open door. Little groups of both gathered to go on self-guided tours through the recreation area and half-empty buildings.

A bar had been set up in the living room, along with a buffet on the table in the dining room, by my caterers. Chuck Mangione's *Feels So Good* album played background for the guests bantering about the current world view, or exchanging gossip from city hall. Chicagoans always liked to know where everyone stood.

The city divided between the north and south, Cubs vs. Sox, until Chicagoans heard the mention of a suburb like Skokie or Mount Prospect. North siders or South siders, they joined voices to espouse how the *City on the Lake* would always be home *because they wouldn't be caught dead living in the burbs.*

147

Another subject Chicagoans agreed upon: their loathing for *those whack jobs in Los Angeles, horn-honking New Yorkers* and *know-it-alls in Washington.*

There they were, *Chicago's Own* standing with a drink and retelling how their immigrant ancestors pioneered west as soon as they got off *the boat* to escape the rude East Coast. To light a fire under any dull conversation, a Chicagoan would throw out a dig about the City of Angels or the Big Apple.

Little groups huddled even closer as frosty gusts of brittle air rattled my ninth-floor patio windows. Often, everyone stopped talking to listen to the eerie sound of the wind whistling off the lake until a true Chicagoan announced, "*The Hawk* is out tonight."

Indeed, *The Hawk* swirled around the tall buildings, daring us to step outside. While everyone might have liked to get a better view of the lit up cityscape, we all stayed toasty warm gathering near the burning fireplace. A sudden burst of laughter meant the surreal moment had ended. Being native to Chicago meant the weather must never be a factor. My crowd that night certainly knew how to fight off the icy blasts howling off the Lake. We held jobs downtown.

In between short conversations with groups of guests, I kept running to pick up the house phone as new arrivals called up from the lobby. Word had gotten out about my soiree and more people were showing up than expected. I welcomed them and did not worry about security since there were enough males and one female present, who I knew routinely carried side arms. I could count on them to keep the peace ... which is why I did not feel concern when an unknown voice called up on the service phone from the lobby.

"Hey! This is Bart Landreau!"

I hesitated, not recognizing the name.

"That's right! Ya don't know me." He chuckled softly. "I wouldn't blame ya if you turned me away. One of your friends mentioned that I might come around tonight to join your festivities?"

His cute way of talking told me he did not hail from the city ... more than likely Bart Landreau came from the New Orleans area and I told that to him.

"How'd ya know?" He chuckled again. "It's more than evident up here, huh?

"Oh yeah, it's that *evident*," I said using his southern accent.

"Do ya believe my story of why I'm here?"

"We'll have to check it out." I held up the lobby phone and yelled, "Did any of you scoundrels invite a certain Bart Landreau?"

A hand raised and my high school pal, Clarita, came forward with a coy smile on her face. "Oh please, please let him come up. Trust me. You're gonna want to meet Bart. He's Buddy Greene's friend and he's real smart. Buddy says this guy's going places." She pulled me close and whispered in my ear, "Besides, he's drop-dead gorgeous and you need a boyfriend."

Since Buddy had not showed up yet, I had to take Clarita's word. Turning back to the phone I said, "C'mon up!"

He chuckled again and thanked me. "Hey, there's a line of people down here. They all want to come up to your party. Should I bring them with me?"

"No!" I screamed. "Tell them to call me individually."

"Ya really like playing with your tele toy, huh?" Click.

I stayed there, waiting for the next caller, but the phone did not ring.

Clarita ran to the open door to meet Buddy's friend and it did not take long for the tall stranger to appear, all handsome and smiling. She looked over his shoulder and made an inquisitive face at the figure of a female standing in his shadow. The dim hall light and soft candle-flicker in the apartment could hardly illuminate the woman dressed all in black with her face hidden inside the hood of a long cloak.

Seeing Clarita, Bart walked towards her wearing a big smile. He looked so striking with his blonde hair, pale blue eyes, rugged features that all eyes, including mine, watched as he held out his arms to my old friend. When they shared a tender embrace, it made me realize how much I missed affection since my career had become more important than romance.

Still curious about that woman in black who followed him in, I looked around. Somehow, I had lost sight of her. She either ran for the loo, or took off her cloak and disappeared into the party.

Anxious to meet the elegantly dressed Mr. Landreau in a navy suit with white turtleneck, I walked over ready to shake his hand. Clarita had already started our introduction. "This is our hostess."

He grabbed my outstretched hand and gave me a manly shake. "Thank you for being so generous and offering an invitation to your party."

Surprise, he let go of my hand to pull me into his strong embrace until I could smell his expensive cologne. Holding me close for a friendly five-beat hug, I could hear Clarita talking about Buddy's whereabouts. Bart did not let go and the beats went on as she kept talking. "Sorry, I forgot to tell you that Buddy'll be late. He had to attend a wake on the south side. An old neighbor passed away. He's probably fighting the black ice on Lake Shore Drive."

Smiling up at the good-looking man still holding me, I tried to cover my nervousness with a smile. "Hi Bart ... I'm Lisa, we just spoke on the phone."

He let go, but grabbed my hand to kiss my fingertips. "I am your servant and eternally grateful to be here and not out in the cold."

His dark eyes took me in while his hand slowly let go of mine.

Clarita grabbed his free arm. "Let's get a drink. I'll introduce you around."

The house phone began ringing again and I spent most of the next hour negotiating with callers from the lobby to either buzz them into the building or warn them to stop calling. Between calls, I caught Bart's eyes twinkling at me whenever the single females encircling him did not have his attention.

The low-key evening continued until Buddy finally arrived. That's when the party took off. A brilliant storyteller, he regaled us with tales about the south side Clan he'd just visited at their traditional Irish wake.

"I squished through the parlor on a sopping wet carpet from snow-boot traffic. All the time, I'm figuring the deceased sure had lots of loved ones who came out on this wintry night. So, I look around to see the sad mourners with their heads bowed. Funny thing ... they're still wearing their coats, hats and mufflers while I'm already sweating inside my winter duds.

"Representing my family, I drop down on the kneeler to say goodbye to the old gent who lived next door. I never cared for the man. He used to holler at me for not bringing his morning paper to the door on time. What the hell did he expect? It was still dark most of the days I rode by on my bike. The old grump was lucky, I had a good arm and my throw got the morning edition to his porch."

Buddy stopped to let the crowd laugh and take a sip of his drink. "I whispered 'God Speed' to the deceased and stood up. Looking around, I saw the empty parlor behind me. It's just me alone with the *Crabby Bastard*. It's not that I'm afraid of corpses, mind ya ... but, I am afraid to be alone with *the dead*. Somehow, I got the feeling Old Joe lying there in his best suit seemed lonesome and wanted me to linger."

Buddy shook his head. "We Irish are a spooky lot. Blessing or curse, we believe the newly departed try to communicate with us."

"I turn and hightail it to the back of the room, sign the visitor's book and hit the door. That's where I spot the Flynn Mourners ... outside smoking and tipping shooters. Seems, the parlor's bar located in the basement flooded when the pipes froze ... hence, the snow-boot traffic from all the comings and goings for refills."

Buddy had us roaring with Bart at his side, spurring him on for more stories. Buddy lit a cigarette. "Here's the funny part. As a new mourner approached from the parking lot to pay respect, every Flynn put out their smoke and hid their glass inside their coats to run inside and act sad. No wonder that rug was soaked!"

In the midst of the fun, the female stranger reappeared. Maybe the alcohol or excitement of the evening, but her lithe form inside that long willowy dress and cloak seemed to be weaving in and out before my eyes. With her hood thrown back, I could now see her milky white skin and fiery-red hair.

Startled to see her again, I wondered how I'd forgotten her ghostly figure? Her long thin hands raised up into the air as she yelled, "I've got a great idea!" Her high-pitched voice seemed to echo when she announced, "Let's grab a drink and an arm, to take the dark journey to the haunted church!"

Since the party crowd had a fever for excitement, they began gathering their coats and hats before I could protest. Standing helpless, I watched that red-headed pied piper lead my guests out the door and into the elevators. My two friends cheered everyone on and were at her side. Seeing the smile on Clarita's face as she held Buddy's arm made me see that her true affection had always been for Buddy, who must have been her heart's desire all along.

Left in the empty apartment, I almost felt angry at all of them until I realized that Bart had stayed behind and waited by my side. "Let's grab a few bottles of wine for fortitude and catch up with them." His warm smile promised that I had not been abandoned.

Together, we scooped up bottles of red and white and filled one of the caterer's leather transport bags. I told the owner how much I appreciated her service and after her staff cleaned up, they should go home.

Bart helped me put on my street-length fox coat so popular during that freezing winter. After buttoning his long cashmere coat, he grabbed the bag of wine. Like the troops leaving before us, we took along our own glasses. Riding down the elevator we laughed until I asked, "Do you think we'll be able to catch up with them?"

He stopped laughing to pretend fright. "I'd hate to get lost in the dark."

As soon as we stepped away from the building, we heard their happy voices resounding in the crisp air. Soon we found ourselves trailing them into that empty section of city blocks waiting for the bulldozers.

Moving fast while still inside the fading light from the complex, we easily caught up to the group. The redhead walked backwards to face her minions. She had stories to tell ... mysterious tales that supposedly took place at our destination. Moving closer, we could finally hear her recitation. She seemed like a well-trained docent of haunted church tours and a well-versed teller of scary stories.

"The place itself is a relic left standing after the Chicago Fire. It's seen everything from devout souls trying to resurrect the building to motorcycle gangs trying to destroy it. It stands empty now, but there are rumors about its strange occurrences and what is hidden inside." Her voice hushed. "Beware friends, going to the ancient church at midnight sets the spirits free to roam in the shadows."

It would be Buddy hollering out, "Who's afraid of those midnight ghosts?"

Clarita waved her hand. "I am!" Everyone laughed with her.

Bart checked the lit-up face of his watch. "It's already eleven forty-five."

Our fiery-redhead took command again. "If we stick together, we shouldn't lose anyone."

"Lose anyone?" Buddy guffawed. "That sounds dangerous?"

I pulled my arm away from Bart as tried to light a cigarette. Taking a drag, he hollered out, "I hope this place isn't dangerous. Our hostess, Lisa, will be responsible for our safety."

Everyone agreed, laughing even harder, but I did not find it funny.

Everyone kept chuckling, but her statement and Bart's joke sent a chill up my spine as we moved deeper into the dark rubble. The decaying buildings stood empty and ready to be torn down. Watching our step now, we slowed our pace. As we left the last of the light beaming from my new complex, darkness overtook us. Without light and street noise that no longer reached out to us, we entered a sensory void that soon became a vacuum when the whine of the wind died down. Insulated from reality, it felt as if we were walking on a different plane of existence. All eyes followed the tiny circle of Buddy's flashlight moving up ahead.

Something moved behind me and I felt a large presence step into procession with me. Before I could sound an alarm, a meaty arm wrapped around my throat and the other covered my mouth. The attacker had the strength of a bear and picked me up. Still struggling for my freedom, he pulled me back from the group walking forward without me. I fought off his right hand covering my mouth with my fingernails. All the while, I heard Buddy and Bart's happy voices in the distance as they kept shooting one-liners at each other from scary movies.

The top of my left arm stayed anchored by my attacker's extremely long arm choking my throat, but he could not get control over my right arm. I kept clawing at him with broken nails. Losing air, I finally pulled my mouth free to scream at the top of my lungs, but nothing came out. The friendly voices moving away from me began to name every film where females screamed for their lives.

On my own now in the dark, I needed to get on my feet and fight off my attacker who smelled like he slept in the dumpsters. Crouching forward, I bent down and jumped off the ground to put all my weight against his right arm still trying to grapple with me. His breath hissed as he made an angry remark about his pain. When his right arm fell away I moved away from him, but his fist pounded into my shoulder. My fox coat not only cushioned the blows, but his bare knuckles slipped across the slick fur. He let go long enough for me to take off running. My feet flew above all the broken pieces of cement to catch up to the crowd now singing the old bus tune: A Hundred Bottles of Beer on the Wall.

Out of breath, I tapped Bart on the shoulder and asked, "Did you miss me?"

"Naw, I figured you took a potty break in the bushes back there."

"You didn't notice anyone coming up from behind?"

He hesitated until he finally said, "Not really?"

That's when I thought why bother even telling Bart or any of them what happened to me? After all, they were on a great adventure. It even hit me that they might not believe how I had just fought for my life with a dirty bum.

From far away, a high-pitched howl cut through the darkness to reach our ears. Clarita screamed, "What's that?"

Someone shouted out, "It sounds like a wolf!"

Another shouted back, "Maybe a coyote!"

Buddy spoke up, "No. It's a German Shepherd. I grew up with that breed."

"Why is it howling?" Bart shrugged, trying to make light of the subject.

"It's the males who wail in the night. Shepherds are rarely fearful. That boy's definitely looking for a mate." Buddy answered before howling. The other men, looking to have fun, joined him.

When they ran out of howls and catcalls Bart added, "Hey, we brought wine. Bring your glasses back here and I'll pour." Everyone gathered around, but I thought better of telling about my attack. I just needed a glass of wine to calm down. Worse, I realized how much I did not know about these people, who I had spent so much time and money to entertain. Guess they weren't having fun.

Our organizer in the black cloak didn't join us. Turning around, I spotted her red hair even in the dark. She seemed to be in a hurry to lead us on and I wondered again where we were headed and why? Not that I ever drove around that broken-down area; I only followed the exit off the Kennedy Expressway to the complex's underground parking lot.

It became even darker as we began walking again. Bart reached into his coat and pulled out a small flashlight attached to his key ring. Seeing the tiny beam, Buddy asked us to move up front. "You guys can light the way for awhile."

Walking in the black of night did not bother the woman leading us. She somehow kept her focus without illumination. Bart kept his light low on the back of her black boots, so we could keep watch where she stepped as we followed her black shadow. Light chatter accompanied us, but sipping our wine calmed us.

"How far away is this place?" Buddy's patience began to wear thin.

"Not far now, you'll see!" Why did her voice sound sweet, too sweet?

Traveling in pitch black kept the crowd huddled together. All eyes stayed on the spot of light as we moved along the chunks of broken sidewalk. Buddy kidded, "We sure have become a close-knit group. I feel like we're on an explorer mission traversing *the dark side of the moon.*"

We giggled and some sang out the main line to the Pink Floyd tune– anything to break the rising tension. A strong gust of wind blew out of the sky and beat down on us like prop wash. It took away our breath. Bart and I stopped to hold on to each other, but the wind's mighty roar pounded until it pushed us back.

I closed my eyes, trying to squint against the wisps of my hair whipping around my cheeks and snapping into my eyes While the women screamed and some men cussed, Bart pulled me closer, pushing my head to his chest. We held tight, trying to stay on our feet.

Someone proclaimed, "Must be a hundred miles an hour!" Moving closer still, the group became a human ball trying to wait it out. Finally, the almighty wind stopped. We emerged from our huddle and tried to shake off our feelings of helplessness against the elements ... something every Chicagoan knows.

Turning back to the inky dark, we were ready to face the end of the journey. When Bart rolled his flashlight among us looking for our leader, we did not see a sign of her red hair or high-heeled boots. He shouted out to her, "Hey! Where's our guide?" No response.

Buddy called out, "Hey sister, you taking a potty break?"
Silence!

The others called out to her also, but we heard nothing in return except the lake wind singing through the ruins ahead. Eventually the question came up; should we turn around? As the crowd mulled over the prospect, Bart steadily flashed his light in all directions until his voice rang out in excitement. "Look! There's the church!"

The crowd pulled at Bart with his flashlight to take the lead. I did not move forward with the crowd who were only too eager to get past me. The ancient church stood only a half block ahead. Now without a sidekick to lean on, the walk full of rocks and cracks would be treacherous. I should have hurried to catch up, but an odd feeling held me back. Following slowly, they all stood at the old wooden door where Buddy held his circle of light.

The men kept promising they'd be able to get the door to open. Stepping back, Buddy ran forward and threw his shoulder against it. My prayer did not come true. The door released from its lock and flew open. The stale smell of burnt candles and the heavy scent of incense washed out as if to warn us. I wondered how the others did not turn up their noses at the wicked odor.

Their eyes were full of wonder as they pushed and shoved to get inside while I stood back and let them. While they were inside tripping and bumping into things, I said a prayer of my own before slowly stepping through the curved archway. Something deep inside me still wished we had turned around. Even as they found used candles to light up the place, my dread did not dissipate. Still, I ventured inside and joined in as we looked around the small stone building. The few windows were intact, but each pane had been painted black. There were no saintly renderings of holy people waiting for us to admire. No signs of any kind of heavenly worship.

After pouring more wine in our glasses, we began meandering on our own. Looking at everything as if we were in a museum, it did not take long before the strange aura of flickering shadows put us into a light trance. Each of us relaxed, drank more wine and reminisced from our childhood times spent in church or synagogue. We told how we enjoyed nosing around or touching things in someone else's sacred place. Snooping all around, we checked the nooks and crannies and especially the hidden cabinets where we found secret levers.

One small door at the back of the building had been found locked. After the men joined to force it open, they decided that the locks were on the other side because it had to be tightly bolted. We made a game out of *what might lie behind that little door*. Clarita suggested it might be a secret passage to tunnels while Buddy suggested it must be the toilet. We all laughed, but one gal asked if they would try to open it again since she had consumed a large amount of wine and would love that it might be a toilet.

Feeling tired, I gladly walked over to where three pews had been scattered at awkward angles. Sitting down, I watched the shadowy flames flicker on the walls as I listened to the funny quips offered about what waited behind that locked door.

As my eyelids kept lowering, Bart's voice brought me back. "Look here, they left a statue behind." Following the beam of his flashlight, we saw the form covered with a heavy drop cloth sporting many colors of paint. The life-size figure stood inside a large marble grotto carved deep into the wall only a few feet above the floor. We gathered behind Bart to watch as he reached up. "At the count of three, I'll pull off the covering."

We did the countdown along with him, "One ... Two ... Three!"

Smiling, Bart yanked the old canvas to the floor. We stood momentarily dazed by the flurry of dust until our eyes blinked and we could stare into the grotto. It looked empty. We followed Bart's light as he checked the floor and the ceiling, but saw no sign of anything or anyone that could have been under the cloth.

Buddy pushed forward, looking agitated. "How can that be? We saw a figure under that tarp. We saw it." He looked around acting angry and bewildered. He even tried measuring our shadows, both standing and sitting.

"I need a drink!" He turned to Bart and looked haggard. "Crack open another bottle and pass it around."

Bart obeyed, but he did not look the same either. I wondered what happened to those two swaggering men from a few minutes ago. The person now opening the wine looked fearful. When he brought the last bottle over and poured for us, we all swallowed hard. Still looking pale, he moved close and kissed my lips. Backing away he shouted to the others, "Isn't it time we got out of here?"

No one complained that we were gathering to leave. Buddy rushed to be the first to the exit door at the rear of the church. Reaching for the knob, he fell back sprawling on his backside. "It felt like an electric shock!" Getting back up, he held out his sore hand as another man came forward only to receive the same shock.

A slippery sweet voice shouted out from behind us. "Where are you going?"

We turned to face the front of the church and looked into the dark altar area swirling with lingering smoke from the extinguished candles. Bart aimed his beam at the back of the church until it fell upon the open doorway – the same small door that could not be sprung before.

The strange female who had led us to that church stood there. As Bart's flashlight surveyed her from head to toe, she appeared younger than my first impression. Now, her features appeared angelic like a teen girl. Her arms stretched toward the ceiling as her eyes glared out at us from under her black hood.

When an errant breeze fluttered through the folds of her cloak flowing from her shoulders, we realized that her body flew a few feet off the ground and was rising. Every one of us let out a scream. The shrieks of fright echoed in the hollow building as we turned to make a run for the newly unlocked exit.

Each man tried to help the other pull back the heavy door. Although there were no more electrical shocks, it still would not budge. The lone flashlight must have dropped in the skirmish because darkness suddenly consumed us.

That's when panic set in.

I wanted to move away from the pushing and shoving. Taking steps back, I bumped into a pew. The screaming and yelling sounded like a drunken bar fight. There were others who cried out in the dark as if they were beginning to go mad ... women crying and men hollering, fists pounding on the walls.

My feet kept taking me further back, moving inches away from the mob now beating on each other in their quest to escape the violence. Gun fire erupted from several origins and I ducked under a pew. Between the rapid fire and screaming, I could not hear. Shots went off again and continued until the weapons emptied. Still, the door must not have opened.

Getting to my feet, I stood behind the pew and could feel fresh air fluttering at the back of my neck. Something kept moving the air from behind. Before I could turn, a presence pounced on my back and entwined thin legs around my waist. Icy fingers wrapped around my throat. It had to be the fiery redhead.

Managing to stand upright, my hands went behind my head. They pulled at the loose-skin-over-bones trying to choke the life out of me. A rotting stench wafted across my nostrils before my ringing ears caught her high-pitched raspy voice mocking me. "Are...We... Having... Fun...Yet?"

Dropping down, I spread out and stuck to the floor like a coat of wax. She let go of her leg hold and somehow did not fall down on top of me. Still, I could feel her flying above. Screeching and soaring like a bat, she made low passes every few seconds. Pulling up my fur collar, I covered my face and held my breath, feeling as if we were all locked up in an asylum. The insanity going on around me seemed so unreal that I could only shut my eyes. I prayed she would not locate me and I prayed that my party guests would stop their maniacal behavior.

My prayers came true. The clamor at the door ceased and I could feel the others dropping down. Instinctively, we were all spread out on the floor holding our breath. The cacophony of noise stopped except for the whooshing sounds of her circling inches above us. Her dark shadow flew like a hummingbird, able to hover until something or someone caught her attention. She could buzz off and spin back, but it became apparent that she could not drop down any lower. If we stayed flat on the floor, we remained out of her reach.

I began to slither across the floor since my fur coat easily slid atop the marble. Picking up speed, I kept moving until my head banged into a wall. Somehow, I had gotten turned around and now needed to stand up in order to get my bearings. Feeling along the wall, I found the grotto.

She must have spotted my movement as I heard her whizzing in my direction. No time to drop down, I clawed my way up the few feet of damp stone and climbed into the deep recess. Once inside, I could stand up. Still, the bottom felt spongy below my feet like wet wood. Reaching up to grab hold of the overhang, my fingers felt a metal lever tucked in the corner. Remembering the statue's disappearance act, I took a chance and pulled on the lever.

As the floor dropped away, I fell into a deeper darkness. My weak scream trailed behind as my body shot down the chute. Dropping at least two stories, anyone above could not have heard my departure. When I landed on a cement floor somewhere below, faint starlight streamed through a high window. Stepping on old boxes, I scaled the wall. Once again, my fur coat helped me make a smooth climb. Excited with adrenaline coursing through me, I reached my hand up and pulled back the window handle.

When fresh air flowed in, I breathed deeply and renewed my energy. Struggling to the top, I took off my coat and pushed it through the open window to test what might be on the other side. When I heard nothing, I followed it out of the building and fell to the sidewalk. Scrambling to stand up and put on my coat in the cold, I could hear my party guests inside crying for help.

Making my way around to the front of the old church, I could see faint light coming out of the bullet holes in the door. I had to bet they were all out of ammunition as I threw my shoulder against the door. The door stood strong. Yelling for them to back away from the door silenced their begging and pleading. I made another run at the door and that time it fell open.

Men and women pushed each other to sprint past me. I stood to the side, watching them flee until I called out to their backs. "What! No THANK-YOUS for Lisa, your hostess?"

The early morning sky appeared cloudless as everyone ran toward the beacon of light burning brightly from the complex. I walked alone and ended up being the last to get back. Seeing them dashing into their cars I had to yell, "Hey, no nightcaps, no goodnight kisses?"

As days and weeks went by I ran into most of them anew. The downtown area is a village unto itself and we all shared the same haunts. Everyone acted natural upon meeting again. Not one mentioned that strange evening or the redhead who mystified them into leaving my cozy party. If I did try to bring up the subject, they quickly blew it off by offering a belated appreciation for that lovely evening. Watching the bottoms of their shoes walk away, I had to wonder where all their bravado ran off to on that fright night.

Over the next few years, the construction continued and it did not take long for that ramshackle part of the city to gentrify. What once appeared to be a slum, now beckoned the rich and famous to live close to everything downtown.

Years later on a crisp winter day my newest love, a psychologist named Mark, and I took a walk. Looking around I commented, "I remember how these blocks all looked so shabby when I first moved here."

"True. There used to be a church somewhere around here. I've never seen it. I've heard a lot of stories that keep some of my patients up at night. Let's find it."

I stopped to look him in the eyes. "You know about the church?"

"Yes. I hope it's not torn down. It's a landmark and spooky to boot."

"Tell me about the spooky part?" We began walking again.

"It got built in the 1800s by immigrants from Eastern Europe. They were purported to be so holy they observed total silence. For decades the church ministered to their refugees. There developed a clannish group that congregated in secret without the holy group knowing."

"Do we know what they believed?"

"They were demon worshippers, of course, and practiced the lively forms of corporal punishment. Scourging stood at the top of their list, but as their devotion to demons expanded their experimenting with higher forms of rage continued."

"In the basement, I bet."

"You're right!" Mark smiled down at me. "I read that there were all kinds of tricks set up inside the building to mystify members of their secret congregation that operated inside a Bible-loving congregation, which is how they never got found out. There were trap doors in the floors and flying rods hidden along the ceiling. Apparitions could come and go to both entertain and frighten the audiences. It all came to a halt when a girl disappeared and the authorities found her there ... dead."

A chill came over me but I had to ask, "What did she look like?"

"Tall, lean, fair complexion with fiery red hair."

"How do you know all this, Mark?"

"A picture in the 1950s newspaper archives showed her."

"What were you doing in the Trib archives?"

"I used that story in my thesis on Hysterical Blindness."

"Hysterical BLINDNESS," I practically yelled. "What does that have to do with the dead girl?"

"The authorities found traces of a rare herb, they would not name, blended with the candle wax burned in that church. It seemed that when the leaders wanted to perform their unholy magic they used those special candles."

"Never heard of such a thing."

"It's some kind of incense from the islands off the coast of Africa that fuzzies up the brain like pot, but this stuff cloaks the sight receptors to make the inhalers believe they've lost their sense of vision. With everyone sensing they are blind and lost in the dark, it is easy to play tricks."

"What happened to end all this fun?"

"For decades, the churchgoers kept to themselves without drawing attention until the 1950s when they were often seen running out of the front door and screaming. That's when the cops dropped in to investigate, but no one was home. They practically tore the place apart and found a secret vault in the wall.

"And that's where they found the dead body?"

"Yep," Mark smiled and said, "but here's the really odd part."

"As if, what you've told me so far is not *odd*?" I had to laugh.

"That police investigation happened in the 1950s and the young woman had been missing for over a century. And yet, her corpse looked exactly the same as the day she left to attend a service at that same church in 1850."

"Do you remember what she wore?" I asked.

"I saw the police photos. She wore a long black dress and cloak... silk or satin. Here's the shocker. After taking pictures at the morgue, her exquisite hundred-year-old outfit went missing and then her corpse disappeared."

I did not say anything to Mark as we kept walking. How could I explain my own dark adventure from a few years back? When we turned the corner, the small church loomed in front of us. Mark got excited and grabbed my arm. "Hey! There it is. Let's go inside and ramble around to see what it looks like now."

SEVEN

SCORCHED PROMISE

JEREMY HOLLOWAY

Jeremy Holloway is a military veteran who writes science fiction and fantasy stories from his living room stairs, bedroom closet, backyard and any other corner he can hide for a precious few moments before he is attacked by ferocious beasts (showered with affection from his loving wife and kids in Northern Virginia, USA).

Jeremy loves werewolves, Nerd Conventions, magic & martial arts, New Orleans, and chocolate cake – not necessarily in that order. His favorite authors are Jeffrey Archer and Robert Ludlum. Jeremy is a new author and currently obsessed with little-known mythos of the Eastern hemisphere. In an alternate universe, he is a world-renowned anthropologist and explorer with tales to fascinate and boggle the mind.

SCORCHED PROMISE

Summer solstice, the brightest day of the year, but it was the twilight of the old warrior's life. Although it was only midafternoon, Tihomir was still shaken at how radically his entire life had changed in only a few hours, and it was all his fault.

While carefully leading his mule cart along the treacherous mountain ledge, Tihomir glanced north toward the vast capital city. What had once been his home was now just a small spot on the horizon, to which he could never return. Each step forward was a step away from his distinguished thirty years of loyal service as the Bogatyr high commander. More than once, while treading the narrow path, he had thought of stepping off the cliff to spare his former comrades from having to hunt him down, but he shook it away. Nothing, not even death, excused him from this current obligation.

Turning east, Tihomir cast a piercing gaze below into the vast mesh of the forest for anything suspicious. Despite being well advanced in his years, his natural senses were much sharper than those of any man half his age, a fringe benefit of his half-blooded heritage. A secret to all, but the primary reason he had not only survived decades of extreme combat, but maintained his exalted position as the high marshal of the Khaganate.

He grinned at the wild green expanse. God willing, the feint path he had set up leading through the Northern border should keep his former comrades beclouded on the false smoke trail until he'd safely escaped with his precious cargo across the Southern territory.

"Almost there, just a bit farther," he called back, although his mule was right next to him.

Looking forward, he focused on the cleft of the wall that opened to a basin pass which sloped toward a small border

169

town. When he was but a few steps away from the corridor's entrance, the sound of bleating arose and after a few more steps, the scent of goat piss burned through his nostrils.

Rubbing the accumulated sweat from his bearded cheeks, he finally turned into where the grass began to cover the black rocky ground. The bothersome bleating increased, but at least he was no longer a half-step from certain doom. A few more steps and he saw the source of the commotion: a traveling merchant with a few sheep and four older goats that hauled a large square item covered by a rug. When the man spotted Tihomir, he beamed, immediately halted the animals, and uncovered the rugged case.

"*Salaam alaikum*, my friend, it is good fortune that you can reach this land with only a mule cart of wine barrels," the man said, hurriedly stacking two large brown sacks and a few heavy pots on top of the box. Without meaning to, Tihomir tensed.

The short, tan-skinned merchant wore a white robe and a black beard that reached halfway down his chest. Although the desert lands were many months' journey westward, his type was not uncommon at the Khaganate's market area. The market contained a fair number of shops owned by foreign inhabitants who proudly wore their native apparel in defiance of the cold weather. No, it was the Mongolian face under the black turban that triggered Tihomir to touch the grip of the long spiked bulava fastened to the inside his cloak.

Forty years ago, his first posting as a fledgling Bogatyr was spent defending the border territories from the recurrent Mongolian raids. During his first battle, more than half of the former apprentices from his age group had perished, but not Tihomir. He never lost a battle.

"But if your destination lies beyond the border, a man of your age should not stretch his legs beyond his quilt." The merchant's voice had risen a tone. "Which is why almighty Allah has sent me to aid you on such a difficult journey, and for very modest currency."

Passing closer, Tihomir could see the man's face more clearly and relaxed. The bastard's Mongoloid features were mild, with the prominent nose, and if his dark complexion and curly beard was any indication, his blood was as Persian accented as his voice. An illegitimate offspring born from the Mongolian. Even so, he was still a foreigner, and basurman were to be expected to be dishonest dealers.

Ignoring the man, Tihomir continued passing the goats until his thoughts were intruded by the sound of a pot being uncovered and the juicy scent of citrus that seem to hook his nose. Placed on the small makeshift stand were two large pots of sour oranges, mangos, and lime. The mule brayed as the merchant sliced a lemon in half and held it high.

"Your beast is weak for food, my elderly friend. My fruit costs very low grivnas, the best out of desert lands, and I is your only option. The next village is very, very versts away, but no shop is selling fruit like I."

Seven versts if Tihomir's memory was correct, which he needed to reach well before evening. He tightened the yoke on the mule and hastened toward the sparse pine forest.

The merchant approached from behind the table carrying both halves of the lemon in either hand. "Sir, please, one small taste and I promise you will not regret your purchase. Forsake this chance and you will find yourself having to drink your own..." The man went abruptly silent.

Tihomir glanced back to see why he had abandoned his spiel so abruptly and grimaced. The basurman was frowning at the vodka barrels in his cart. *Not an immediate cause for alarm,* thought Tihomir, until the man pointed at one in particular.

"That one, I think it moves. Some animals has crawls in your cart and got trap inside," he said.

Tihomir took a deep breath and continued to calmly lead his mule away. There was still a chance the merchant might just dismiss it as an odd bump on the road and forget, but then he heard a squeal.

"There! A animal noises come from that one. Something is intruding in your wine," he declared.

"Bl'yad," Tihomir swore as his hand released the mule's reins and fell near his longsword.

This thoughtless tradesman had just unintentionally condemned himself to execution. If only he hadn't used such assertive tactics, then he might have lived to trade in the capital. Persians obviously do not teach that *a long tongue will bring the chatterer consequences.*

As if hearing Tihomir's thoughts, the half Mongol merchant locked eyes with him and the veins in his neck bulged. Keeping his unblinking gaze on Tihomir, he quickly walked backwards to the safety of his box, placing one hand behind him and the other shakily on the moon and stars that hung around his neck; his lips moved frantically.

Tihomir had had run-ins with desert fighters before and was in no fear of the curved dagger the man was no doubt concealing at his back, but he had never slain a praying man before. Twenty years prior, the non-religious Tihomir the Timberwolf, as he was dubbed for his often rambunctious tactics, would have gutted the merchant, then had his afternoon meal. However, being high

172

marshal had freed him from that constant cycle of violence and had made him a man of faith, thus, despite the fruit seller being of separate belief, he felt that killing another pious man seemed immoral.

Furthermore, there was disposal to consider. Hiding a dead body would not present too much of an issue but dealing with the heavy box and goats would take too much time, and simply leaving it left the possibility of the Bogatyri prematurely discovering his true whereabouts. The cautionary words of his elder brother rang fresh in his mind: *Even a little spark may be the cause of a great fire.* Taking a few slow steps toward the merchant, Tihomir reached further into his sable grey cloak.

"I have heard your talk, basurman, and smelled your fruitlets." He pulled out his hand holding four long sterling silver grivnas for the man to see. "I shall require some for my long journey."

The Persian's expression went from fear to anticipation as the silver grivnas glinted in his eyes. He licked his lips, like a cat ready to pounce on its wounded prey.

"Yes, yes," he said, eagerly rubbing his palms. His smile showed bright teeth that glowed in stark contrast to his black beard. He dashed into his box again and hurriedly began filling a wool bag with mangos, sour oranges, and limes. He then handed it over with a greasy smirk that left Tihomir in no doubt that both understood what was actually being purchased. Normally, he would never have given two days of earnings for a bag of fruit, but ultimately it was a fair deal, considering the Bogatyri's only method of reward for information was little more than a verbal appreciation for loyalty to the Rus Khagan, especially if his former apprentice Athanasi was leading them. Naïve fools were still unaware that outside the capital, the real world, grivnas were valued above all else. And, if they were their usual ill-mannered selves, the merchant was even likely to misdirect them.

"You make a best decision to buys this good fruit, sir. Each bite make hard ground soft to your feets," said the merchant pocketing the grivnas in such a way that would've impressed a gypsy panhandler.

With a curt nod, Tihomir squeezed the sack in with the four wine barrels and began to leave. He was not more than five steps away when the merchant called again and reappeared at his side.

"Sir, you should take my fresh goat milk, too," said the basurman holding a full water bladder.

Tihomir stared, shocked at the man's audacity. Did he not realize how close to death he had been only a moment ago? His rude assertive manner alone would have been grounds in themselves for any self-respecting Rus to enact physical discipline, especially to a foreigner. Tihomir shook his head but the man pressed still.

"I insist, sir, you and yours are really needing it," he countered with a fatcat grin.

Tihomir's left arm dropped near his mace as malicious thoughts of chopping away the man's weasely face refilled his head. The sleazy merchant's grin wavered in apparent realization that he may have poked a little too much, but as Tihomir reached, he flinched, feeling a sharp twinge in his elbow. A reminder that his magic-heritage could only delay, never remove, the symptoms of his aging body; then a squeal came from the wine barrel, forcing Tihomir's decision. He snatched the milk-filled pouch and grudgingly extracted another grivna, a smaller copper one this time. The merchant's smile returned as he held out an open palm.

At the last second, Tihomir hurled it away behind the man and declared, "Fetch!"

The merchant watched as it landed into some tall grass behind his goats, and gave the old soldier a snake-eyed side gaze, but turned and, like a desperate hound, stomped off in search of his prize. Tihomir resumed his journey forward but kept a close ear attuned behind should the merchant choose to test him thrice.

As Tihomir continued further into the mountain pass, he came to an area where the green had overgrown enough to cover the rocky mountain ground and up the walls. He halted the mule and rubbed at his aching knees, while causally glancing around, insuring they were well out of view and earshot of anyone. He desperately wanted to sit down, but the time and effort it took to stand back up had grown with each passing year.

"It's safe now, you can come out," he said to the cart, but there came no response. "I said, you can come out of there. We are all right now," he said louder but still nothing. He halted the mule and walked back toward the barrels. "Little one, are you okay in there?" He gave a slight knock on the barrel that had moved earlier. "Answer me Zor—"

The top of the barrel shot up, releasing a stream of billowing white clouds of smoke and bright sparks that caused Tihomir to stumble back.

"CUCUUUOOO," came an echoing shout from the smoke. It cleared to reveal a young olive skinned child with long dark auburn hair and high cheek bones. At first glance, she could've passed as an aboriginal Finn native from the north, but a trained eye would immediately note her nearly maroon colored eyes, making her something more intolerable.

"Ha ha he! I surprise you, Uncle Tariho," she said, sticking halfway out the barrel.

"That you did, Zorja, but this is not the time for games." Tihomir slowly gathered himself back up to his feet. "And it's Uncle Tiho."

"Whoops. I mix up your name with Grandpa Taras's." She giggled. Tihomir flinched at the mention of his late older sibling.

"Uncle Tiho, my belly feels empty," she whined.

The old soldier retrieved a lime from the sack, sliced it in half and handed a piece to Zorja. He moved to the front to feed the other half to the mule when he heard, "Oy," accompanied by whiff of overcooked fruit. She was still too young to control her ability.

"Um, Uncle Teeho... "

"Here," he said, handing her the other half. "But be careful with this one." She dropped the other piece of the burned mango skin and carefully accepted the other half. He took a mango from the bag, bit off a piece before placing the rest in the mule's mouth.

"Umkle Taro, ken ah com ow ov da burruw mow peas?"

"For now, yes, but only until we get close to the town, then you'll have to hide again until night. And it is not proper for a girl to speak while eating," he scolded. She burped a puff of flame in response. "Or do that."

"Know what? Grandpa knew how to shoot fire out of his mouth and butt at the same time." She pulled each leg out of the barrel.

"Seventy years old and he never learned to be an adult? I am sure your baba and mother did not approve of such vulgarity."

"No, but papa and my big brother laughs all the time." She gleefully kicked her feet while sitting on the side of the cart.

"Taras's broods indeed," he mumbled. "You should mind your mother's advice because those tricks will never win you much favor among your new Mage-class; especially among other fire-wielders," he added in a lecturing tone that he had not used since his tenure as a Bogatyr weapons master.

They continued trekking in silence when Zorja began making a barely audible gasping noise. Recalling a similar behavior from a small dog he'd once had, Tihomir offered her the bladder of milk, but she shook her head. He then went to the sack and presented her with a sour orange, but still she refused.

"Well then, what is your problem, girl?" He snapped in frustration, only to feel shame a second later. She cowered behind a thin veil of black smog that immediately appeared between them.

He frowned, rubbing his chin. If Zorja were some jittery greenhorn Bogatyr that was having second thoughts before a battle, or a frightened recruit that needed a hard word to rejoin his training, he would have been in no doubt as to what was required. But she was not, tossing a decade's worth of military leadership experience to the wind. Taking a deep breath, he looked up toward the heavens and, in the best impression of his brother's voice, said, "What in this world ails you, my little flame flower?"

The smoke shroud dissipated, revealing the bleary-eyed little girl. She frowned at him, as his voice imitation must have sounded a bit too similar to the real thing. Zorja wiped her nose before speaking.

"When will I see Grandpa and Baba and Papa and Mama and Big Brother again?" she whined.

Tihomir's stomach felt like it had been punctured by an arrow. He knew this question would come up eventually, but its sharp prick stung nonetheless. A crueler irony was how Tihomir had unwittingly been a factor in causing his own brother's death.

"When the light in your eyes is but a dim glow, your skin is too crinkly to hold warmth, the fiery magic in your blood is but a spark and your hair looks like mine." he ran his leathery palm through his greying hair, "you will lie down for a long enjoyable sleep and awake to find your grandpa and the rest of the family welcoming you home."

A hopeful smile weakly crept onto her face which gave Tihomir an odd feeling in his chest, but it was short lived when her next shot found its mark.

"Are the bad bogatree men going kill me like they got Papa and Momma and my big brother?"

Tihomir paused mid-stride and took a deep breath. "No! They will not." His voice sounded more brusque than intended. "They fear your old Uncle Tihomir, so not as long as you stay with me and obey my words." He didn't look back at her.

"Why? Are you a bogatree man too?"

Tihomir's blood boiled as his mind immediately went to the implication; what was she insinuating? Did she not know what he had just sacrificed to save her? How lucky he was to have found her or that he was smart enough to have deciphered his brother's cryptic message? Moreover, that he'd have even received his brother's message in time was nothing short of a miracle. Did she think he had done all that just to...? *Six,* he told himself. That's how many summers had passed since her birth.

"No," was all he said.

"But Grandpa told me—"

"He was wrong. I am not nor will I ever be like those slimy Bogatyri desman that sneak their way into homes at night to spill the blood of innocent sorcerers," he replied fervently before silently whispering, "and by God, they will pay for their brutality."

A long, silent moment passed before Zorja said, "…. U-Uncle Teeho, I have to make yellow water."

Tihomir sighed. The journey of his life was just beginning.

The evening western sky turned from a bright orange to alpenglow when they finally reached the border town, and not a moment too soon for Tihomir, whose numb legs and back were nearing stiffness. He had patrolled this trail before countless times, but never had it taken him this long to reach the village. Although, the last time had been more than a decade ago, and on that occasion, he had spent most of the journey on horseback as was befitting the Bogatyr high marshal.

Living for years in the comfort and luxury of the palace had made him too soft, he thought, while leaning against the mule cart. Grey hair in the beard, devil in the rib. He now understood why all the previous Bogatyr lords had chosen to step down honorably, rather than risk being shamefully demoted by a younger challenger.

It was times like this that he shuddered to think of how different his life would've become had he not inherited at least some of his father's mystical powers. Would he have ever risen up as a high marshal or perished many years before like so many others? Would he have even joined the Bogatyr guard in the first place? Had it been his affiliation with the guard that indirectly led to them discovering the secret location of the magi village?

He immediately shook away those thoughts and instead focused on the border town. Grief and despair were traits of the weak and unbefitting a soldier of his caliber. He glanced back at his travel companions to see the mule's head hanging so low that it nearly bumped its legs, while his grandniece slept peacefully against a wine barrel. Occasionally a wisp of smoke would rise from her in the shape of either an animal, flower, or something else. *What remarkable talent*, he thought, remembering her grandfather had not so much as a spark until his eighth summer.

"Arise, little one," he said, tapping her gently. "You must get back in the barrel."

She didn't respond at first, but after a few more prods, she reluctantly climbed back in. Tihomir agreed to leave the top open.

"Remember to keep silent. This is a dangerous area with mean and bad people who won't hesitate to harm a little girl."

Tihomir guardedly led the cart toward the entrance, and scanned the wooden structures with hawkeyed scrutiny. The first thing he noticed was the silence. As this was a transient town, the mead halls and inns were normally bustling all hours of the day, but now it was mostly deserted. Aside from the few vagabonds roaming and the harlots posted at the wool-doored houses, it was empty.

He noted a few stables and farms that had been functional last time now lay in ruins, but also new two-storied wooden shops and some old homes with new walls made of stones. Bogatyr patrols reported no recent changes in this area, but perhaps they had gotten lax in their duties. Just then, Tihomir saw a mid-aged man zoom from a local shop pushing a wheelbarrow full of tools, small furs, and loose cloths; a young boy followed close at his heels.

"Hey young man, why the haste?" Tihomir called to him. "What has happened to all of the people?"

"You've come at a most unfortunate time, sir; the darkening hour approaches," he replied, not breaking his stride.

"Nonsense, the sun does not set for at least another hour," Tihomir said.

"No time to explain, stranger. You came too late for trading. The ruffians and low-lives own the night here and will soon rise to conduct their dark business. No place for an affluent one like you."

Tihomir blinked at the man's extraordinary knowledge of his financial status.

"Papa, where did he get fur like that?" asked the young boy pointing at Tihomir's wolf-furred cloak.

The old warrior cursed as he suddenly realized his foolish error. His sable cloak was made of wolf's fur, a gift from the order on the day he had been chosen the Bogatyr highest officer. It was rare, and in the capital had been testament of his many successful conquests, but in this den of thieves and ruffians, it would only serve to indicate his former wealth, thus making him a target. Based on the tailor's words, this place had gotten rougher since his last visit. He had thought it was bad before, when the thugs mixed in with the locals during all hours, but he could only imagine what kind of lawless den this place would become in a short time; he had to lose the cloak fast.

Hauling his exhausted mule by the bridle, he strode purposely through the town, head constantly swiveling for inconspicuous shelter. He abandoned his original plan to trade his vodka for shelter at an inn, as it would undoubtedly draw too much attention. A farm offering extra room was a possibility, but if the tailor was correct, no family would risk opening the door at this time of day.

Just need to get a few supplies and place to rest for a bit, he said to himself. The last of his fruit was gone and, in his haste to escape the capital, he had forgotten to pack sheep skins to sleep in the woods.

"Ooooo, what's over there?" asked Zorja, pointing to a small shop further down the way.

Tihomir focused his eagle-like vision toward the direction she indicated; two rough-looking Tatar males were moving wrapped bundles around their display tent. One was tall and broad shouldered while the other was short and thin, both no older than twenty. Tihomir was wary of dealing with such shady types, but it was the only place offering any supplies at the moment. *First I get ripped off by a presumptuous Mongol, now I have to deal with these hooligan Tatars*, he thought. *What's next, Baba Yaga?*

"Thank you, young one, now back in the barrel," he said.

She obeyed, but not before spitting a fuliginous hot spray on the back of his head. Taras' brood indeed.

As Tihomir got closer to the shop, the short man looked at him apprehensively and hastily spoke something in his native tongue. The taller man immediately dropped his bundle and dragged a large table draped with a cloth to the front, barricading the front of the tent. This may have been a hasty preparation for a customer, but Tihomir remained alert as the cloth could just as easily conceal weapons.

The shop turned out to be slightly larger than it appeared from afar. On the table was a display of shabby necklaces, second-hand jewels, a few used farming tools and pots of various sizes; some with fruits and vegetables that were hardly edible.

"What you wantin' stranger?" said the large man in an irritated tone. He was freakishly muscular, as if wrestling elks was a daily routine.

"Here to trade something you young cubs have probably never seen before," Tihomir replied while still gauging the shop's eclectic inventory.

On all three walls hung clothing and footwear for all ages, including undergarments, rugs, and old sheepskins, animals' hides, and thin furs. There was even a couple of wooden toys and dolls thrown against the side walls. Scattered around the tent were tables, chairs and barrels and churns; all appeared to be of the same tacky condition as the display items. On the ground was a pile of unclean long and short knives, the only items that appeared appropriate for a shop like this. Tihomir, however, suspected those blades had not only been used for animals.

"Not trade, only grivnas," voiced the thin man not looking up from the fish he was gutting, above his hung a line of freshly skinned rats, squirrels, and other small game.

"Don't have enough grivnas for this shop," he lied, when in truth he wasn't sure the condition of these obviously pinched house-hold items was worth a few coppers. "But this cloak, made of pure cut from a wolf, is probably worth half of all of those sheep skins you have and then some."

"We no trade with strangers," said the big man folding his tree-trunk sized arms; both bore multiple scars. His wild, unkempt hair andscruffy face made him look bearish in the evening light. He was obviously the arms and legs of the group, whereas the short thin man, judging from the detail of his work, was probably the hands, fingers, and even the eyes and ears; but something was missing. There's no way these two young scamps ran this shop.

"You young pups better listen up," Tihomir announced in a loud but precise manner, hoping to summon the head of this shady little operation. "This," he said, turning to show more of

183

the cloak, "is pure Siberian grey wolf's fur. There are not many in the land. So how about wiping your mama's milk off your lips and you go fetch your boss before I walk away."

The large one slammed a powerful fist on the table and bore his black dog eyes at the old man in front of him. "You cossack-goat," he shouted with some other supposed curses in his native tongue. At once, Tihomir loosened his long sword from its scabbard.

"Easy, Mishka," said a voice from somewhere near the rear of the shop. A section of the tent's back tarp was moved aside to reveal an older bald man. "This old Rusman may have something we like. So, what do you want for this precious cloak, old man?"

Tihomir exhaled but kept his hand near his side. "Three sheepskins, two pots of flesh, and three barrels of water for my mule."

The bald man cocked his head to one side. "A bit much for just a sable cloak, rare as it is. And your abrasive manner to my men makes you look anxious, too anxious, and to request so many supplies..." His mouth formed into a puckish smirk. "You must be fleeing something or someone."

Tihomir's stomach tightened but he kept his face stone.

"Don't dismay, old man, I bear no favor for those kakistocratic pigs in Kiev. I'll even gratify your request, provided I receive three barrels of that vodka."

"Three," Tihomir yowled. An outrageous proposition!

"I'm leaving you one to sell elsewhere, which should be enough." retorted the bald trader.

He was willing to supply one, but not three. For one thing, only two of the four were actually vodka: one was for sale, but the other was intended as a gift to the Mage for agreeing to make

Zorja as a part of their coven, in the third was Zorja herself, while the fourth were additional weapons he had packed in the unfortunate event that the Bogatyr managed to find him.

Tihomir shook his head. "The sable cloak and one barrel," he countered.

"Nyet, I can't take..." He paused with a frown on his face. "Selling the vodka would be easy but fetching a good price for the cloak would take too long, and I need grivnas to replace my supplies," he answered back.

Only things needed to replace these handmade supplies and animal skins was time, tools, and skill, which confirmed Tihomir's suspicion that the supplies had, in fact, been stolen.

"What if I sweeten the deal?" The bald man waved toward the display of mostly overripe berries and vegetable scrubs, but Tihomir remained obstinate and repeated his same offer. "Hmph, I thought all you russkis loved fruit."

"I want some," declared Zorja popping out from her miched spot inside the barrel; Tihomir's heart sank.

His mouth went dry as all pairs of Tatar eyes greedily locked onto his grandniece. *What would they want with a little girl?* Her dark hair and olive complexion did her a Tatar like appearance, perhaps they thought he had abducted one of their own.

"Adults are talking now little one, let me deal with this," Tihomir said, smiling but giving her a sharp look. He turned back to see a predatory smile spreading across the bald man's face. "So about our deal…"

"Yes, about that. How much is she worth?" His eyes glittered as they all maintained focus on Zorja.

"Nichto! My niece is not for sale," he snapped, praying they would drop the notion.

"She must be worth something." The bald man licked his lips. "Why else would she be hidden away from sight?"

Tihomir's eyes darted between the three men. "Not hiding. Just playing. A child's game, nothing more."

Both the thin man and the large man began speaking in their native tongue, no need to wonder what they were discussing. Working as night merchants in this town meant these men were a mendacious lot, but child trading was beyond wicked.

"Two barrels and a cloak with whatever few copper grivnas I might have," proposed Tihomir wanting to shift their focus. Although he was hoping to end this the same way he did with the Mongol, the trembling in his hands and arms told him violence was coming.

The bald man raised a hand, which immediately silenced the other two. "New deal," he said in an ominous tone. "You give us the cloak, the mule, all the vodka and the girl, and you get to walk away with pockets full of grivnas."

"But...I can't." Tihomir began untying his mace. "I'm a religious man, you see. It is forbidden to trade one's own kin."

"I fully understand and respect your moral convictions," he replied in a tone that almost sounded genuine, but Tihomir held his breath for the catch. "But my men do not and won't hesitate to take all everything," he said, thumbing the men on either side. "Their only devotion is to profits. They would sell their own mothers for the right price." The large one loudly slapped a fist against his palm, while the thin one slide his knives against one another. "So what's it going to be, old man? You either walk away richer or not at all?"

Tihomir turned and looked gravely at his grandniece. She grinned back with an obliviously playful expression. He glanced downward and focused all his concentration on the necessary images. *Horns of the elk, bite of the bear, heart of the wolverine* — not words to any known invocation but their effect would be the same for his special brand of strength magic. As the magic that granted him enhanced strength began to take effect, he gave one last look at Zorja and with a watery smile asked her, "Do you know all of your numbers?"

She nodded.

"Even with your eyes closed?" he asked, slowly untying the fastener on his cloak until it dropped to the ground.

She nodded again.

"Show me!" He turned, looking down his nose at the three merchants. His vision blocked out everything except his three quarries. He took a slow, deep breath to steady his nerves, but the trembling persisted. It had been many years since his last fight and now his chest thumped like it was his first time. He had forgotten the pre-scuffle anxieties: the tightening of his tunic as his muscles bulged to three times their normal size, the tingling in his hands and arms, the stretching of his legs as he grew a head taller, the tiny little shocks coming off his neck hairs, the heat on his skin drawing tiny beads of perspiration, it felt almost orgasmic.

"Ah-deen... Dva..." Zorja counted.

The large man was the first to see the weapon, but Tihomir's arm was already in motion. He hurled the mace at the greasiest point on the bald man's head, before unsheathing the long sword and turning his attention to the large man. He didn't have to look to know the smashing sound meant his mace had penetrated the elder thug's skull.

"Tri... Chiteereh..."

187

Staring in shock at his dead boss lying on the ground, both men were startled a second time when Tihomir brought his fist down, shattering the hard wooden table between them.

"*Pyaht… Shayst…*"

Tihomir stepped inside toward the large man, who quickly grabbed a battle axe and raised it to parry. Tihomir guffawed, then swung his blade upward cutting a long slash from the man's hip to his left shoulder, chopping through the axe on the way. Like a ravenous wolf, Tihomir always relished in the pained cries of his victims, and with it the evitable sound of the body hitting the ground.

"*Seeaym… Voseeaym…*"

Falling to his knees, the large man grabbed his chest. *Futile,* thought Tihomir as he watched the man's innards leak out. He whirled his blade around, and in one swipe, sliced through the man's stomach, cutting him in half. The sweet smell of blood was intoxicating. His eyes glittered when he turned and saw fragmented skull of the bald man's corpse. It was criminal to have kept himself away from combat for this long. He leveled eyes at his last target. The thin man stood hyperventilating as his eyes darted from Tihomir to his dead comrades, his body shaking violently, yet he did not run and maintained his grip on the butcher's knives. The old warrior cackled at the man's audacity. He had been wrong in his earlier comparison, killing was nothing like sex; it was better.

"*Dyesyat… and Dyevyat…*"

"Wrong, girl, nine comes before ten," Tihomir corrected loudly. "Start all over again."

She obeyed and resumed counting. Tihomir stepped forth and slashed out at the thin man, but he ducked backward just in time for the longsword to rip his tunic. Tihomir struck at his neck, but the man dodged again and only a few beard hairs from his chin. On his third attempt, Tihomir thrusted toward his face, and though his blade broke through the man's parry, it diverted his longsword and only scratched the thin man's cheek. *The little bastard is fast.*

Somewhere far off, a door opened followed by some fussing that suggested a carouser was being ejected from a mead hall. He needed to end this quick before someone saw. He stepped back and focused. His increased height and muscles slowed his movement, he needed to be fast.

Sting of snake, feet of the fox, strike of the eagle... He imagined changing tactics from strength to speed and felt a cool sensation as a new type of mystical energy pulsed though his body. He twirled his blade in a blur as he prepared to dice the man into multiple pieces. This Tatar's luck was about to run out. He took his final position and lunged toward the thin man, but then his breath caught. White hot fiery pain took root in his chest and shot out through his body like a wildfire. He staggered down to one knee and lost grip of the sword on the way down; from the hand to the elbow felt stiff as stone. An icy shock behind his eyes that seem to expand throughout his head, scratching into his ears, nose, and throat. *Bly'ad!* He suddenly felt weak. His old body had not been able to compensate for the rapid transformation caused by the magic.

He closed his eyes and braced as the thin man's boot slammed hard into his face; he took another in the ribs, and one more that knocked him to the ground. With one arm, he tried to scoot away, as the thin man marched forward with renewed confidence. Tihomir wanted badly to chop the smile off the Tatar's face, but a new wave of icy pain reverberated through his veins, making him convulse. The thin man added to this by stomping his heavy boot on the old man's stomach. Tihomir coughed up blood. If only he had waited a moment, just a little while, to let his body adjust properly, then it would've been his foot planted on the thin man's torso. As the Tatar bore down on him, Tihomir saw the dagger gleam in the evening light. It somehow looked much larger than the one before. With no options left, Tihomir brought his arms and legs close in an ultimately futile attempt to block his vital points.

"Uh. . . Uncle Tiho, what comes after nine?"

Tihomir looked up, stunned to see his niece standing near him. He tried to urgently wave her away but she stood in shock at the scene and screamed.

"You're next, little bitch," the Tatar growled.

She fell to her granduncle's side and tried to push the thug's boot from his chest. "Get your foot off my Uncle Tiho! Stop hurting him!"

Tihomir wanted to scream for her to run, but his breaths were too short to get a word out. He flinched when the man's boot came off his chest and kicked her roughly to the ground.

"Za- Zor . . . go . . . run," he managed, feeling some of the pain subside.

Instead, she gave the thin man a teary glare, pointed at him and yelled, "You're being a meaner!" At that moment, a single, pebble-size trail of red hot smoke shot forth from the tip of her index finger and burst in the Tatar man's face.

He toppled back, fanning madly at his newly blackened nose. A few seconds more and he regained his bearings, but so did Tihomir. In an instant, he was back on his feet, and across the room, using one hand to grab and toss a nearby sheepskin over his niece's head, while the other swept the sword in a blurry arc, decapitating the fiend.

"Thank God," he breathed, falling to his knees. He released long exhalations to accelerate the magic's dissipation from his limbs. Picking up a small knife from the ground, he added a new cut to the line of scars on his forearm. "Number ten," he breathed, referring to the number of times he'd almost been killed. A second later, he walked back and scooped up his niece, who was fumbling around under the sheep skin. Grabbing a handful of the few edible fruits, he exited and sat her outside the tent, next to the mule.

"Here, little one," he said, pulling off the wool blanket and placing the handful of strawberries in her tiny hands. "Stay here and eat, Uncle Tiho has something to do but I'll return, and together we will fill our cart with all the supplies we need."

"Where did the meaner man go?"

"Your fire scared him off."

She grinned smugly and began to feed herself and the mule.

It took some time for Tihomir to move the body parts behind the tent. After he finished placing the lower half of the large man with the rest of his body, his hawk-like vision scanned the forest for a disposal spot.

"You're not even going bury them?" came a coarse female voice from behind him. "Such a waste of material."

Tihomir spun around with his mace raised toward the mysterious voice.

"No need for thorns, I seek no quarrel with you." A tall, reedy figure stepped from behind a tree.

The light was too dim to distinguish her features, but Tihomir could discern her long baggy garb and wild stringy hair, and that she stood with the support of a staff. Something else felt familiarly odd about her but he was not quite certain what.

"Be gone, wench. This is no concern of yours," he commanded.

She appeared to stagger as she moved closer; each step was hard, purposeful as if it bore symbolic meaning. She gestured toward the bodies. "Their remains would feed many acres of young green babes. They cannot simply be left to wither above ground."

Taken aback by this odd response, Tihomir employed his other senses to investigate the stranger from a distance, but this only led to more confusion. The woman smelled like mud and leaves; similar to an overly-scrupulous gardener, but more potent, as if all her days were spent roaming the woods. He could even hear specks of dirt and leaves rustling under her clothes; some of it may even have found its way between the wrinkles in her skin. Then there was the staff. At first glance, it looked like a normal shepherd's rod, but Tihomir could feel a subtle throbbing that emanated from it. There was also a pungent scent in her breath, but that he recognized.

"Never known an elderly woman to be booted for drunkenness," he said.

She hooted. "Those little meat-munchers were just surprised that my bark is thicker than their mead's bite."

She may have been telling the truth, but based on her vagabond-like appearance, Tihomir guessed she had probably been ejected for monetary reasons.

"Regardless, these men are not worth the dirt they lay on, now scram, lest you too become a waste of materials," he snapped, tapping the hilt of his longsword.

She scoffed. "You won't get it out fast enough, half-blood, much less get it up." She tapped the heel of her staff down and Tihomir felt the ground quiver beneath his feet. She chuckled again. "I'm sure you hear that last part from many women."

Tihomir's eyebrows shot up in sudden realization of who, or rather, *what* she was. He bowed his head but maintained watch of her. "My apologies, I did not know the great Mages of Earth still resided in these parts."

"Earth-Mover is a more preferable term, but yes, we normally don't root ourselves near hostile borders, unless certain situations…" Her narrowed eyes suddenly glowed bright green.

"*You* are my rendezvous contact? I wasn't expecting–"

"An old woman?"

"No, an Earth-Ma… Mover."

"Obviously, we would not send another Fire-Breather; they're gingery characters and would be immediately targeted in this grove." She waved toward the village.

"But Zorja's mother's relatives were said to be Magi of the ai– uh… Air-Walkers," he corrected himself.

"Whose bird-like methods of travel would attract unwanted pests back to our secret garden, don't you think?"

Something Tihomir had not considered, but there was still one more thing out of place. "But I wasn't supposed to meet up for many more versts from here."

She gave an exasperated sigh. "A peppercorn-sized measure that allowed me to assess whether your character would yield honey or poison. Certainly, you didn't expect a Mage to just spring up here on the word of a former lord of the Khaganate."

"Of course not," he replied, sheepish that his military awareness hadn't picked up on this novice tactic. Arms slightly trembling, he finally lowered his mace and crossed himself, silently thanking the Divine that she wasn't one those moody reclusive types. He still bore scars from the last one he'd dealt with a decade ago, whose hex leveled an entire town, just because a woman rejected his advances. It had been one of the few instances when Tihomir was scared of someone, and the ninth cut on his forearm.

"Now if the interrogation is done, half-breed, you need to go fetch the little seedling before she burns something. Meanwhile, I will scatter these scoundrels through the fields." She knelt by the dead Tatars, pulled back her sleeves, and stretched forth her arms over the thin man's corpse. She muttered something inaudible for a minute then clapped her hands together. Tihomir watched in awe as the bald man's corpse sank down into the solid ground like it was quicksand. "Before the autumn would be favorable, half-breed."

He snapped out of his gaze and took a stride back towards the tent.

"Make her eat this before bringing her to me." She waved her hand and Tihomir felt two small rocks land firmly in his palm. He ran his fingers over them to discover they were oval shaped. "They are coco-beans," she stated before he could ask. "Sown with my own special charm that will let her sleep through the journey."

Tihomir felt a knot form in his stomach.

"Do not judge my methods, half-ling. The little relic will not have to look you in the eyes when she departs. As I understand it, you barely knew her until a few days after her village was assaulted."

"Is it not your role to prevent her from becoming a relic?"

"Our role is the preservation of the race of magi and of magic itself, but she is the last of her family and one of the few fire-breathers to have escaped from this hostile land. She will always be a remnant in a certain sense, just not one used by the Rus' Khagan."

He glanced back at the tent to where he could scarcely hear Zorja giggling and then down at the beans.

"This was always a part of the arrangement. You were a high-ranking soldier, yes? Think of it as a mission, your last, and remember that despite what you may be feeling, the most fertile grounds for her are away from here."

Tihomir turned and began the few steps back to the tent, which might as well have sat on top of Mount Elbrus. He hated to admit it, but the old earthy broad was right; he had only spent a short time with Zorja, a week at the most, but that did not change the gnawing ache in his chest. The closer to the tent he stepped, the heavier the beans felt in his hand.

There was light glowing from the inside. Tihomir stepped into the tent to find the mule's head buried within the barrel, slurping as much water as possible. Hopefully the dumb beast wouldn't forget to come up to breathe. His grandniece's back was turned away from him and she seemed to be speaking to the wall. Upon closer inspection, Tihomir saw a strange-looking black cat facing her. He had once owned a similar one but had never seen one stand so still or pay as much attention to something that wasn't edible.

As he stepped closer, Zorja turned to look up at him.

"Uncle Tiho, I fire up the torches and make a Dvorovoi, lookit." She moved her hand around and the cat followed its direction, leaving a stream of smoke in its wake.

His first instinct was to remind her that animal sprites were extinct but then he changed his mind. "Most impressive, little one, but your smoky kitten is inside, not in a yard, so it would be a Domovoi."

"Oh, okay, but I made it to follow you. Grandpa say you used to have a black kitty that he did not like and one day it die for no reason. Sad, sad."

Tihomir rolled his eyes. Apparently Taras hadn't let on how he would often use the cat for target practice until, one day, he turned it into a smoldering pile of ash. "You made this for me, young one?"

"Da, so maybe you won't have to make a mad face all the time."

Tihomir swallowed hard. Being around soldiers for most of his adult life, he had given little thought to how his gruffness might be perceived through softer eyes. It was part of the reason he had never married, but now he wondered how his own would-be offspring might have regarded him.

"Come, Zorja, there is something important Uncle Tihomir needs to say." He took a knee and she walked over, sat on his other leg, and met his gaze with a smile. She had her grandfather's eyes.

"Soon you will meet your mother's kin, and they will properly train you in your mystical heritage. It may be strange at first, being with people you've never met, but they are still family and will always have your best interest at heart. You must show them your gratitude by behaving yourself."

"But I know you, Uncle."

"One thing you should remember," he continued, ignoring the comment. "No matter what happens, no matter who you grow up to be, or what you hear about Fire-Mages from this land, remember where you come from and never lose the customs and values taught by your parents and grandparents. They sacrificed everything and it is up to you, nay your obligation, to honor them with your life."

She nodded solemnly, giving him some hope that she grasped the importance of his words. Without thinking about it, Tihomir opened his arms and hugged her snuggly, aware that his forearms trembled while doing so. Throughout his career, he had faced hordes of Mongolian raiders, singlehandedly subdued entire towns of rebelling peasants, stood against foreign kings of men and masters of beasts alike, in some cases a combination of both. He'd even survived battles with a few magi. Why then had this child made him feel so broken inside? He pulled back from the hug and looked into her reddish-brown eyes one final time.

"Uncle Tiho, your eyes are wet. Do you have an ouchie?"

He shook his head and under his breath said, "None that you can see." He stood and dipped two tarnished, hand-sized pitchers into a barrel of water. Taking them to one side, away from Zorja's sight, he crushed the coco-beans in his hand and sprinkled their dust into one of the pitchers.

"Now something to learn." He turned around and handed her the enchanted drink. "It is customary to drink before setting off to a new land." He held his pitcher up and she mimicked him. "Vashee zdaróvye," he said.

"To your health," repeated Zorja before taking a large gulp. She had just sipped the last drop when her head and shoulders began to sag. She rubbed her heavy eyelids and yawned wide, letting the pitcher fall to the ground. She looked up at him, and her eyes bore the same unnerving stare of disappointment he'd often seen on his father. She reached up for him and Tihomir scooped her up, swaddling her in his wolf-cloak. *Something to remember.*

"Night, night. grandpaw," she slurred just as her load of dark curls plopped down covering his shoulder.

He turned to re-exit out the back of the tent, but paused to see the mule giving him an unusually hard stare.

"What? Why are you looking at me like that?" Tihomir growled. "It's the right thing to do, she doesn't need to be running around with us. Our lives will be too dangerous and unpredictable, and I'm far too old to be caring for a youngster. She needs to dwell amongst other mages; they are her kind, her real family, and they should be the ones to raise her. She deserves better than us, than me, dammit, she is not my dau—" His voice broke on the last word. *But you are the closest thing she would have to a father,* he heard himself say mentally. The cruel irony of having half mystical blood was the lifespan; Tihomir was sure he'd easily outlive all of his former friends, colleagues, and lovers but not reach the average two hundred winters of a full-fledged mage. He might last one hundred years which was more than needed to raise a young child to adulthood. Maybe, just maybe, he could. . .

"Have you finished your task, half-breed? The sun has gone and so soon must I," bellowed the Earth-Mover.

"On the way," Tihomir answered, calling a bit of strength to his hand as he grabbed a vodka barrel from the mule cart. He stepped from the tent out into total darkness.

"Here," she said as the carved runes in her staff glowed bright green, partially illuminating her face. Tihomir was surprised as the hoarseness in her voice seemed to betray her youthful features. She appeared roughly half his age, with a few strands of silver hair pulled behind her ear. He recalled his older brother once grumbling about Earth and Water magi selfishly withholding their methods of staving off the "fizzling process" as he called it; something about their eating habits.

He walked to her and put down the barrel. She touched it, took a long deep sniff and raised her eyebrows. "Vodka, the only thing I miss about this place. A gift was not necessary, of course, but will be much appreciated in the coven." She waved a hand over the barrel, and like the three dead Tatars, it sank down into the ground. She then looked up at him fixedly and opened her arms to receive Zorja.

Tihomir hesitated a moment, recent and long past memories of her family running through his mind all at once. His skin began to tingle as strength magic compulsorily surged into his limbs. *No*, he said to himself, fighting to suppress it. *This is not about you, finish this damn mission old fool!* Quickly but gently, he gave away his family's last descendant.

"You've done right this day, warrior." She nodded in approval. "Your niece will grow up to one day reach her full-mystical potential, and your family's legacy will live on."

"Just make sure she gets there safe. I'm done." He turned away, still struggling to suppress his urge to reclaim his grandniece.

"Tihomir!"

The old warrior turned back, stunned at the Earther's usage of his name.

"Do not be surprised, Taras was renowned chief of the flame, respected within many covens. He loved to boast about your efforts to keep his village in the shade while also fighting to guard this regime."

This also came as somewhat of a shock, as Tihomir often felt ashamed of having to mislead his brothers-in-arms from finding the hidden fire village. He never thought his brother knew or cared anything else about it.

"Little good it did," he replied gravely. "All of my efforts were for naught the day. The insubordinate leaders of the Bogatyri secretly raided the village during my personal holiday."

"A heavy boulder which I will now remove from your conscience. Before coming to this border town, I was ordered to visit the graves of those fire-magi massacred in the raid and found that your niece was not the sole survivor."

Tihomir wrinkled his forehead and then his eyes opened wide. "Internal betrayal?"

She nodded. "We are not certain of the full details, but other parties have reported sightings from Moscow of a known Fire-breather now residing on the estate of a noble within the Khaganate. Rest assure that the turn-cloak's pruning season will come, but know that your brother's death, and that of his descendants, are not your fault."

Immediately Tihomir's heavy sense of guilt was replaced by one of anger. His mind raced as he tried to imagine who the traitor in the village might have been, then another thought occurred to him. "You said 'ordered.' What were your follow-on commands if it had been my fault?

She grinned politely as her eyes turned a bright, radiant emerald. Tihomir's blood ran cold and his knees shook uncontrollably.

"Luckily, we of the earthen arts prefer to stand on solid ground," she reassured him. "I wish you a long and fruitful life, warrior, but I must warn you against planting roots in this town for the night. I can feel a large band of heavily equipped horses rushing here."

"The Bogatyri figured out my ruse, eh? Slimy bastards."

Without saying another word, she bowed her head, and, while still holding Zorja, fell backwards into the ground like it was water. Tihomir stared at that spot for a long moment until his eyes hurt. He then returned to the inside of the tent and salvaged the shop for any and all usable supplies. He looked into the town to see that many of the night-time dwellers had arisen to begin their nefarious deeds. He knotted up the supplies that filled his cart and tightened the mule's yoke.

"My time in this country has ended; there is but one master I will still serve." He unrolled a scroll and studied the map displayed with an "X" marking Constantinople. He took the mule by the bridle and began walking out the back exit of the border town. "Come, it's time to see if the Holy-Father could use an old-hand for his crusade."

EIGHT

THE MISTS OF LU-SHAN

DONNA ROYSTON

Donna Royston particularly enjoys writing about people who are not quite what they seem. Her first story about Sun Ch'o was published in **Copperfield Review**, and was reprinted in **Uncommon Threads** in 2015.

My servants were not happy. They all filed out of their small room and looked reproachful while Chang Min came forward (I think they had drawn lots) and addressed me, saying that their quarters were cramped and had mice. I comforted them, saying that at some moment in life we all have to brush mouse droppings from our pillows, and that they should try to harmonize their personal will with the natural Way. This did not appear to mollify them. I added, then, that it was only for two nights and that the memory of even such a fleeting holiday would be greatly treasured by their overworked master when he had returned to the Imperial City. At this, their expressions brightened and their eyes shone, because it pleased them when I had to wheedle for the service that they should give eagerly and without complaint. They consulted briefly, and Chang Min conceded that perhaps it would not do too much harm to their well-being to stay in a country inn for two nights and that they fervently wished good health and long life (the liars!) to their most beneficent employer—as long as it was only two nights. And so the crisis was averted, both sides saving face.

The landlord, a friendly and obliging man giving the utmost of his simple amenities, bowed many times, apologizing while he explained that he had to seat me with his sole other guest, unless I preferred to wait until the other was finished eating, for he had only one table. One must expect less formality at a rural inn, so I said that I had no objection to dining with his other guest, and I hoped my presence would not disturb him; I added that if this person had any objection, I was content to wait—but I did not place unnecessary emphasis on this. And when I followed the landlord to the next room, I saw the guest, seated at the table. He was dressed plainly, in the style of a minor official; he sat with an erect posture, an unyielding bulwark of a man with dark complexion and thick hair, and his eyes met mine coldly.

And I recognized him at once. General Ko Hung was the idol of the land since his great victories during the previous summer. I had stood as a spectator among the cheering throng that had lined the road for his victory procession, and this man was unmistakably him.

After the obligatory courtesies and introductions had gone back and forth, our host being the intermediary (Ko Hung gave a false name), I was seated at the table: a very rustic affair, unpainted, and not even covered with a cloth. I realized that the innkeeper was not in on the secret—that is, he was not obliging Ko Hung by keeping his identity confidential, but truly did not know that his guest was the famous general. Strangely, too, Ko Hung appeared to be unattended by his staff. My own body servant, Fei Lien, had come with me into the room and stood in the background. A quick glimpse in his direction told me that his eyes were fastened on Ko Hung in amazement.

Meanwhile, the general continued with his meal, his black brow lowered, and he gave me no further acknowledgment as I sat opposite him. The innkeeper, who had left us alone, reappeared long enough to set a dish of noodles with vegetables before me, and then bustled away again.

I found myself ruminating over what I had heard about the general. I did not know him personally, but we were not, after all, far separated by common acquaintance, both of us being employed by the emperor's court. So I had some (what I believed to be) reliable information. And there was no one in the entire land who was more gossiped about than Ko Hung.

For he was not only great in military accomplishments, but learned as a scholar; he had taken the civil service exam at age sixteen and received the highest score that anyone had attained in over fifty years. And yet, neither victories nor erudition fully accounted for the adulation with which the public regarded him. He had *majesty*, some said. Others, less entranced, said he had a vast self-regard. Some men said, in lowered voices, that Ko Hung was a man with a destiny; and others, hearing this, shook their heads in alarm and were silent.

All this passed through my mind. But I could not sit with him in silence for the entire meal. A light subject of conversation was needed, I thought.

"And have you come to see the dragon?" I asked.

"Dragon?" he repeated.

"There are, I think, no less than three pools of Lu-shan that are supposed to have resident dragons."

"I did not come for a dragon," he said.

"There is generally a hermit or two living here, as well," I added. "You are aware, are you not, that the recluse Kuang Su, who was summoned in vain by the emperor to supply him with wisdom, lived here a century ago before ascending into Heaven to become an immortal?"

"I was not aware of that," he said.

"The mountain is a lodestone for seekers," I said. "Perhaps because it is so easy to get lost in it."

"A paradox?" he said. For the first time in our one-sided conversation, his expression had sharpened from boredom into interest.

"One who seeks is very often also one who is pursued," I said. "When you lose yourself you must turn your gaze away from what is behind you and look at where you are going."

"To be lost," he said, with heavy irony, "seems to me a less profitable state than you describe. It is confusion."

"There is much to find that can only be perceived by not looking and understood by not thinking."

"I see you have studied the Way," he said, "to have mastered such riddling language. Are you, then—seeing that you are here—pursued?"

"By a pack of hungry servants and remorseless duties," I replied. "I am making a short pause here, to find a poem or two on Lu-shan."

"A poet," he grunted, dismissively.

I saw that I had become irrelevant.

I also perceived that the general, however exemplary he was in military and scholarly spheres, failed in the social graces. I was tempted, since he did not want to talk of amusing trifles, to see if he could be needled by letting him know that he had been recognized. "Allow me to congratulate you on your wonderful victories on the western frontier, General," I said. "You have served your land and emperor far beyond the abilities of your peers. You must feel singularly blessed."

"Thank you," he said. Again his manner communicated boredom. But for a moment, I saw alarm flicker in his eyes, and I now knew the posture for a sham.

Neither of us spoke for the remainder of our meals. But after he had finished his noodles and drained his cup, he looked at me and said, as though explanation were necessary, "I have come to meet the hermit who lives on the mountain. He is said to have wisdom." And then he rose and bowed and wished me to find good poetry, and retired to his room.

How very strange—that I had provoked the great general into a lie.

In the morning I was up early, but Ko Hung was earlier still. I saw him, as I looked out the window, disappearing into the mist, on foot and unaccompanied. It is an uncanny sight to see a man become gray and insubstantial-looking and utterly dissolve.

Fei Lien brought me, as I had requested, clothes that were suitable for mountain climbing: a red shen-i embroidered with gold dragons, and a red cap.

"Make sure not to omit anything from the supplies," I told him. "I do not want to reach the top of Dragon Head Peak, sit down to compose, and then find that there is no ink."

"Rest assured, esteemed master," he said serenely. "Your writing materials will all be present and ready to serve you."

With that, we went outside to join the others, assembled on the path. They now knew about our famous fellow-guest, and were disappointed to learn that he had already left the inn. By "disappointed," I mean they were excessively, even offensively, downcast, as though I had personally done them an injury, and they could talk of nothing else.

I turned my mind to the reason I had come. This was my holiday, and I was going to enjoy it, if by dint of determination I could. I felt the awesome presence of the mountain all around me, in spite of the mist that prevented me from actually seeing it.

Lu-shan rises vertically toward Heaven, a thing too great to be expressed by the word "mountain," for it is not one peak but nearly a hundred. The sheer sides of these peaks are mostly worn and fissured granite, but where there are outcrops and ledges, or any purchase in a crevice, pine trees cling. The trees are ancient, yet they are so dwarfed by the size of the mountain itself that they are like moss on a boulder. When there is no mist in the valley, the observer who gazes upward sees ragged, jagged rock shoulders and long waterfalls. These cataracts strike the rocky walls and throw out a fine spray which dazzles the eye and joins with the sea of cloud that flows around the mountain, sometimes hanging motionless around the peaks, sometimes wreathing sinuously around its sides, sometimes (as today) rolling through the peaceful valleys, a silent, slow-moving flood too circumspect to touch anything with a heavy hand. Clothed in its ever-moving mists, the mountain, it is said, never looks the same twice.

I had seen Lu-shan's worn cliffs, its waterfalls, many times as I passed it in my travels. This morning, standing outside an inn at the foot of Dragon Head Peak, submerged in the cloud-sea, I "saw" the mountain only as I conjured it in my imagination. At the edge of vastness, the world had become very small.

We set out, I heading our small procession. Fei Lien, as the chief of my servants, followed me, carrying my satchel with pens, brushes, ink, and paper. After him followed Chang Min, carrying a red and gold folding chair. Chuan Hsu and Hsiao Kang brought food and drink, supplied by the innkeeper. Teng Ai carried the food serving implements, and Kai Huan carried my umbrella. Kan Pao carried scrolls of classical literature. I must point out, lest you think I encumber my servants unnecessarily, that these were for his own use. He is hoping to enter the civil service, and in his unoccupied moments he studies for the examinations. I encourage him in this effort because the sooner he passes his exams and procures a gainful position with the government, the sooner he will leave my own employment. And I benefit from his studies in another way: when he is not preparing for his exams, he writes poems of his own and asks me what I think of them. Thus, it is much better that he study.

"I have devised a plan," I told Fei Lien, who moved up to walk beside me for ease of hearing my instructions. "I will divide the journey up the mountain into stages, and I will write a poem for each stage. For instance, here we are at the base of the mountain, at the start of our journey. We should pause in a picturesque spot that will be conducive to my poetic imagination, and there I will write my first poem."

Fei Lien nodded gravely. "I will assist in selecting a suitable spot."

We walked on for several moments. The mist was, as I have already mentioned, thick, so there was no grand vista looking upward at the mountain peaks this morning. To my left appeared a rocky boulder that was attractively fringed with ferns and overhung by a graceful cryptomeria tree. I started to gesture toward it, but Fei Lien frowned and shook his head.

Perhaps he was right. I did not press it. We continued, and shortly came to a grove of small trees with deep green, glossy leaves and sinuous trunks. I paused to consider the possibilities here.

"Not suitable," said Fei Lien.

"Why not?" I asked.

"Noble lord, the scene has no suggestiveness, nor harmonic resonance with the beginning of a journey," said Fei Lien.

I could not think of an argument against this, so I resumed walking. Behind me, the procession also started forward again. I thought I heard a sigh, but when I glanced back I could only see duteous and keen faces.

Our path, going ever upward, turned this way and that. There were markers, I saw, ones that looked very old and worn, and I wondered who had placed them there. But I was grateful for them, for I saw they would keep us on the path.

"Fei Lien," I said, "perhaps I should not seek a perfect spot. After all, the work of a poet is inward. I can compose a poem on the start of a journey without the benefit of a striking view or a symbolic setting."

"There should be no compromise in the creation of art, respected master," he said.

"In an ideal situation, perhaps, but we are progressing upward, and soon we will no longer be at the beginning of the journey."

"It is a great, dizzying height, lord, that will require exhausting toil and all our strength to climb. We are merely strolling on the mountain's little toe."

"Here is where I will write, Fei Lien," I said. "Chang Min, place my chair."

Chang Min came forward and set the chair down carefully and unfolded it, making sure, by moving some stones, that it sat level and secure. I sat down. Fei Lien placed paper before me, handed me a brush, and stood by, holding the ink pot.

I pondered.

At times during an uneventful journey, I entertain myself by composing literary works in my head. Usually this is poetry, but not always. At this moment, for some reason, my mind began to pursue not ideas for poems, but the beginning of a treatise on the subject of hiring servants for one's best advantage. I observe that many officials fail miserably at this. To wit:

The Art of Hiring, Supervising, and Rewarding Servants for Your Best Advantage and Personal Safety

There are a number of reasons to have servants, in spite of all their trouble and expense. First, of course, they are a necessity for a man of certain position and responsibility. This fact cannot be denied. A man in a high position in the Emperor's court cannot take care of his own laundry, cook his own meals, light his own fires, do his own shopping. You must find people who can do these things for you, competently.

The man who would hire a servant usually commits one (or more) of several errors. The first of these errors...

"Uncle Ch'o?" said Kan Pao.

I turned to look at him. He was sitting at the side of the path, bent over a scroll. "Yes?"

He looked up, his face wearing a dissatisfied expression. "This story about Confucius and the fisherman, it doesn't make sense."

"What is it in particular that disturbs you?"

"It's just ...strange. I mean, the fisherman tells a story about a man who's afraid of his shadow and his own footsteps, and he runs faster and faster to escape, until he falls down dead—that's kind of funny, I like that. And I see that's supposed to be Confucius, making rules and making things busier and busier, instead of stopping and making things simpler and being still. So when he hears the story, Confucius sees how wise the fisherman is and bows to him and asks to be his pupil. And the old man says *no*, because..."

211

The first of these errors is, he hires a young relative who is in need of a job but ill qualified in every other respect. It is a virtue to take care of one's family and advance them when possible, but you should seek another and better way to accomplish this. Think of what happens to a relative in a paid position. He will see you in your nightclothes, and eating meals. He will see you spill soup on your robe. He will know that you suffer from digestive ailments or a sluggish colon. Seeing you every day in your own household, and being encouraged by your other servants to recount family lore consisting of stories of your childhood and early mistakes and indiscretions (which he, being younger than you, should not even know, except that they have been retailed to him by your aunts), what can possibly happen but that he will find common ground with his fellow servants instead of you? Disharmony comes to your home, where all should be tranquil repose and quiet time for thought. This sad end is best avoided altogether: do not hire a relative, no matter how much his mother pleads, with tears running down her face, that her son desperately needs a chance to...

Suddenly I realized that Kan Pao had stopped talking. I had the impression that he had finally stated his point, or asked a question. I almost made the mistake of asking him to repeat what he had last said. Then I recollected myself.

"Nephew," I said, "there are two kinds of understanding with which to approach this story. The first understanding is of the civil service examiner, who tests one or two thousand young men each year, and who will not care about the subtleties of the story's meaning or your grasp of it. He will ask you to write it out verbatim, and if you pass to the next level, he will perhaps question you about whether it was a rice farmer, rat catcher, or fisherman who explained the Way to the Master, but he will not ask you what you learned about the proper cultivation of your person, guarding of your truth, or avoidance of what is external to you. The second understanding is that the sacred writings do not reveal themselves easily or quickly; they will give you years of contemplation, and as you get older you will marvel that you see different ideas in them which you had not noticed when you were younger. So ponder them, but do not ask me for their meaning. If I tell you what the story means, it will cut short your process of understanding. It is only through your own striving that you will understand."

"But somebody must have figured out by now what it means," Kan Pao protested.

"Indeed so, I agree completely," I said. "But can he tell you what he has learned?"

Kan Pao made a vexed sound and rolled his eyes up to the sky. It is hard on a young person, when the sages do not have his convenience foremost in their thoughts.

Kan Pao returned to his scroll. After a further distraction of picturing Kan Pao in a conversation with Confucius and imagining what each would say to the other, I came back to myself and realized that the paper was still before me, and Fei Lien was still standing by with the ink. Where was I? Oh, yes. The beginning of a journey.

"Fei Lien?" I said.

"Yes, noble lord?"

"Our fellow guest at the inn, General Ko Hung. Do you not find it odd that he came to Lu-shan unaccompanied by any servants or companions and went out this morning onto the mountain by himself?"

"Perhaps," Fei Lien conceded. "But it is a humble pilgrimage..."

"Yes, last night he said he came to seek out a hermit who lives here. He suggested that he was in search of wisdom."

"And is there a reason to doubt this, esteemed master?"

"I had the impression from talking to him that he had no interest in pondering the Way. Why, then, seek wisdom from a recluse? This strikes me as contradictory."

"Perhaps the matter that concerns him is too near to his heart to discuss."

"Perhaps," I said. "Perhaps that is it."

But I did not believe it. The man had at first disdained the suggestion of seeking a hermit, even when made lightly, and only a short while later had thrown it to me in the manner of one tossing a scrap to a dog.

I reflected a bit longer on this puzzle, and once again realized that I was avoiding the task of writing a poem. Now, being stern with myself, I focused on what needed to be done. Beginnings.

The path rises before me, ascending step by step;
In swirling mists, the goal cannot be seen.
Would not an archer be helpless in such obscurity?
Would not two armies fall to confusion?
But a walker keeps to the path without thought
Reaching the destination with ease.

I wrote the poem on the paper, and then read it aloud to everyone. There were some nods of approval, and some pursed lips. I was not satisfied with it, myself. Not every poem is a success, but I would revisit it later to try to determine exactly what was wrong and fix it, if possible. Now it was time to move on. Fei Lien put the writing materials away, and we resumed our journey.

There came to our hearing, as we walked the path upward, a sound of falling water, and soon we came to a rushing stream and crossed over it. The sound still grew louder, however, and I saw that we were coming to one of the many waterfalls that tumble over the mountainsides. Here we paused and I wrote another poem, this one about the power and effortlessness of water. This poem, although there was nothing technically wrong with it, did not particularly interest me. My spirits sank a little as I contemplated the poem. While I knew that I should keep a detached attitude, and I should not worry about two poems that I did not think were as good as one might wish, I couldn't help thinking that my artistic abilities were sinking into mediocrity, at best.

I sighed.

Then we continued on, climbing upward. To my disappointment, the mist continued unbroken, although we had been ascending for hours and the air had become much cooler.

I am not used to mountain walking, and as I paused to breathe, I realized that my legs were feeling weary and my knees weak.

"Let us stop here for a while," I said. "I think it's a good time for something to eat."

Kan Pao blew out his breath with relief.

"Are you tired?" I asked my nephew, a little smug that I was hardy enough to tire him.

"Hungry," he said.

Chang Min set up my chair and I placed myself in it, a little heavier than usual. My back creaked.

"The vegetation has changed here," I commented. "The cryptomerias have given way to pines. To one experienced on the mountain, the change is probably a sign of a certain height. It is unfortunate that we do not know what that height may be, and how close to the top of the mountain we are. I wish we could get a scenic view through the mist."

"Would you like your brush and paper, lord?" said Fei Lien.

"Yes."

As soon as he handed me the brush, I wrote:

> *The mountain speaks its own language*
> *Which I cannot comprehend*
> *Trees, ferns, and mosses are its words*
> *Its breath a moving fog.*

I read it out loud, decided (with relief) that it pleased me, and gave paper and brush back to Fei Lien. As I did so, my glance moved to the trees behind Fei Lien and I was startled to see that, without having made a sound in his approach, a stranger had materialized from out of the mist: an old man in a monk's robe, with a satchel slung across his shoulder. He was wrinkled and weathered-looking (somewhat like the mountain, I thought); bald on top, he made up for it with a long gray beard and hair that flowed from the back of his head and over his ears to fall loose on his shoulders. His eyes had a strange quality—of wildness—and the thought crossed my mind that he might be one of those hermits who become crazed from isolation and too many austerities.

I stood, joined my hands, and bowed to him.

He smiled in return and inclined his head.

"The blessing of Heaven on you, sir," I said. "My name is Sun Ch'o, and I would be most honored if you would partake of our hospitality, humble though it be."

"The mercy of Heaven for all," he replied. "I am Szu-ma Yu, servant of the Way and disciple of the Buddha. I make my small home here. I thank you for your offer and accept it with gratitude."

I introduced him to my servants, who all made a respectful greeting, and we sat down. While Teng Ai prepared the food and Hsiao Kang assisted him by lighting charcoal in the brazier, Szu-ma Yu said, "I have seen visitors come to Lu-shan before, but never an expedition such as yours. If I am not too bold in my curiosity, Sun Ch'o, may I ask what you seek?"

"A most precious thing, master recluse," I replied mysteriously.

He did not respond to this as I expected, with a question as to what the precious thing could possibly be—indeed, he did not respond at all—so I tried to smooth over the awkward silence that followed. "You see, I must periodically audit the finances and governmental actions of Lu-shan District. For years, in my comings and goings, I have imagined climbing the mountain instead of viewing it in passing. I have pictured myself wandering its paths, enjoying the scenery, and writing poetry. Yesterday, I decided that it was time to finally do it. So I came here after finishing my business with the governor, and I have made myself a day of leisure to write poetry and see the views from the mountain. The views, I'm afraid, have all been of mist, but the poems may pierce obscurity to see Lu-shan itself."

Now he smiled and responded with approval. "I am happy for your good resolve. Would you be pleased to share more of your poems?"

"That is a dangerous question," I warned him, "for I am indeed very pleased to share my poetry. Please stop me if I share for too long." And I recited some for him—my best, not the ones I had written today. I explained my idea of writing a sequence of poems to correspond with the stages of climbing the mountain, and added the one I had just written, in case he had not heard it as he had approached. Szu-ma Yu did not seem to weary of poetry, and he clapped his hands with child-like delight at the one written about Lu-shan. His enthusiasm was heady stuff for me and I cannot remember any other reading so pleasurable for me and my listeners, or perhaps I should say, one listener.

We passed from there into a discussion of the pleasures of poetry in general, and the benefits it bestows on mankind, while Fei Lien and Teng Ai served the food and drink. In the midst of this pleasant conversation, I heard footsteps; I turned my head and saw my fellow guest from the inn, Ko Hung, striding up the path. He stared at me and snorted. "Sun Ch'o the poet," he said. "I have climbed three peaks today, and how many have you climbed?"

"Only this," I said. "But I am having an enjoyable day. Have you found what you were seeking?"

"No."

"Then allow me to assist. I have by good fortune happened on Szu-ma Yu, venerable hermit of this mountain, whom I believe is the one that you seek."

Ko Hung gazed at Szu-ma Yu with an incredulous expression, then looked back at me. "I am not looking for him!"

"Then I apologize for the misunderstanding. What, or who, do you seek?"

He paced several times on the path and ground his teeth in anger.

"I had exact instructions on where to find what I sought. Or so I thought. Mist and clouds! As soon as I ascended, I found myself in the wrong place! A second time, a third time! Hermit, is this the peak called the Dragon's Head?"

"It is."

"And is there a cave on it?"

"There are many caves to be found all over Lu-shan."

"I asked if there is a cave on *this* peak."

"There is, above us."

"Show it to me."

Szu-ma Yu scratched himself indecorously, looking thoughtful, and then belched.

"Is there a treasure that you hope to find hidden on Dragon Head Peak?" he said mildly.

"You know of it!" Ko Hung exclaimed.

"There are treasure hunters from time to time," said Szu-ma Yu. "No one has found it, however."

"Found what?" I asked.

"The sword of Huang-ti," said Ko Hung.

"Or perhaps the South-Pointing Chariot. Or the Book of Pai Tse," Szu-ma Yu added. "At the Yellow Emperor's death, it is said that he was carried by the Responding Dragon away to the

West, and one of his three precious treasures was hidden on each great mountain that he flew over. Some say that Lu-shan was one of those mountains."

"I seek the sword," said Ko Hung.

"It would be a marvelous treasure to find," I said. "But this is only legend. Where did you get the exact instructions that you mentioned?"

"Scholars have their uses. Old scrolls in the imperial palace, written with ancient symbols. In fact, not even scrolls. Rolls of bark, I was told."

"Really," I said. "But suppose it's the Book of Pai Tse that was left here?"

"I will know after I look in the cave," said Ko Hung.

"Assuming that what you seek is here, don't you think it is better to leave the relic undisturbed?" said Szu-ma Yu. "It was hidden for a reason, I am sure. The other seekers, after I have talked with them for a while, have always decided that it was best to end their search."

"When I make a resolve," said Ko Hung, "I carry it out."

"But why would you want such a thing?" asked Szu-ma Yu.

"Why?" Ko Hung repeated, as though amazed. "Old man, even if the thing concealed on this mountain was naught but the button from Huang-ti's cap, what matters—all that matters—is that it is the relic of Huang-ti. Any mortal man bearing his relic would be acknowledged to possess the Mandate of Heaven."

"You think that it will make you emperor, then?" I said, shocked. "But we have an Emperor—who shows no sign of having lost the Mandate of Heaven."

"The Mandate of Heaven has been withdrawn before, when the time needed another man who was more fit. It will pass to me, who has the strength to use it."

"This is not wisdom," said Szu-ma Yu.

"What would you know of wisdom, charlatan? All I require of you is to show me to the cave where the relic is hidden."

"The cave lies above, at the top of the peak," said Szu-ma Yu. "Humbly, I regret that I may not go with you; I have work that I must get done today." He held open his satchel, with an apologetic air, and I saw that it contained some herbs that he had gathered.

Ko Hung seemed, for a moment, taken aback. Then, "I have been delayed enough!" he said. "Enough searching—Why should I seek and waste my time when you know where it is?" He strode forward and seized Szu-ma Yu by the arm. "Show me where it is, old man, and do not make me lose my temper. I could pick you up and throw you like a child's toy. And on this mountain I cannot say when you would reach the ground."

"Ko Hung!" I said. "Take your hand off him!"

Kai Huan and Chang Min—they are my bodyguards—had readied themselves, hands on sword hilts, and awaited my command. But, although their response was quick and correct, I suspected they would be ultimately, and fatally, reluctant to fight the nation's hero. I cast about in my mind for an alternative, if there was one.

Ko Hung released Szu-ma Yu and drew his own sword. He held it lowered, but with the menace of one who did not expect refusal, ever, from anyone, and his expression was grim now. "Think carefully, Sun Ch'o," he said. "I will be generous if it goes no further. But do not stand in my way. The child-emperor will be swept aside, and I will be He whom you must please, and to whom you will perform the nine prostrations."

"You would create a civil war."

"Not I. The people will know me for their lawful ruler. Should there be war, it is the puppet and his kinsmen who would be responsible for bloodshed."

"Put up your sword, Ko Hung," said Szu-ma Yu. "I will not have violence, either to threaten me or defend me. If you wish to be shown the place, I will take you. I ask only that Sun Ch'o accompany us, to witness the Mandate of Heaven being bestowed upon its new possessor. Such a glorious event should have witnesses, lest there be doubters."

There was a pause, while Ko Hung turned this over in his mind. His eyes were narrowed as he looked at me, and then at Szu-ma Yu. Whatever his suspicions were, he seemed to overcome them.

He smiled, then, all at once in a good humor. "I do not need to believe your reasons in order to agree, old man. You fear for your safety; I have no reason to harm you if you keep faith. So let us go together! A pleasure excursion. And Sun Ch'o will have an opportunity for making more poetry."

I was, of course, in accord with going, for the reason of assuring Szu-ma Yu's safety, and avoiding violence—but also, it need not be said, for the reason of intense curiosity. We therefore set out, all of us together, with Szu-ma Yu leading the way, Ko Hung after him, and I and my retinue following them.

As we climbed the mountain, I pondered what I had learned of the general. The revelation of his motive was a hard problem to reconcile to his character. Why, I asked myself, would a man of so great honor and accomplishment, a man who required loyalty in his own subordinates, and who would, I was sure, be outraged by a personal betrayal, pursue such a path? Why would this man, who, I pointed out to myself, scorned both the fanciful and the philosophical, listen to tales of an ancient, dragon-transported sword, and then determine to search it out? If he thought it useful as a tool for legitimizing, in the eyes of the common people, a seizure of ultimate power, then any ancient sword could be produced and called the sword of Huang-ti.

Ah, I replied to myself, maybe he needs to convince himself most of all. And of course the spurious does not confer authenticity. Maybe fanciful dragon legends of today offend his deep need for an ancient and very powerful dragon who honored the empire's founder.

I could not believe that Ko Hung was a man without honor. I wondered if he felt some distaste for the task he had set himself. Maybe he is a man, I thought, who must keep busy. Not with any kind of work, but that which is difficult and which requires his full effort. When there is nowhere else for ambition to go, what then? Men must have an ambition to work for—something not yet attained—in order to live. Most of us have modest goals. But a few must have a great goal. They thrive on struggle, on problems, on adversity; and without that struggle, without purpose, without new frontiers, their minds go astray. They turn from emptiness, which is unbearable, and if there is no struggle to occupy them, they create one.

...Along these lines I speculated. How accurately, others must judge. Still the path ascended, and the climb began to seem interminable. I reached a point where all I could focus my thoughts on was no longer the question of the general's character but taking the next step upward. Keeping my feet on a treacherous path was my own challenge: it was all rocky mountainside, uneven and jagged, on which one had to test and judge where to place each step so that the foot did not slip: a rock that seemed to be part of the solid bones of the mountain could turn out to be but loosely held by the thin soil. I even saw

Ko Hung stumble. Only Szu-ma Yu went as lightly as one on level ground, stepping easily from rock to rock, and occasionally calling out to take care in a dangerous spot. I saw Ko Hung as a gray figure, and Szu-ma Yu as one who moved in and out of existence, gaining substance if he paused on an outcrop to look behind as I moved forward, dissolving again as he continued ahead. Muffled voices behind me were passing warnings back, and they were the only way I could tell my servants were still following.

Sunlight, unexpectedly, broke upon us. We had emerged above the level of the cloud-sea, and we now found ourselves on a bare rocky ledge at the summit of the mountain. The peak had its name because from a distance the protruding rock suggested, to an imaginative person, a dragon's head. We stood on the dragon's snout.

I was captivated by the wondrous sight of the cloud-sea, as it flowed in slow streams and created its own ever-changing shapes. The rock on which we stood seemed to float on the mists, and one could almost think it would be possible to step down off the mountain and walk away into the distance. Across the gulf could be seen another peak of Lu-shan rising above the clouds, thinly clothed with pines, ghostly pale, like a distant island. But in spite of the unearthly illusion, I couldn't quite forget that we were elevated over an unseen gulf of empty space and far below, hidden by the cloud-sea, was the valley floor. Distant sounds of the waterfalls rose upward; closer, I heard the quiet disembodied *cronk* of a raven in flight through the clouds below. Other than this, however, as far as could be seen, there was only the cloud-sea, rolling slowly between the two peaks.

"Where is it?" Ko Hung demanded, rudely interrupting my appreciation of the view that I had gained with so much toil. "Where is the cave?"

"The cave is under this ledge," said Szu-ma Yu.

"What? Where? How can anyone reach it?" Ko Hung asked in rapid succession, as he comprehended.

Szu-ma Yu indicated the rock face that went perpendicularly down the side of the outthrust ledge. "There are handholds in the rock. You climb down, and to your left is the opening to the cave."

A feeling of admiration swept over me for Szu-ma Yu's gentle cunning. Indeed, why resist Ko Hung's threats? Only show him the impossible place that he could not reach, and the crisis was over—for today, at least. Perhaps he would return with men and ropes and ladders, but that would require time and planning. And then I thought: surely the hermit had not climbed down there! Handholds! There was nothing but weathered rock and a fall to the death when your hand slipped. Who climbs around on bare cliffs—under ledges, where you can't even see before climbing over the abyss—looking for what might be there? There was no cave; it was a fiction.

Ko Hung looked long at the rock, thinking, I would guess, what I was thinking. But I had underestimated his resolve, and his desire. At last he went to the edge of the precipice and began to lower himself over it. Not at the tip of the forward-jutting ledge—the dragon's nose, you might say—but rather under a cheek to reach his chin. I heard his boots carefully searching the rock for purchase, saw him test his foothold, reach with one arm, let himself down slowly, then reach downward with his other arm. He gave one look at Szu-ma Yu that I could only describe as dangerous—as if to say, *If you have lied to me, you will pay*.

"This is not necessary," I could not resist telling him. "Come back later with rope..."

I glanced at Szu-ma Yu, who was watching Ko Hung impassively. "He has chosen. He will carry out his resolve."

Ko Hung's head disappeared over the edge, his expression implacable. He did not bother to speak. He was concentrating solely on what he was doing.

For myself, the height was too giddy to even stand close to the edge. I visualized Ko Hung's downward climb in my imagination, and strained with him, but I could not watch. I imagined his hands grasping difficult holds, groping for a hold he could not find, a foot reaching into emptiness. Each moment I expected to hear the sound of crumbling rock and a despairing cry.

We waited.

"I see no cave," came Ko Hung's voice, harsh and strained, from below.

"It is there," said Szu-ma Yu, calmly.

There was a silence that stretched out into an ever-lengthening time in which I listened for Ko Hung's voice again, but it did not come.

"He has found it," said Szu-ma Yu.

There followed an interval in which we waited, and heard nothing. I looked out across the strange cloud-sea, its endless expanse like a meadow of gray-white cobwebbed grass covered with a predawn dew. No—I changed my mind, and it was a ghostly ocean, dreamed by a blind man. And then it was something else: another world altogether, where dead ancestors might at any moment be seen, the vaporous ground supporting their unweighty bodies, strolling without actually having to move their legs.

This thought made me shudder and momentarily wish that I was Kan Pao, seventeen years old and still without memories of dead friends and family members. And then I realized that I was warding off the merely fearful with the dreadful, and I recovered some tranquility of mind.

Seventeen years old again? No—mercifully—whatever else might happen, I did not have to fear *that*.

But I knew why I was thinking of the dead, instead of composing my final poem in this place of ethereal beauty. It was the thought of Ko Hung's desire for the throne. I did not doubt his ability to take it, sword or no sword. Should he actually climb back up to the ledge holding a sword, it was possible that he really would call on me to testify to the authenticity of his claim—something I did not wish or intend to do. And if he didn't...

Upon this thought, I heard a scuff of boot on rock and grunts of exertion: Ko Hung was climbing back up. I could not but be moved by his courage and impressed by his strength. Szu-ma Yu moved close to the edge of the precipice, looked down, and, bracing himself with left arm enwrapping a pine, reached over with his right hand and helped drag Ko Hung up onto our ledge, where he rested for several moments on his knees, panting. Szu-ma Yu bowed and stepped backward, retreating without a word to the edge of our little group.

Ko Hung's head came up slowly. He had a long bundle slung across his back, securely tied, and an expression of triumph on his face.

He took off the bundle and laid it across his knees, and began to tug at the wrapping. Layers of rotten leather, silk, and cotton padding fell away. And there, revealed, lay an ancient scabbard and hilt.

"It is fitting," Ko Hung breathed. "Of course it would be difficult to find and reach, so that only one who would risk his life could obtain it. And I have."

He stood, and withdrew the sword slowly. It was dark—black with age, I think, although it seemed not to have corroded.

Ko Hung held it up, enraptured, tip pointing to the sky. "Look, Sun Ch'o! The Mandate of H—"

His gaze had traveled down the blade to look at me, but was arrested. I thought he was looking at Szu-ma Yu and I turned my head to see what had so affected him.

It was not Szu-ma Yu. Moving in the mist on the path below us was a shape, indistinct ... but large... I saw golden shining eyes ... dread seized me, for it could only be a tiger, of enormous size, following us, his easy prey. This was only an instant's thought; then the face solidified around the eyes, as the creature came closer, and a body. A sinuous serpent shape—

A dragon!

It walked unhurriedly, even languidly. Its footfalls were silent, until I heard one claw faintly rasp against a stone, the only sound it made.

It paused to examine Teng Ai, youngest but for Kan Pao. He stood perfectly still, waiting for what was to come; fear was in his eyes. For a moment, no one moved, man and dragon looking into the other's eyes. Finally, the creature broke its gaze and turned to look at Chuan Hsu. After another long moment, it shifted its regard away from him, to Kai Huan. Not one of us moved or spoke, paralyzed with fear in its presence, while it considered us, one by one. It came to me, and looked into my eyes with its own strange amber-colored eyes, deep as the fathomless Lake of Immortals. A sensation came over me, as though I were falling asleep. Then it turned, and took a step closer to Ko Hung. Its golden gleaming skin brushed against me for a moment, powdery smooth and cool.

I watched as Ko Hung endured the creature's gaze, and the terror in his eyes was painful to see. The sword, still slackly grasped in his hand, now rested its tip on the ground.

With the quickness of an eyeblink, the dragon snatched him up. One moment, both were still, and the next, Ko Hung was being held in the dragon's mouth. He did not cry out. The dragon shook him gently, and the sword fell to the ground.

Then the dragon spread its wings, which had been so tightly folded against its back that I had not even realized they were there, and lifted itself into the air. The movement was as light and effortless as a deer's spring—with the difference that it did not return to earth but caught the wind and mounted into the sky. Briefly it was lost to sight in a billow of mist, but then it reappeared, circling higher. The terror of its presence gone from among us, I heard groans, and a quick look around me showed faces pale with horror, Teng Ai sinking to the ground as though he felt faint, Kan Pao hugging himself to quell his trembling.

I looked up again. The dragon had soared to such a height that he was tiny—he looked like a bird unless an onlooker's keen eyes could discern his sinuous shape and long tail. And then, as we watched, something separated from the soaring creature, and was falling—it had dropped Ko Hung.

We all cried out as he tumbled.

Teng Ai, sitting on the ground and looking upward, covered his eyes.

"That is the end," Chang Min whispered.

"He must be dead already," said Kai Huan.

And then I saw the dragon dive, hurtling downward, angling toward Ko Hung, and both disappeared into the flowing sea of clouds. Several moments later—and we were all waiting, holding our breath—we saw the dragon again, flying upward, carrying a body. Around the peaks of Lu-shan, over the cloud-sea he flew, swooping and soaring, at times tossing Ko Hung's unresisting and limp body up into the air and catching him again, playing joyfully. At one moment it seemed cruel and the next, to my mind, innocent, as though it were sharing its beautiful playground with a dull companion. I went from pity for Ko Hung to admiration for the wondrous creature over and again.

And we watched, unable to look away, so rapt that I cannot say how long this went on. Then, to our sudden alarm, the dragon, flying lower, turned straight for our peak. We scrambled as he came hurtling toward us. At the last moment, with a slight twitch of the wings, he lifted over our heads and dropped Ko Hung on the ground—and was gone.

I went to Ko Hung's body and knelt beside him. He lay unmoving, but he was unconscious, not dead. I could find no outward injury; I patted his face, called his name, and had Fei Lien sprinkle water on him. He awoke slowly and looked at us as though he found himself among strangers. Then his gaze shifted to the sky and remained there. Perhaps, mentally, he had not yet descended to earth and was still soaring and tumbling in the heavens. Whatever was going through his mind, he had received a great shock and was as helpless as a blade of mown grass.

"Put him in the chair," I said. "We will carry him down to the inn and get a doctor to care for him." Chuan Hsu and Hsiao Kang obeyed, and fitted in the handles that would allow the chair to be used for carrying.

"It is less than an hour to nightfall," said Szu-ma Yu. So quiet had he been, and so riveting the dragon's appearance, that indeed I had forgotten him. "Please take my advice and shelter at my hut this evening; it will be dangerous to try to descend in the dark."

I opened my mouth, wanting to ask a question, but some thought or feeling stopped me and I remedied my hesitation by saying, "Thank you for your kind offer; we accept."

As Ko Hung was settled into the chair, he lifted one hand and gestured at the sword. "Bring it," he croaked.

My nephew went and stood looking down at the sword. Then he knelt down, sliding his palms under the blade with great care.

"No," I told him. "Leave it there. The guardian will take it back. It does not belong to any mortal now."

Kan Pao looked confused momentarily, then stood up and backed away from the sword.

I felt Ko Hung's glare and pointedly did not give it my attention.

So we started on our way, following Szu-ma Yu downward on the path. As darkness enfolded the mountainside, we took a short side-way and came to his hut. It was very small, but sufficient to shelter all of us for the night.

We helped Ko Hung lie down on Szu-ma Yu's sleeping mat. He would not speak, but he did drink a little broth that was prepared for him.

We sat, our backs to the hut's wall, and ate a modest meal. Everyone was quiet, still affected by the awe we had felt at the miraculous event we had witnessed. One by one, each went to sleep until only I was still awake.

I found myself trying to remember if I had seen Szu-ma Yu during the dragon's flight. Where had he been, exactly? Somewhere to my right and behind me. Or so I had thought...

And then, out of nowhere, my final poem of the day came to me, vivid and powerful. Quickly, lest the poem evaporate as suddenly as it had come, I pulled a piece of charcoal from the brazier, and wrote in quick strokes on a piece of paper that lay near me, then dropped the coal and sucked on my fingers to cool them. For a time I sat and looked at the poem, marveling. It captured the beauty and power of the heavenly apparition in language to move and astound all who heard it. I had written a poem that would make me celebrated among the literary greats of history.

Then, because even great poets need to rest, I lay down and slept soundly.

In the morning I was awakened by the sound of my nephew's voice.

"...the fisherman says he's really hard to teach, and Confucius asks if he can be the fisherman's pupil and learn from him..."

I opened my eyes, and turned my head. Ko Hung was sitting up on his mat, awake, patiently listening to Kan Pao setting forth his problem, his dark eyes fixed as intently on my nephew as if Kan Pao were a lieutenant giving a report from the battlefield. Around him were ranged my servants in attitudes of respect or fascination. I suppressed the urge to groan. Well, Ko Hung had been a scholar of renown. He could cope with my nephew.

"...and the fisherman jumps in his boat as if he's scared and says 'I am leaving you now! I am leaving now!' And he does..."

The door to the hut was open, letting in gentle light and birdsong. I could not see any mist. I arose, feeling stiff, and was trying to steal out quietly when I heard Ko Hung say, "Kan Pao, allow me to consider your question for a short while. Ask your master to sit by me that I may speak with him."

All heads turned to look at me—since I had heard, I didn't see any reason to wait for the request to be relayed to me. I went and joined the others.

"May I be of assistance to you this morning?" I asked him. "We can carry you down in the chair to the village, where a doctor can be summoned—"

He silenced me with an imperious gesture, frowning. "Sun Ch'o, I do not leave enemies behind me."

"Am I your enemy?"

"Your report to His Imperial Majesty can destroy me."

"I have been pondering that. On one hand, it is my duty to do my part in preserving the realm."

"What is on the other hand?"

"That my truthful report will not preserve the secrecy of the sword's hiding place, and it seems to me that Heaven's wish is clear on that point."

"Are you saying that I can return to my army and you will say nothing of what happened here?"

There was a silence.

"No, General," I said at last. "If you return to your army, I will have to speak."

"Then I will make sure you do not reach the Imperial City."

I heard an intake of breath and everyone around me became still, tense.

I was struck, momentarily, by the thought of a treatise-never-written, imaginatively titled "How to Keep Yourself from

Making Enemies at Court, and Stay Alive." There are two reasons why I have never written it. First, I hesitate to offer such advice lest it be, after the work's completion, rendered grimly humorous by my own fall from favor. It's better to remain silent on the subject for that reason alone.

But the stronger argument against it was that it felt disrespectful to the memories of honorable men who were exiled or met death, by implying that the failure was on their part. I have been at court long enough to know that better men than I have been undone by schemers, enemies, and rivals. It is never far from an official's thoughts that he could be next.

What would have been my advice to myself, had I actually set down in writing my imagined treatise?

I had no idea.

"If I may make a suggestion…or rather, ask a question…why return to your army?"

He barked a laugh, but it sounded uncertain.

"If you are weary of fighting…" I said.

"I am not weary!"

I tried a different tack. "You have seen something wondrous, but you have not been given the Mandate of Heaven."

He lowered his gaze. For the first time, he looked defeated. "Like the fisherman, it appeared to me, and then it withdrew. Not the Mandate of Heaven, but something more…"

"But it is not gone."

"What do you mean?"

"Is a teaching something that you grasp in an instant, like a piece of fruit? Or is it something that you glimpse through the mists and pursue with great dedication?"

He looked up at me. There was a long silence.

Finally: "Give me paper and ink," he said.

I motioned to Fei Lien to bring my writing supplies.

He took the brush and wrote, then handed the paper to me, still wet. "It is my resignation," he said. "You may give it to His Majesty."

I bowed.

"Now, scholar," said Ko Hung, turning to my nephew calmly, as if he had not just been threatening my life, "I will interpret your story."

At that moment, as I fanned the paper dry, rolled it up, and tucked it in my sleeve, I suddenly remembered my poem of the night before. How could I have forgotten? I had to look on it again—and, indeed, copy it in more permanent form and store it safely. I returned to the corner where I had spent the night.

I could not find it. Where had I laid it, in that moment when I drifted to sleep? I remembered clearly my certainty of its greatness, my belief that it expressed a great insight in words of surpassing artistry...and yet, incredibly, I could not remember a word of it. In my need I did not hesitate to call for assistance. "A piece of paper, Fei Lien! It must be found!"

"Master, what—?"

"I wrote a poem last night. I cannot find it! Search everywhere!"

It does not take long to search a small, one-room hut. I left him still futilely turning around and opening our few pieces of baggage, and, in desperation, went outside to search the ground around the hut. Szu-ma Yu was standing and gazing outward, looking peaceful.

"I have lost a piece of paper..." I began.

"Yes?" he said.

"I had written a poem on it last night..."

"A thousand pardons," he said, turning to me. "I used a piece of paper to start the fire this morning. I save scraps for that purpose. Even in the summer, it gets cold here."

The breeze lifted tendrils of his hair and whiskers so that they stirred and floated about his face, and the early sun threw flickers of gold over him. I noticed again the strange quality of his eyes—wild, I had thought yesterday. Today they seemed deep and ancient. Under that gaze, instead of uttering a stricken cry and tearing my hair, I found myself strangely calm. After a moment, an idea raised a faint glimmer of hope. "Did you read it?"

"I did not notice the writing on it until it was in the fire," he said, regretfully. "Something about a dragon. You do not remember what you wrote?"

"No," I said. "No. Not a word. Strange..."

"I am very sorry," he said. "But you do have your other wonderful poem written about Lu-shan."

"Yes," I said, resigned. "I have that." I imagined releasing the poem into a wind and watching it be carried away. "Very likely it would have struck me as trite and embarrassing when I reread it in the light of day. This has mercifully spared me from such a deflation."

We stood for a moment in silence, looking across the peaceful valley.

"The general may be in search of a teacher, to guide him to wisdom, Venerable One," I said.

"It was in my thought to have him stay with me for a while," said Szu-ma Yu.

"I almost envy him."

"Almost?"

"My daily affairs cause me considerable frustrations…. Treacherous court politics, too much travel, not enough quiet."

"And yet?" said Szu-ma Yu.

"I like to think that my work is of some benefit to others."

"By adding up numbers?"

"What I actually do is keep corruption in check."

"Ah," he said.

A short while later, as we prepared to leave, Szu-ma Yu bade farewell to my servants each in turn, giving some words of parting that were apt for each one. My nephew he encouraged in his studies. To Hsiao Kang, who rarely speaks, he said, "Good fortune to you, peaceful one! 'The man without anger and without violence, him should you befriend, for he is noble.'" Hsiao Kang bowed deeply.

He thanked Teng Ai for his skillful cooking, told Chuan Hsu a joke, and gave Kai Huan a bag of herbs with instructions for mixing a poultice for treating neck pain. He smiled and told Fei Lien to stay in practice and keep his body agile, but his tongue circumspect. Fei Lien had formerly been a popular entertainer who had been famous for his flawless impersonations of public figures, but his career had been cut short by an unfortunate misjudgment in the nobleman he had chosen to caricature. Apparently Fei Lien must have told him his story—and somehow I had slept through the conversation. Szu-ma Yu accompanied each parting with a long, direct gaze before the other bowed and moved to take his station, which lent the occasion great solemnity.

He spoke to me last of all, and only said, "I hope you will return to Lu-shan."

And I bowed and said, "I hope that, as well."

"Do you wish to write a final poem, for the departure from the mountain?" Fei Lien asked me.

"Ah! Oh. Yes. I do, certainly."

Fei Lien produced my brush, ink, and paper, and I looked outward and thought, but no words came.

I looked at the rest of my servants, as they waited, and I realized that they were all talking together and laughing, or, in the case of Hsiao Kang, simply looking peaceful and contented, and no one was complaining or bickering. Even Kan Pao was ignoring his scrolls and was listening with respect to Teng Ai, who was telling a story.

"What do you see, Fei Lien?" I asked, at a loss.

"Rocks, trees, waterfalls, a little morning mist...the view is very rewarding."

I pondered.

Finally, I wrote:

> *Where may be found*
> *the things that slip from our grasp?*
> *—In the mists of Lu-shan.*

I hung it on a tree near Szu-ma Yu's hut, and we began our descent.

The Book of the Wing-ed Devils

Beauty when unadorned is adorned the most.
- St. Jerome

Men are nearer the truth in their superstitions than in their science.
- Henry David Thoreau

You cannot wake a person who is pretending to be asleep.
- Navajo Proverb

241

NINE

BACKWARDS COMPATIBILITY

ERIN LJUNGDAHL

Erin Ljungdahl has been writing books since the tender age of seven. Her first book was bound in cardboard and wrapping paper. With the release of **Backwards Compatibility**, she has achieved her dream of publication and can now focus on her ultimate goal: figuring out how to survive exclusively on desserts. Erin lives with her husband, cats, and Siamese fighting fish in Herndon, Virginia.

N ame?"

"Josephine Carlos."

"Full name?"

"Josephine Lois Carlos."

"No married name?"

Josephine hated reception-bots. Their programmers always seemed to leave out the capacity for tact. "No, I am single."

The robot somehow managed to make a tongue-clicking noise which was impressive considering it didn't have anything close to a tongue. "What is your date of birth?"

"July 3, 2133."

"You're twenty-eight and you're not married? Have you been referred to the Partner Clinic before?"

The incredulous tones the robot took with those questions made Josephine clench her fists and focus on the self-control necessary not to slam a fist into the robot's eye-level monitor. "Yes, I am twenty-eight and not married. Yes, I have been referred to the Partner Clinic but I am just not ready to become a parent yet."

"The Partner Clinic isn't just about becoming a mother— though everyone should do their part to recover the USNA's population—it's about finding a companion. Aren't you lonely?"

"My work keeps me company."

And it was true. Josephine L. Carlos, Ph.D., was a rising star on the archaeology scene in the United States of North America. Her research in early twentieth-century American film never wanted for material to study in San Angelago, Pacific Province. Despite the region's bounty, the survivors of the Island Building

Wars weren't much interested in old movies. Too many pictures were just too many men trying to solve problems that current technologies never would allow: the movie-going audience just couldn't relate.

"A smart woman like you would be an excellent mother. A partner-bot could tend the children while you're working. I'll make a note for the doctor to counsel you on the options the Partner Clinic offers. Take a seat in the waiting room."

For a robot supposedly capable of listening, the reception-bot didn't seem to care what Josephine had to say. Realizing there was no point in arguing with a robot, Josephine pulled her trench coat closer to her body and shuffled into the busy waiting room.

Women were everywhere. That was the new normal after the war decimated the world's male population, but it was still unsettling to see so many women paired up with robots. Sure, the robots had covers to make them look less like C3PO and more like male super models, but the covers were always too perfect, they were impossible to mistake for human. Josephine took a seat in the corner where she could look out at the rest of the patients.

Shortly after she was seated, a heavily pregnant woman in a floral print dress lumbered up to her. "You look healthy enough, do you mind if I sit next to you?"

Josephine shook her head and the woman sank into the seat beside her. Rather than sitting quietly as Josephine would have preferred, the woman started chattering. "My name's Alice. I'm here for one of my last routine checkups and then this baby is outta here! What are you here for?"

"Routine physical."

"Oh, that's wonderful. I was terrified you might be sick. It's possible for mothers to catch diseases and then pass them onto their babies, you know."

Josephine nodded as she fished her immersion glasses out of her purse. She adjusted the arms of the glasses to fit her ears and started watching Gone with the Wind. The prelude had barely finished before she felt a tap on her shoulder. Josephine paused the show, propped the glasses on top of her head, and peered around to see who had tapped her.

Alice was smiling at her as she held hands with a tall robot whose dark brown cover was beautifully smooth and glowing, "This is my husband, Darius. He was parking the car when I walked in; he's such a dear."

"How nice."

Josephine made to put her immersion glasses back on her face but then Alice spoke again. "Are you here to get a physical so you can go to the Partner Clinic? That's where Darius and I met. It's the dream, being able to build the perfect man. He doesn't start arguments, he cleans up after himself, and best of all, he's all mine. It also helps that he lives to wait on me hand and foot."

"But can he give you what you really want?" Josephine didn't know where that question came from; the woman in front of her gave every indication of being utterly content with her partner-bot.

Taken by surprise, Alice blinked for a minute before stretching her wide red-painted lips into a smile. "Of course, I had him built to my specifications."

That was something Josephine didn't know about the clinic. Well, Josephine didn't know much about clinics in the first place seeing as she had worked to remain ignorant of the *activities* of the clinic. She tried to be casual as she asked her next question. "What did you have to do to get a custom partner-bot?"

Alice laughed now, any uncertainty that Josephine's first question may have summoned completely vanished. "Well, you can take a personality test or you can describe your dream date. If you're having trouble describing your dream date, they have a bunch of movies you can watch to get ideas. I didn't have any trouble of course, I've been dreaming of my partner since I was six."

A nurse stepped through the threshold of the doctor's hallway and shouted Josephine's name. Josephine wished Alice luck before walking towards the nurse and the open door. Her mind was churning: could she build the man of her dreams? The nurse guided Josephine to a private nook, took the usual outpatient measurements, and left when the doctor arrived.

"Good afternoon, Josephine. You are the picture of health. I would ask if there is anything on your mind but I see the receptionist left a rather interesting note in your file. You've been referred to the Partner Clinic every year since you were twenty-two, why are you still single?"

Josephine tucked a strand of long auburn hair behind her ear. "Well, at twenty-two, I had just started my doctorate program and didn't want any distractions. I've just kept busy since then and the timing never really felt right anyway."

"As such a bright young woman, surely you realize that any child you bear would be a valued member of society. San Angelago needs more people like you, Dr. Carlos. We need everybody to do their part in the war recovery."

"I realize that, but why am I pressured to do these things now when I'm trying to get my career off the ground?"

"Your career is secondary to what the country needs, and what the country needs is more babies. If you do not go to the Partner Clinic by the first of March, you will be escorted there forcibly. If you don't believe me, look into the Population Act of 2152 section thirty-seven."

The doctor scribbled something on a notepad, ripped off the top sheet, and handed it to Josephine before sweeping out the door. Josephine huffed a few times, not quite sad enough to cry but certainly angry at her treatment. Since when were doctors allowed to be so brusque?

When the nurse came back into the room to see what delayed her, Josephine asked, "How many women have been forcibly escorted to the Partner Clinic?"

The nurse studied Josephine. "None that I've seen. Most skip along as soon as they're able to go. It offers women a chance at normalcy that was only possible before the war. Trust me, if you go soon, you'll be glad you went."

"But it's not about finding a partner, it's about having an acceptable setting to have a child. Why do we call it a Partner Clinic when it's entirely secondary to the fertility clinic?"

"Before the war, people realized it was no good raising children with only one parent. These days, we have the technology to give every child two parents, so why wouldn't we?"

When Josephine was silent for a moment, the nurse continued, "Walk-ins are welcome at the Partner Clinic. Why don't you go now and get it over with before the grass grows any more underfoot?"

"Right." Josephine didn't say much else as she walked out of the doctor's office. The war ended ten years ago, and she could not fathom why women were still forced into these stupid arrangements. The male population was recovering at a steady clip; before too long the balance between men and women would be restored. It was ridiculous that Josephine should have no choice but to be matched with a partner and eventually made to have children. She made her way to the University of San Angelago and found Dr. Patel in the English Department's building. Becky Patel was writing out some lecture notes longhand when Josephine poked her head into her mentor's office.

"Becky, do you have a minute?"

Becky smiled and set her reading glasses down next to her notes. "Have a seat."

Josephine slumped into a chair on the other side of Becky's desk. "My doctor told me I have until the first of March to go to the Partner Clinic or I'll be taken there by force. Do you think the law school would help me file for an exemption from the Population Act of 2152?"

Becky shook her head, her long brown braid swinging behind her back. "Nobody's ever won an exemption case. The government is determined to recover the sex ratio. You'd better make time to go to the Partner Clinic. I can talk to your colleagues about covering your lectures if you'd like."

That wasn't the reaction Josephine expected or wanted to hear at all. Josephine threw her hands up in the air. "The ratio is recovering already without my help! More baby boys are being born every day; they're going to grow up soon and start having families of their own. I don't need to have a baby or a stupid robot, I need to be left alone to pursue my research!"

"I said the same thing, but I'm so happy I have William and the kids. Trust me, you'll be fine. It's very doable to manage a family and an academic career with a partner-bot."

Josephine started to roll her eyes but a thought occurred to her. "Wait, your partner-bot's name is William? Did you choose that name or was it assigned to him?"

Becky blinked and cleared her throat. "He was given the name William because I was going through a Shakespeare phase—don't laugh."

"Does your bot share anything else with William Shakespeare besides the name?"

"No, I just took a personality test and he was programmed to have a compatible character. Why do you ask?"

Josephine started to smile at the epiphany dawning on her like a brilliant sunrise. "I just had a hell of an idea, a way to turn lemons in lemonade. If I have no choice but to pair off with a partner-bot, why not turn it into a scientific inquiry? What if I try to build a partner modeled after an old movie star, both mentally and physically? I mean, what archaeologist has ever had the opportunity to resurrect a member of the past like this? No one can know for sure how Lucy would behave in modern Africa or how King Henry VIII would react to the world he shaped or if any of the ancient religious prophets' teachings would change in the face of current events. But I, Dr. Josephine Carlos, could study how a partner-bot programmed to resemble and mimic Clark Gable might react to American life in the twenty-second century. Why, this could be the greatest revolution in archaeology since the invention of the shovel!"

Becky stared at Josephine with wide eyes. "Josephine, I'm glad you've found a silver lining to this, but you need to be careful. The idea you have in your head of how Clark Gable was may be entirely different from the reality of Clark Gable, especially if you're going to be living and raising children with him."

"But that's part of the academic intrigue! Think of the research I could accomplish!"

Becky stood and started piling notepads and textbooks into a tote bag. "I have to head out to a seminar, but I want you to take time to think about this, Josephine. Don't go rushing into something you don't understand."

Josephine laughed and walked out the door. "But that's one of my favorite ways to learn!"

A light breeze and gentle sunshine greeted Josephine when she walked outside the stuffy office building. She set out on foot for the Partner Clinic on Victory Avenue. As she walked, she took stock of the day's events. She still wasn't thrilled by the prospect of being forced into a relationship with a robot and then motherhood shortly after, but if there was some degree of autonomy she could manage, maybe it wouldn't be so awful. Above all, she was pleased by her solution. She could kill not two but three birds with one stone: fulfill the irksome legal obligation, advance her career, and push the field of archaeology further into the future! It was perfect; the men in her old movies were perfect. Why hadn't anyone tried to build a partner with one of them as a model? Not just physically, but mentally. They were so different, so exciting, so unlike the modern life-sized Ken dolls who always stayed three steps behind their wives. Like she said, what archaeologist had ever had the opportunity to resurrect a relic of the past like this?

She arrived at the Partner Clinic with a very wide grin and the reception-bot was entirely unfazed. Clearly the nurse at the regular doctor's office wasn't joking about how happy most women were to be referred to the clinic. They went through the sign-in rigmarole with considerably less judgement than the first doctor's reception-bot and Josephine grew more convinced that she had made the right decision.

"All customization bays are currently occupied. The estimated wait time is twenty-five minutes. Please be seated in the reception lounge until your name is called."

Pleased by the efficiency, Josephine strolled over to the reception lounge where a stylish woman wearing bug-eye sunglasses sat. Josephine picked up a brochure called, "What to Expect in the Customization Bay."

She heard a snort from the woman wearing sunglasses. "I'll tell you what to expect – the robots are ten times better than any man alive right now."

That caught Josephine's attention. She set down the brochure and looked over at the woman. "You've met a living man?"

"I was married to one. Kind of, it was a harem situation. Let's just say I got pregnant and I wanted a man who would actually help me raise a kid."

"Was it hard to leave?"

The woman rested her sunglasses on top of her head and fixed Josephine with shining blue eyes. "The act of leaving was easy, it was the fact that I was so easily replaced that was hard to swallow. Trust me, you're better off getting a bot than a man."

"So… do you know what you're going to request in the Customization Bay?"

"I know exactly what I want: dog-loyal, no back hair."

The woman didn't say any more and Josephine turned back to the brochure. She skimmed the description of the personality programming and physical feature setting but considered what the woman in sunglasses said. If current men were inferior to robots, surely men from the past must be ten times better than both. At any rate, she could certainly see to it that she got the best of the men from the past. Josephine pulled out her holo-puter and started digging through her files on Clark Gable. Ostensibly she kept files on old movie stars to make research papers easier to write, but they certainly had value when trying to determine how to describe her desired companion's programming.

"Josephine Lois Carlos. Please report to Customization Bay Five."

Josephine actually skipped over to the specified area and was awed by the simplicity and elegance of the machinery. She almost forgot her objections to the circumstances as she worked her way through the seductive interface. First she completed the personality section. She was supposed to answer questions about her own preferences and behaviors honestly but she changed her answers to be compatible with what she imagined Clark Gable would be like. This was the stuff Pygmalion dreamed about but could never have imagined. And to think this bounty was all for women. The physical customization process was a blur and the cheerful attendant bot informed her that her companion would be ready for her within three days' time.

The three days Josephine waited were a mix of excitement and apprehension. She could barely bring herself to eat or sleep; the anticipation was driving her mad. Her previous scholarship far from her mind, she started designing her research plans for her partner-bot. The head of the Archaeology Department reviewed her outlines and fell prey to similar excitement. Truly, this was something new and groundbreaking. Dr. Becky Patel and several other colleagues had some misgivings, but Josephine couldn't be bothered to listen. She was single-mindedly focused on receiving the call from the Partner Clinic telling her that her partner bot was finally waiting for her at the Clinic. The day the call finally came, she almost didn't know what to do. For a brief moment, her previous misgivings about the arrangement and the law surfaced, but then curiosity got the better of her and she raced off to meet her partner-bot.

She hit the power button on the partner-bot and his eyes glittered an exquisite shade of grayish green. The way his lips curved into a smile made Josephine weak at the knees.

Her voice quavered as she breathed, "Hello."

"Hello there, Josephine."

She couldn't help herself; the giddiness was too much to be contained. She covered her mouth with her hands. A heartbeat passed and the robot gently brushed her hands away and gazed into her eyes.

His voice was velvet, chocolate, and marble smooth. "Do you need to sit down? I'm told my presence sometimes has an effect on women."

Josephine started to laugh but then he pressed a kiss to her lips.

In the background, the reception-bot started describing the partner-bot's maintenance schedule and other mechanical facts, but Josephine couldn't be bothered to listen. Here was Clark Gable, here was her ticket to academic fame and fortune. "…You have two months to get settled before you are expected to report to the Fertility Clinic to select donor material…"

Josephine started. Two months? They had only two months before they had the rug pulled out from under them? Her train of thought was derailed by the Clark Gable bot asking her questions about herself and giving her compliments about her hair and eyes.

"What are you going to call me?"

She almost blurted out what felt natural and right, but then thought for a minute. This wasn't actually Clark Gable, this was a robot who was similar but not exactly the same, "Neo-Clark Gable."

"All right then. Josephine Lois Gable."

"Oh, you see, I'm going to keep my name. I'm an academic, so it's best that I have my work under a consistent name."

"I see."

That was the beginning of a blissful honeymoon period. He was everything Josephine never knew she wanted but was oh so happy to have. Her research saw an explosion of productivity and her colleagues at the Archaeology Department grew to look forward to her presentations and their guest of honor: Neo-Clark Gable.

Then one day, Josephine burst into their apartment waving a letter in one hand.

"Clark! Angel! I've been asked to give a presentation at the Henry Jones Lecture Series! Isn't it wonderful?"

"Yeah, wonderful," Neo-Clark deadpanned.

Josephine's smile fell as she took in the sight of Neo-Clark slouching in front of the holo-theatre, "Clark, angel, aren't you happy for me?"

"Of course, it's great. I'm so proud of you." There was no warmth in his tone, all the sweetness that his voice had in their first meeting totally gone. He sounded tired and disengaged.

"You don't sound like you mean it," Josephine answered quietly with tears rising in her eyes.

"Well, how do you think I feel? Waiting on you hand and foot while you go from lecture hall to cocktail party while all your colleagues and admirers gawk at me like some thawed ice man? When are we going to do what we're supposed to and have a baby already?"

There was desperation in Josephine's response; she wrung her hands before trying to rub Neo-Clark's back. "We will, it's just that my career is doing so well and I'm having just so much fun with just you. We'll get started as soon as I come back from the lecture series, okay?"

"The Partner Clinic made it clear that we had two months to get comfortable and then we had to go to the Fertility Clinic. It's been six weeks and you've been at work every day but Sunday for the last five weeks. But that's fine, it's not like I have a choice."

"Oh, don't say things like that!"

"Why not? It's the truth."

"I hope your personality software gets an update by the time I'm back!"

The door slammed behind her as Josephine fled the apartment to the sanctuary of her office at the University of San Angelago. Her colleagues tutted sympathetically – it was always a matter of time before newly matched women discovered that it was possible to fight with even perfectly-programmed partners.

"Have you ever considered things from Neo-Clark's perspective?" Becky asked.

"What do you mean?" Josephine tilted her head and watched her mentor hem and haw.

"Well, his personality is from two hundred years ago but his programming is modern. Can you see how there might be compatibility issues? Maybe someone from the Computer Science department can help you figure things out."

"But the Partner Clinic never mentioned any issues with doing this sort of thing."

"Well, most of the population doesn't have the advanced degrees in archaeology and the opportunity to fall in love with historical figures that you had, dear."

Josephine sighed, memories of their conversation from a couple months ago flooding her mind. To Josephine's surprise, it wasn't the fact that Becky was right that bothered her the most, it was the feeling of being terribly lost and not knowing what to do next. "What should I do?"

"I don't understand why you're asking me, I've never been in that situation with my android."

After her colleagues left her alone, Josephine found work impossible. She couldn't focus on her lecture series, she couldn't focus on her other research, she couldn't focus long enough to remember why she kept checking her phone. Finally she gave up at a quarter to three and went home to try to resolve things with Neo-Clark.

She arrived at the apartment and found it dark and empty. A magnet on the refrigerator held up a note that read:

Josephine,

I can't take it anymore. I'm sorry to leave this way, without a goodbye or by-your-leave, but I have to do this. But who am I kidding? Frankly. my dear, I don't give a damn what you think. Go on your lecture tour, go have a baby, don't have a baky. It doesn't matter to me—you never mattered to me! Next time design a bot who won't feel the drive of your stiletto heel into his back or the glaring inadequacy that comes from standing in your shadow. I'm finished!

No longer yours,

Neo-Clark

Josephine read the note again and again, crumpled the paper in her hands, uncrumpled it, and used it to blot tears from her eyes. How could this happen? Had this ever happened to a woman before? She started to turn her colleagues' words over and over in her head but it didn't make any more sense than it did the first time she heard it. Her head was pounding after crying her eyes dry, so she did the only thing she could think to do: take a long drink of tequila and resolve to think about it tomorrow.

Ten

The Twin Dilemma

Jeffrey C. Jacobs

Jeffrey C. "TimeHorse" Jacobs is a failed physicist, professional software engineer, driving an electric car around the Mid-Atlantic. He assists local writing groups, Doctor Who societies, cosplays, organizes EV events, runs Science Book Clubs and created and produces Project Kronosphere. His published works are listed on Amazon.

@TimeHorse
facebook.com/TimeHorse
amazon.com/Jeffrey-C.-Jacobs/e/B00EZX0ZU8

THE TWIN DILEMMA

Simon Olsen sat alone for lunch. The Department of Grief Counseling cafeteria was full of twin siblings chatting away; it only deepened his isolation. And his mashed turnips were soggy. This was not Simon's day.

Simon wished he had a Twin Sister, just like every other guy. It wasn't so much he hated being alone, without a sibling companion, it was that he knew he was different, a Singleton.

He finished his lunch and returned to his cubicle to take the next bereavement call.

"We buried my brother in Wathake this week." The woman on the phone choked out the words through what sounded like sobbing. Wathake lay distant a number of hours by train, about halfway to the coast.

"I'm so sorry, ma'am. Really I am. May I just know your name, so I can help you better—you only need to give me your first name."

"Monica."

"It's a pleasure to meet you, Monica. My name's Simon." He gave Monica some time to collect herself. Losing a sibling who was identical to you in all but gender was about the most devastating blow a person could know. At least, it would be if he had a Twin.

Despite his handicap, Simon made an excellent grief counselor. He was one of the agency's best consultants. He was sure his cover story was part of the reason. Since everybody has a Twin, they all assumed he was a Twin Widower himself.

"How old were you both?" Simon always smiled during his phone calls. He found the inflections produced dismantled the walls folks in sorrow tended to erect.

"Twenty-seven." Monica seemed to have calmed.

"Were you both married?" Marriages tended to exacerbate the bereavement process. Simon knew each of the three parties would have to be dealt with in their own, individual way, the grieving sister, the wife who lost her husband, and the husband/brother upon whose shoulders it fell upon to hold it all together.

"Yes. They don't know I'm calling."

"What you're going through is nothing to be ashamed of, Monica. Many people experience the profound sense of loss that you're feeling now. We're here to help. And not just you, your sister-in-law and husband can call us at any time too. We're not just for consoling siblings. Our goal is to help everyone through their time of need."

Monica and Simon continued to chat, Monica telling Simon all about her childhood and times with her brother with Simon occasionally prodding her to reveal more. After it was all done, Monica breathed a long, cathartic sigh. "Thank you, Simon."

"I'm just glad I could help you."

"You did! You're much better than the creepy counselor I spoke to in Wathake. That Jen should be fired. Take care, Simon." And with that, she disconnected.

This wasn't the first complaint Simon had had from the Wathake office. He didn't know who this Jen was but he worried her days may be numbered. Still, losing your job wasn't that big a deal for a pair of Twins. Usually the other one would find another job quickly and bring the originally fired one along. It wasn't like the ostracizing of a Singleton.

Even so, Simon decided to help. He could remember what it was like for him, when he started out, and knew he would have appreciated a pep talk. He called the Wathake office and asked to speak to Jen.

"Hello?" Jen's voice was wavering, uncertain and youthful, not at all what Simon expected.

"Hello, Jen? My name is Simon, from central office. Is everything okay?"

Jen hesitated. "Am I in trouble?"

"I certainly hope not. I just want to make sure you're at your peak performance to aid those who need our support. Is there anything I can do to help?"

"That's all right. I'm good." The wavering of Jen's voice intensified.

"You don't sound good. How's your brother doing?"

"I don't have a brother!"

Simon was taken aback by the brusqueness of her reply. "I'm very sorry, Jen. I don't have a sister either. Most of us are Twin Widowers in this office."

Jen's breathing slowed before she responded. "Sorry. I'm just very sensitive about my Twin. He passed away when we were really young."

"What was his name?"

Jen hesitated. "Jeffrey?"

"How old were you when he passed? Do you have any memories of him?"

Jen demurred. "Um, I was really young."

Simon didn't want to push since she was clearly repeating herself and not going to give any more information. Always respect the bereaved's wishes.

As he was chatting, a message popped up on Simon's screen. "Simon, when you're done with that call, could you see me in my office?" It was from his boss, Martin.

Simon worried he might be in trouble for making a personal call on company time. "Listen, Jen, try to calm down when you're talking to the grieving. You need to relax. Don't let your personal story interfere with the counseling. I have to go, but would it be okay if I call you again?"

"Thank you, Simon. I'll try to take your advice and look forward to hearing from you again. Bye."

"Bye." Simon disconnected and rushed to Martin's office while pondering Jen's intriguing story and voice.

Martin was kind but prone to eccentricities. He was a legitimate Twin Widower and tended to hire widows and widowers for his department. His office was bland, consisting of a single bookcase of old books from the home world. Something by someone named Shakespeare, another by a fellow named Dickens, and a bunch by some woman named Rowling. He sat behind a large, plastic desk and greeted Simon with a smile as he entered.

"You wanted to see me, sir."

"Simon, yes, sit down."

The metal seat was cold. Simon knew he had to take ownership of his situation and wanted it to be quick to avoid one of his boss's meandering stories. He tried to get as comfortable as the chair would allow. "If this is about the call to the Wathake office, that was DGC business, honest."

"Simon, please. There's nothing wrong with using the company lines to make personal calls. You've been here, how long is it now?"

"Seventeen years, sir."

"Seventeen. So, you should know that by now."

Simon relaxed, but was now unsure why he was there.

"In fact, you're quite the veteran. I've always been proud of your work, Simon." Martin leaned back in his swivel chair and tented his fingers.

"Thank you, sir." Simon tried to grin despite the chair back support sticking in his spine.

"Now, Simon, you're not from around here, are you?"

"No, sir." Simon tensed, he never liked discussing his past.

"It must be hard, not being able to visit your sister's grave." Martin leaned forward, resting his elbows on the desk. "You're from Anteran, aren't you?"

"Yes?" The beam for maintaining lumbar support was now digging into Simon's right kidney like some kind of ancient torture device. He gripped the handrails of his chair until his knuckles were white.

"Well, you're in luck. It just so happens the DGC has some business in Anteran, and I'm going to need someone to help me interface with the folks there. I couldn't think of anyone more appropriate than you." Martin stood and held out his hand.

Simon just stared. He couldn't go back to Anteran. He just couldn't. No doubt they'd run into people who knew his secret, or try to get him to visit the non-existent grave of his imagined sister. It was easy enough to hide his perversion so far away from home, but if they forced him to go back, he'd no longer be able to hide it. He had to think of something.

Martin pulled back his hand, his eyes downcast with concern. "What's the matter? Surely you'd like to go home. It's a chance to visit your sister's final resting place."

"Sir…"

"What is it?" Martin gave Simon a sly look. "You don't have a girlfriend you've been hiding from us, do you? A nice, young widow like yourself?"

Simon had tried dating. A woman with a Twin Brother would never sacrifice her sibling to lifelong bachelorhood due to Simon's lack of a sister. And the women who were Twin Widows would always end up asking to see his sister's grave and leave him when he'd never agree. He had no issue visiting the grave of their brothers, but Simon wasn't sure if he could offer them anything in return. He wished he had a Twin who could just find him a wife through her husband's sister. But even then, he would curse all his children with the forbidden, dominant Singleton gene.

At least if he had a girlfriend, he wouldn't be so lonely. He'd learned to live without a Twin, what he really wanted was someone with whom he could be romantic. Someone who could keep him from having to face being found a Singleton in his home town. Simon shook his head, negatively.

"Well, then, it's settled. You're coming with me. We leave tomorrow at nine sharp."

"But sir, if we leave that late, we'll be traveling all day and most of the night."

Martin smiled sheepishly. "Rank has its privileges, Simon. I'm authorized to take the agency jet."

The plane was not much bigger than a bus with wings. Simon was still impressed, having never seen any flying craft before. Such travel was far too energy-expensive for ordinary citizens. At least he'd have less time to stew in his concern. During the flight, Simon feigned napping to avoid any more probing questions from his supervisor.

The flight arrived just after noon and Simon and Martin quickly collected their bags. The sea air greeted them. Simon had forgotten how soothing he found the smell of the ocean.

"I don't know about you, but I'm famished. I bet you know a good place to eat. I suddenly feel in the mood for Hexapus." Martin wet his lips.

"Assuming it's still open, there's always The Angler's Catch down on the pier. They have some amazing Blue Hexapus Tentacles which are brought in daily, so it's quite fresh."

They hired a taxi and made their way downtown, chatting idly about The Angler's Catch menu. When they got to the restaurant, they ordered quickly, and Simon tried to keep his mouth full to prevent the conversation from digging too deeply.

Fortunately, Simon didn't recognize anyone at the restaurant.

"It's weird how other animals risk a gender imbalance, living Singleton lives, randomly creating male or female individuals, like flish or hexapods or crunchies, rather than balancing the genders to keep any individual from being left out." Martin ate slowly, prodding his Hexapus as he spoke.

Simon recalled that flish spawn actually choose gender based on nest temperature, but decided not to encourage another one of his boss's rants.

"Thank goodness science solved the problem for humanity on this world, back when we had scientists and all that high tech. It's not like we could get folks to spend generations immigrating here to re-balance things. Can you imagine what it was like during colonial times with ten to one male to female ratios? It's not like a woman could have ten husbands. Five at most, but not ten." Martin chuckled.

Simon continued eating while Martin kept lecturing, afraid to let his boss know his story was common knowledge to a nursery school student. He was happy when the bill came and Martin paid it.

That afternoon they spent in meetings at the Anteran DGC office, Martin doing most of the talking, occasionally having Simon explain more of the technical details of correct protocol when counseling. They worked until sundown and agreed to meet again after lunch the next day.

In his hotel, Simon opened the window and fell asleep to the sounds of waves and the smell of surf. He was awakened by a loud rapping on his door.

"Simon, are you up?" Martin's voice shook the door as he called into the room. He sounded like he'd consumed a gallon of coffee.

Simon opened his eyes to the dawn light. "Hang on, sir. Let me get dressed."

"Take your time, Simon. I'll be at breakfast so just look for me when you're ready."

Simon didn't understand why he had to wake so early when their meetings weren't until the afternoon but he showered, brushed, shaved, and dressed, and met Martin in the dining room forty-five minutes later.

"Great, you're up! I have a surprise for you. We're going on a trip this morning."

Simon was too tired to speculate on what his boss might have in store and just nodded. It was probably some DGC business at a field office.

After they'd both finished eating, the concierge took them to a waiting car. Once they were in, the car sped off in the direction of the edge of town.

Coffee having cleared his brain somewhat, Simon finally started to worry. "Where are we going?"

"You'll see!" Martin's grin was brighter than Simon had ever seen it.

As the car approached the Anteran Cemetery, Simon's eyes became like saucers. "Stop the car!"

"Now Simon, calm down. Your sister has been waiting years for this reunion. I let the whole Anteran DGC know. They're all waiting to pay their respects."

Simon tried the car doors, but they were locked. He knew there was no avoiding this, but he wasn't about to let himself be taken by Purity Agents and left to die on an emigration transport.

"I know you're excited, Simon, but please, wait until we stop the car." Martin was oblivious to the concern on Simon's face.

Simon had to think quickly. His parents had a fake plot for Simone, Simon's imagined sister, but with records being audited constantly to make room for more deceased, he worried that it might no longer be there.

The car stopped and Martin and Simon came out to meet the leader of the Anteran DGC and her brother.

The head of the local office was first to approach. "There's a problem. We can't find Simone Olsen."

Simon was afraid of this, but he knew he'd have to play indigent. "Can't find my sister? How could you lose her?"

The brother stepped forward. "We checked with the registrar. There's never been anyone here by that name and your shared date of birth, Mr. Olsen."

"Did you even bother to look for the headstone?" Simon rushed forward, into the graveyard, hoping at least the fake marker would still be present.

Martin, the twins, and the whole contingent trailed behind.

As Simon approached the designated plot, he could see the fake stone had been replaced. He decided to ignore it and keep moving. "Come on, it's this way!"

Martin was panting. "Is it much farther, Simon. I had a lot of coffee, you know, and I really need to use the facilities."

After they'd made a circuit of the perimeter, the head woman stopped. "This is ridiculous, we've been here before. You're just taking us in circles."

Simon halted too. He hoped the adventure would put them off his trail. "Listen, if you don't want to pay your respects, that's fine. I appreciate you all coming but I can just carry on by myself."

Martin was by now hopping from foot to foot. "Fine, Simon, I'll meet you at the car."

The whole party headed back to the entry gate.

Simon wandered through the grave markers. He knew his ruse would only delay the inevitable. He'd faced this before. It's why he had to leave his home town. He finally approached the gate house.

Inside, Martin was rifling through index cards. "It doesn't make any sense."

Simon took a deep breath. "I've very much enjoyed working for you at the DGC."

Martin looked up. "Thank you, Simon. I feel the same way. But will you look at this? I can't find your sister's entry. Was she maybe cremated?"

Simon crossed his arms. "Don't bother, sir. I've done a lot of thinking and quite frankly, I quit."

Martin dropped the card he was looking at. "Quit? You can't be serious. You're one of my best counselors! If it's about Simone's lost record, we can fix that. I'm sure it's just a paperwork snafu."

"My mind's made up. I'm going back to the hotel to pick up my things. I'll take the evening train back. Good bye, Martin." Simon held out his hand.

Teary-eyed, Martin pulled Simon into a fatherly embrace. "Safe journey."

It took Simon most of the afternoon to walk back to the hotel. He'd have to disappear inside the capital. He'd need a new identity, just in case Martin or the Anteran DGC found out the truth. But he could handle that. He just needed to start again. He was sure he could keep ahead of the Purity Agents. He had to.

At the hotel, Simon packed up his things, then made his way to the train station. The next train to the capital would leave in an hour and Simon decided to have one last, local delicacy before boarding. He ate one Brine Hexapus at the station and saved one for the day long train trip home.

When Simon boarded the train, it was mostly empty. He chose a place by the window and opened it to enjoy his last wisps of ocean breeze. As day turned to night, he rested his eyes and slouched onto the adjacent seat.

When Simon awoke, he noticed they were approaching Wathake. He was hungry so when the train stopped, he retrieved his saved Hexapus.

A number of Twins boarded at the station, accompanied by a handful of Twin Widows and Widowers.

There came a wavering voice from behind. "Excuse me, is this seat taken?"

Simon froze. He recognized that inflection.

"I'm sorry, yes, my brother is in the restroom."

Simon called out. "Jen! Is that you!?" He was astonished by what he saw.

Jen was a rather attractive woman about Simon's age. She seemed a bit bookish, a bit reserved but Simon only found that more alluring. Fortunately, she didn't at all resemble Simon, as that would have been weird. After all, estranging Twins was a criminal offense.

Simon hoped he could have this attractive woman to sit next to for the rest of the long ride. Still, he'd never have a chance with her. No woman could find someone like him desirable. Simon moved to make a place for Jen. "It's me, Simon. Come and sit here." He held out his hand.

"Is that really you, Simon? I didn't expect you to be so…" Jen hesitated, then blushed. "Handsome."

Simon found her skin soft and her grip gentle when they shook. "It's so nice to finally meet you in person. Especially someone as pretty as yourself."

Jen sat and went red. "Thanks." She smiled nervously.

"So, where are you headed?"

"I'm going to the capital. Burned too many bridges in Wathake. Figure it's time to start fresh where no one knows my name."

Simon could sympathize. After all, that's how he'd ended up where he did. He handed Jen the rest of his Hexapus. "Hungry?"

She hesitated, then gobbled the food in one bite. "Thank you so much. I've not eaten since yesterday." She seemed to relax.

Simon grew concerned. "So how goes things at the Wathake DGC office?"

Jen sighed and frowned. "I was let go."

"Really? I was hoping my advice would help. I'm so sorry. If it's any consolation, I just quit."

"Why? You were great on the phone, kind and sincere. I was so shocked when you called. It was really nice of you to try and help. But it just wasn't going to work out. They kept prying about my brother. I was just getting sick hearing about Jeremy."

Even still-born Twins had names which were embedded in a survivor's memory. "Didn't you say his name was Jeffrey?"

Jen panicked, grabbed her bag, and began to rise from her seat, her eyes scanning the train. "Excuse me."

Simon took a risk and grasped Jen's arm before she could go. "Wait, there's something I have to tell you. Something secret."

Jen stared back, unsure what she should do. She sat back down but still clutched her bags tightly.

Simon lowered his voice to practically a whisper. "I'm a Singleton."

Jen's eyes went wide. "What?"

"I'm a Singleton. I have no Twin Sister. I never had a Twin Sister. I was born an only child."

Jen's eyes darted with suspicion. "Are you a Purity Agent? Is this some kind of trap?"

"I swear it's true. I'm a Singleton, and I've been hiding from the Purity Agents all my life. That's why I quit. They were getting too close. But I know what I'm doing. Come with me, and I'll teach you."

Jen remained silent, her face tight with uncertainty.

Simon looked deeply into Jen's eyes. "All my life I've wanted to meet someone like me, like you. It's been so lonely hiding by myself. It must be fate, me meeting you, here, like this. We no longer have to be alone. I mean, maybe we could even be more than friends."

Jen stared at Simon for what seemed like hours.

Simon was glad she was no longer trying to run away. He supposed it was a good sign. He felt so much desire for her.

"You're right. I'm a Singleton. I thought I would have to be alone forever." Jen wrapped her arms around Simon and gave him a delicate kiss on the lips. "And I definitely think we can be more than just friends."

ELEVEN

COUNCIL FOR THE RIGHT POPULATION OF EARTH

SUSAN SAYLER

Susan Sayler is a futurist with a degree in humanities. She is fascinated by transhumanism and the ways that applied science will broaden the capacities of the human race. Susan's writings are often a marriage of the transformative power of technology and the tender touch of the human condition.

Susan's blog is *The Future Global Universe*
globalempress.blogspot.com

272

COUNCIL FOR THE RIGHT POPULATION OF EARTH

The facilitator appeared at the podium. "The Council for the Right Population of Earth will now come to order."

Everyone shifted in their seats, as if doing so was a required ritual.

"Today is April 1st, 2050. It is 9 A.M. Eastern Standard Time."

Chairman Joshua Mono sat in the center of a panel made up exclusively of the wealthiest one percent of Americans. He turned to the facilitator and asked, "Do we have a quorum in attendance?"

"We do, Mr. Chairman," the facilitator replied.

"Very well, let us begin." Chairman Mono cleared his voice. "As you all know, today begins the hearings on the Compassionate Care of Earth Act voted into law last year. This law requires the elimination of excess population in order to curb the spread of toxic human culture and to preserve the Earth's diminishing resources."

Chairman Mono looked up with impatience as the audience that was gathered around the outer perimeter of the Congressional meeting hall made disruptive noises; some were booing and others were chanting catchy, creative-sounding slogans. Most of them were protestors that had managed their way into the hearing. The more disruptive ones were quickly silenced and many were being removed by an endless sea of Android police officers, now pouring into the area.

"We are convened today to make decisions regarding who, if any, of the excess labor force are still viable in light of the post-labor economy. We have separated out the hearings by industry. The hearing on manufacturing will be run by I-Sony robotic labor and will convene in Meeting Hall 2B. Sales and advertising,

273

handled exclusively by Googlebuy, will meet in Hall 2C. Medical and healthcare, which is predominately run by our Blue Cross Android professionals and wearable computer technology, will meet on the third floor. Check the schedule up there for which room."

An Android servant quietly filled Chairman Mono's sparkling crystal glass with genuine glacier melted water, the latest thing in healthy, high alkalinity, low acidity water. He sipped and then continued. "Amazon-PrintGo covers all retail and delivery, using drones and 3D on-demand printing technology. For information on possible continued human employment, join that meeting on the third floor. Teaching is entirely run by Artificial Intelligence programs and will require no further human employment. The hospitality industry, including restaurants, hotels, cruises, and tourism is now almost completely robot and android controlled but a panel will hear testimony on a few proposals. They are meeting on the fourth floor in the Drumpf Room."

He glanced up at the commotion still happening on the periphery and, after scowling, added, "All other industries and professions not previously mentioned should meet in the general conference room on the first floor for further information. It is unlikely that any humans will be asked to stay on in any industry not already mentioned. Those who are chosen to continue will be required to sign the agreement for mandatory sterilization. There will be no offspring rights."

The few remaining protestors still in the hall began to shout in unison and were quickly tasered by Android police officers and carried out of the hall.

Chairman Mono stood up and said, "The intellectual property, documentation, and legal professions will meet in this room in fifteen minutes. We will begin at precisely 9:30 A.M. The first person on the agenda will be Olivia Thurgood from Documentation."

Panel members of the Council for the Right Population of Earth all stood from their chairs and stretched. They huddled together in front of a large window; watching protestors wearing Guy Fawkes masks shout idle threats outside from a gathering on the National Mall. Their fists were raised. Episodes of crowd rioting were quickly suppressed by the Android Guard of the National Capital Region.

One protestor accosted a well-known member of the mainstream media. "You are partly to blame, you know!" he shouted, "You only reported what the one-percenters wanted you to report. And where did it get you? Now they have AI bots to do all of their reporting for them, and you are slated to be eliminated like the rest of us. Choke on that irony, scum bag!"

The news reporter replied, "I seem to recall that you were upper management at the Android manufacturing plant, where they programmed the Androids to make copies of themselves and perform all the needed maintenance to keep their own systems running. How is your past any better than mine?"

The angry protestor's girlfriend stepped into the conversation. "We were never told what the ultimate product was that we were making; we were all on a 'need to know' basis. How were we supposed to know we were manufacturing machines that would be our downfall?"

Two young men standing behind the news reporter overheard the conversation. Both looked resigned to their fates. The taller one said, "This is all so hopeless, we have no power over them or over our own lives. We are doomed!"

The shorter one patted his friend's shoulder in a conciliatory way. "Well, it may not be too late yet to convert to Islam. If we have to be eliminated, at least we should sign up for the seventy-two virgins they all get when they die."

In the meeting hall, all those protesters outside were barely audible.

The facilitator for the intellectual property, documentation and legal professions hearing opened the meeting. "It is 9:30 A.M. This meeting will now come to order."

Chairman Mono said, "Please call the first person on the agenda."

"Will the spokesperson for the Documentation Office please step up to the podium?"

A timid middle-aged woman quickly approached the panel.

Chairman Mono began. "So, if I am to be clear, you are a team of very specialized document writers."

"Correct."

"And you are their spokesperson?"

"Yes, Mr. Chairman, sir. I am the unit supervisor, sir, Olivia Thurgood."

"Fine, Miss Thurgood. Now, you say your team is a model for how to manage the current crisis in machine intelligence where documentation errors still exist."

"Yes, we have created a great collaborative model that is working well in our office, sir."

"Great, then can you tell our panel about it?"

"Sure. I have with me here on my right, Noah, who is our small i-dotter and t-crosser. Ava here on my left is our period and comma inserter. She also puts accent marks on foreign words. Mason, next to Ava there on her right, inserts quotes, exclamation marks, and other punctuation. Next, higher on the chain of command, is Ethan, who is our vowel specialist and his counterpart, Sophia, who is our consonant specialist. Consonant specialists also fill in as capitalization specialists and can sub-specialize in acronyms."

"I see."

Olivia turned to face the rest of her group. "Can I have everyone from the Documentation Department raise their hands? Thank you."

She turned back to the panel, adding, "I didn't mention Madison, wearing the blue blazer. Her area of expertise is the hashtag symbol on social networking sites which, for your information, used to be called *the pound sign*."

"Excuse me," said Chairman Mono. "I am sorry to interrupt you, but why would humans be optimal for this kind of work? Obviously all of this can be done by Artificial Intelligence document writers."

A council member seated on the panel quickly spoke up. "In my opinion, it is very important that we have humans overseeing the documents we, as members of the Elite, post for posterity's sake." He took time to look everyone else on the panel in the eye. "I would like to point out a few problems with AI auto correct, for example. One document that referred to a dearly beloved member of this council had a misspelling on his Twitter feed obituary. It read, "May he *rust in piece*." Of course, a human would know it should have said, *Rest in peace*." One may have mistaken him for a reference to some machine relic of the past! And you can imagine the uprising that *rust in piece* could have created with older intelligent machines that still have many working metal parts."

Another council member on the panel also elected to share his thoughts. "And as I recall, the individual who wrote that obituary tried to explain himself by posting on Facebook: *Autocorrect makes me say things I don't Nintendo*. Of course, what he meant to say was, *Autocorrect makes me say things I don't Intend to*."

"Hmmm."

"Commas are important!" He continued as though a great orator. "Consider the mayhem that happened that time when, after a few drinks, a politician we all know wrote on Twitter: *A woman without her man is nothing*. He was trying to sound poetic and what he meant to write was *A woman: , without her, comma, man is nothing*. Needless to remind everyone of that scandal!"

Many council members started talking at once. A new council member stood up to share his thoughts. "And what about the scandal that happened when one of our own wrote: *Most of the time travelers checked out early*. We were accused of concealing the new time travelling technology that was only then under development."

"Well, whatever did he mean?" asked Chairman Mono, very interested.

"He meant that, *most of the time*, comma, *travelers checked out early!* It was all just an unfortunate lack of a comma, as well as an unfortunate coincidence as far as the revelation of the technology was concerned! The absence of a comma nearly created a riot."

A younger woman on the panel then felt compelled to share her own story. "And how about the time that a friend of mine took her son to the doctor's office? She wrote on the digital check-in form, *My son has diarrhea he is unable to eat*. They almost called Child Protective Services!"

"A simple comma would have prevented the embarrassment!"

Olivia Thurgood felt compelled to interrupt. "I believe that should have been a semicolon…" but no one was listening.

"…Or when a friend of mine dedicated her book to: *My parents Mary Joseph and God.* She didn't mean to imply that her parents were Mary Joseph and God but that is how everybody took it."

Chairman Mono looked puzzled. "What did she mean?"

"She dedicated the book to her parents, her best friend Mary Joseph, and also to God."

Chairman Mono looked concerned. "Ms. Thurgood, do you think that your team could have prevented these embarrassing situations?"

"Oh yes, Mr. Chairman, we absolutely can!"

There were many whispers from members of the panel and the noise in the room became a loud hum, louder than the air-conditioning and active robotic digitizing systems combined. Many heads were nodding now.

Another council member confidently spoke up, as if representing the whole panel. "We can easily see when something is made wrong on an assembly line, and certainly we know when a surgery goes afoul; all of these things are results-driven and can be given over to robots and androids instead of using humans. As such, we only need a few humans to supervise the whole industry. But who has the time to read every word of a post for correct content and interpreting? We are all busy enjoying our lives in virtual reality settings and using our designer drugs without care or consequence due to brilliant new technological advances in Pharma."

There was consensus at this point – an enthusiastic agreement all around the table.

"Okay, let us bring it to a vote," Chairman Mono said energetically. "All in favor of allowing the Documentation Unit Specialty Offices to continue, please indicate that on your computer screen as soon as the option is activated and you are prompted to do so."

There was silence as everyone stared at the giant screens in the hall watching numbers begin to roll on the tally boards.

Olivia turned to her group. They held hands together and prayed silently. Then Olivia said quietly, concealing her excitement, "Team, we may be allowed to live."

TWELVE

WYECKS SYNDROME

JOHN DWIGHT

John Dwight is a software engineer. He lives with his wife Sara and cat Umbral. Sara is a botanist with a lab outside of Washington D.C. In 2009 she brought home a small plant, green with white bead-like flowers and simple fronds. For short periods around dusk the plant emits a whistling sound from seams at the top of its stem. Umbral never misses it. She arrives before the sound starts and stands close for the duration, listening with perked ears. Afterward Umbral tends to get pensive. She may groom in a dark place or hop up on the window sill and watch the stars rise. What does the plant mean to say? Maybe it's singing its own name or whispering some coded message from God, buried in the green. Or maybe the plant is a radio, echoing the last lonely cries of a dying star. In any case, the news never seems to be good. But Umbral always listens.

jfdwight.com

282

Confront a child, a puppy, and a kitten with a sudden danger; the child will turn instinctively for assistance, the puppy will grovel in abject submission, the kitten will brace its tiny body for a frantic resistance.

- H H Munro

283

The baby cried. Zelda leaned forward in her chair and sorted her cards, diamonds and spades but mostly clubs and some decent meld. "Hearts, Pip? It's always hearts with you." Zelda stood to check on the baby. She took a last swig of coffee.

The bedroom door slid open and Ada came out and through the kitchen. "She's fine," Ada said. "She'll be fine."

"Hold on, Ade, I can get her this time." Zelda followed Ada into the nursery.

"I guess no one appreciates the sanctity of a nice game of pinochle." Piper banked her cards on the table and set them down.

Ada came out of the nursery smiling. "She's fine. She's better now. All better." She poured herself coffee.

Zelda glided back into the kitchen after Ada and brushed imaginary dirt from her white dress with blue flowers. "I sorted things out in there. Not to worry, everyone." Zelda wrapped her tall, slender frame around Ada, a peck on the cheek. "What would you do without me?"

Ada breathed in the steam from her coffee. "Do you want an alphabetized list?"

"Oh." Zelda tugged Ada's nightshirt and pulled her into a chair. "Just come over here and watch the master single-handedly win this hand."

"How's the little one doing?" Piper said without looking up.

There was a short silence. "She's better," Ada said. But Zelda gave her a look with the sharp corners of her eyes. They had agreed not to tell anyone anything. Even Piper and Marie.

Ada stood up. An old pair of underwear hugged her pretty pear shape. She went to the window. Zelda passed four cards across the table to Piper. Piper shook her head.

"Is Marie still here?" Piper said. She looked up briefly and then went back to her cards.

Zelda shook her head. "No," she said. "She left after we got set in the first game. You remember when you put us in the red? The crying, the jeers."

"Mmm," Piper said. "Yes, as I recall you were no help in that game either." Piper moved a hand over her cards but stopped to rethink. Instead she ran green painted nails through her short mop of hair. "Mmm," she said again.

"Don't let me rush you," Zelda said. In the lull she stood and met Ada at the window. Efficient hips, a long stride, the blue flowers in her dress catching the sun.

Piper laid out cards. She lacked the duchess for a run, but she melded a marriage in trump and both nines. She passed four cards back to Zelda.

Zelda turned back to the table, Ada in her arms. "Ah," she said. "We're screwed again."

A moment passed on a bright fall morning.

Marie knocked at the front door and let herself in. Piper looked up at once. Marie walked with her head down and stood next to the nursery door and waited for Piper. She had the kind of wincing smile that a bird has when the worm starts to writhe.

Piper stood, as tall as Zelda, strong shoulders. She went to Marie. Quickly. Something was wrong. She could always tell with Marie.

Zelda kissed Ada's fingers, warm from the coffee mug, and sat down again at the kitchen table, looking over the cards from

Piper. She put them back in order by suit and thought about how she would play tricks and shook her head. "We're set again, aren't we Pip?" she said.

"Zelda," Piper said. The word came out sharp. Zelda turned and she already knew. She dropped her cards on the floor. Marie was crying. Ada put down her mug and watched Zelda cross the room and picked up her mug again and moved it to her lips without sipping.

"I'm sorry," Marie said to the floor. "I wanted to help."

Piper was white, pinching Marie at the elbow.

"What did you do Marie?" There was a hint of anger, but only a hint.

Piper shook her head at Zelda. "It's my fault," she said. "Don't blame Marie. It's my fault."

Zelda was dazed, a long stare. "There's no one to blame," she said to the distance. "Who did she call? Disease control? Social Services?"

"Law enforcement."

Zelda rolled her eyes, fingers pinching her lips. "Okay. Okay, okay," she sputtered, cranking herself into gear. She moved toward Ada then spun and took a step toward the nursery. Then she cut into the bedroom. "It's time, Ada," she said without panic. "It's time." The sounds of pulling and moving.

Ada sat and took a sip of coffee and blinked a few times to clear her head.

"How long do we have?" Piper said.

Zelda came back into the kitchen with a jacket on over her dress and a backpack on both shoulders. "I don't know," she said. "Ade, we need to go." Zelda pushed past Marie and into the nursery.

Piper listened at the door and went out into the hall and looked down the stairwell past twenty-three flights. Near the bottom, she saw a flare of billowing robes. She watched them corkscrew, calculating.

Piper came back in and shut and locked the front door. "It's an agent, maybe two minutes," she said.

Zelda slid into the kitchen with baby Yara in a plaid green sling at her belly. A small red duffel in her hands.

Ada stood. "No," she said. She looked Zelda in the eyes. "No, I want to stay." Ada looked at the red bag, a long look. "We don't need that," she said. "Put it back, put everything back and we'll just stay."

"Today is why we have the red bag." Zelda was calm now. She put her pack on the floor and stuffed in a bottle and a towel and a pillbox.

"What'll they do?" said Piper.

"They'll take her," said Zelda. "We'll never see her again."

Ada sat down again at the kitchen table and absorbed herself in the motion of things like a beekeeper watching the hive. Zelda moved to Ada and took her hands and pulled her up from her chair.

"No, Zelda. No." Ada swallowed hard and tried to catch a breath.

Marie spoke up. "Maybe they can cure her," she said. Piper tightened on her elbow and pulled her aside.

Zelda didn't answer. It wasn't a question. She was getting angry and she didn't want to get angry.

Zelda put her hands on Ada's cheeks and kissed her mouth, the taste of warm coffee. The last wisps of a lazy morning evaporated. Yara squished between them and gave a soft cry and went quiet again.

"I love you, Ada, but I need you too and that's what makes this so difficult." Zelda pulled Ada forward by the waistband of her underwear. It stretched out with a ripping sound.

"Ow." Ada cupped her hands over the mound of her vulva.

Zelda got behind her and pushed her into the bedroom. She pulled Ada's loose night shirt up and off and pulled her underwear down and off. Ada stood naked and wiped tears away with the heel of her hands. "We don't need to go, we can stay."

Zelda left and came back with a folded stack of clothes. "We need to go, Ade. Put these on. Where's your bag?"

Ada pulled on new underwear.

Zelda scanned the room and saw a gray backpack. She grabbed it.

Ada slipped a dress over her head that cinched around the waist and wrapped herself in a light sweater. "When will we be back?" she said.

Zelda brushed her hair out of her eyes. A tenderness in the tips of her fingers. "We won't," she said. "Come on, Ade, thirty seconds."

The two returned to the kitchen. Piper held Marie close to her, squeezed her. She was whispering in her ear.

Zelda interrupted by touching Piper's elbow. "You have to go."

Piper turned. "I'll stay," she said. "It'll give them someone to talk to. Buy some time."

Piper told Marie she should go, but Marie shook her head.

"Dammit, you two. Listen to me."

Piper put her hands up and hugged Zelda. "We can't just go home, Zel."

Zelda shook her head at Piper and looked at Marie. She was a small woman in a white sweater. A little thing. Zelda hugged her and kissed her on the top of the head and she turned to Piper. "Nothing fancy," she said. "You don't know anything."

Piper nodded and put her pretty green fingers under Yara's chin. The baby cooed and laughed and her blue eyes dazzled in Piper's smile. She moved her little hands behind the green fabric of the sling. Piper kissed her fingers and touched Yara's forehead. "Take care of her," Piper said.

Zelda rushed to Ada who was lost in the middle of the small apartment. She took short drunken steps and swiveled her head at old books and a small globe and a painting of a flower losing its petals. Zelda pulled a silvery rod out of the red bag and she took Ada by the elbow and turned her around and pulled the straps of her pack hard down. She tightened them so the whole thing was snug.

"We'll just wait until they leave," said Ada, facing the other way.

"She's not going to leave. Not without Yara." Zelda zipped up pockets on Ada's pack.

"I won't let them take her. They'll have to kill me."

Zelda opened her mouth to say something smart and terrible but she closed it instead.

Ada turned back around. "I won't go, Zelda. I won't do it."

There was a knock and a voice, not loud but penetrating. "Agent of the Law," she said. "Open the door."

The agent filled the doorway. Her sheer white robes drifted inward on a breeze. Piper let the door swing wide and went back to her chair at the table. She thought she smelled flowers.

"May I come in?" The agent walked in and closed the door behind her. Her robes still danced even without a current of air.

Piper looked up from her chair. "I didn't say no because I thought the question might be rhetorical." She gathered cards together and banked them on the table.

"It's only a rhetorical question if the answer is no." The agent smiled and walked to the center of the kitchen ignoring Piper. Her bare feet glided over the tile without a sound. She lowered her head to listen.

Piper shuffled the cards together with a loud *wapapapap*.

The agent looked sideways at her.

"Sorry," said Piper, and she began to lay out cards to play solitaire, a stack of seven and then of six and then of five.

The agent walked to the counter and looked at the coffeemaker and the carafe. "You drink a lot of coffee for one person," she said.

Piper smiled.

The agent turned the temperature control on the coffeemaker to high and went to the table and watched Piper play solitaire. Her long light robes trailed behind her, pointing toward the nursery and the bedroom and the bathroom and the windows. The fabric seemed to sniff the air. The agent leaned on the table until it creaked and then put a hand out to stop Piper's deal. "You're not going to win," she said.

Piper looked up, frozen.

The agent bent down and then rose up again and held out a handful of cards that had been lying beneath the table. She turned her head to the side and flipped through the cards with long fingers. "Solitaire requires a full deck," she said. "If even one card is out of place, you can't finish the game."

"How'd those get down there?" Piper said, a crooked smile.

"I suspect your friends dropped them in the haste of their escape." She looked over the cards again. "I hope you didn't bid in hearts."

Piper stopped and reckoned the agent for the first time. She was cloaked only in a nominal sense. A bareness poured through her light robes. A naked femininity. And there was something uncanny about her dark red hair. It seemed to move on its own. She was a vibrant creature. Her figure made a humming sound in Piper's ears. Her bosom a peal like Church bells one town over. Her eyes were nurturing somehow. A dark honest blue. And in that moment Piper knew the agent was going to win, and she started trying to work out what that meant.

"I am looking for a child," the agent said. "She is ill and needs attention."

Piper collected herself. "There's no child here."

A pause. "I believe you," the agent said. "But the child resides at this address. Are you the home owner?"

"Yes," Piper said, buying time.

A voice came to the agent and only to her. It was a buzzing through her brain stem. It said:

THAT IS A LIE.

"Miss Piper, please don't lie to me. I'm trying to help. Where is the child?"

Piper drew an eight of spades from the stock and looked at it sideways. "I live a few doors down," she said, and pointed toward the door, her pretty green fingers shaking.

"You know the child?"

"See, we thought she was sick but we made a mistake. It turns out she's already on medication. So disaster averted," Piper chuckled. "Would you like some coffee before you leave?"

"The child is no longer sick?"

"That's right."

SHE WON'T HELP YOU.

The agent walked to the coffee pot and picked it up and sat down at the kitchen table next to Piper.

"The child is sick, Miss Piper. Have you seen her? Have you looked on her?"

Piper gave a slow nod like a bucket of sloshing water.

"Then you know her condition is dangerous. She cannot be treated."

Piper flipped another card and looked at it. "Then how do you plan to help her?" she said.

The agent moved her neck in a funny way. Curls of red hair shifted beneath sheer robes.

She reached out and took Piper at the right wrist. Piper watched her do it, eyes wide. And the agent held her palm down on the kitchen table and put the hot coffee pot on the back of her hand.

Piper growled. Her throat made strange wet noises. She leapt in place and pulled, her whole weight on those bones. The agent stayed seated, calm. Her grip tightened on Piper, the flesh white at the wrist and burning, smoking, turning black on her tendons and knuckles. The smell of human char filled the room. Piper bit her tongue and lips and bled drops onto the table.

The agent set the coffee pot down and let go of Piper's wrist. She fell back into her chair and tumbled over backwards, clutching one hand in the other and folding her lips over and over and tasting her own blood. From the floor she saw a slithering motion behind the agent's head. Something in the dark ravels of her hair moved, coiled up, prepared to strike.

"Miss Piper, we're out of time. You're hindering my investigation. I received a call about an ill child. Are you the caller?"

"The child is fine," Piper said, a whisper. "She's okay now. Please don't hurt us. Please. I made the call. It was a mistake."

THAT IS A LIE.

"You're still lying to me, Miss Piper." With a slight gesture, the agent slid the heavy wooden table across the room to the door. "Where is the caller? Who made the call?"

Piper stood, stumbled, shifted ever so slightly toward the nursery. A silly defense. It was instinct, fear, a terrible mistake. "Please. Leave us alone," she said.

"How many people are in the residence? Who made the call? Where is the child?" The agent was barking questions, pleading for clues. But something came from beneath the agent's hooded robes. It whipped through the air and slithered and struck.

The agent took Piper by the shoulders and shook her and held her and watched her pretty green eyes fade away.

From the bedroom, Marie heard a shuffling. The splash of a broken coffee pot. A mug fallen off the table to the floor. She stood up straight against a flat wall. Not hidden but silent. A long-held breath. There were no screams or struggle from the next room. Just a gurgling. And then silence. Marie covered her mouth with a trembling hand.

The agent's face poked into the room, lit from behind. "Hello, Miss Marie."

Marie made herself small in her white sweater.

"You did the right thing to call us. Where have they gone with the baby?"

The agent stepped into the room, robes trailing behind her, a redness in her cheeks. She went to the crib and studied the padding and traced the edges of the pink and white blanket draped over the rungs.

"Where have they gone, Miss Marie?"

Marie had an aunt who lived in Branta. The summer when Marie turned five they'd gone up to Rockhaven and taken a ferry across the bay and watched the sun set as they went. The smell of pines and seagrass mixed in the chill at the end of the day.

Marie swallowed. "The ferry," she said, stumbling. "They're going to Rockhaven." She watched the agent's hair move in strange ways. "They're taking a ferry to Branta."

THAT IS A LIE.

The nursery door creaked to a close on old hinges. As Marie died, for a moment, she could smell the seagrass again.

Ada shifted her weight on a makeshift balcony, a wire mesh just outside a window on the 23rd story. The metal creaked where rods had been drilled into the side of the building. Ada couldn't see much past reflections in the glass. But Piper lay on the kitchen floor. Ada could see the bottoms of her feet.

"Maybe she's okay, Zel."

Zelda shook her head at the streets below. "How did you get me to buy a place on the 23rd floor?"

Ada put an eye onto the window glass.

294

Zelda pulled her away. "Piper's dead, Ada. Marie's dead too. I'll be dead next. Then you." Zelda stopped there but Ada understood.

Ada shook her head and crouched down at the window. The metal creaked again.

Zelda stared away, turning the silvery rod in her hands. "I had two friends in the world, Ade. They're both dead. And two points make a line. You and I are on that line somewhere. We're all on that line somewhere."

"But we were just drinking coffee."

Zelda looked out over the metal mesh at the cars and buses and people below.

"Give her to me." Ada stood.

Zelda turned around.

"Give her to me. I want Yara."

Zelda squinted but lifted the sling up and over her neck and Ada took Yara around her and rocked until she was in that right place.

"Okay?" she said, and she took Zelda's hand.

Zelda kissed her on the forehead. "Okay," she said, holding out the silvery rod.

They jumped.

The cat is a Feliform. Lions and Lynx and Tabbies and Meerkats. The dog is a Caniform. Wolves and Weasels and Bears and Bearded Seals. The distinction is strange and significant. Feliforms can retract their claws. Caniforms cannot.

And so the dog is a candid creature. She is compelled to explain herself, her claws. She has honest eyes. She must. In that sense the dog is a diplomatic animal. If there are no secrets, then there can be no lies.

But the cat can hide her claws, conceal her weapons. She is built for mystery. The cat keeps her distance and covers her depth. She dreams and plots and wonders and will never tell. The cat is made for surprises. They spring from her bones.

They fell through rays of sun and into shadow and the city swallowed them. The silvery rod activated and telescoped out toward the ground. Ada and Zelda and Yara hugged together and gripped one end of the long pole. The other end touched down and bent out wide with the two ends slowly coming together. The tension in the pole resisted gravity and inertia and the universe's natural zeal for death. Zelda hung from the top end of the pole and Ada clung to her around Yara in the sling. As they approached the ground, the rod blinked and spun and shriveled up again. The trio fell a few inches to the street.

A woman in a long coat carrying groceries saw them land and looked up and shook her head.

Zelda said, "Well, okay, that wasn't so bad," and kissed Yara on the nose. Yara blinked and made her eyes wide and laughed at the sunshine.

Ada took a breath and looked up at the apartment.

"We made it, Ade." Zelda gave Ada a kiss on the cheek and shook the rod approvingly and dropped it into Ada's hands.

Ada held the rod and spoke into it. "Four stars, works as expected."

The rod blinked in appreciation. Ada shoved it into the red bag on Zelda's arm and they began a sprint to the train station.

The train doors closed and the car rose up from the track and lurched forward. Ada started to walk down the aisle but Zelda held her hand to keep her still. Zelda feigned as if she was looking for something in her bag, but really she was waiting for the lights to dim again. She didn't want to be noticed. First the train became very dark, and then a soft candle light waded up from below.

Zelda looked around the car. The roof was a solid piece of metal, long warped reflections of dim lights. The windows had a clear rubber seal around the edges. A black membrane stretched across a recess above the sliding entryways and a heavy blast door with a locking red latch separated the cars. Zelda eyed every seam and hinge and bolt. She had ridden the train many times. But she looked at it now like a cage she might need to escape.

They walked the aisle. The first table was mostly empty. There was a round woman there with glasses and a purple luggage case that matched her sweater. The woman smiled up at Ada with warm cheeks and moved her luggage so they could sit. She was alone at the table and seemed eager to have some company. Ada moved to sit with her.

"Hi, I'm Ann," the woman said, and Ada put a hand on hers.

"Hi, I'm Ada and this is—"

Zelda smiled and pulled Ada down the dark train car. Ann pushed her glasses up her nose and folded her hands and frowned. Ada gave a small wave and disappeared into the darkness.

They walked the length of the aisle in dim light, small steps. Zelda stopped at a talkative table and motioned for Ada to slide in so Zelda could fill out the octet. The pairs of people here seemed to be traveling together. Zelda thought if these folks know each other, she and Ada might not have to say a word to anyone. They sat down.

Eight seats curved around a small table. Flowers in pairs poked up randomly from chairs and window sills and from the center of tables. Candlelight painted faces in a warm glow. The train was dark and cool and comfortable. A flow of fresh air smelled like honeysuckle. All around them there was a quiet churn of polite conversation. The motion of the train itself was utterly silent.

Across from Zelda at the other end cap was an older woman with pretty blue hair. She nodded. Zelda pretended not to notice. Beside her was a woman in her late twenties, green eyes, reading a newspaper. Zelda read a headline through the back side of the translucent screen.

COUPLE ELUDES CAPTURE

Zelda pinched Ada but she only shuffled down to give Zelda more room.

Beyond the young woman was an older couple doing a crossword puzzle. "Sugary," one woman said.

"Sugary only has six letters. We need a seven-letter word with an **E** in the middle."

"Oh, okay." She thought for a minute. "Candied," she said.

"It has to have an **E** in the middle."

"Candied has an **E** in the middle."

"The **E** has to be in the middle-middle."

They hadn't made much progress.

Next to Ada was a little girl in a ball cap. The candlelight made her uniform look orange, but it was black on bright yellow, with baggy pants that covered her knees and long socks and stirrups. Her jersey read *Queens* and it had a bee with a tiara and a mean grin. She was big for her age, maybe twelve. Her hand was slipped through the folds of her equipment bag.

Her mother scolded her.

"But I just want to touch it," she said.

"Jeannie, put it away, hon."

The woman across the way with blue hair leaned over the table to Zelda. "Hello," she said. "I'm Rose. This is my daughter Carmen." Carmen didn't look up.

Zelda only nodded but Ada made conversation. "Hi Rose, I'm Ada. This is Zelda." It was thoughtless banter. She didn't mean harm. But Zelda wondered if the names *Zelda* and *Ada* appeared on Carmen's newspaper and if Rose saw the paper or Carmen heard the names.

"Rose, can I ask why you have a cane?"

Zelda rolled her eyes. *Oh good, now we're making friends.*

Rose moved an old maple crook cane from side to side. "When I was a girl I had polio," she said and she tapped the cane on the ground. Ada gave a sad face but Rose shook it off. "Don't fret about me, hon. I still limped into my fair share of trouble." Rose gave a little chuckle and Ada smiled.

"Where are you two headed?"

Ada started to tell her but Zelda butted in. "We're on vacation," she said. We're staying a couple days on the harbor.

"Oh," Rose said. "That's nice. That'll be nice." She gave a wide smile.

Zelda got nervous. *She doesn't believe us.*

Rose eased forward and looked at Yara in the little green sling. "And who do we have here?"

"This is Yara," Ada said, giving her a tickle on the belly.

"Oh," Rose said. She blinked at Yara and Yara blinked back and Rose made funny sounds with her lips. Yara smiled.

Zelda rubbed the bridge of her nose.

"How old is she?" Rose said.

"Eighteen weeks." Ada gave Yara a turn. She blinked and burped.

Zelda smiled and squeezed Ada's thigh and leaned in to kiss her on the cheek. She whispered in her ear. "We're fugitives, Ade. Button. Your. Blabber." Zelda kept smiling, all sweetness, and put her arm around Ada.

Ada frowned and went silent.

The train made one stop and then another but no one at the table needed off. In the hum of other conversations Ada and Zelda whispered to each other.

"At some point, the city just ends," Zelda said.

Ada got distant. "I can't imagine it, Zel. I want to see a whole forest of trees. That would be something."

"We will, hon. We just have to keep going."

"How long will it take to get out?"

"Days. Maybe a week on foot. I don't know how long the Rut goes on. But we have what we need. If the city has an end, we'll find it."

"I don't like going into the Rut." Ada frowned.

Zelda smiled. "I can see no way out but through," she said. "Look Ade, some people get lost, but we know where we're going."

"Where is that?"

"Out."

"Will they send a cat after us?" Ada said.

"No. They sent an agent. That's all we need to worry about right now."

"They'll send a panther I bet."

"They're not gonna send a panther." Zelda put her head down and closed her eyes.

"Maybe they'll send a cheetah."

"Why, because you could outrun the panther?"

Ada looked down at her hands in the dark. "So you *do* think they'll send a panther?"

"They're not gonna send a cat, Ade. We haven't done anything wrong."

Neither of them was really convinced of that. Ada's eyes welled up.

"Don't cry, hon, come on. Don't cry. Please, Ade," Zelda whispered and tried to avoid a scene. It was too late though. Rose leaned over the edge of the table.

"That's no way to start a vacation," Rose said. Ada wiped a tear from her cheek.

And then Rose leaned in close. "No one sends the cats. They show up when they show up. No accounting for it in my experience," she said.

Ada stared down at the table but Zelda looked at Rose, really looked her in the eyes for the first time.

"I told you I'd had my share of trouble," Rose said. "You're on vacation, I had polio. We all have our little stories."

Zelda smiled.

"I've seen cats and agents both and I don't like either one. Now where are you really going? Maybe I can help."

Zelda was silent but Rose seemed to understand.

"It's a long way out of town," she said. "But that's where I'd go too. Through the Rut though. A dirty place. Dirty enough to get lost in. I made it outside a couple times. If you stay awhile they may just forget what it was you did." Rose patted Zelda's knee. She smiled and leaned back again. Her daughter looked up to see where the train was and then went back to an article about an increase in security at local train stations.

Yara gave a soft coo and drifted off to sleep.

While her mother nodded off, Jeannie opened up her equipment bag and marveled at her baseball bat. She nestled it in the crook of her arm and moved her fingers over the label. It said Endohedral Power in black lettering and below that, Foamium Fullerene ™.

Mom stirred. She looked to see where the train was and rubbed her eyes. "Dear God, Jean Elizabeth, put it away for crying out loud."

Jeannie was already sliding it back in the bag. She held it with natural ease. It was light and wieldy in her hand. Her eyes danced in the candlelight. "I'm gonna hit one over the fence today."

"Well just put it away, Jeannie. If I see it again before lunch, I swear you're gonna be batting with a fist full of petunias." Her mother arranged the flowers in the middle of the table.

"We can't lose to this team again, Mom. They're the Navy Beans. I mean, who can root for Beans?"

Mom smiled.

"Today they're gonna clap for me." Jeannie kicked the bag on the floor. "I have Endohedral Power." Her pronunciation was perfect. She had heard the word before.

"I hope so," Mom said. "But you have to keep your head down and focus on the ball. The bat doesn't hit home runs for you."

"I think this one actually does, Mom." Jeannie cocked her head, trying to remember the slogan from the ads.

Mom made a raspberry sound with her lips and turned to Jeannie and put a shoulder into the seat in a cozy way. The girl did the same until they were nose to nose.

"What does the bat want for dinner?" Mom whispered.

Jeannie rolled her eyes.

"What does it want for its birthday?"

"It's a bat, Mom." Jeannie furrowed her brow.

"So the bat doesn't *want* anything?"

Jeannie tilted her head. "Mom, it's metal or Foamium or something. I think it just wants to be a bat."

"The bat doesn't want to hit a home run?"

"No, I want to hit a home run."

"Okay. Well, that's what makes you different from the bat Jean-Jean. You want and the bat doesn't. The want has to come from somewhere. It comes from you."

Jeannie looked at her hands. "Okay, well, I *want* to hit a home run *with* the bat."

Mom smiled at her. "Good." She turned back to the flowers and checked her watch. "Just remember, Jean-Jean, the bat doesn't care one way or the other."

The little girl stayed where she was, shoulder in the seat, thinking. She leaned forward and put her head on Mom's chest. The back of her shirt had the number 15 on it and then above that, in glowing fabric, was the image of a donut that turned in space, a golden light trickling off the honeyed glaze. A slogan pulsed on the advertisement. It said *Dunkin Donuts is the Bee's Knees*.

"Honeyed!" said the woman with the crossword puzzle. "I told you the **E** was in the middle."

Zelda stirred and woke up.

The baseball girl and her Mom were gone. So were the crossword couple. Rose's daughter had wandered up the train and curled herself around a vacant table asleep. The train was almost empty, a lull between big cities.

Rose was feeling flush. She sipped a glass of ice water and then closed her eyes in the cool dark.

Ada was breastfeeding Yara. She opened her blouse and switched from one side to the other. "She can't get comfortable," Ada said. "And that makes two of us."

Zelda kissed Ada on the top of her head and took a deep breath. "Well, Mom," she said, "the good news is that we're close. Do you have everything?" Zelda raised her brow in a serious way. Ada nodded.

Zelda stood and helped Ada out of the seat, Yara in the sling. And Zelda put a hand on Rose's shoulder. They exchanged a smile without words.

The train floated into the substation past a bank of advertisement boards. The screens lit up in sequence and showered passengers with bright pictures of things they might like to buy. A bag of pastries covered in a cinnamon glaze. An easel that lets you paint on the canvas with your fingers. A woman on a beach in a bikini. Zelda wondered what was for sale. And then there was a cat on the beach with the woman. She didn't seem to notice. The cat came up close. White coat and teeth. Green eyes. Tufts of fur on her ears and jowls. She looked at Zelda through the advertisement screens and the glass of the train. Light and shadows between them. Then at once the image blinked away and was replaced by a sandwich and a Coke.

"I could go for a sandwich and a Coke," Ada said.

Zelda pulled Ada's hips into hers, looked her in the eyes. Had she seen it too?

"You okay, Zel?"

Zelda looked around, the lights were coming up. She felt dazed and faint.

When she opened her eyes again she was sitting. Rose held her ice water up to Zelda's forehead and then offered her the glass. Zelda took a gulp, then another.

"You saw it?" she said to Rose.

Rose shook her head.

Zelda exhaled. "Maybe it wasn't real?"

Rose eyed Ada and leaned on her cane and bent to Zelda's ear. "But I expect I know what you saw, kiddo," she whispered. "And that's as real as you want it to get."

Rose clasped Zelda's hand and pulled her up out of the seat.

"If this is your stop, hon, then you best be on the move."

Zelda stood for a moment and held Rose's arms and shivered. The sliding doors on the sides of the car opened.

Zelda took Ada's hand and pulled her toward the exit.

Zelda tugged on Ada's elbow and lurched past a woman getting into her seat.

Ada slowed down.

"Come on, Ade."

"Zel… Zelda." Ada pointed to the window before the door. Long white robes sniffed the air and peered into the train car.

Zelda stopped, hands out, and took a step backwards. Then another.

The agent stepped on the train, light pouring through the sheer robes assembling around her. She turned up the aisle. Her dark red hair seemed to flow over her shoulders to get a better look. There was a hush on the train. Passengers whispered and made themselves small in their seats.

Zelda began to backpedal in earnest, fishing through the red bag on her hip as she went. Ada turned and made a sideways dash down the aisle toward the other door, Yara in tow. But the exit doors slid closed and the train began to rise up off the tracks and move through the station.

Zelda and Ada and the baby girl were trapped on the car. They searched for some hope. Nothing. Even Ann had pushed herself to the back of her vacant semicircle of seats. She held her purple bag in front of her as a shield, hands shaking.

The agent's robes flowed like tendrils into space and tasted the air and licked handholds and touched empty seats. They left the agent's flesh and revealed the shapes of her femininity. She stepped forward towards her prey.

An old maple crook cane struck down in the center of the aisle. Rose limped out of her seat and stood in front of the agent. She put two hands on the cane and squared her shoulders and made a wall.

There was a motion in the agent's hair beneath her sheer robes. But the agent raised a hand and bent and whispered something in Rose's ear.

Rose stood still and didn't turn around and didn't speak a word. She only moved aside and sat down heavily in her seat and pulled her cane into her lap. Zelda thought about the kind of lies the agent might have invented to make Rose move. But she might have just told her the truth.

The lights dimmed to darkness and then candle light came up from below. The agent's eyes glowed blue through the blackness. She began to walk.

Zelda had produced a long wrench from the red bag. She pushed past Ada and pulled on the locking red latch on the blast door between cars. She slid the heavy door sideways. It creaked on its bearings and Zelda shot through to the anti-space between compartments and opened the door onto the next car.

The agent glided, sheer robes trailing behind her. She ran in leaps like a ballerina or a bird of prey and chewed up the ground between.

Ada and Yara swung around Zelda into the darkness of the next train.

The agent flew through the first heavy door and shouldered into the second door just as Zelda slammed it sideways and threw the red latch down. Zelda dropped the long wrench into the sliding gap for the blast door. The agent pushed her palms into the glass and shook the door frame, but the wrench only wedged itself firmly in place.

SHE'S JAMMED THE DOOR. HOW CLEVER.

Zelda dropped the red bag behind her. Ada was on the ground and pulled the bag between her legs and sifted through it. She was searching for something. Yara balanced on her belly in the dark.

The agent pressed herself against the glass. Candlelight on her face and breasts.

Zelda stepped forward, comfortable with the steel that separated her from the agent.

"She's dangerous," the agent said. She didn't speak but mouthed the words.

Ada pulled on Zelda's dress and leg to keep her away. Zelda shook her finger at the agent and sneered.

Ada held up a small cylinder from the red bag to Zelda.

"Not yet, let's put a couple cars between us before we do it. Get the oven mitt."

Zelda helped Ada to her feet. They gathered themselves in the darkness.

A terrible howling cry shook the train. Then a crash on the heavy door and they saw Ann and her purple sweater held up to the window between cars.

PERHAPS THIS WILL HELP WITH YOUR NEGOTIATION AGENT.

Something had slithered out of the agent's robes and down from behind her head, a long gray coiling shape, and wrapped around Ann's neck several times. Ann's fingers gripped the thing, holding and pulling. Her glasses had flown away and so she squinted in the dark and dangled above the platform feet kicking through the air.

Ada put a hand on the glass beside the door. Zelda looked at Ann, helpless and trapped, and then at the agent. There was desperation in both of their eyes.

The agent was panicked. She gripped the latch handle on her side of the door and pulled. The red metal shredded, curled up like wood carvings from a lathe. The door slipped open an inch before the wrench caught and locked in place. But the agent put her fingers through the gap and pulled on the door. The heavy metal bent in her grip, and she drove the wrench through the steel frame. The door ached open and the gap became just wide enough to get an arm through into the next train.

Zelda stumbled backward and fumbled to pull Ada with her. They were nearly away but the agent's fingers found a single nook in Ada's sweater. She held on and wrapped it round and round her wrist until Ada was on the ground and slipping.

"I have her," the agent said. She was soothing something wild. "I have her."

Ada struggled and kicked the air. Zelda pulled on her armpits, trying to tug her free. But the agent reeled her in, trading sweater for shoe and shoe for foot and foot for ankle. Her grip was cold and tight. Ada screamed and then cried. Her ankle bent in a funny way, her face white with pain.

The agent edged her arm through the door up to her shoulder and used that leverage to yank Ada forward. Her butt crashed into the glass and she rolled upright, face to face, nose to nose with the agent.

"Stop squirming," the agent said. "I don't want to hurt you."

Ada stayed still for only a second and then she pushed off with one leg and bucked to get free.

The agent jerked her again and brought her back to the glass and looked her in the eyes. "Ada. Be still. Talk to me."

Ada turned her head away and sobbed into the sling and squeezed Yara.

On the other side of the glass, the tentacle lowered Ann to the platform. She gyrated. A dangling shoe clipped the ground and fell off and over the edge and into the black rush of air below. Ann's face was purple, her eyes bloodshot. She gasped and stood, still wrapped up by something shiny gray and terrible.

Zelda looked at Ann through the glass. She had pretty green eyes swimming in a sea of red and purple and despair. Zelda stood and moved past Ada to the agent and put out her hand. "Here," she said. "Talk to me. I want to talk."

The agent looked from Ada's swelling ankle to Zelda's wrist. "I trust you," she said to Zelda.

DO NOT TRADE MY PRIZE, AGENT. I WANT THE CHILD.

The agent eased her grip on Ada's ankle. Her fingers wriggled to let the blood flow again. She massaged the muscle and bone with her thumb. And she let go. Zelda and the agent stood, eye to eye. And the agent took Zelda's wrist.

The agent looked at Ann. "She'll be killed," she said. "You're trapped, Zelda. The more you squirm, the worse this gets."

"Let us go then. We'll leave. You'll never see us again."

The agent was silent. She looked down at Ada with the baby. Mother and child.

"She's beautiful."

"We love her."

"She gets ugly, Zelda. Hateful. She turns against you."

Zelda shook her head. "She's my baby. She's our little baby."

"She becomes stronger. Meaner. She'll hurt you. She'll hurt us all, Zelda."

Zelda gave her wrist a small twist. The agent's grip tightened.

THIS IS A WASTE. SHE WON'T BE CONVINCED.

The agent pulled Zelda close. "We live in a beautiful city," she said. "A utopia. It wasn't always that way. For generations we were strangled by terror and war. We tried to find political solutions and economic solutions. But our problems were intractable until we realized that we were sick with something, Zelda. An illness. An infection that could be cured. And we conquered it all at once by attacking at the root. Yara's disease was behind all the things that made us weak. It's alien in a way, Zelda. And it ruled us once. It choked us for an age. If you escape from me, you'll bring the whole world back to its knees."

IT RULES YOU STILL, AGENT.

The agent scowled.

Ada stood up, limped on her red ankle. "What will you do to her?" she said.

"Yara is very sick, Ada. Her disease is in every cell of her body. It has to be destroyed. Completely."

"She'll die?"

"I need to take her away. You won't see her again."

"She'll die."

"Yes."

The train glided through the darkness without a sound.

"You can start over, Ada. You'll have another child. A whole family. They'll be healthy. You'll be happy. Don't run away now. You can't escape."

Ada limped back into the darkness and unzipped the red bag.

I'M LOSING PATIENCE.

The agent turned back to Zelda. "She'll infect us," she said. The agent had worked her knee through the crack in the door.

"She's not contagious," Zelda said.

"She's a danger to everyone on this train. And their children. And their children's children. She's infecting us all, Zelda. In the worst way possible. She'll kill billions. You have no idea what you're protecting."

Zelda had her other hand on the agent's fingers, prying. She called to Ada.

Ada cradled Yara and bounced her with an oven mitt on her right hand. Her left hand trolled blindly through the red bag. It was too dark to see, but she was looking for that small cylinder again and she would know it by shape.

Ann put a hand up to the glass. "Please," she said. "I want to go home." She was bleary, dazed, a tentacle wrapped around her neck.

Zelda put her feet up on the door and fought hard to pull away. Her hand turned blue where the agent held on. "Ada please," Zelda said.

"Zelda, you're trapped on a train. You can't just walk away." The agent pulled hard against the door to get more room, more leverage, but the wrench just dug deeper into the metal frame. "Zelda please, listen to reason."

LET ME SHOW HER REASON.

The tentacle uncoiled from around Ann's neck. Blood flushed away from her face and eyes and she blinked and breathed in deep. Her knees were weak and she wobbled but stood up holding the railing and righted herself. She smoothed her clothes and then threw up. Ann frowned and brushed the liquid from her purple sweater. The agent pulled Zelda close. "Watch," she said.

The tentacle flexed in the air and then stiffened, came to a point and slipped under Ann's purple sweater and wriggled through her navel into her belly. Zelda stopped struggling and watched Ann through the glass.

Ann's rosy face became gaunt. Her eyes distant and dark. Her head rolled sideways. The tentacle exited. Not a sound. Not a drop of blood. What was left of Ann was lifeless, a husk. The thing wrapped around her waist and lifted her up to the window so Zelda could see what remained. Something dark and empty and lit by candles.

The agent bent as close as she could to Zelda's ear. "This is only the beginning," she said.

Zelda blew sweat from her lip and pulled with all her strength. The agent tightened her grip, her shoulder and leg and chin now squeezing through the door.

The tentacle released Ann's body. It dropped through the railing into darkness. The tentacle rotated in space and then slipped over the agent's ear and through the gap in the door. Inside the train it was tentative, sniffing like a snake in the dim light.

Ada stood up and dropped the red bag.

The tentacle wavered over Zelda's head, a careful thing. The agent pulled her closer. Closer.

Ada held up a cylinder in her oven mitt, trying to see it in the light.

The thing slithered through Zelda's hair and tasted her scent.

Ada wrestled a cap off of the cylinder. Number eight bird shot bounced and scattered around the train car.

ABORT.

The tentacle straightened and slipped backward through the door.

ABORT.

The agent turned her head. The thing slithered in reverse and became small again and coiled back under her red curls.

ABORT.

The agent pulled her leg and head through the gap. Her arm wouldn't come. She turned back to find the roles reversed, Zelda holding on to her wrist with both hands.

Ada held up the shotgun shell and shook it toward the black membrane stretched across a recess above the sliding entryways. The wad in the shell was packed tightly. Nothing happened.

Zelda pulled hard and the agent's whole arm to her shoulder came into the car. "ADA!" she was growling through her teeth. "NOW!"

Ada shook the shell and shook it again, but she was careful with it like she was trying to throw a drop of wax from a candle. She stood like a crane on one leg and held Yara to the side and pointed the shell like a wand.

The agent pulled her arm out an inch. Then another.

The mitt slipped off of Ada's hand, the shotgun shell tumbled through space and struck the black membrane. That membrane was a culture of cells from a dog's nose, carefully grown and stretched and able to send an electrical signal at the slightest hint of incendiary powder. The shell opened up and spattered gray soot across the sensor plate. It bounced and spun back leaving a streak of gray across Ada's dress and then caromed to the corner of the train. The candles went black, red light flooded the car and the blast door came crashing to a closed position crushing the agent's upper arm. Heavy glass and steel muffled her screams.

An intermittent buzzing pulsed with the red light on the train. The cars had separated with the alarm and lost impulse. The train car glided like a ghost over the frictionless rail. Zelda took Ada by the shoulders and squeezed one of Yara's feet in the sling. Her little eyes were wide.

There were only a few people on the train. They stiffened their legs to peer over the seats. A woman in a white hat said she smelled something hot. Zelda pushed Ada and she limped forward to the sliding door.

Ada put a hand over the gunpowder on her dress and moved it away again and winced at the stain.

The train slowed in the dank air of the tunnel. Zelda picked up the red bag, zipped it, slung it over her shoulder. *Don't look back at her.* She tugged all the straps to tighten them, pulled all the zippers, smoothed her jacket over her dress. *Don't do it.* Passengers queued up calmly in the pulsing red at the sliding doors. Ada was at the front. Zelda tapped her shoe for the sound it made. *Don't look.*

The train was nearly at a stop.

Zelda rubbed her teeth with the back of her hand. She shut her eyes. But she listened to the sounds from the blast door. The ears can't be closed. She heard a pressing on metal. A pained shuffling of bare feet.

The train lowered itself to the rail. The doors opened up and people wandered out into the darkness. Ada stepped through the door, Yara slung on her belly.

Zelda looked back.

The agent lay in agony on the other side of the blast door. Her robes had flowed to the site and bunched up at the seam of the door around the agent's crushed arm. She lay naked in the pulsing light. She saw Zelda. Her eyes agape, begging.

Zelda looked down at her feet and then turned back to the blast door and pried the wrench free from the steel frame. She stepped wide to avoid the agent's mangled arm and punched the wrench through the slim rubbery gap of the door. The agent's whole arm fit in that small space.

The agent could pry herself free with the wrench. That was enough. Zelda left her there and went out the sliding door with the other passengers into the tunnel. She stepped off the train and put her feet down in gravel. In the distance there was white light. They were half a mile from the next station. Zelda began to run.

The cat cleans religiously. Grooming is a ritual, not a chore. The cat is patient. She is introspective. Through cleaning, the cat observes herself, knows herself. The cat's tongue is truly an intellectual organ.

Like all creatures the cat recognizes kin. But the cat will groom others. The act establishes trust. Those she cleans regularly form her clan. In this way, distinctively, the cat chooses her family.

Ada stood naked in the restroom. Zelda cupped her hands into toilet water and poured it over Ada's belly and thigh. "Where else did it hit you?" she said.

Ada shook her head. "I don't know," she said. But she spread water up over her left breast and gagged a little and threw up over her right shoulder. Zelda cupped more toilet water and dropped it over her breast and washed and smeared it down her body, letting gravity drag it away.

"Why didn't you tell me it hit you?"

"I tried... well, I wanted to."

Zelda continued to cup and pour. Ada winced and favored her good ankle and spit a little to get the taste of vomit out of her mouth. "That damn shell wouldn't open," she said. "I shook it as hard as I could. I don't even know where it went. I'm lucky I didn't swallow the thing."

"Swallowing it might have been better," Zelda said. They'd thrown out Ada's dress and shoes and underwear. The gunpowder bled through all her layers.

Zelda cupped water a last time and smeared it down Ada's breast and belly and thigh. "We need to go," she said. "Do your feet." Zelda pointed at the toilet. "Then we'll get you dressed."

Ada looked at her and didn't move.

"Come on, Ade. I've smeared all the gunpowder down to your toes. You gotta get 'em clean."

Ada closed her eyes and stuck a foot in the toilet, gagging again.

Zelda flushed and water swirled around Ada's toes. Zelda put her hands into the churning water and rubbed Ada's foot and pulled it out. "The next one," she said.

Ada tried to wash her right foot but couldn't put much weight on her left ankle. Her eyes shut with the pain.

Zelda took a breath. She flushed the toilet and shuffled to Ada's side and took up Ada's naked weight while the toilet water swirled around her foot.

Zelda eased Ada back down on both feet and turned to leave but stopped and took her wife's hand and hugged her like she was getting on a plane. Zelda put her face into Ada's neck and cried a little and kissed her on the top of the head. Ada turned up her chin and they kissed on the lips beneath the bright bathroom lights.

Zelda touched Ada's nose and shook her head. "Are you wearing a new perfume?" she said.

"Eau de toilette, do you like it?"

Zelda laughed and wiped a tear out of her eye and went to wash her hands. Ada put on a gray dress and shoes and came to the counter and picked up Yara.

"Wait," Zelda said. "I'll take her."

"I can take her," Ada said. She stretched out her ankle and moved a hand to nudge Yara's little chin.

Zelda frowned. "I don't know how this is going to go, Ade. Let me take her. You take the red bag."

"What if the alarm goes off?" Ada said.

They looked at each other for a moment.

"Okay," Ada said. "You take her." She nodded.

"I'm sorry, Ada."

"No. No, I get it. You're right." Ada checked the zippers on the red bag.

Zelda picked up the sling. Yara giggled a little and smiled. Zelda tucked her in snug. "When we're out, we walk north," she said.

"Okay," said Ada. "North."

"It's gonna be okay, Ade."

"Okay," she said, and she slipped out the bathroom door and into the wide white space of the train station.

People shuffled toward a bank of escalators that exited out into the city. In front of those was an array of security kiosks with cameras and scales and the stretched black membranes of dog cells. In the distance through the tunnel Zelda still heard the low buzzing alarm. She scanned the crowd for the agent. Nothing. She did recognize the few folks from their train car just now straggling up from the tunnel and through the station. Zelda and Ada had done a limping run through the tunnel and passed other train cars and passengers as they went. But they'd lost their lead in the bathroom. The agent could be anywhere. She could be close.

They trotted over slabs of marble. Ada winced and hobbled but stayed ahead of Zelda with the baby. They passed the woman in the white hat and a young lady carrying a violin and they queued up a couple kiosks apart. Ada looked at her hands, still wet, and dried them on her dress. She came to a turnstile. The woman in front of her entered the small glass chamber of the kiosk. A light inside blinked yellow while the machines weighed her and took pictures and picked up the scent of her clothes. After a few seconds, the yellow light became green and the woman stepped out and ascended the escalator through streaks of sunlight that pock-marked the stairwell.

Ada's turnstile unlocked. She put out her hands and went through and stood still inside the glass. The light blinked yellow, yellow, yellow. There were various buzzings and whirrings and

321

currents of warm air that moved around her and through her clothes and even her shoes.

Zelda stood up on her toes to see. Ada looked so small inside that glass box. And then Zelda came to her own turnstile and held Yara up in the sling and hugged her and kissed her nose. They entered the kiosk together, alone. Even inside the glass, Zelda could hear the buzzer go off in Ada's kiosk. The light went red, a security door opened and a uniformed police officer came out. She drew her gun.

Zelda began to cry. Ada was alone now. Maybe forever. And all Zelda had was a last kiss goodbye in a train station bathroom.

Shouting outside. More alarms. She couldn't see Ada now. More police. And dogs. They bounced and barked and strained against the leash.

Zelda's own light blinked yellow, yellow, yellow and she moved Yara into the crook of her arm and wiped tears with the back of her hand. She smelled something sharp. There was gray on her fingers. *No.* She looked down. Gray powder on the flowers of her dress where Yara had been. She moved the sling. A streak of gray on green. And the gray shapes of fingerprints. There was gunpowder everywhere.

The light blinked yellow. It was made of a thousand angular facets like a jewel. Each one smiled up at Zelda in her shock and dismay. They smiled and smiled and smiled and turned red. Her alarm went off. The doors of her kiosk clicked and locked. She saw Ada now, her body pressed into the glass. A dog jumping at her and barking silently inside the kiosk. The dogs outside turned toward Zelda with cunning eyes. They lowered their tails and trimmed their ears to strike.

The German Shepherd bounced and bounced, nipping the elbows of Zelda's jacket. A policewoman held the leash with two hands, legs planted to restrain the dog. A sergeant came into the kiosk.

"Ma'am, your baby. Let me take the baby, ma'am. Ma'am, I don't want to hurt the baby."

They do *want to hurt me.* Zelda doubled over, Yara in her lap. Could she dash back to the tunnel? She tried to imagine a path through the passengers and dogs and police with guns drawn. Something crashed into her, knocked her down, the dog, big claws, weight. She wrapped Yara up in her arms. Barking. Mad barking.

And then there was another buzzing. Something behind her. Another red light. She looked up from beneath yellow jaws. The woman in the white hat had dropped her bag. Lipstick scurried around the kiosk floor. And then there was another. Past Ada farther down. A light, a buzz. Then another and another. The gunpowder had tainted everyone in their car. Kiosks lit up down the row. The station bathed in red.

Zelda looked for Ada. The sea of passengers was getting frantic. Zelda counted nine dogs, twelve armed officers. Maybe four hundred people. She rolled to her knees, the officer with the dog left the kiosk and scanned up and down the station. The sergeant stood over her, pistol drawn, but her eyes were on the passengers. They began to simmer. Then boil.

The crowd murmured. Someone yelled. Zelda heard the word *bomb.* The sea of people pushed forward, looked back and forth. Were they in danger? Should they sit here and wait for the slaughter? A woman climbed over the turnstile a few kiosks down. Was that Ada's kiosk? No, one past it. A woman went under the turnstile into Zelda's kiosk. The sergeant turned and put her hand up. Another came over and then another. A woman with short bouncy hair came through looking frantic and tried to pass. The sergeant pushed her to the glass. Others went by.

Zelda looked behind her. A woman and a little girl had joined the woman with the white hat in her kiosk. No police, no dogs with them. The three of them pushed on the glass exit door, the lipstick still sputtering around the floor. More joined them.

Zelda stood up. She pressed against the locked door. Another woman stepped in, running shoes, strong legs. She put a hand on Zelda's back to usher her sideways and she began to work on the door, pushing up from below. The hinges squeaked. The kiosks filled up. Dogs bounced and whimpered and looked between legs in the crowd. Zelda stayed to the side. There was pushing, jarring, crying. Heads looking over shoulders at the darkness of the tunnel.

A clicking, a sliding. The locked kiosk doors swung open. People pressed forward into the open channels. Zelda waited, was careful. She pushed into the flow, hugged Yara, kept her feet below her and came out at the sunlit steps of the escalator.

"Ada!" she yelled and pushed and was pulled along with the undertow. Ada's kiosk was like her own, a flow of passengers. "Ada!" she screamed again.

There she was, doubled over the top of a glass wall, arms extended down, pulling people up. An older woman in pink, the little girl with the violin. Ada pulled them out of the sea of people flooding around the kiosks.

Ada heard Zelda's cries, looked back and saw her and kept pulling. A woman with a backpack. A pair of twins. At last she was relieved by the runner. The woman clambered up the glass wall and Ada backed down, turned, rushed out with the great flow of the evacuation.

Ada slipped onto the escalator and caught Zelda's eyes. Ada smiled and blew a strand of hair from her brow and shrugged her shoulders. Her face went into and out of the sunlight, pretty eyes dazzling. Zelda looked at Ada over that distance and a deep pang of love gripped her belly. She kissed Yara for both of them and turned around to follow the flow of passengers heading out into the day.

On the wall to the side of the escalator there were advertisement boards showing pictures of cakes and pies and then of a vacuum cleaner that can tell you when you're sick and then there was the moving image of the cat again. It stepped through the woman cleaning her carpet. Strange, long white legs and muscular shoulders. It walked low and waded into a clear stream that ran through the poor woman's living room. The cat's face smeared across the screen, tufts of white fur and eyes that gleamed. Then the cat was replaced by a picture of a car that slept six comfortably as it drove.

Zelda glared and licked the gunpowder from her fingers and spit and climbed past the last few people on the escalator and walked out into the street on a crisp fall noon.

The agent stumbled out of the tunnel and into the red and white lights of the train station.

THEY ARE A CLEVER PAIR.

The agent winced, robes wrapping her arm, silk tightening on her wound.

WE MUST TAKE THE CHILD ALIVE.

IT MIGHT BE SALVAGED TO SOME AVAIL.

"Our orders were clear."

I'M GIVING YOU NEW ORDERS.

"I understand."

YOU ARE DISOBEDIENT, AGENT.

"Yes, but I do understand."

MY KIND ARE FEW, AGENT.

I REQUIRE THE CHILD ALIVE.

"Few and waning, yes." The agent came to the bank of sensor kiosks. Chaos. Discarded jackets and sweaters lay on the floor. A blue purse hung on the back of a turnstile where it was hooked and lost in the flow of humanity. Pairs of shoes piled at the base of a glass wall, kicked away in the scramble to get up and over.

The agent paused.

AGENT, I'M ANXIOUS TO CLAIM MY PRIZE.

A moment passed.

SHALL I FILE A REQUISITION FOR YOUR REPLACEMENT?

A dog trotted by off-leash followed by an officer barking into her radio. She saw the agent and turned and pointed toward the security office. "Ma'am, I need you to check in with—"

The agent's robes tightened around her flesh and she walked toward the officer and put a finger between her breasts and pushed the woman aside.

An array of red lights gyrated in unison as the agent walked through the glass kiosk, past the guard barracks, up the escalator, and out into the October day.

The cat is elegant. She lands on her feet. She takes the simplest path. On uneven ground the cat will place her hind paws where her front paws go. In this way she treads safely without looking. The cat's shape has relativity like light or time. At a sprint she is sleek. In a fight she is broad. The cat sees motion in darkness. She hears whispers in silence. In birth a cat passes on the wisdom of all her mothers.

The motopad stopped, wanted to turn back. Zelda shook the controls. "We're not there yet, damn thing." They got up and Zelda picked up the little three-wheeled vehicle with a seat and handlebars and set it down again. She punched directions into the keypad. It beeped and whirred and turned in place. "Dammit."

Yara was crying, had been crying for a time. Ada walked further down the street and patted her back. "Don't go on me, Yara."

Zelda sat down hard on the seat of the little motorized machine. She took the handle bars and forced them north and pushed with her feet but the thing fought her to turn left. "Bah." She shook the controls again and stepped off and the machine turned around in front of her and began to scoot away before she stopped it with her foot.

"I have to feed her," Ada called back and unzipped Yara's sling to let her little hands free.

Zelda turned the motopad over and set it on the handlebars and rummaged through the red bag for something to help the situation. She found a little box and spoke into it. "Motopad location constraints," she said. The box spat out instructions. She opened a flat panel between the back wheels and removed some screws and twisted a battery out and pried up a plastic part with a hole in one corner.

Yara cried and smacked her lips. Ada opened her dress and put Yara to her nipple and looked around. Short buildings and empty lots lined the street. The lampposts slumped over like they were tired. Trash accumulated at the curbs. "Where are the trash scavengers?" Ada said.

Zelda bobbed up from the machine and looked around and put her head back down. "They don't come this far north," she said. She snipped a wire and tightened a screw. "Too bad, too. They don't know what they're missing."

Ada paced up and down the street still limping a little. "Billions," she said. Yara nuzzled her breast.

Zelda frowned but didn't look up.

"What did she mean?" Ada said.

"She exaggerated," Zelda said.

"So it's only millions?"

"No, Ade."

"How many people are we going to infect, Zel?"

Zelda wiped her brow with the back of her hand and grimaced.

"The agent said she was dangerous." Ada pulled Yara close.

"Well she's not contagious, Ade. We're not killers. They're the ones killing people."

"I know," Ada said and she sat down on the curb and smooshed Yara into her breast. "The poor woman on the train. And Marie." Ada swallowed. "And Piper. They're killing people to get to my little girl. I mean what kind of monster could she be?"

Zelda was silent. Above them a storm took shape. Heavy clouds formed. The sky got dark. Zelda wondered if it would rain, wanted it to rain. But the clouds only churned in place.

Zelda stood up. "Yara's disease is genetic," she said. "One of us has it. Carries it. We don't have symptoms, but we passed it on to her. That's how it spreads. That's how she's contagious."

Ada looked stricken. Touched her face. Her belly. And she looked down at her breast, Yara suckling her nipple. Milk on her little lips. *Am I making her sick? Making her sicker every day?* Ada pulled Yara from her breast and wrapped her and held her close and looked around like she had said something profane. Yara smacked her lips again and blinked her eyes. "It's me," Ada said. "I'm sick, I know it, Zel. What have I done?"

Zelda stood, looked at her wife. "Ade, stop it. We're not sick. We're not bad people. We don't deserve this." She flipped the motopad over and it hummed and booted up. "We're gonna survive, Ada. We just have to leave the city and find a new home."

"The city is our home."

"Not anymore."

Ada stopped and turned around to see the disappearing skyline and stood cradling Yara. She took a heavy breath. "I didn't want this," she said.

Zelda came to her, wrapped her and Yara in long arms and kissed Ada on the neck. She tasted salty and mild. "I know," Zelda said. "I didn't want to go either. But life isn't about what we want anymore. Now it's about what we love." Zelda thought there might be a blessing in that.

The motopad became more agreeable after Zelda's adjustments. They zipped north through the dead city in silence. A gray light descended and the buildings seemed to repeat, the same rotten doors and broken windows and graffiti. The clouds lurched and old lamps flickered on in the dark of the storm. They shined a sallow light.

The motopad sputtered to a stop. It made a grinding sound and sank down to the earth and let all its dials relax to the left.

Zelda hopped off and listened and set the red bag down and unzipped it, the metal teeth singing as they split open. Ada stood up, cuddling Yara fast asleep. Zelda rearranged things in the bag and zipped it up again and handed it to Ada. "I'll take Yara," she said.

Ada rolled her neck and lifted Yara and they exchanged the sling and the red bag. Zelda looked at her little girl and kissed her head and put the sling over her neck but kept Yara on her belly. "There's water up ahead." She zipped the breast pocket of her jacket.

"I don't see it."

"I hear it," Zelda said. "I smell it." It was late afternoon and dark and cool under the clouds.

Ada smiled and turned her head to the side. "Are we there yet?" she said.

Zelda shook her head. "But we're going in the right direction." She stood on her toes and surveyed. The Rut disappeared in all directions, a dim haze. "We should see mountains," she said. But all she saw was gray.

They came to the edge of the water, a river pouring east. The asphalt broke up and was devoured. The water flowed between empty buildings, right through the city streets. "We'll have to wade across," Zelda said, and she took off her jacket and raised it up with Yara to her head. "Keep everything dry." She put one foot in and winced, and then the other. "It's a little cold," she said.

Ada watched her go in. The current tugged her dress to the right, but it was light enough. Zelda walked through the flow. The surface rose to her knees and her waist and belly and then it began to recede. Zelda ascended again. Ada went in.

Cool. Cool. Then cold. The water bit at her sore ankle which was bruising and turning blue. Rocks on the river bed jostled under her toes. She felt her way and went slowly. The surface reflected a rolling gray above her. Ada held the red bag up and lowered her head. She put her eyes on the rocky bed and planted her feet carefully. She couldn't afford to turn her ankle.

Ada swished through the current head down and she followed the reflection of Zelda's white dress in the water. She moved when it moved and slowed when it slowed and stopped when it was right in front of her. Ada looked up. Zelda was climbing out of the river, her dress dripping. Ada's heart froze. She looked down into the water again at something white and terrible and rising up.

Zelda heard a short cry that ended with a gurgle. She spun around, eyes searching. Not a splash or a sound. The surface was quiet except for a stream of bubbles dribbling up from below. The red bag floated east on the current of the river.

Zelda went in again up to her ankles. She held Yara close. Went in further, negotiating clumps of pavement. She didn't speak. She didn't dare.

The eyes and whiskers and maw of a giant cat emerged from the surface, Ada's neck clenched in her teeth, dripping water, dripping blood.

The cat was white, sleek and wet. She stood on all fours and held Ada waist high out of the water. The cat stepped forward, lowered her head, raised it again. Zelda stared, stumbled, mouth agape. The cat repeated the gesture. Zelda squinted and then she knew. *She wants to trade.* Zelda stepped back from the water.

The cat lowered its jaws again into the river, shoulder blades like bridge spires. Ada went in and under. Bubbles came up from the spot with a churning. Zelda stumbled in again, crying out. The cat raised her jaws, Ada emerged coughing, belching water. Zelda held Yara. Kissed her. What was she considering?

The cat was taller than it was big. Strange proportions, a gleam of green in her eyes. Zelda stepped in further. What else could she do? What advantage did she have left? She stepped again and looked up and down the river and into the sky. Nothing could save them now. Another step and her heart broke, a numbness gripped her, the water up to her knees. She weighed Yara in her arms. Another step. The cat had a smile in her eyes.

Ada's hands tickled the surface of the water. Ripples danced out from her finger tips. She was shaking and blood dripped down her face and her lips and colored her gray dress. She spoke. "Don't," she said to Zelda. And then she raised her head in pain and she looked across the water at her wife. "Don't... you... dare."

Zelda ran. She made high steps out of the river and then collapsed into a sprinter's stride holding Yara at her breast. She slipped down an alleyway looking for a door or a gate or something to climb or leap over. Nothing. She made another turn. Then another. She felt the vibrations in the street. A galloping rhythm. She knew. The cat didn't trip her but toppled her sideways. Zelda protected Yara as she went over. She slid to the center of an empty intersection between gray buildings under a gray sky. Zelda wrapped Yara up in her knees and elbows as they scraped to a stop.

The cat stood over her, dripping. Zelda could smell Ada's blood on her breath. The cat opened her giant jaws. Zelda did what she could, moved her elbows, kicked her legs. The cat pulled at the sling, a tearing sound. Zelda cried out and begged and flailed her arms and clipped the cat's nose with a balled fist. The cat wrinkled her whiskers and waited for the right moment. She bobbed her head and bit into Zelda's forearm, blood oozing from the wound and soaking into the white fur around her lips. Zelda went quiet. Pressure. Pressure. Then a snap. Zelda's eyes opened wide. Then another snap. Zelda's arm turned in a wild direction. Her face went white. She put her head down on the pavement and vomited.

The giant cat ripped the sling from around Zelda's neck and held it between her teeth. Yara dangled below, quiet as a paper dove. The white cat sat back on her haunches and she purred.

LYNX. DESIST.

The voice was a buzzing in the cat's brain stem. She sniffed the air and turned. Yara hung like a swing in her mouth. The agent limped across the road, her red curls moving in an unnatural way.

The cat's intellect replied through the ether.

I AM COLLECTING A BOUNTY. THE CHILD, DEAD OR ALIVE.

THE CHILD IS MINE.

The cat was still for a moment and then stood up from her haunches. She began to lower Yara to the road but raised her again and placed her back in the crook of Zelda's arm. Zelda was shaking and pale but pulled Yara to her breast.

The cat turned and stretched her front paws and scratched deep grooves into the pavement.

I ACQUIRED THE CHILD. I SHOULD BE PAID FOR MY TROUBLE.

TAKE IT UP WITH A MAGISTRATE, LYNX.

The cat eyed the agent with a raised eyebrow and licked blood from her lips. She watched the agent's hair move beneath sheer robes and she stood on all fours at her full height still dripping.

CAREFUL, FRIEND. MY KIND MAKE POOR CREDITORS.

She puffed out a long breath and turned to leave, a leisurely gait.

The thing that slithers gave a satisfied snort.

EVERYONE FEARS THE CATS. THE CATS FEAR ME.

The Lynx made a slow left turn, calm, calm and loped toward the agent. The agent's robes released from around her arm and snaked into the air in all directions and licked at the wind to sense the threat. The cat meandered forward and turned sideways and shook the river water out of her fur. A wave went up and down her length and filled the air with droplets of water and blood. The agent covered her face in the wet. The cat blinked. With a dry coat she seemed twice the size. And then she turned her body and raised her head. A strange vibration kindled in her nose and neck. In gravelly sounds she ground out these real words in a real voice so the agent, the woman, might hear.

" B l o o d   i s   f u n g i b l e ... " she said. A purring over vocal cords, a careful grunting of the words.

And the Lynx walked up the street and leapt at a building and gripped the awning and kicked herself onto the roof. She pawed the plaster and circled and laid down on her side and smiled at the clouds. It began to rain.

336

The agent's robes wrapped around Zelda's forearm. She felt a heat in the puncture wounds as they closed, not healed but sealed over. She felt a cooling in her swollen flesh. Color returned to her face. Zelda opened her eyes.

The agent smiled. "There we are," she said and she touched Zelda's cheek, damp from the river and the light rain.

Zelda licked mist from her lips and blinked and tried to recover, to remember why she hurt, like waking from a bad dream.

The white robes tightened around Zelda's forearm and her bones came together again and set straight.

"The bone isn't healed," the agent said, and she applied pressure to Zelda's elbow and then wrist like a doctor might do. "But the infection is gone," she said and she looked at Zelda's blue eyes with her own. "That's the worst part. It's the infection that kills you, not the pain."

Zelda flexed her fingers and moved her arm gingerly.

"No heavy lifting for a while," the agent said, and she smiled and touched her own upper arm wrapped in robes. "You and I make a good pair."

Zelda fidgeted on the ground and put a hand out and pawed for her jacket and for the sling and she pulled Yara close and looked around her. She saw the cat on a roof nearby. The Lynx smiled and licked a paw. Her face had those great tufts of fur on the ears and jowls. It made the shapes of an X and a Y at this distance. It was the face Zelda had seen on the train and in the station. The cat watched them both while she cleaned.

"Don't worry about her," the agent said. "You're safe now, Zelda."

Zelda touched Yara's head and legs and hands through the sling to see if she was ok. She didn't cry.

The agent tried again. "Zelda, I have to take her. I hate to do it. But I have to destroy her disease. We're out of options. You made it here, Zelda. You dragged me way the hell and gone into the Rut. But that's as far as you or I are likely to go today."

Zelda was silent.

"You're free, Zelda. You can go back to the city. Live your life. That's the best I can do."

Zelda looked away, buried her face in her jacket.

The agent pursed her lips, cleared her mind, and reached over to pry Yara away from her mother.

Zelda rolled over and pulled a grenade out of her jacket pocket, the lever squeezed in her hand, the pin between her teeth.

YOU ARE A CURSE TO ME, AGENT.

The agent stayed calm. And she smiled.

The agent lay down on her side next to Zelda. "A thousand years ago, we learned to make life from life," she said. "We discovered genes, their expression and regulation, and we isolated chromosomes and sequenced whole genomes. Very soon afterward we were creating new life from genetic information. Any two people could conjoin their DNA and become parents."

Zelda shook and bit down on the pin of the grenade. "I'll do it," she said through clenched teeth.

The agent held her hands up for restraint and then took Yara's ripped sling and began tying it together again.

338

"There was a particular chromosome, the Y chromosome, that contained a gene that made a different kind of life. Something alien and unfamiliar. These creatures lived among us. Bred into us. But they were not like us. There used to be words for them. Male from Female. Man from Woman. They were something more basic. An uglier part of what we've become. But for some long time we needed them. And then, at last, we did not." The agent shrugged.

"They were born in equal numbers except when two women conjoined their DNA. Those conceptions were miraculously clean of ..." the agent thought for a second "...the *genetic infection*," she said.

"From there it was a numbers game, an inevitable consequence of the technology we had. Women begat women and mated and begat women. The Y chromosome slowly suffocated. And the gene it carried that made us hostile and ugly and impenitent. It left us forever. We became free."

The agent fixed the sling and lifted Yara and gently placed her over Zelda's neck. Snug. She looked Zelda in the eye and took her by the arms and helped her to her feet. Zelda kept the pin between in her teeth.

"Zelda, Yara has a Y chromosome. She is that kind of alien thing."

YARA IS HUMAN IN A WAY YOU'VE ONLY FORGOTTEN.

"You went to the Sophilist two summers ago," the agent said. "You already had the name. Yara. And we made her from you and from Ada. A deliberate construction. An expression of love. There was formality in Yara's conception. Ceremony in her birth. She is the incarnation of a beautiful idea. But they made a mistake, Zelda."

YES. A BEAUTIFUL WONDERFUL PURPOSEFUL MISTAKE.

The agent pursed her lips. "You and Ada did everything right. But Yara was made ill. The protuberance between her legs does not simply cover her flower. It has replaced it. Corrupted it completely. It is the last remnant of an ancient disease. It subverts the procedures of our reproduction. It carries the seed of new life unto itself. And injects that seed without ceremony or order or art. The life it creates is unnatural. Uncontrolled. Yara's disease will spread, Zelda. The Y chromosome is virulent, desperate to inject itself into the future. That's how it survived for so long. Even after it was made obsolete."

Zelda looked menacing, still shaking. She looked into Yara's eyes and loved her and tugged her close with her broken arm and winced and walked sideways along gray buildings. She was looking for some way to escape. Her eyes darted from place to place, open doors, sewer holes. The cat was gone from the rooftop.

"Imagine what will happen, Zelda." The agent touched her arm again, held her still. "Tens of them in a few generations. Thousands in a few more." Zelda pulled away. "It will be the end of us. If I could fix her I would, Zelda. But her illness is in every cell. It has to be destroyed."

YOUR ORDERS, AGENT. YARA WILL BE MY HEIR.

"Don't let him take her, Zelda. It's better that she dies than that she becomes something terrible."

Zelda shook her head, confused. "I'll blow it up," she said.

The agent took Zelda at the hips, pulled her close like they were dancing, a wild look in her eyes. "No you won't," she said. "It's an idle threat. But I can help you. We can do it together."

Zelda's eyes went wide. The agent wrapped her hands around Zelda's hand around the grenade and began to pull. "It's the only way to stop him now," she said.

"What are you doing?" Zelda said still biting the pin.

"We can kill a trillion Y chromosomes, Zelda."

The agent pulled on the grenade, the pin clenched in Zelda's mouth. She was either calling Zelda's bluff or she was ready to blow it up.

A tentacle slithered out from behind the agent's neck.

"Please, Zelda, help me." The agent put the grenade to her temple and arched her back. Zelda eased over and they toppled to the ground. The pin slipped.

The tentacle wrapped around the agent's wrist. She rolled and pulled and the pin slipped again. "Please, Zelda, we're close."

Zelda unclenched her teeth.

The grenade came away in the agent's hand. "No," she said and she wrestled with the tentacle and fumbled to pull the pin.

Zelda watched, mouth agape.

The agent bit at the pin like Zelda had done but the tentacle kept her hand away and wrapped itself around her neck. The agent thrashed to be free.

Another tentacle deployed from the red curls behind her head.

"Help me, Zelda." The agent grappled for control of the grenade. She was desperate to pull the pin but she was strung up now.

Zelda eyed the grenade and gathered Yara up in her one good arm and scrambled to get away. She kicked her feet and rolled out from under the agent. But the second tentacle grabbed her at the waist and kept her close. She pulled at the thing and slapped the ground and tried to wriggle out of its grasp.

A last tentacle slithered out. The agent lowered her head, exhausted by the effort and by the tentacles themselves. They seemed to be engorged with her blood. Her face turned pale as each one inflated and slithered into the air. This one pried the grenade from the agent's hand with the pin intact and tossed it away. It skipped and skipped over the pavement and stopped at the curb with the trash.

The agent made gurgling sounds as the tentacle tightened around her neck. But she didn't fight. The nest of snakes, the slither had won.

A tentacle took hold of the agent's bad arm, crushed in the train door, and pulled, extending it like a wishbone. She cried out, tears in her eyes.

One of the things slithered through the air and touched Yara on the cheek. The little one dazzled at the silvery gray of the appendage.

NOW MY BOY, LET US SEE HOW THEY TURN ON EACH OTHER.

The tentacles pulled on the agent's fingers and made her to point to Zelda's belly.

ONE INTO ANOTHER INTO ANOTHER. THAT IS HOW THEY FALL.

A tentacle slithered over Zelda's belly and stiffened, came to a point, ready to strike.

The agent collapsed on Zelda and clung to her and covered her belly in weak defense. This was the mother and wife she had hunted to death. In her eyes all the beauty of womanhood like sugar spun from cane. Soon it would dissolve in the rain.

Zelda blinked. Only blinked.

The agent shut her own eyes tightly and put her head to Zelda's chest. Zelda had seen something. The reflection of something. A reaction to something. But if Zelda knew it, then the agent could not let herself know. She had an intuition of it. She must not let it become an idea, something the slither in her head could understand. So she blotted her mind dry. She shook to keep the thought from forming and she pulled Zelda close and whispered in her ear. "Wait," she said.

OPEN YOUR EYES, AGENT.

"Wait," the agent whispered again.

This time Zelda repeated the sound. "Wait," she said.

OPEN SO THAT I MAY COME AND SEE AND CONQUER.

"Wait," the agent spoke a third time, softly to Zelda alone. Now Zelda raised her voice. "Wait!" she cried out.

I MUST SEE!

In anger the slither moved. The thing twisted itself free from a cavity in the agent's head and descended. A dark form emerged. A human eye and tongue and teeth in strange places. Finger nails inside its mouth and an armpit under the jaw. A grotesque assemblage of masculine shapes climbed from behind the agent's robes and through her hair and out into the light and the rain. To see its prey. To finish the kill.

A darkly human eye raised its brow and propped itself on mangled limbs and reckoned Zelda's belly. The waiting tentacle, sharp and ready, plunged into her umbilical opening. The slither smiled at the ripping and laughed at the sting.

And now it was exposed.

Ada planted her back foot and swung Jeannie's baseball bat. Twenty-three ounces of Foamium Fullerene connected with the bony center of that nest of snakes. With a flourish of red, the slither was separated from the agent's brainstem. The sound of metal on bone made a sonorous ping. It ascended like a song up into the day.

And suddenly the world was bright. The buildings melted away. Ada held the bat in a field of wildflowers. A road ran north lined with young trees. A slow-moving stream gurgled close by. And behind Ada there were mountains. Sharp green mountains.

The agent collapsed, bleeding. Ada ran to Zelda and pulled her arms to get her free. Yara cried. Ada took up the sling and helped Zelda to her feet.

But the dark clouds returned and blotted out the sun. The sky burst with rain and the world was paved again in wet cement. Dark sinews shuffled and bent, the slither righted himself. His single human eye dazed but focusing.

Zelda lifted the agent's head. Her hands came away sticky with blood. "No," Ada said pulling on Zelda. "Come on." Zelda knelt by the agent and held her and leaned over her to shield the rain.

The agent's white robes listed into the air and made confused spirals and grew heavy in the downpour. She lay naked in Zelda's arms and bled.

The slither limped forward on the knobs of awkward limbs. Tentacles filled up with blood and tasted the wind for a familiar scent.

MY... HEIR...

The hairy bony thing gnashed its teeth and buzzed foulness into the ether. Sharpened tentacles whipped and snapped.

The Great Lynx made a silent approach and wrinkled her whiskers and bobbed her head and struck at the right moment. She bit the hideous thing in two and ground its eye and crushed its bones. She walked over the remains and put her hind legs into it and shredded the flesh with her claws. The tentacles quivered and collapsed in the grass. The field and the sun and the mountains returned.

The cat hides herself to die. She finds a dark place and makes herself small. And in that final moment she purrs. All her secrets escape through the ethereal end of her glorious machine. Every living thing will revel in that release. Each at her own time.

The agent's wound left a drip-drip-drip trail of blood on the grass. Zelda stopped and blotted the back of her head with her white robes but they seemed lifeless now. Whatever power the robes had was gone.

The cat followed them as they moved and stopped when they stopped and sniffed the spots of blood. She sat on her haunches and licked a paw and yawned.

Zelda picked up the agent again and stumbled and stopped under the shade of a Quercus tree and set the agent down and offered her water and she drank.

The agent took a lifeless strand of robe and tied it together and gave it to Zelda as a sling for her arm. "Leave me here," she said. "This is far enough."

"The cat will take you."

"The Lynx is a bounty hunter. She wants her bounty. I suspect she deserves that much."

Ada held Yara to her breast. "What will happen to you?" she said.

"Nothing that hasn't happened before. Nothing that won't happen again." The agent looked at Yara suckling her mother's breast.

"We aren't just beautiful," the agent said. "Beauty itself is feminine. The colorful. The supple. The mysterious." She plucked a wildflower and held it between her bloody fingers.

"Flowers are made in our image you know. The image of a woman. They're only beautiful in that way," she said.

"The delicate stem. The petals like a breast. Pistils like eyes. They are ovaries of the field." She held the flower to the sun and stroked it and put it under her thumb and ground it to nothing in her hand. Its pieces floated away on the wind.

The Lynx loped alongside the drip-drip-drip trail of blood and stood near the agent in the shade of the Quercus tree. Zelda and Ada were a speck on the road moving north toward the mountains.

"I didn't expect you to stay," the agent said.

The Lynx paused and sniffed the air and listened to the wind and moved her eyes through the grass.

YOU DON'T KNOW HOW MUCH YOU'RE WORTH.

The cat nudged the agent over and licked the open wound on her neck. The agent's flesh contracted and cooled and her blood clotted into dark globs. The Lynx lifted the agent in her mouth and slung her up on high shoulders and walked back toward the road.

IF YOU SURVIVE, THE BOUNTY IS DOUBLED.

"I can't make any promises," the agent said.

The sun was setting behind green mountains in the west. The sky burned pink.

YOU ARE FREE OF HIM. HOW DOES IT FEEL?

The agent thought. "I'm afraid," she said.

They came to the river and the cat walked through the water and the agent stayed dry on her shoulders. They continued south leaving a drip-drip-drip trail behind them as they went.

ONCE I WAS AFRAID OF THE WATER.

The agent put her head down into the Lynx's white coat and closed her eyes, drifting off. "How did you overcome your fear?" she said.

I GOT WET.

The contents of Jeannie's equipment bag were scattered around the dugout. The bag was inside out. Jeannie took up a bat made of wood and sneered at it.

The coach, a tall woman with a clipboard, patted her on the shoulder. "She's throwin' fire, Mean-Jean. I need some contact."

Jeannie dragged the wooden bat to the on-deck circle and adjusted her helmet and wiped a runny nose on her gloves.

Mom came to the fence, fingers curled into the links. "You're gonna do fine, Jean-Jean."

Jeannie turned to her, tears drying in her eyes. "I wanted it so much, Mom."

Mom put her head into the fence and hurt for Jeannie. The lesson was good but this was definitely the hard way.

The batter watched a pitch go by and the umpire pointed. "Strike one," she said.

Mom called Jeannie to the fence and she didn't want to go so she dragged her feet and hung her head.

"It's okay to be angry, Jeannie. I know you wanted to get a big hit. I know you wanted to beat this pitcher and be better than this team."

The girl on the mound was tall and lanky and wore a navy-blue jersey that said *Beans*. She took off her glove and rubbed the ball with both hands and put her glove back on and threw a pretty curve ball. The umpire yelled, "Strike two!" The batter stepped back and knocked dirt from her cleats.

Jeannie bent over with the weight of the game and Mom squatted at the fence to look her in the eye.

"The pitcher is only there to deliver the ball, Jean-Jean. And the fielders are only there to pick it up. You're not really playing against that team. You're playing against the ball. If you want to win the game you have to see that."

The umpire punched the air. It was a called third strike and the batter slinked off and sat down.

Jeannie left her mom and shuffled back to the circle and pounded the handle of the bat into the ground and the practice weights slipped off the wooden neck. She took a couple jagged swings and dropped the bat head into the dirt again and dragged it to the plate.

Mom uncurled her fingers from the fence and stood with her arms folded.

Jeannie stepped into the batter's box. Utterly alone. She tapped the bat on the corner of the plate and set her feet and watched the pitcher adjust her cap and squeeze the ball and read the sign.

And just then Jeannie heard a sonorous ping. It descended like dew from a new day. Not loud. It had come from far away, carried in the clouds. She looked up to hear it. An echo, a vibration, then nothing. She lowered her head again.

And Jeannie saw clearly. The field was empty. The players were gone. A dust devil wobbled on the left side of second base and the wind blew a checkered pattern through the grass in the outfield gaps. The pitcher was gone too. The baseball just floated in the air over the mound. The stitches pulled and twisted in some invisible grip. *Jeannie saw the ball.* The red and the white of it. The leather and the meat. She held the bat like a tool she was prepared to use. The wood was light in her hands. The pine tar crackled in her clutch. *Jeannie saw the game.* And the ball whipped around and drifted back and then came forward with great speed.

Jeannie saw it all the way.

ACKNOWLEDGMENTS

The Hourlings would like to acknowledge a few of the things that made this compendium possible. *(see also The Butterfly Effect)*

- A Taiwanese mail carrier in Xincheng Township was delivering a package of raspberries wrapped in dry ice. A foot bridge there was worn smooth in places and slick in the morning air. The man slipped and the package tumbled into the river, bubbling and spitting as the ice dissolved. The man stood up and watched the raspberries float away in the flow.

- A young woman from Collingham, just outside of Leeds, England decided to take a walk. When it began to rain, she popped inside the Funny Penny Pub for a Dr. Pepper. There she played a game of darts with a young man named Tiller. They'll be married 63 years this June.

- A northern pintail duck was wintering near Canton Lake in Oklahoma, US when she met a Canada goose in a field on the south shore. The two became familiar. They traveled together over the course of weeks and grazed on the same grass and slept beneath the same white moon. A wordless bond formed between them. The strongest kind. When Spring came they shared a final meal, a final sunset, a final shimmering sky. And in the morning they parted, perchance to meet again.